Karl Pearson

The Ethic of Freethought

A Selection of Essays and Lectures

Karl Pearson

The Ethic of Freethought
A Selection of Essays and Lectures

ISBN/EAN: 9783337277819

Printed in Europe, USA, Canada, Australia, Japan

Cover: Foto ©Andreas Hilbeck / pixelio.de

More available books at **www.hansebooks.com**

THE ETHIC OF
FREETHOUGHT

A SELECTION OF ESSAYS AND LECTURES

BY

KARL PEARSON, M.A.

FORMERLY FELLOW OF KING'S COLLEGE, CAMBRIDGE

Freiheit, aber vereint mit der Freiheit immer den edlen
Ernst und die Strenge des Lebens, die heilige Sitte
HAMERLING

𝔏𝔬𝔫𝔡𝔬𝔫
T. FISHER UNWIN
26, PATERNOSTER SQUARE
MDCCCLXXXVIII

TO THE

Members of

Ring's College, Cambridge,

AS A SLIGHT

TOKEN 'OF GRATITUDE

FOR SEVERAL SUNNY YEARS OF

COLLEGE LIFE

AND SOME INVALUABLE

FRIENDSHIPS.

PREFACE.

THE lectures included in this selection have been delivered to Sunday and other audiences, and the essays have been published in magazine or pamphlet form during the past five years. The only paper written especially for this volume is a criticism of the President of the Royal Society's recent contribution to Natural Theology; some few of the others in the section entitled "Sociology" have been revised or partially rewritten.

A few words must be said about the method and scope of my book. The reader will find that neither the sections nor the individual papers are so widely diverse as a glance at their titles might lead him to suspect. There is, I venture to think, a unity of purpose and a similarity of treatment in them all. I set out from the standpoint that the mission of Freethought is no longer to batter down old faiths; that has been long ago effectively accomplished, and I, for one, am ready to put a railing round the ruins, that they may be preserved from desecration and serve as a landmark. Indeed I confess to have yawned over a recent vigorous inditement of Christianity, and I promptly disposed of my copy to a young gentleman who was anxious that I should read a work entitled: *Natural Law in the Spiritual World*, which he told me had given quite a new width to the faith of his childhood. Starting, then, from the axiom, that the Christian 'verities' are quite outside the field of profitable discussion, the first five papers of this volume endeavour to formulate the opinions which a rational being of to-day may hold with regard to the physical and intellectual worlds. They deduce—with what measure of success I must leave the reader to judge—a rational enthusiasm and a possible basis of morals. They insist on the almost sacred nature of doubt, and at the same time emphasize scientific and historical study as the sole path to knowledge, wisdom, and right action. The Freethinker's position differs to some extent from that of the Agnostic. While the latter asserts that some questions lie beyond man's power of solution, the former contents himself with the statement that he does not know at present, but that, looking to the past, he can set no limit to the knowledge of the future. He has faith in the steady investigation of successive generations solving most problems, and meanwhile he will accept no myth as supplement to his ignorance. The Freethinker is not an Atheist, but he vigorously denies the existence of any god hitherto put forward, because the idea of one and all by contradicting some law of thought involves an absurdity.

The second or historical group of papers regards one or two phases of past thought and life from the Freethinker's standpoint. The selection was here somewhat more difficult, as I had more material to choose from. The first two papers are fairly closely related to points treated in the first section. The last three deal with a period in which the forces tending to revolutionize society were in many respects akin to those we find in action at the present day. The man of the study, the demagogue, the Utopian, and the fanatic were all busily at work in early sixteenth century Germany, and to mark the success and failure of their respective efforts is not without interest.

The last section of this book is the one which is most likely to meet with severe criticism and disapproval. It deals with great race problems, which, in my opinion, are becoming daily more and more urgent. The decline of our foreign trade will inevitably force upon us economic questions which reach to the very roots of our present family and social life. It is the very closeness of these matters to our personal conduct and to our home privacy which renders it necessary and yet immensely difficult to speak plainly. For

another five years 'Society' may hold up its hands in
astonishment at any free discussion of matters which are
becoming more and more pressing with the great mass of
our toiling population; deprecation may be possible, I repeat, for another *five* years, but in *ten*—if respectability is
still sitting on the safety-valve—well, then, it is likely to
learn too late that prejudice and false modesty will never
suffice to check great folk-movements, nor satisfy pressing
folk-needs. There are mighty forces at work likely to revolutionize social ideas and shake social stability. It is the
duty of those, who have the leisure to investigate, to show
how by gradual and continuous changes we can restrain
these forces within safe channels, so that society shall emerge
stronger and more efficient from the difficulties of our nineteenth century Renascence and Reformation. Its possibility
will, I believe, depend to a great extent on the Humanists of
to-day keeping touch with the feelings and needs of the mass
of their fellow-countrymen, otherwise society is likely to
be shipwrecked by a democracy trusting for its " spiritual "
guidance to the Salvation Army, and for its economic
theories to the Social-Democratic Federation. One word
more: the last papers of this section are essentially tentative; they endeavour to point out problems rather than
offer final solutions. Their purpose will be fulfilled if they
induce some few earnest men and women to investigate and
discuss; to prepare the path for the social reformer and the
statesman of the future.

KARL PEARSON.

SAIG, *September*, 1887.

ERRATA.

Page 98, l. 25, *for* wass, *read* was.
Page 206, l. 11 *from bottom, dele first* s.

CONTENTS.

FREETHOUGHT.

The order of Mind is one with the order of Matter ; hence that Mind alone is free which finds itself in Nature, and Nature in itself.

I.

THE ETHIC OF FREETHOUGHT.[1]

The truth is that Nature is due to the statuting of Mind.—Hegel.

IT is not without considerable hesitation that I venture to
address you to-night. There are periods of a man's life
when it is better for him to be silent—to listen to others
rather than to preach himself. The world at the present time
is very full of prophets ; they crowd the human market-place,
they set their stools at every possible corner, and perched
thereon, they cry out the merits of their several wares to as
large a crowd of folk as their enthusiasm can attract, or their
tongue reach. Philosophers, scientists, orthodox Christians,
freethinkers—wise men, fools, and fanatics—are all shouting
on the market-place, teaching, creating, and destroying,
perhaps working, through their very antagonism to some
greater truth of whose existence they and we are alike
scarcely conscious. Amidst such a hubbub and clatter of truth
and of falsehood, of dogma and of doubt—what right has
any chance individual to set up his stool and teach his doctrine ? Were it not far better for him, in the language of *Uncle
Remus*, to "lie low" ? Or if he do chance to mount, that
a kindly friend should pull his stool from under him ?

I feel that no man has a right to address his fellows on
one of what Carlyle would have termed the 'Infinities' or
'Eternities' unless he feels some special call to the task—
unless he is deeply conscious of some truth which he *must*

[1] This lecture was delivered at South Place Institute on Tuesday,
March 6, 1883, and was afterwards printed as a pamphlet.

communicate to others, some falsehood which he *must* sweep away. The power of speech is scarcely to be exercised in private without a holy fear; in public it becomes a most sacred trust which ought to be used by few of us, and then only on the rarest occasions.

Hence my hesitation in addressing you this evening. I have no new truth to propound, no old falsehood to sweep away; what *I* can tell you, you have all probably heard before in truer and clearer words from those who may rank as prophets of our modern thought. I come here to learn rather than to teach, and my excuse for being here at all is the discussion which usually follows these papers. I am egotistical enough to hope that that discussion will be rather a sifting of your views than a criticism of mine—that it should take rather the form of debate than of mere question and answer. With this end in view I shall endeavour to avoid all controversy. I do not understand by a discussion on Freethought an attack on orthodox Christianity;—the emancipated intelligence of our age ought to have advanced in the consciousness of its own strength far beyond such attacks; its mission is rather to teach than to quarrel—to create rather than to destroy. I shall assume, therefore, that the majority of my audience are freethinkers—that they do not accept Christianity as a divine or miraculous revelation; and I would ask all, who holding other views may chance to be here to-night, to accept for a time our assumption, to follow us whither it leads, and to mark its re-sults. For only by such sympathy can they discover the ultimate truth or falsehood of our relative standpoints; only such sympathy distinguishes the thinker from the bigot.

In order to explain the somewhat criticized title of my lecture I am going to ask you to accept for the present my definitions of Religion, Freethought, and Dogmatism. I do not ask you to accept these definitions as binding, but only to adopt them for the purpose of following my reasoning. I shall begin with an axiom—which is, I fear, a *dogmatic* pro-ceeding—yet I think the majority of you will be inclined to accept it. My axiom runs as follows: " The whole is not

identical with a part." This axiom leads us at once to a
problem: What relation has the part to the whole? Applying this to a particular case, we state: The individual is
not identical with the universe; and we ask: What relation
has the individual to the universe? Now I shall not
venture to assert that there is any aim or end in the universe
whatever; all I would ask you to grant is that its con-
figuration alters, whether that alteration be the result of
mere chance, or of a material law, or of a superior cogitative
being, is for my present purpose indifferent. I simply
assert that the universe alters, is 'becoming'; *what* it is
becoming I will not venture to say. Next I will ask you
to grant that the individual too is altering, is not only a
'being,' but also a 'becoming.' These alterations, whatever their nature, be it physical or spiritual (if there is any
distinction) I shall—merely for convenience—term *life*. We
may then state our problem as follows: What relation has
the life of the individual to the life of the universe?—Now
without committing ourselves to any definite dogma I think
we may recognize the enormous disparity of those two
expressions, the 'life of the individual' and the 'life of the
universe.' The former is absolutely subordinate, utterly
infinitesimal compared with the latter. The 'becoming'
of the latter bears no apparent relation to the 'becoming'
of the former. In other words, the life of the universe does
not appear to have the slightest ratio to the life of the individual. The one seems finite, limited, temporal, the other
by comparison infinite, boundless, eternal. This disparity
has forced itself upon the attention of man ever since his
first childlike attempts at thought. The 'Eternal Why'
then began to haunt his mind. 'Why, eternally why am I
here?' he asked. What relation do I, a part, bear to the
whole—the sum of all things material and spiritual? What
connection has the finite with the infinite? the temporal
with the eternal? Primitive man endeavoured to answer
this question off-hand. He found a power within himself
capable apparently of reviewing the whole; he rushed to
the satisfactory conclusion that that power must be itself

infinite; that he, man, was not altogether finite, and so he
constructed a doctrine of the soul and its immortality. Then
he built up myths, superstitions, primitive religions,
dogmas, whereby the infinite was made subject to the finite
—floating on this huge bladder of man's supposed immortality. The universe is given a purpose, and that purpose is man—the whole is made subordinate to the part.
That is the first solution of the problem, the keystone of
most concrete religions. I do not intend to discuss the
validity of this solution. I have advanced so far merely
to arrive at a definition, and that is the following: *Religion
is the relation of the finite to the infinite.* Note that I say religion *is* the relation. You will mark at once that as there
is only one relation, there can be only one religion. Any
given concrete system of religion is only so far true as it
actually explains the relation of the finite to the infinite.
In so far as it builds up an imaginary relation between
finite and infinite it is false. Hence, since no existing religion lays out before us fully the relation of finite and
infinite, all systems of religion are of necessity but half
truths. I say half truths, not whole falsehoods, for many
religions may have made some, if small, advance towards
the solution of the problem.

The great danger of most existing systems lies in this—
that not content with our real knowledge of the relation
of the finite to the infinite, they slur over our vast ignorance
by the help of the imagination. *Myth* supplies the place of
true knowledge where we are ignorant of the connection
between finite and infinite. Hence we may say that most
concrete systems of religion present us with a certain small
amount of knowledge but a great deal of myth. Now our
knowledge of the relation of finite to infinite, small as it
may be, is still continually increasing—science and philosophy are continually presenting us with broader views of
the relation of man to Nature and of individual thought to
abstract Thought. It follows at once, therefore, that, since
our knowledge of the relation between the finite and the infinite,
that is, our acquaintance with the one true religion, is, by

however small degrees, ever increasing, so in every concrete religion the knowledge element ought to increase and
the myth element to decrease, or, as we may express it, every
concrete religion ought to be in a state of development.
Is this a fact ? To a certain small extent it is. Christianity,
for example, to-day is a very different matter to what it was
eighteen hundred years ago. But small as our increase in
knowledge may be, concrete systems of religion have not
kept pace with it. They persist in explaining by myth,
portions of the relation of the finite to the infinite, concerning which we have true knowledge. Hence we see
the danger, if not the absolute evil, of any myth at all. An
imaginary explanation of the relation of finite to infinite too
often impedes the spread of the true explanation when man has
found it. This gives rise to the so-called contests of religion
and science or of religion and philosophy—those unintelligible
conflicts of 'faith' and 'reason' which can only arise in the
minds of persons who cannot perceive clearly the distinction
between myth and knowledge. The holding of a myth explanation of any problem whereon mankind has attained, or
may hereafter attain, true knowledge is what I term enslaved
thought or *dogmatism*. Owing to the slow rate of development
of most concrete religions, they are all more or less dogmatic.
The rejection of all myth explanation, the reception of all
ascertained truths with regard to the relation of the finite to
the infinite, is what I term *freethought* or true religious
knowledge. In other words, the freethinker, in my sense of
the term, possesses more real religion, knows more of the
relation of the finite to the infinite than any believer in myth ;
his very knowledge makes him in the highest sense of the
word a religious man.

I hope you will note at once the extreme difficulty according to this definition of obtaining freedom of thought. Freethought is rather an ideal than an actuality ; it is, too, a
progressive ideal, one advancing with every advance of positive knowledge. The freethinker is not one who thinks
things as he will, but one who thinks them as they must be.
To become a freethinker it is not sufficient to throw off all

2

forms of dogmatism, still less to attack them with coarse satire; this is but negative action. The true freethinker must be in the possession of the highest knowledge of his day; he must stand on the slope of his century and mark what the past has achieved, what the present is achieving; still better if he himself is working for the increase of human knowledge or for its spread among his fellows—such a man may truly be termed a high priest of freethought. You will see at once what a positive, creative task the freethinker has before him. To reject Christianity, or to scoff at all concrete religion, by no means constitutes freethought, nay, is too often sheer dogmatism. The true freethinker must not only be aware of the points wherein he has truth, but must recognize the points wherein he is still ignorant. Like the true man of science he must never be ashamed to say: Here I am ignorant, this I cannot explain. Such a confession draws the attention of thought, and so of research to the dark points of our knowledge, it is not a confession of weakness but really of strength. To slur over such points with an assumed knowledge is the dogmatism of philosophy or the dogmatism of science, or rather of false philosophy and false science—just as dangerous as the dogmatism of a concrete religion. Were I to come here and tell you that certain forces were inherent in matter, that these forces sufficed to explain the union of atoms into molecules, the formation out of molecules of chemical compounds, that certain chemical compounds were identical with protoplasm, and hence build up life from a primitive cell even to man,—were I to tell you all this and not put down my finger every now and then and say, this is an assumption, here we are really ignorant; this is probable, but as yet we have on this point no exact knowledge; were I to do this I should be no true scientist—it would be the dogmatism of false science, of false freethought,—every bit as dangerous as that religious dogmatism which would explain all things by the existence of a personal god or a triune deity. Hence, *materialism* in so far as by dogmatism it slurs over scientific ignorance; *atheism* in so far as it is merely destructive; *positivism* while it declares the relation

of the finite to the infinite to be beyond solution; and
pessimism which also treats the problem as beyond solution,
but replaces belief by no system of enthusiastic human
morality—these one and all are not identical with freethought.

True freethought never slurs over ignorance by dogmatism;
it is not only destructive but creative; it believes the problem
of life to be in gradual process of solution; it is not the
apotheosis of ignorance, but rather of knowledge. Thus I
cannot help thinking that no true man of science was ever a
materialist, a positivist, or a pessimist. If he were the first,
he were a dogmatist; if either of the latter, he must hold his
task impossible or useless. I do not by this identify freethought with science;—far from it! Freethought, as we have
seen, is knowledge of the relation of the finite to the infinite,
and science, in so far as it explains the position of the
individual with regard to the whole, is a very important
element, but not the totality of such knowledge.

I trust you will pardon the length at which I have discussed *Religion*, *Freethought*, and *Dogmatism*, if I have succeeded in conveying to you what I understand by these terms.
Religion I have defined as the relation of the finite to the
infinite; *Freethought* as our necessarily partial knowledge of
this one true religion; and *Dogmatism* as that mental habit
which replaces the known by the mythical, or at least supple-
ments the known by the imagination,—a habit in every way
impeding the growth of freethought.

You will say at once that it is an extremely difficult, if not
impossible, task to be a freethinker. I cannot deny it. It is
extremely difficult to approach closely any religious ideal.
How many perfect Christians have there been in the last
nineteen hundred years? Answer *that*, and judge how many
perfect freethinkers fall to the lot of a century! No more
than baptism makes a man a real Christian, does shaking off
dogmatism make a man a freethinker. It is the result of
long thought, of patient study, the labour of a life,—it is the
single-eyed devotion to truth, even though its acquirement
may destroy a previously cherished conviction. There must
be no interested motive, no working to support a party, an

individual, or a theory; such action but leads to the dis-
tortion of knowledge, and those who do not seek truth from
an unbiassed standpoint are, in the theology of freethought,
ministers in the devil's synagogue.   The attainment of
perfect freethought may be impossible, for all mortals are
subject to prejudice, are more or less dogmatic, yet the
approach towards this ideal is open to all of us.   In this
sense our greatest poets, philosophers, and scientists, men
such as Goethe, Spinoza, and Darwin, have all been freethinkers; they strove, regardless of dogmatic belief, and
armed with the highest knowledge and thought of their time,
to cast light on the one great problem of life.   We, who
painfully struggle in their footsteps, can well look to them as
to the high priests of our religion.

Having noted what I consider the essence of freethought,
and suggested the difficulty of its attainment, I wish, before
passing to what I may term its mission, to make a remark
on my definition of religion.   Some of you may feel inclined
to ask,—" If you assert the existence of religion, surely you
must believe in the existence of a god, and probably of the
so-called immortality of the soul?"   Now I must request
you to notice that I have made no assertion on these points
whatever.   By defining religion as the relation of the finite
to the infinite, I have not asserted the existence of a deity.
In fact, while that definition makes *religion a necessary logical
category, it only gives god a contingent existence.*   My meaning
will be perhaps better explained by reference to a concrete
religion, which places entirely on one side the existence of
god and the hope of immortality.   I refer to Buddhism, and
take the following sentences from Rhys Davids' lectures :—

" Try to get as near to wisdom and goodness as you can
in this life.   Trouble not yourself about the gods.   Disturb
yourself not by curiosities or desires about any future
existence.   Seek only after the fruit of the noble path of self-
culture and self-control."   The discussion of the future of
the soul is called the " walking in delusion," the "jungle,"
the " puppet-show," and the " wilderness."   " Of sentient
beings," we are told, " nothing will survive save the result of

their actions; and he who believes, who hopes in anything else, will be blinded, hindered, hampered in his *religious* growth by the most fatal of delusions."

Such notions render Buddhism perhaps the most valuable study among concrete religious systems to the modern free-thinker.

I can now proceed to consider what seems to me the mission·of the freethought I have just defined. In the beginning of my lecture I endeavoured to point out how the disparity between the finite and the infinite,—between the individual and the universe,—forces itself upon the attention of man. Struggle against it as he may, the 'Eternal Why' still haunts his mind. If he sees no answer to this question, or rather if he discovers no method by which he may attempt its solution, he is not seldom driven to despair, to pessimism, to absolute spiritual misery. Note, too, that this spiritual misery is something quite distinct from that physical misery, that want of bread and butter, which, though little regarded, is yearly crying out louder and louder in this London of ours; though distinct, it is none the less real. The relief of physical misery is a question of morality, of the relation of man to man—an urgent question just now, pressing for immediate attention, yet beyond the limits of our present subject. The relief of spiritual misery, also very prevalent nowadays, owing to the rapid collapse of so many concrete religious systems—that is the mission of freethought. I do not think I am assuming anything very extravagant in asserting that it is the duty of humanity to lessen in every possible way the misery of humanity; it is really only a truer expression of the basis of utilitarian morality. Hence the mission of freethought to relieve spiritual misery is the con-necting link between freethought as concrete religion and freethought as morality. Let us examine a little more closely the meaning of this mission.

The individual freethinker, except in very rare cases, can advance but little our partial knowledge of the relation between the finite and the infinite. He must content him-self with assimilating so far as in him lies the already ascertained truth. Now, although the already ascertained truth be but an infinitesimal part of the truth yet undiscovered, nevertheless the amount of truth added to our stock in any generation is in itself insignificant compared with what we have received from the past. In other words, the greater portion of our knowledge is handed down to us from the past, it is our heritage—the birthright of each one of us as man. Every freethinker, then, owes an intense debt of gratitude to the past; he is necessarily full of reverence for the men who have preceded him; their struggles, their failures, and their successes, taken as a whole, have given him the great mass of his knowledge. Hence it is that he feels sympathy even with the very failures, the false steps of the men of the past. He never forgets what he owes to every stage of past mental development. He can with no greater reason jeer at or abuse such a stage than he can jeer at or abuse his ancestors or the anthropoidal apes. Even when he finds his neighbour still halting in such a past stage of mental development, he has no right to abuse, he can only endeavour to teach. The freethinker must treat the past with the deepest sympathy and reverence. Herein lies, I think, a crucial test of much that calls itself freethought. A tendency to mock stages of past development, to jeer at neighbours still in the bondage of dogmatic faith, has cast an odium over the name freethinker which it will be difficult to shake off. Such mocking and such jeering never can be the mission of true freethought.

Let us suppose now our ideal freethinker has educated himself. By this I mean that he has assimilated the results of the highest scientific and philosophical knowledge of his day. It is not impossible that even then you may turn round upon me and say he has not solved the problem of life. I admit it. Yet in so far as he is in possession of real knowledge—that is, of truth—he has made a beginning of his solution. For this very word truth itself denotes some absolute, fixed, unchangeable law, and therefore a connection between the finite and the infinite. But not only has he made a beginning of his solution; he has started himself .

also in the true direction, wherein he must continue to work out the problem. No myth, no dogmatism can lead him astray; the freethinker of to-day has this advantage over the past, that where he is ignorant, he confesses it, and this in itself increases the rate at which the problem of life will be worked out. At every step there will not be an ever recurring myth to be swept away; at every turn his own dogmatism will not act as a drag upon his progress.

Hence it seems to me that the true freethinker can relieve a vast amount of spiritual misery; he can point out how much of the problem, albeit little, has been solved; he can point out the direction in which further solution is to be sought. Thus we may determine his mission—the spread of actually acquired truth—the destruction of dogmatism beneath the irresistible logic of fact. It is an educational, *creative*, not merely a destructive mission. Do not think this mission a light one; it is simply appalling how the mass of truth already acquired remains in the minds of a few; it is not spread broadcast among the people. I do not speak so much of the so-called lower classes, who, so far as the present serfdom of labour allows, are beginning to inquire and think for themselves, but rather of those who are curiously termed the ' educated.' Take the average clergyman of whatever denomination, the church or chapel-going lawyer, merchant, or tradesman, as a rule you will find absolute ignorance of the real bearings of modern philosophy and of modern science on social conduct. Here freethought has an infinite task of education. A remedy scarcely seems possible till science and philosophy are made essential parts of the curriculum of all our schools and universities.

The mission of freethought, however, lies not only in the propagation of existing, but in the discovery of new truth. Here it finds its noblest function, its holiest meaning. This pursuit of knowledge is the true worship of man—the union between finite and infinite, the highest pleasure of which the human mind is capable. It is hard for us to appreciate the intense delight which must follow upon the discovery of some great truth. Kepler, after years of observation, deducing the laws which govern the planetary system; Newton, after long puzzling, hitting upon the principle of gravitation; or Sir William Hamilton, as the conclusion of complicated analysis, finding the existence of conical refraction and verifying the wave theory of light—in all these and many other cases the conviction of truth must have brought endless pleasure. Even as Spinoza has said, " He who has a true idea is aware at the same time that he has a true idea, and cannot doubt of the thing." So with truth comes conviction and the consequent pleasure. Yet this is no self-complacency, but an enthusiastic desire to convey the newly-acquired truth to others—the intense wish to spread the new knowledge, to scatter its light into dark corners, to sweep away error and with it all the cobwebs of myth and ignorance. Hence it is that those from whom freethought has received the greatest services have been, as a rule, either philosophers or scientists, for such men have done most to extend the limits of existing knowledge; it is to them that freethought must look for its leaders and teachers. Here note, too, a very remarkable difference between freethought and the older concrete religions; the priest of freethought must be fully acquainted with the most advanced knowledge of his day; it will be no longer possible to send " the duffer of the family " to make a living in the church; the thinker only can appeal to the reasons of men, although the semi-educated has too often served to influence their undisciplined emotions.

But I have wandered somewhat from my point, that portion of the mission of freethought which relates to the discovery of new truth. It is in this aspect that the essentially *religious* character of freethought appears. It is not a stagnant religious system with a crystallized and unchangeable creed, forced to reject all new truth which is not in keeping with its dogma, but one which actually demands new truth, whose sole end is the growth and spread of human knowledge, and which must perforce adopt every great discovery as essentially a portion of itself. From this pursuit of religious truth ought to arise the enthusiasm of freethought; from this source it ought to find a continuous supply of fuel which no

dogmatic faith can draw upon. If freethought once grasped
this aspect of its mission, I cannot help thinking the consequent enthusiasm would soon carry it as the mastering
religious system through all grades of society. So long as
freethought is merely the cynical antagonism of individuals
towards dogma, so long as it is merely negative and destructive, it will never become a great living force. To do so, it
must become strong in the conviction of its own ·absolute
rightness, creative, sympathetic with the past, assured of the
future, above all enthusiastic. No world-movement ever
spread without enthusiasm. In the words of the greatest
of living German poets—

> Wisset, im Schwärmgeist brauset das Wehen des ewigen Geistes!
> Was da Grosses gescheh'n, das thaten auf Erden die Schwärmer!

It is no little future which I would paint for this new religious movement, yet it is perhaps the only one which has
a future; all others are of the past. It will have to shake
itself free of many faults, of many debasing influences, to take
a broader and truer view of its mission and of itself. Yet the
day I believe will come when its evangelists will spread
through the country, be heard in every house, and be seen on
every street preaching and teaching the only faith which is
consonant with the reason, with the dignity of man. Not by
myth, not by guesses of the imagination is the problem of life
to be solved; but by earnest application, by downright hard
work of the brain, spread over the lifetime of many men—
nay, of many centuries of men, extending even to the lifetime of the world; for the solution of the problem is identical
with the mental development of humanity, and who can say
where that shall end? Such then seems to me the mission
of freethought, and the freethinker who is conscious of this
mission may say proudly in the words of the prophet of
Galilee, " I come not to destroy, but to fulfil."

There still remains a point in which, perhaps, above all
others, my ethic of freethought may seem to you vague and
unmeaning. I refer to the nature of that truth, that knowledge of the relation between the finite and infinite, which it
is the principal duty of freethought to seek after.

If we could assert that all things happen by chance, that there is no invariable relation between one finite thing and another finite thing; that precisely the same set of circum-stances concludes to-day with a different effect from yesterday; that the lives of worlds and of nations, phases of being and of civilization, are ever passing without ordered beginning or end into nothingness; that everywhere huge chance up-heavals are eternally starting, eternally ceasing without co-ordination and as the mocking playwork of chaos,—were this the case, all hope of connecting the finite and the infinite would be impossible. Not only the recorded experience of our own and all past ages tell us that this is not the case, but I venture to assert that it is absolutely impossible it should be the case; and for the very simple reason that no man can conceive it. The very fact of such chance, of such chaos, would render all thought impossible—conception itself must cease in such a world. Once obtain a *clear* conception of any finite thing, say water, and another clear conception of any other finite thing, say wine; then if one day these concep-tions may be different and the next day the same—it is obvious that all clear thinking will be at an end, and if this chance confusion reigns between all finite things, it will be impossible for man to form any conceptions at all, impos-sible for him to think.

The very fact that man *does* think seems to me sufficient to show that there is a definite relation, a fixed order between one finite thing and another. This definite relation, this finite order is what we term *Law*, and hence follows that axiom without which it is impossible for any knowledge, any thought, to exist, namely: " The same set of causes always produces precisely the same effect." That is the very essence of the creed of freethought, and the rule by which every man practically guides his conduct. What is the nature of this Law, this ordered outcome of cause in effect ? Obviously it is not a finite changeable thing, it is absolute, infinite, independent of all conceptions of time or change, or particular groups of finite things. Hence it is what we have been seeking as the relation between finite and infinite. It is that which binds together the individual and the universe, giving him a necessary place in its life. Law makes his 'becoming' a necessary part of the 'becoming' of the universe; neither could exist without the other. Knowledge, therefore, of the relation of the finite to the infinite is a knowledge of law. Religion according to the definition I have given you to-night *is* law,[1] and the mission of freethought is to spread acquired knowledge and gain new knowledge of this law.

Let me strive to explain my meaning more clearly by an example. Supposing you were to grant me the truth of the principle of gravitation and the theory of heat as applied to the planetary system. Then I should be able to tell you, almost to the fraction of a second, the exact rate of motion and the position at a given time of each and all the planetary bodies. Nay, I might go further, and describe the 'becoming' of each individual planet, its loss of external motion, motion of translation and rotation; then, too, its loss of internal motion, motion of vibration, or heat, &c. All this would follow necessarily from the laws you had granted me, and the complicated work of mathematical analysis would all be verified by observation. Now note, every step of that mathematical analysis follows a definite law of thought, one step does not follow another from chance, but of absolute necessity. I can *think* the succession in *one* way only, and that one way is what? Why, the very method in which the facts appear to me to be occurring in so-called Nature!

This enables me to draw your attention to another phase of law—namely, the only possible way in which we can think things is precisely identical with the actual way in which they appear to us to occur. When the thought-relation does not agree with the fact-relation the incongruity is always the result of unclear thinking, or unclear facts—false thought or false conception of facts. Let me explain more closely my meaning. When we say that two and two make four, we recognize at once a law which, if contradicted, would render

[1] A fact partially grasped by the Jews, and even suggested by the Latin *religio*.

all thinking impossible. Now it is precisely this aspect of the so-called laws of nature which I wish to bring into prominence. Take, for example, Kepler's laws of planetary motion ; these he discovered by the tedious comparison of a long series of observations. At first sight they might appear as certain laws inherent in the planetary system— empirical laws which chanced to regulate that particular portion of the material universe. But mark what happens : Newton discovers the law of gravitation ; then thought can only conceive the planets as moving in the manner prescribed by Kepler's laws. In other words, the planets move in the only way thought can conceive them as moving. Kepler's laws cease to be empirical, they become a necessary law of thought. The law of gravitation being granted, the mind must consider the planets to move precisely as they do, even as it must consider that two and two make four. You may perhaps object : "But at least the law of gravitation is an empirical law, a mere description of a blind force inherent in matter ; it might have varied as the inverse cube or any other power, just as well as the inverse square." Not at all ! It is not my object to explain to you to-night how near physicists seem to be to a proof of the absolute thought necessity of the law of gravitation,—what wondrous conceptions the very existence of an universal fluid medium forces upon them. But as a hypothetical case I may mention that, if we were to suppose matter to consist ultimately of spherical atoms capable of surface pulsations,—and there is much to confirm such a supposition —then, owing to their mere existence in the fluid medium, thought would be compelled to conceive them as acting upon each other in a certain definite manner, and as a result of analysis this manner turns out to be something very akin to the so-called law of gravitation. Thus gravitation itself, granted the atom and the medium, would become as necessary a law of thought as that two and two make four ! We should have another link in the thought-chain.

At present our positive knowledge is far too small to allow us to piece together the whole universe in this fashion. Many of our so-called laws are merely empirical laws, the result of observation ; but the progress of knowledge seems to me to point to a far-distant time when all the finite things of the universe shall be shown to be united by law, and that law itself to be the only possible law which thought can conceive. Suppose the highly developed reason of some future man to start, say, with clear conceptions of the lifeless chaotic mass of 60,000,000 years ago, which now forms our planetary system, then from those conceptions alone he will be able to *think* out the 60,000,0years' history of the world, with every finite phase which it had passed through ; each will have its necessary place, its necessary course in this thought system—And this total history he has thought out ?—It will be identical with the actual history of the world ; for that history has evolved in the one sole way conceivable. The universe is what it is, because *that* is the only conceivable fashion in which it could be,—in which it could be thought. Every finite thing in it, is what it is, because *that* is the only possible way in which it could be. It is absurd to ask why things are not other than they are, because were our ideas sufficiently clear, we should see that they exist in the only way in which they are thinkable. Equally absurd is it to ask why any finite thing or any finite individual exists—its existence is a logical necessity—a necessary step or element in the complete thought-analysis of the universe, and without that step our thought-analysis, the universe itself, could have no existence.

There is another standpoint from which we may view this relation of law to the individual thinker. There has long been apparent antagonism between two schools of philosophical thinkers—the Materialists and the Idealists. The latter in their latest development have made the individual ' I ' the only objective entity in existence. The ' I ' knows nought but its own sensations, whence it forms the subjective notions, which we may term the idea of the ' I ' and the idea of the universe. The relation of these two ideas is, as in all systems of philosophy, the great problem. But in this idealism the idea of the ' I ' and the idea of the universe are, as it were, absolutely under the thumb of the individual ' I '—it is objective, they are subjective ; it proudly dictates the laws, which they must obey. It is the pure thought-law of the ' I ' which determines the relation between the idea of the ' I ' and the idea of the universe. On the other hand, the materialist finds in nature certain unchangeable laws, which he supposes in some manner inherent in his undefinable reality, matter; these laws do not appear in any way the outcome of the individual ' I,' but something outside it, with regard to which the ' I ' is subjective,—which, regardless of the thought of the ' I,' dictates its relation to the universe. Is the antagonism between these two methods of considering the ' I ' and the universe so great as it at first sight appears? Or rather, is not the distinction an idle one of the schools? Let us return to our idealist. Having made his thought the proud ruler of the relation between the idea of the ' I ' and the idea of the universe, he is compelled, in order to grasp his own position, to regulate his own conduct in life, to place himself—his ' I '—in the subjective attitude of the idea of the ' I ; ' to identify himself with the idea of the ' I.' This act is the abnegation of his objectivity, he becomes subjective, and the objective entity which rules his relation to the universe is an abstract ' I,'—pure thought—it is this which determines the connection between the ' I ' and all other finite things,—between finite and infinite. In other words, idealism forces upon us the conception that the law which binds the finite to the infinite is a pure law of thought, that the only existing objectivity is the ' logic of pure thought.' But this is precisely the result to which materialism, as based on physical science, seems to point,—namely, that all so-called material or natural laws will ultimately be found to be the only laws thought can conceive ; that so-called natural laws are but steps in the ' logic of pure thought.' Thus, with growth of scientific knowledge, all distinction between Idealism and Materialism seems destined to vanish.

Religion, then, or the relation of the finite to the infinite, must be looked upon as matter of law ; not the mindless law of chance, but a law of thought—even akin to : ' Nothing can both be and not be.' We have to look upon the universe as one vast intellectual process, every fact as a thought, and every succession of facts as a succession of thoughts; as thought only progresses in logical order of intellect, so only does fact. The law of the one is identical with the law of the other. To assert, therefore, that a law of the universe may be interfered with or altered, is to assert that it is possible to conceive a thing otherwise than in the *only* conceivable way. Hence arises the indifference of the true freethinker to the question of the existence or non-existence of a personal god. Such a being can stand in no relation whatever of active interference to the law of the universe ; in other words, so far as man is concerned, his existence cannot be a matter of the least importance. To repeat Buddha's words, " Trouble yourselves not about the gods! " If, like the frogs or the Jews, who would have a king, we insist upon having a god, then let us call the universe, with its vast system of unchangeable law, god—even as Spinoza. We shall not be likely to fall into much error concerning his nature.

Lastly, let me draw your attention to one point which has especial value for the religion of freethought. We have seen how the disparity between finite and infinite tends to depress man to the lowest depth of spiritual misery, such a depth as you will find portrayed in James Thomson's *City of Dreadful Night*. This misery is too often the result of the first necessary step towards freedom of thought, namely, the complete rejection of all forms of dogmatic faith. It can only be dispelled by a recognition of the true meaning of the problem of life, the relation of the finite to the infinite. But in the very nature of this problem—as I have endeavoured to express it to-night—lies a strange inexpressible pleasure ; it is the apparently finite mind of man, which itself rules the infinite ; it is human thought which dictates the laws of the universe ; only what man *thinks*, can possibly *be*. The very immensities which appal him, are they not in a sense his own creations ? Nay, paradoxical as it may seem, there is much truth in the assertion, that : *It is the mind of man which rules the universe.* Freethought in making him master of his own reason renders him lord of the world. That seems to me the endless joy of the free-thinker's faith. It is a real and a living faith, which creative, sympathetic, and above all, enthusiastic, is destined to be the creed of the future.

Do you smile at the notion of freethought linked to enthusiasm? Remember the lines of the poet :—

" Enthusiasts they will call us—aye, enthusiasts even we must be :
Has not long enough ruled the emp● word and the letter?
Stand, oh, mankind, on thine own feet at last, thou overgrown child !
And canst thou not stand—not even yet—must thou still fall to the
    ground
Without crutches, then fall to the ground, for thou art not worthy to
    stand ! "

(Hamerling.)

II

THE PROSTITUTION OF SCIENCE.

How fertile of resource is the theologic method, when it once has clay for its wheel !—*Clifford.*

An interesting psychological study might well be based on a comparison of the mental characteristics of the present and the late Presidents of the Royal Society. The former un-rivalled in his analysis of intricate physical problems, demanding every accuracy in mathematical reasoning, and ever ready to destroy the argument from analogy or the flimsy hypothesis—witness his earlier polemic against the pseudo-hydrodynamicists—the latter spending the greater part of his energies on the investigation and elucidation of a branch of science which as yet has hardly developed beyond the descriptive stage. Place before these two men a complex problem needing the most cautious reasoning, the most careful balancing of all the arguments that can be brought forward, and the most stringent logic—can there be a doubt that the mathematically trained mind will see farther and more clearly than that of the descriptive scientist ? The argument from analogy, while shunned by the former, will seem natural to the latter, who has been accustomed to qualitative rather than quantitative distinc-tions. Yet how totally opposed to this plausible conclusion is the actual state of the case ! How much more than scientific training is evidently needed to give the mind logical accuracy when dealing with intellectual problems ! It is Mr. Huxley, who, well versed in what the thinkers of

3

the past have contributed to human knowledge, shatters with irresistible logic the obscure cosmical speculations of Ezra and Mr. Gladstone. It is Professor Stokes, who, like a resuscitated Paley, discovers in the human eye an evidence of design, and startles the countrymen of Hume with a physico-theological proof of the existence of the deity! Poor Scotland! What with yearly Burnett Lectures and three Gifford Professors of Natural Theology, thou wilt either be driven into blatant atheism or have thy mental calibre reduced to the level of a Bridgewater treatise! It is true one Drummond has written a work wherein, by the light of analogy, dogma is seen draped in the mantle of science—a work, whose sale by the tens of thousands is, like the Psychical Society, gratifying evidence of a widespread and almost desperate craving for a last stimulant to super-sensuous belief. It is true the neo-Hegelians of Glasgow can deduce the Trinity by an ontological process almost as glibly as their brethren of Balliol; yet it remained for Professor Stokes to present Scotland with a new edition of the rare old "argument from design." [1] We doubt whether his fellow natural theologians will thank the Professor for the gift, for they are already well on the road to the discovery of a hitherto neglected category which shall supersede causation—at least for the physiologists. It is worth while, however, to consider this gift a little more closely because it is quite certain that if the 'natural theologian' does not regard it with favour, the supernatural theologian, in other words the work-a-day parson, will only be too glad (like the mediæval schoolman who cancelled one twenty-five authorities by a second twenty-five) to cancel one president of the Royal Society by another.

Let us approach the problem by trying to state briefly what is legitimately deducible from the 'order' of the universe, and then expose the fallacies of Professor Stokes' reasoning. The first and the only fundamentally safe conclusion we can draw from the apparently invariable sequence

[1] *On the Beneficial Effects of Light.* Burnett Lectures. By George Gabriel Stokes, M.A., F.R.S., &c. Fourth Lecture, pp. 78–97.

or 'order' of natural phenomena, is that: Like sensations invariably occur to us in similar groupings. This is no absolute knowledge of natural phenomena, but a knowledge of our own sensations. Further, our knowledge of the 'invariability' is only the result of experience, and is based, therefore, upon probability. The probability deduced from the sameness experienced in the sequences of one repeated group of sensations is not the only factor, however, of this invariability. There is an enormous probability in favour of a general sameness in the sequences of all repeated groups of sensations. In ordinary language this is expressed in the fundamental scientific law: "The same causes will always produce the same effects." In any case where a new group of causes produces a novel effect, we do not want to repeat this new grouping an enormous number of times in order to be sure that the like effect always follows. We repeat the grouping only so often as will suffice to acquaint us with the exact sequence of causes and effect, and then we are convinced that the effect will always follow owing to the enormous probability in favour of the inference as to sameness in the sequence of a repeated grouping.[1] Our knowledge of the 'order' of natural phenomena is thus only equal to our consciousness of an enormous probability based upon wide experience in the sameness of the sequence which groupings of sensations adopt whenever they are repeated. The 'order,' so far as we are able to trace it back, lies in the sameness of the sensational sequence, not necessarily in the *Dinge an sich*. The sensations reach the perceptive faculty under the fundamental forms of time and space; sequence of sensations in time, and sometimes apparent conjunction in space, have led mankind to formulate the category of causation. If the sensation A invariably

[1] A good example of this is the solidification of hydrogen, which has perhaps only been accomplished two or three times, yet no scientist doubts its possibility. The criticism of Boole on the probability basis of our knowledge of sequence in natural phenomena (*Laws of Thought*, pp. 370–75) has been, I think, sufficiently met by Mr. Y. Edgeworth (*Mind* 1885).

follows B, or even if B is invariably found associated with
A, we speak of them as cause and effect. But as yet there
is not the slightest evidence that the ' order ' extends beyond
our perceptive faculty and the laws of our perception to the
Dinge an sich. The 'order' of the universe *may* arise from my
having to perceive it, if I perceive it at all, under the forms of
space and time. My perceptive faculty may put the ' order'
into my sensations. To argue that because this order exists
there must be an organizing faculty is perfectly legitimate.
To proceed, however, from the human mind to the order in
sensations, and then assert that the order we find in the
universe (or the sum of our sensations) requires an 'universe
orderer' on an infinite scale, is the obvious fallacy of what
Kant has termed the physico-theological proof of the existence
of a deity. It is to reflect the human mind into phenomena,
and then out of them into the unreachable or unknowable
god ; to argue like savages, because we see ourselves in a
mirror, that there is an unknown being on the other side!
From our sensations we can only deduce something of the
same order as our sensations, or of the perceptive faculty
which co-ordinates them ; from finite perceptions and conceptions we can only pass to finite perceptions and conceptions ;
from ' physical facts ' to physical facts of the same quality.[1]
We cannot put into them anything of an order not involved
in their nature. From sequence in sensations we can reach
a perceptive faculty of the finite magnitude of the human,
and nothing more ; we cannot logically formulate a creator
of matter, a single world organizer, an infinite mind, nor a
moral basis of the universe such as the theologian, the
reconciler, or even Kant himself really require. An ontological, never a physico-theological, process *may attempt* to deduce
the existence of a moral basis. The dogma of identifying
the human with the divine mind will, indeed, enable us to get
out of the argument from design a pantheistic, but never a
moral basis of the universe. The last page of Professor
Stokes' work proves that he was himself dimly conscious

---

[1] Kant, *Der einzig mögliche Beweisgrund zu einer Demonstration für
das Dasein Gottes.* Ausg. Hartenstein. Bd. ii. s. 165, 203, &c.

of not having 'deduced' exactly the sort of deity he was in search of. By a series of assumptions, not to say fallacies, he could reach a deity, either 'too anthropomorphic' or else a 'sort of pantheistic abstraction'; as he only started with the human mind, these results are not surprising. To obtain the divine being of the theologians he must finally appeal to *revelation*. We need scarcely remark that had he begun with it, he would have saved us some bad logic and left his own position quite unassailable; the theologian, who fences himself in behind belief in revelation, and disregards natural theology and the neo-Hegelian ontology of our modern schoolmen, is beyond our criticism, and at least deserves our respect, in that he does not seek to strengthen his conviction in the accuracy of Peter and Paul's evidence by arraying dogma in the plumes of science and philosophy.

If the law of causation, the 'order' of the universe, be really, as we have stated above, a result of the human perceptive faculty always co-ordinating sensations in the same fashion, it is obvious that the basis of the 'order' in the universe must be sought in the perceptive faculty, and not in the sensations themselves; the ultimate law of phenomena, as we perceive them, will be a law of the perceptive faculty, and more akin to a law of thought than a law of matter in the ordinary sense of the term. Indeed no so-called law of nature based upon observation of our sensations is anything more than a description of their sequence; it is never, as is often vulgarly supposed, the cause of that sequence. Although Professor Stokes undoubtedly recognizes this, there are one or two phrases in his book not unlikely to encourage the vulgar belief. Thus he speaks in one place (p. 79) of "matter obeying the law of gravitation," and in another of gravitation "as holding together the components of the most distant double star as well as maintaining in their orbits the planets of our system." The careless reader might be led to look upon the law of gravitation as the cause of planetary motion, although this is, of course, not Professor Stokes' intention. The law of gravitation answers no *why*, only tells us a *how*; it is a purely descriptive account of the sequence in our sensations of the planets; it tells us more fully and generally than Kepler's so-called laws the *how* of planetary motion; it tells us that the planetary and other bodies are changing the speeds with which they move towards each other in a certain fashion. *Why* they thus change their speeds it does not attempt to tell us, and the explanation of the law of gravitation, which we are all waiting for, will only throw us back on a still wider, but none the less a *descriptive* law of the motion of the parts of the universe. Even if we were able to throw back the whole complex machinery of the universe on the simplest motion of its simplest parts, our fundamental physical law could only, as dealing with sensations, be a *descriptive* one. To pass from that descriptive law to its *cause* we should be thrown back upon the perceptive faculty, and be compelled to answer why it must co-ordinate under change in time and place, or under the category of motion (and in this case motion of a particular kind), the simplest conceptions to which it can reduce the universe, or the sum of its sensations. Granted that I do see one and not a series of coloured images of an object, it is obviously necessary that when I come to study the build of my eye I must find it a fairly achromatic combination, otherwise one series of sensations would be opposed to another; our perceptions would contradict each other, and thought become impossible. I can only think according to the law that contradictions cannot exist, and there is no more wonder that I find the eye a fairly achromatic combination than that I see only one image. Given that I have a sensation of a single image of an object, my perceptive faculty compels my sensations of the structure of the eye to be in harmony with the former sensation. To argue from the harmony existing among my sensations to a like harmony and order in the *Dinge an sich* is to multiply needlessly the causes of natural phenomena, and so break Newton's rule of which Professor Stokes himself expresses approval. If the human perceptive faculty is capable of so co-ordinating sensations that all the groups maintain their own sequence, and are in perfect harmony with each other, shortly that 'order' and 'design' appear in natural phenomena, what advantage do we gain by needlessly multiplying causes and throwing back the 'order' and harmony of our sensations upon the *Dinge an sich*, and an unknowable intellectual faculty behind them ?

To sum up, then, the conclusions of this brief treatment of the problem, in order to investigate by their light Professor Stokes' fourth lecture, we find :—

1. That nothing can be deduced from our sensations, which is not of the same order as those sensations or the faculty which perceives them ; we can deduce only the physical (or descriptive law) and the perceptional (or true causative) law.

2. That there may or may not be order and harmony in the *Dinge an sich*. It is a problem we have not the least means of answering by physical or psychological investigation. To assume, however, that the order of our sensations connotes a like order in the *Dinge an sich* is to " multiply needlessly the causes of natural phenomena."

3. That physical science must remain agnostic with regard to such order and with regard to an infinite mind behind it among the unknowable bases of our sensations.

4. That theology cannot obtain aid from science in this matter because the latter deals only with the sensational, and cannot proceed from that to quantities of an entirely different nature—to the supersensational. To reach the supersensational, theology must take the responsibility on her own shoulders of asserting the unthinkable — of asserting a revelation, an occurrence which lies entirely outside the sensations and the percipient with which alone science has to deal. Theology must cry with Tertullian : *Credo quia absurdum est.*

It will be seen from the above that revelation and matter —the *Dinge an sich*—are the unknowable wherein the theologian can safely take refuge from the scientist. Let him remember that our only conception of matter is drawn from the sensation of motion, and that the ultimate phase of this motion we can only *describe*, not explain, then he will have no hesitation in shaking hands with Ludwig Büchner, and sharing the unknowable with that prince of dogmatists. . Strange as it may seem, it is nevertheless true, that in materialism lies the next lease of life for theology.

Let us now turn to the remarkable fourth lecture of the third Burnett course. Had the President of the Royal Society been writing on a purely scientific as distinguished from a theosophical subject, there is little doubt what his method would have been. He would have referred to what previous researchers had ascertained on the subject, he would have clearly stated the relation of his own work to theirs, and if in any case he had come to conclusions differing from those of first-class thinkers, he would have been careful to state the reasons for his divergence, and shown that he had not lightly put aside their results. Why should Professor Stokes, when he approaches an intricate intellectual problem, think he may discard the scientific and scholarly method? When an argument, which orthodox and heterodox philosophical thinkers alike have set aside for nearly a century as valueless, is drawn in a state of rust from the intellectual armoury, and, without any pretence to much furbishing, is hurled at the head of our trusty Scot, surely we may demand some explanation, and not, like a distinguished Scotch mathematician, hail as an "exceedingly clear statement"[1] a lecture which gives no evidence whatever that the writer has duly weighed the lucid dialogues of Hume, or the elaborate arguments of Kant and the post-Kantians. Whatever may have been Hume's own opinion, whether he thoroughly agreed with Cleanthes as he states, or merely used Cleanthes as a mask for his real opinions as propounded by Philo, there cannot yet be a doubt that Cleanthes gives no valid reply to Philo's arguments ; and as Mr. Huxley has observed, Hume has dealt very unfairly to the reader if he knew of such a reply and concealed it (*Hume*, p. 180). As

[1] Professor P. G. Tait, in a characteristic article in *Nature*, June 2, 1887. But then the author of *The Unseen Universe* probably means by a 'clear statement' one not encumbered by the lengthy processes needful to logical proof.

for Kant, he found, even in his pre-critical days, that the "only possible proof" for the existence of a deity was ontological, and the process by which, in his post-critical period, he deduced the second "only possible proof" of the existence of a deity from the need of a moral world-orderer (when transcending the limit of the human understanding he discovered the *Dinge an sich* to be Will), was the very reverse of the argument from design. As for Hegel, let us for once quote from a metaphysician a paragraph which Professor Stokes would do well to take to heart :

"Teleological modes of investigation often proceed from a well-meant desire of displaying the wisdom of God, especially as it is revealed in nature. Now in thus trying to discover final causes, for which the things serve as means, we must remember that we are stopping short at the finite, and are liable to fall into trifling reflections. An instance of such triviality is seen when we first of all treat of the vine solely in reference to the well-known uses which it confers upon man, and then proceed to view the cork-tree in connection with the corks which are cut from its bark to put into wine-bottles. Whole books used to be written in this spirit. It is easy to see that they promoted the genuine interest neither of religion nor of science. External design stands immediately in front of the idea ; but what thus stands on the threshold often for that reason gives the least satisfaction." [1]

"Whole books *used* to be written in this spirit," Hegel tells us, and now Professor Stokes gives us a whole lecture without so much as suggesting that his method of argument has been subjected to the most severe criticism. But perhaps this absence of reference to previous writers is excusable ; it may be that Professor Stokes' own arguments are so conclusive that the criticism of the past falls entirely short of them. Let us investigate this point. Our lecturer commences by telling us that he is going to devote his last lecture to the illustration afforded by his subject to the theme proposed by old John Burnett in his original endowment (1784), namely—

[1] *The Logic of Hegel,* Trans. Wallace, p. 299.

"That there is a Being, all-powerful, wise, and good, by whom everything exists; and particularly to obviate difficulties regarding the wisdom and goodness of the Deity; and this, in the first place, from considerations independent of written revelation,"—and so on.

It must be confessed that the only way we see, in which old John Burnett's bequest could have been made available for obviating the before-mentioned difficulties, would be the proper encouragement of internal illumination, so that the world might possibly have been provided with oral revelation of a more modern type than that 'written revelation,' which in the first place is to be neglected. However, Professor Stokes has thought otherwise, and in the *Beneficial Effects of Light* he hopes to obviate our intellectual difficulties as to this all-powerful, wise, and good Being.

He commences by telling us of the order which the law of gravitation has introduced into our conceptions of the planetary system, and how, if we went no further than that treatment of the subject which concentrates the planets into particles, and so deals only approximately with one side of their motion, we could predict indefinite continuance in time to come for the planetary system. All this is admirable truth, or very near truth. Then we are told how the physical condition of the planetary bodies no longer treated as particles, but as worlds, is solely but surely changing; the sun is losing its heat, the planets their volcanic energies, the earth her rotation owing to tidal friction,—shortly, the physical condition of the solar system is changing even as its position in the stellar universe. Again very true, and what is the just conclusion? Obviously: that solar systems may be built up, develop physically for billions of years, and then collapse; perhaps in long ages to form again parts of other systems. So much we may conclude, and nothing more. But what has our lecturer to say on this point? Let us quote his own words:

"The upshot is that even if we leave out of account all organization, whether of plants or animals, we fail to find in the material system of nature that which we can rest on as self-existent and uncaused. The earth says it is not in me, and the sun saith it is not in me " (p. 82).

That worlds may come into existence and again pass away, and that the period during which human life can exist upon them is limited, have long been evident to every one except the endless progress worshippers of Mr. Frederick Harrison's type. But what is there in the evolution of worlds more than in the birth and death of a cock-sparrow to justify us in assuming that the one more than the other is 'caused'? The shape and physical constitution of the universe at one instant differ from what they are at the next; and to say that no phase of universal life is self-existent, is merely to say that universal life is ever changing. The human being is continually gaining new cells and losing old ones, but shall we argue from the fact that these cells are not self-existent, that the human being also is not self-existent? Because the universe loses one solar system and gains another, is this any evidence that the universe is not self-existent? If it be, we may at least content ourselves with the modest example of a cock-sparrow whose death is a more obvious fact than the decay of the planetary system to the ordinary observer.

" When, from the contemplation of mere dead matter, we pass on to the study of the various forms of life, vegetable and animal, the previous negative conclusion at which we had arrived is greatly strengthened." Although Professor Stokes sees the possibility of the evolution of worlds without a definite act of creation, he still speaks of a *previous conclusion* (as if any real conclusion had been reached at all !), and proceeds to confirm it by showing that animal and vegetable life is not self-existent or uncaused. Before we examine this next stage in the argument, we would draw attention to the almost Gladstonian phrase, ' mere dead matter.' As we have previously pointed out, we know nothing whatever of the nature of matter, our simplest physical conceptions are those of motion ; we have some reason for believing the ultimate elements of the universe to be in motion, but why they are in motion, and apparently uncaused motion,[1] we have

---

[1] For example, the vibrational energy of the concept 'atom.'

not the least means of determining. Self-existent motion is not exactly what we associate with death, and in fact the whole phrase, 'mere dead matter,' might lead the uninitiated to suppose we had a complete knowledge of the cause of our sensations, while in fact we are in absolute ignorance with regard to it.

Having disposed of 'dead,' let us turn to living matter. Here there are two problems to be investigated. What is the origin of life in any form on the earth ? and, What is the origin of the diverse forms of life that we find upon it ? These are problems to which science has not yet given final answers; in which we at present deal only with probable hypotheses, but hypotheses which we must judge according to Newton's rule, " which," in the words of Professor Stokes, "forbids us needlessly to multiply the causes of natural phenomena."   In attempting to answer the first question we must keep the following possibilities before us :

1. There never was any origin to life in the universe, it having existed from all time like the matter which is vulgarly contrasted with it ; it has changed its form, but never at any epoch begun to be.

2. Life has originated " spontaneously from dead matter."

3. Life has arisen from the " operation in time of some ultra-scientific cause."

These possibilities, which we may term the perpetuity, the spontaneous generation, and the creation of life, are not very clearly distinguished by Professor Stokes.   He appears to hold that life *must necessarily have had an origin*, because we have ample grounds for asserting that those phases of life, with which we are at present acquainted, could not have existed in certain past stages of the earth's development. Recognizing only known types of life, he proceeds to question whether their germs might not have been brought to earth by Sir William Thomson's meteorite—an hypothesis which he not unnaturally dismisses.   But granted the meteorite, Professor Stokes continues :

" Of course such a supposition, if adopted, would leave untouched the problem of the origin of life ; it would merely invalidate the argument for the origination of life on our earth within geological time " (p. 85).

We see clearly that the writer supposes life, even if it did not originate on the earth, must have had an origin. But why may not life in some type or other be as perpetual as matter? We know life which assimilates carbon and eliminates oxygen; we know also life which assimilates oxygen and eliminates carbon—yet between the lowest forms of these lives we cannot draw a rigid line. Shall we dogmatically assert, then, that types of life which could survive the gaseous and thermal changes in the condition of our planet are impossible? The word *azoic*, as applied to an early period of our earth's history, can only refer to types of life with which we are now acquainted. There is a distinct possibility of other types of life, and of these types gradually evolving, owing to climatological change, into the types of which we are cognisant. Some of the most apparently simple forms of life with which we are acquainted must really have an organism of a most complex kind. The spermatozoon, bearing as it does all the personal and intellectual characteristics of a parent, must have a far more complex organism than its physiological description would lead us to believe; the potentiality of development must in some way denote a complexity of structure. *Size* thus appears to be only a partial measure of complexity, and the minuteness and apparent simplicity of certain microscopic organisms by no means proves that they are the forms of life which carry us back nearest to the so-called azoic period. The types of life then extant may have been complex as the spermatozoon and as small as the invisible germ, if one exists, of the microscopic organisms found in putrefying substances, for aught we can assert to the contrary. It is obvious that of such types of life the geological record would bear no trace, and we cannot argue from their absence in that record to the impossibility of its existence. That no life such as we know it could exist in the molten state of our planet may be perfectly true, but that is no proof that germs of a different type of life may not have survived in the gaseous mass, and developed into known forms of life as the climato-physical conditions changed. With regard, then, to the hypothesis of the perpetuity of life, the scientist can only remain agnostic, and cannot draw any evidence, as Professor Stokes seems to think, of the "operation in time of some ultra-scientific cause." The perpetuity of life is, however, a more plausible hypothesis than creation, as it does not "needlessly multiply the causes of natural phenomena." Professor Stokes simply extends his premise, 'no living things *that we see around us* could exist in the incandescent period,' to 'no living things at all,' and thus arrives at the origin of life in an 'ultra-scientific cause.'

Passing on to the hypothesis of spontaneous generation, we may note again the same logical fallacy :

" The result of the experiments which have been made in this subject by the most careful workers is such that most persons are, I think, now agreed that the evidence of experiment is very decidedly against the supposition that even these minute creatures can be generated spontaneously."

The minute creatures in question are the microscopic organisms in putrefying matter. The statement may be perfectly true, but before it would allow us logically to reject the possibility of the spontaneous generation of life, we should have to show—(1) that the organisms in question were the particular types of life which generated spontaneously ; their 'minuteness' is certainly no evidence of this, unless, *accepting the doctrine of evolution*, we have shown that these organisms are with great probability the earliest types of life known to us, and therefore nearest the type which arose after the 'azoic' period ; (2) that we have reproduced in our experiments the physical conditions extant at the time when life may be supposed to have been generated. There is no evidence to show that a turnip or urine wash, subjected to a very high temperature and preserved in a hermetically sealed vessel, at all represents the physical and climatological conditions of the earth at the close of the azoic period. It is obvious that these conditions can hardly be fulfilled in experiment ; we cannot imitate the climato-physical state which possibly only in long course of millions of years produced a type of life totally different from anything known to us, and which type, if reproduced, would not necessarily fall within the limits of our organs of sense. No *negative* experiment can lead us to reject the hypothesis of spontaneous generation, however much a positive experiment might prove it. Hence, when Professor Stokes postulates a commencement of life on earth, negatives spontaneous generation, and arrives at a cause "which for anything we can see, or that appears probable, lies altogether outside the ken of science," he is simply piling Pelion upon Ossa, one dogma upon another, and so ruthlessly thrusting aside the logically agnostic attitude of the true scientist. As to the third hypothesis, that of creation, the only arguments that can be produced in its favour are (1) from the process of exhaustion—*i.e.*, the logical negation of all other hypotheses, or the proof that all such destroy the harmony existing between various groups of our sensations ; (2) from the evidence of revelation. This latter we are not called upon to deal with under the heading of natural theology.

When we turn for a moment from descriptive science, or the classification of sensations, to the simplest intellectual concepts that the mind has formed with regard to the ulti- mate elements of life and matter, we find very little to separate the one from the other, certainly nothing which enables us to assert that there is perpetuity in the one more than in the other. We analyze our sensations of both, and find our ultimate concepts very similar. In the ultimate element of matter, apparently self-existent motion, and capa- city, owing to this motion, of entering into combination with other elements, our conception of the ultimate element of life might almost be described in the same words. Why this self-existent motion is our ultimate concept, is at present an unanswered problem, but, as we have pointed out, its solution is more likely to be reached by a scrutiny of the perceptive faculty, and the forms under which that faculty must perceive, than by any results to be drawn from de- scriptive science. Be this as it may, it is sufficient to note that there is nothing in the perpetuity or, on the other hand, in the spontaneous generation of life (which is really only another name for the perpetuity, as the universe will probably always possess systems in the zoïc stage) that contradicts the harmony of our sensations, or bring confusion into our concepts of life and matter.

Professor Stokes next devotes one brief page to statement, and another to criticism, of the doctrine of evolution. His second problem being the origin of the variety in living types, we have next to inquire what natural theology has to say about it ? *Apparently* it is content, after stating the stock objections, such as small amount of transmutation of form in actual experiment, the absence of connecting links, and the deterioration (or *degeneration*, as Professor Ray Lankester has termed it) of types of life, to remain agnostic in the matter. The concluding remarks of Professor Stokes on this point are, however, suggestive of his real opinion :

"Suffice it to observe that if, as regards the first origin of life on earth, science is powerless to account for it, and we must have recourse to some ultra-scientific cause, there is nothing unphilosophical in the supposition that this ultra-scientific cause may have acted subsequently also " (p. 89).

The fallacies in this reasoning are almost too obvious to need comment. It assumes (1) that life has had an origin ; (2) that because science has not hitherto explained something (which possibly never existed), therefore it must alway remain unable to do so ; (3) that if we have recourse in one case to an ultra-scientific cause, there is nothing unphilosophical in doing so again. Indeed there is an obvious rejoinder which seems strangely to have escaped the lecturer—namely, that it would not accordingly be unphilosophical to attribute all natural phenomena we have not yet fully explained to ultra-scientific causes, and so do away with the Royal Society and other scientific bodies as useless and expensive institutions, 'unnecessarily multiplying the causes of natural phenomena '!

The argument may be paralleled by the following, which we may suppose drawn from the lecture-room of a mediæval schoolman : Since science is powerless to explain why the sun goes round the earth, and we must have recourse to some ultra-scientific cause, there is nothing unphilosophical in supposing the same cause to raise the tides. *Ergo*, God daily raises the tides.

From this point onwards the lecturer turns more especially to the argument from design, and takes as his example the extremely complex structure of the human eye. Contemplating all the intricate portions of this organism and its adaptability to the uses to which it is put, Professor Stokes finds it "difficult to understand how we can fail to be impressed with the evidence of Design thus imparted to us." This evidence from design goes, we suppose, to prove the existence of old John Burnett's "all-powerful, wise, and good Being." We wonder if Professor Stokes' audience would have been equally impressed with the evidence from design had he chosen as his example the leprosy *bacillus*, which is also wonderfully adapted to the use to which it is put, and the organization and life of which is equally evidence from design of the most interesting kind. But perhaps, notwithstanding the term 'beneficial,' it is not the anthropomorphic qualities of wisdom and goodness in the deity which are to be deduced from the evidence from design. It is only the existence of 'constructive mind.' If this be so, we may well inquire whether complexity of construction is always evidence of mind, and we cannot prove the fallacy of the argument better than by citing the words in which Philo demolishes Cleanthes.[1]

"The Brahmins assert that the world arose from an infinite spider, who spun this whole complicated mass from his bowels, and annihilates afterwards the whole or any part of it by absorbing it again, and resolving it into his own essence. Here is a species of cosmogony which appears to us ridiculous, because the spider is a little contemptible animal, whose operations we are never likely to take for a model of the whole universe. But still here is a new species

[1] *Dialogues concerning Natural Religion.* Part vi. Green's Edition, p. 425.

of analogy, even in the globe. And were there a planet wholly inhabited by spiders (which is very possible), this inference would there appear as natural and irrefragable as that which in our planet ascribes the origin of all things to design and intelligence as explained by Cleanthes. Why an orderly system may not be spun from the belly as well as from the brain, it will be difficult for him to give a satisfactory reason."

The absurdity of the argument from analogy is well brought out in these lines. Till Professor Stokes has proved beyond all question that it is not the human perceptive faculty which produces harmony and order in *its* world of sensations, it seems idle to suggest that at the basis of that harmony and order there may be something analogous to the human mind. The basis of those sensations—the *Ding an sich*—may after all be a gigantic spider who spins from the belly, not the brain.

But even if we adopt for the sake of argument the crude realism which separates a 'dead matter' from something else which it terms 'mind,' we find in the 'law of the survival of the fittest' an apparently sufficient cause for the adaption of structure to function. Professor Stokes remarks, it is true, that even if this probable hypothesis were proved, it would not follow that no evidence of design was left; but it would follow that the remnant of Professor Stokes' natural theology, so far as he has expounded it in this work, would collapse. The evidence for design would be thrown back on those great physical laws which a certain school of thinkers delight to describe as 'inherent in dead matter,' rather than as forms of the perceptive faculty. Although Professor Stokes gives us no real arguments against the *possibility* of the law of the survival of the fittest being able to explain the adaption of structure to function, still he tells us what he *believes*; namely, that this law may account for some (if for some, why not for all ?) features of a complex whole, "but that we want nothing more to account for the existence of structures so exquisite, so admirably adapted to their functions, is to my mind incredible. I cannot help

regarding them as evidences of design operating in some far
more direct manner, I know not what ; and such, I believe,
would be the conclusion of most persons."

In other words, the last standpoint of natural theology is
belief, and belief as to what the belief of the majority of
persons may be.

Natural theology having thus thrown up a plausible hypothesis as to the orderly arrangement of phenomena in exchange for a belief in, not a proof of an ultra-scientific cause,
its further stages are easily marked. Returning to its unproven dogmas that neither matter nor life are self-existent
—dogmas based on a misinterpretation of the obvious facts
that planetary systems decay, and life, such as we know it,
was once non-extant in the world—natural theology concludes
that the mind, found by *analogy* in the order of the universe,
is self-existent, and therefore God. But the self-existence
thus deduced as an attribute of the deity is precisely what
revelation has foretold us : " I AM hath sent me unto you.
Here is the unity between science and revelation we have
been in search of! Here natural theology finds itself in
unison with Moses' views as to the nature of his tribal god.
" It is noteworthy," remarks Professor Stokes, " that it is
precisely this attribute of self-existence that God himself
chose for his own designation." The identification of the
' ultra-scientific cause,' of the Jewish tribal god, and of God
(with a capital G), is complete !

It is needless for us to follow Professor Stokes through his
remaining pages ; having once got on to the ground of revelation, it is not for us to pursue him further. We should expect
to find, and do find, arguments from analogy, and a repetition
of the dogmas deduced by a false logical process ; *e.g.*, " We
have seen that life can proceed only from the living " (when
and where ?)—by analogy, why not mind only from mind ?
" The sense of right and wrong is too universal to be attributed to the result of education " (but why not to the survival
of the fittest in the internecine struggle of human societies ?),
—and so forth !

In our whole treatment of this contribution to natural

theology we have endeavoured to keep clearly in view the
function which this absurd 'science' sets before itself,
namely, to deduce from the physical and finite sensation a
proof of the supersensuous and infinite. It disregards the
possible influence of the laws of the human perceptive
faculty on the sensations which that faculty co-ordinates ; it
argues from present scientific ignorance to the impossibility
of knowledge. It neglects entirely a rule of equal importance with Newton's, which may be thus stated : that where
we have not hitherto discovered a sufficient physical or perceptive origin for natural phenomena, it is more philosophical
to wait and investigate than seek refuge in ultra-scientific
causes. Such ultra-scientific causes may be matter for belief
based on revelation, they can never be deduced from a study
of our sensations. From the order and harmony of our sensations we can only proceed to the law descriptive of their
sequence, to the law of physical cause—to this and nothing
more. We cannot help thinking it regrettable that the *doyen*
of English science, a man to whom every mathematician
and physicist looks with a sense of personal gratitude, should
have closed a most suggestive course of lectures on light by,
what appears to us, a perversion of the true aims of science.
He has endeavoured to deduce the self-existence of the deity
by a method of argument long since discarded by thinkers ;
he has only achieved his object by a series of logical fallacies
based on erroneous extension of terms. Authority weighs
more than accurate reasoning with the majority of men, and
on this account the course taken by Professor Stokes is
peculiarly liable to do serious harm. If the human race has
now reached a stage when more efficient conceptions of
morality than the Christian are beginning to be current ;
when more fruitful fields for research and thought than the
theological are open to mankind ; when the inherited instinct
of human service is growing so strong that its gratification is
one of the chief of human pleasures ; then, assuredly he who
attempts to bolster up an insufficient theory of morals, an
idle occupation for the mind, and a religious system which
has become a nigh insupportable tax on the national re-

sources—assuredly this one will be cursed by posterity for his theology, where it would otherwise have blessed him for his science! "You have stretched out your hands to save the dregs of the sifted sediment of a residuum. Take heed lest you have given soil and shelter to the seed of that awful plague which has destroyed two civilizations, and but barely failed to slay such promise of good as is now struggling to live among men."[1] So cried Clifford to two scientists of repute who stooped in 1875 to dabble in the mire of 'natural theology.' It is a noteworthy and melancholy proof of the persistency of human prejudice that in 1887 it is necessary again to repeat his words.

[1] *Fortnightly Review*, June, 1875.

NOTE TO PAGE 48.—It seems to me extremely probable that a wave of life representing the zoic stage moves from the lesser sun outwards across each planetary system. Such a wave has now reached our earth, and, following the physical development, will pass on to the external planets, leaving at most a fossil-record behind it. This wave depends on the thermal conditions of the individual sun, and may be only a ripple of a larger wave which flows outward through stellar space from a central sun.

III.

MATTER AND SOUL.[1]

On earth there's nothing great but man, in man there's nothing great but mind.—*Sir William Hamilton.*

I DO not think I shall be making a great assumption if I suppose the majority of my audience to have read or at least heard about Mr. Gladstone's recent article in the *Nineteenth Century.* It is not my intention to criticise that defence of what our late Prime Minister terms the "majestic process" of creation described in the first chapter of Genesis. The writer exhibits throughout such a hopeless ignorance of the real aims and methods of modern science, that even the humblest of her servants may be excused for treating his article not as a matter for criticism, but as an interesting psychological study. It unveils for us the picture of a mind which is not uncommon at the present time. A mind, whose emotional needs require it to imagine behind natural phenomena a will and an intellect similar in kind, if differing in degree, from the human will and the human intellect; which places behind nature an anthropopathetic, if not an anthropomorphic deity. On the other hand, this mind finds in what science has to say of the growth of the universe only a 'mechanical process.' It is longing for the 'intellectual,' it finds the 'mechanical.' From this feeling arises the revolt against modern scientific thought. Such a mind refuses to allow that the universe is nought but 'bits of matter attracting and repelling each other,' and we have the

[1] This lecture was delivered before the Sunday Lecture Society at St. George's Hall, December 6, 1885. It was afterwards published by the Society as a pamphlet.

remarkable spectacle of a person, to whom at least our nineteenth century knowledge and culture is not a forbidden field,
preferring the "majestic process" of the Mosaic account of
creation to all that truth which the world's great thinkers
have been slowly discovering from the age of Galilei to that
of Darwin! Remarkable indeed is the spectacle of a mind
which finds it almost a catastrophe that the myth of a semi-
barbaric people should be replaced by the knowledge gained
by centuries of patient research!

I venture to think that this confusion of ideas, which is of
undoubted psychological interest, is really due first to the
want of a clear conception as to what meanings must be
attached to the words 'intellectual' and 'mechanical,'
and secondly to a very slight acquaintance with the real
concepts of modern science. If for a moment I were to use
the word mechanical in what appears to be Mr. Gladstone's
sense, as something opposed to spiritual, I should be
compelled to describe the "majestic process" of the Mosaic
creation as mechanical, while the theories of modern
science as to the development of nature, so far from being
mechanical would appear to me spiritual. They would
for the first time raise the universe to an intelligible entity.
From them I should for the first time be led to suspect that
intellectual sequence and natural law do not differ *toto cœlo*;
that thought and physical phenomena cannot in any way be
scientifically opposed; that so far from stuff and soul, matter
and mind, having in reality utterly different attributes, the
little we have yet learnt of them points rather to similarity
than difference. What, if it be the function of modern science
to show that the old distinction of the schools between
idealism and materialism is merely historical and not logical?
What, if after analyzing the concept of matter peculiar
to modern science, we find that the only thing, with which
we are acquainted that at all resembles it, is mind? Surely
this will be rendering the world intelligible rather than
mechanical,—using the latter word not in the scientific, but
in Mr. Gladstone's sense. To show that possibly idealism
and materialism are not opposite mental poles, that pos-

sibly matter and spirit are not utterly distinct entities, will
be the endeavour of my present lecture. Its thesis, then, is :
That science, so far from having in the popular sense mate-
rialized the world, has idealized it; for the first time rendered
it possible for us to regard the universe as something intelligible rather than material.

Let us begin our investigations by striving to ascertain all
that science has got to tell us of matter, and here I must
warn you that science, like theology, has had an historical
past. That she has retained prejudices, even dogmas from
the past, and is only to-day throwing off these old confused
ideas, and distinguishing what she really knows from
plausible theory, and plausible theory from gratuitous assumption. There is no fundamental conception of science
about which more gratuitous assumptions have been made
than matter, and curiously enough matter is a thing which
physical science could afford to entirely neglect. It does
require a physical concept called mass, but it has been a
misfortune of the historical evolution of science that mass
has been connected with matter. This connection was rati-
fied by Newton in his famous definition of mass as the quantity of matter in a body. As every physicist knows what
mass is, and no physicist can offer anything but plausible
theories as to what matter may be, the magnitude of the
misfortune must be obvious to all. If I may be allowed to
express my own opinion, I should say that matter was a
popular superstition which had forced itself upon physical
science, much as the popular, or at least theological superstition of soul has forced itself upon mental science. In
order to explain to you more clearly what I mean, let me
endeavour to analyze the popular superstition with regard to
matter.

To the ordinary mind matter is something everywhere
tangible, something hard, impenetrable, that which exerts
force. The ordinary mind cannot exactly define, but it is quite
sure that it understands matter—it is a fact of everyday
experience. This deliciously naïve conception has reacted
upon science, and more than one recent writer describes

matter as "one of the inevitable primary conceptions of the mind." If all the primary conceptions of the mind were so confused as this one of matter, I venture to think the mind would make very little progress indeed; science would be mere dogma, based on confused ideas. If we question what is meant by the terms hard or impenetrable, we are thrown back on the conception of pressure, or of resistance to motion; we are thus finally driven to the last refuge of the materialists —*force*. Matter is that which exerts force; matter and force are two entities always occurring together, and by means of which we can explain the whole working of the universe. In order, therefore, that we may approach matter, we must understand force. Let us see if we can understand force, or if it can in any way help us in our difficulties. If any of my audience were to ask the first person they meet after leaving this lecture hall, *why* the earth describes an orbit about the sun, I have little doubt that the answer would be: Because of the law of gravitation. Being further questioned as to what the law of gravitation might be, the answer would not improbably consist in the statement that a force varying inversely as the square of the distance, and directly as the product of the masses, acts between the sun and the earth. Now I boldly assert that Newton has not told us *why* the earth describes an orbit about the sun any more than Kepler did. The man who shall tell us *why* the earth describes an orbit about the sun will be even a greater philosopher than Newton. I should be loth to say the problem is insoluble, but it is very far from being solved at present. Kepler described *how* the earth moved round the sun, and that is precisely what Newton did too, only with far greater clearness and generality. The law of gravitation is a *description* and not an explanation of a certain motion. The motion of the earth, said Newton, is such that its change can be described in such and such a fashion. But why does its motion change in this fashion? Newton did not answer that question. Nobody has yet answered it; and he who fully answers it will have probably discovered the relation between matter and mind. Force is not then a *real cause* of change in motion, it is merely

a *description* of change in motion. Force is a *how* and not a
why. It is a description of how bodies change their motion,
and how they change their motion we can only discover by
experience. Force is, then, not a physical entity, but a statement of experimental fact. Could anything be more completely absurd that the definition: "Matter is that which
exerts a statement of experimental fact "?

But force being the 'how of a motion' may naturally
suggest that matter is that which moves. This is a suggestion well worth considering, although it has brought us
very far from the popular conception of a hard, impenetrable,
force-exerting entity. There can, in fact, be little doubt that
all the sensations which a thing—a so-called external body
produces in us—its visible form, its smell, its taste, its touch,
are all due to various phases of motion which exist in it.
Once put an end to those motions, and we should have no
sensations, the thing for us would cease to exist. It is no
dogma, but downright common sense to assert that if everything in the universe were brought to rest, the universe would
cease to be perceptible, or for all human purposes we may
say it would cease to be. The sensible existence of matter
is entirely dependent on the existence of motion. Force
having failed us, let us now see if we can approach matter
better through motion. I do not think it is necessary for me
to explain to you what we understand by position and shape,
—these are things of which the mind can form very clear
ideas; it can also form clear conceptions of change of position
and change of shape; but such changes are what we term
motion. Motion is something, then, which is intelligible to
all of us, although all of us may not be able to measure it
with scientific accuracy. Can we now state any great law
of motion which, without requiring us to dogmatize as to
matter, will help us on our way? I think we can. Suppose
we take two bodies and let them in any way influence each
other, what do we observe? Why, that they change each
other's motions. This is the great fact of all physical
experience: Bodies are able to change each other's motions.
So sure is this fact, that we might even make a general

statement and say that everything in the universe is to a
greater or less extent changing the motion of every other
thing. *Why* is everything in the universe changing the
motion of every other thing in the universe? The scientist
does not know, and he says so; the metaphysician does not
know, but he does not say so. *How* is everything in the
universe changing the motion of every other thing? The
scientist knows in a great many cases, and he says so; it
is, in fact, the whole object of the physical sciences to
investigate this *how*. The metaphysician does not know, but
he generally asserts he does, and for this reason he is worth
reading—like Mr. Gladstone, as a psychological study.

Physicists, solely by the processes of experiment and reasoning upon experiment, have discovered certain rules by which
bodies change each other's motion. These rules are merely
empirical rules, but they have so invariably given true results,
that no sane person would hesitate to accept them. One of
the most remarkable and valuable of these rules is the following : If any two bodies change each other's motion, then the
ratio of the rates of change in their motion is a number,
which remains the same for the same two bodies however
they may influence each other; that is to say, whether one
is placed upon the other, or they are tied together by a string,
or charged with electricity, or whatever the relation may be.
This rule is the great law of motion that we have been seeking for, and is the basis of most physical science. There are
many rules subsidiary to this which have been discovered by
experiment connecting the numbers which represent the ratios
of rates of change for different bodies, but upon these I shall
not now enter. It will suffice here to add that physicists
give a name to these numbers; they term the inverse of such
number the *ratio of the masses* of the two particular bodies with
which the number is associated. The point to which I wish
particularly to draw your attention is this, that the only
thing a scientist knows of mass is that it is a ratio of changes
of motion. This is perfectly intelligible ; motion is a clear
idea, rate of change of motion is a clear idea, and a number
representing what multiple one rate of change of motion is

of another is also a perfectly clear conception. We can all understand motion, we can all understand mass or this ratio of the rates of change of motion. But upon motion and mass the whole theory of modern physics depends. You will see at once, if this be true, that such obscure ideas as force and matter are quite unnecessary to modern physics, and you may be pretty certain that, if any one describes the universe to you as consisting of portions of matter exerting force upon each other, and supposes therewith that he has given an explanation, he is still labouring with confused ideas, that he is still under the influence of the old superstitions, the old conceptions of matter and force. Of matter we know nothing, and such knowledge is not *necessary* for physical science ; of force we can say that it never tells us *why* anything happens, but is only the description of a certain kind of motion discovered by experiment or observation.

Science has indeed reduced the universe, not to those unintelligible concepts matter and force, but to the very intelligible concept motion ; for, all we can understand at present or require to understand of mass, is its measurement by motion. Newton's assertion that 'mass is the quantity of matter in a body' is gratuitous. It endeavours to explain something of which we can form a clear idea by something of which we know absolutely nothing. How then did it arise? Merely from a singular result of experiment being linked with the old superstition of an impenetrable something—matter—filling space. The singular result of experiment is this : that the numbers we have called the masses of bodies are found for bodies of the same material to be proportional to their sizes. Hence, mass for such bodies being proportional to size, it was taken to be a measure of the stuff which was supposed to fill size. By 'bodies of the same material,' I only mean bodies, every element of which produces in us the same characteristic sensations, whether chemical or physical. So long as we consider the universe made up of things moving, and altering each other's motion, we are on safe ground. But you will ask: Why not call the things which move matter? Is it not a mere quibble as to terms? I have no objection to calling the moving things matter, but we must ever bear in mind that the moving things may be the last things in the world which accord with the popular conception of matter, they may even be its negation. What if the ultimate atom upon which we build up the apparently substantial realities of the external world be an absolute vacuum? or, what if matter be only non-matter in motion? I do not say that the moving thing is of this kind, because nobody as yet knows what it really is, but let us endeavour to imagine something of the kind. It will help us if we examine one or two atomic hypotheses. Descartes, great geometrician as he was, held extension not impenetrability the essence of matter. "Give me extension and motion, and I will construct the world," he cried. There is much to be said for this view of the moving thing; that all matter is shape, and not shape necessarily filled with something, approaches very near some of our modern hypotheses. "Give me motion, and space capable of changing its shape, and I will explain the universe to you," is far more rational and much less mere boast than Kant's "Give me matter and I will create the world." For, matter being granted, not much universe is left to be explained.

But there have been hypotheses of matter—hypotheses which have played no inconsiderable part in scientific theory — which denied it even extension. We may especially note that of Boscovitch. For him the ultimate elements of matter were mathematical points, that is, points without extension ; these points he endowed with attractive and repulsive forces. Remembering that all we can under-stand of force is a description of motion, we must consider the universe of Boscovitch as made up of points which move in certain fashions. Boscovitch's matter—a point without extension — would thus only be distinguished from non-matter by the fact of its motion, or we might well describe it as *non-matter in motion*.

A more probable and more recent hypothesis is the vortex-atom theory of Sir William Thomson. There are very strong reasons for believing that all the intervals and spaces between what we term matter are filled up by something, which, while it does not perceptibly resist the motion of matter, is yet itself capable of motion. The existence of this medium, capable of conveying motion, is especially suggested, almost proven, by certain phenomena of light. Now this medium, or ether as it is termed, is quite intangible, it does not seem to influence the motion of what is generally termed matter, and we are compelled to treat it either as non-matter or else as a second and totally different kind of matter. This dualism bears in itself something unscientific, and the brilliant idea occurred to Sir William Thomson that matter might only be a particular phase of motion in the ether. The form of motion suggested by him was the vortex ring; the atom was a vortex ring of ether moving in the ether, somewhat as a smoker might blow a smoke-ring into an atmosphere of smoke. The reason the vortex ring was chosen is because it has been shown that in a certain kind of fluid such a motion once started is like the atom indestructible. Sir William Thomson thus treated what we popularly term matter as ether in motion. Could we once stop that motion the universe would be reduced to that apparent void which separates our planet from the sun. In popular language this is again very like asserting that matter is non-matter in motion. Unfortunately Sir William Thomson's ether vortex rings do not appear to move in exactly the same fashion as that in which we require our atoms to move. The whole theory is still, however, *sub judice*.

Immaterial as the ether seems to be, we might even suggest the possibility that an atom is a small portion of space in which there is no ether, or in other words void of anything, even the immaterial ether. A theory which supposes the boundaries of these voids to be endowed with a certain amount of energy will indeed account for some of the phenomena of gravitation and cohesion. I only refer to this theory as showing how delusive may be the common conceptions of matter; what we term the atom, the ultimate basis of matter, may be the negation of all that is currently termed material—a void capable of motion.

Finally, let me mention a hypothesis suggested, but never

worked out, by the late Professor Clifford. Suppose I were
to take a flexible tube of very fine bore; if I held it out
straight it might be possible for me to drop a thin straight
piece of wire right through it. On the other hand, if I were
to make a bend in it, the wire would not go through unless it
pushed the bend before it. Now let us suppose the bit of
wire replaced by a worm, or some being which can only conceive motion *forwards*, not sideways. If the worm were in
the straight tube it could move ahead, and as it never had
moved sideways it might seem to itself to have perfect freedom of motion—there would be no obstacle in its space.
Now let us suppose a wrinkle or bend in the straight tube;
then if the worm itself were perfectly flexible, it could go
forwards and find no obstacle in its space, notwithstanding
the wrinkle. But, alas! for the worm if it were like the bit
of wire, incapable of bending, then when it came to the
wrinkle, the tube, its space, would appear perfectly open
before it, but it would find itself incapable of advancing
further. The worm must either push the bend before it, or
else regard it as something impenetrable, as something which,
however intangible, still opposed its motion. The worm
would look upon the bend very much as we look upon matter.
Yet the bend is really geometrical, not material; it is a
change in the shape of space. Such an example may faintly
suggest to your minds how Clifford looked upon matter;
matter was something in motion, but that something was
purely geometrical, it was *change in the shape of our space*.
You will note that in this hypothesis space itself takes the
place of the ether filling space; instead of a vortex ring in
the ether, we shall have a particular bend, possibly a geometrical twist-ring in space as an element of matter. Matter
would not necessarily cease to be, because motion ceased,
but would at once cease if space became even, if all the
bends, wrinkles, and twists were smoothed out of it. Matter
would only differ from non-matter in its shape.

Without laying stress upon any of the theories of matter.
which I have briefly described to you, I would yet draw your
attention to a common feature of them all. They one and

all endeavour to reduce that obscure idea, matter, to something of which we have a clearer conception, to our ideas of
motion or to our ideas of shape. Matter is non-matter in
motion, or matter is non-matter shaped. The ultimate element of matter is something beyond the reach of experiment;
it is obvious that these theories of matter are really only
attempts to explain our sensations by reducing them to motion and extension, categories of which we can form clear
conceptions. The sensible universe is for us built up of extension and motion; observation of the manner in which
bodies influence each other's motion enables us to lay down
laws of motion by which we render intelligible all physical
phenomena. Theories of matter are but attempts to render
intelligible the various kinds of motion which bodies produce
in each other, to explain the *why* of motion. No theory of
matter can be considered as a satisfactory, or at least as a final
solution, which only reduces matter of one kind to matter of
another. Thus, if the vortex-atom theory of Sir William
Thomson be true, we are only thrown back on the question:
What is the ether that it acts like a perfect fluid? Or in
other words, what is it that causes the parts of the ether to
exert pressure on each other, or to change each other's motion? We are again thrown back on the *why* of a particular
kind of motion. The fact that it is impossible to explain
matter by matter, to deduce the laws which govern motion
from bodies which themselves obey the laws of motion, has
not always been clearly recognized. It is no real explanation
of gravitation and cohesion, if I deduce them from the motion
of the parts of an ether, which again requires me to explain
why its parts mutually act upon each other. I may invent
another ether for this purpose, but where is the series to
stop? To explain matter on mechanical principles seems
to me a hopeless task, since our next step would be to deduce
those mechanical principles from the characteristics of our
matter. The laws of motion must flow from the nature of
matter, and cannot themselves explain matter. Hence if we
explain our atom by the laws of motion we may have gone
back a useful and a necessary stage, but we can be quite

sure that the atom we are considering is not the ultimate element of matter.

The problem of matter may be insoluble, but at least it cannot be solved on mechanical principles. If the laws of motion are ever to be raised from the empirical to the intelligible, we must find the cause of mechanism in matter. As to what the nature of that cause may be, science is purely agnostic; the cause may be of the nature of mind, or it may be of a nature at present inconceivable to us; it cannot, however, be material, it cannot be mechanical, for that would be merely explaining matter by matter.

Now although science must as yet remain purely agnostic with regard to this problem, it is still of value to keep in view every possibility as to the nature of matter. We find, although we are in no way able to account for it, that two bodies in each other's presence influence each other's motion. We have often been able to state the *how*, but never as yet the *why*. Is there any other phenomenon of which we are conscious that at all resembles this apparently spontaneous change of motion? There is one which bears considerable resemblance to it. I raise my hand, the change of motion appears to you spontaneous; the *how* of it might be explained by a series of nerve-excitements and muscular motions, but the *why* of it, the ultimate cause, you might possibly attribute to something you termed my *will*. The will is something which at least appears capable of changing motion. But something moving is capable of changing the motion of something else. It is not a far step to suggest from analogy that the something moving, namely matter, may be will. This step was taken by Schopenhauer, who asserted that the basis of the universe, the reality popularly termed matter, is *will*. I must confess that I cannot fully understand the argument by which Schopenhauer arrived at this conclusion. It seems to me as pure a bit of dogmatism as Boscovitch's mathematical point. Still, dogma as it is, there is nothing absolutely absurd in such a hypothesis; it at least does not attempt to explain matter through matter. As a mere suggestion, it will serve to remind us of the possible nature of this unknown, if not unknowable, entity matter.

We are now in a better position to form general conclusions as to the part matter plays in the scientific conception of the universe.

1. The scientific view of the physical universe is based upon motion and mass, the latter being merely a ratio of rates of change of motion, hence we may say it is based simply on motion. The rational theory of the physical universe deduced from this view depends upon certain experimental laws of motion. Once grant these laws, and science is capable of rendering intelligible the most complex physical phenomena.

2. With regard to the nature of matter science is at present purely agnostic. It recognizes, however, that if the nature of matter could be discovered, the laws of motion [1] would cease to be merely empirical and become rational.

We may, I think, add to these statements the following:—

3. It does not seem possible to explain matter on mechanical principles, because to do so is merely to throw back a gross matter on a possibly less gross matter, and is in reality no explanation.

4. That, while the science is purely agnostic with regard to matter, it is well for us to remember the various attempts which have been made to render matter intelligible; notably, Clifford's, which attempts to explain matter not on mechanical but on geometrical principles—which would deduce mechanism from geometry; and Schopenhauer's, which attempts to explain matter by the analogy of will.

While science is not called upon at present to declare for Clifford, Schopenhauer or any other material theorist, it is as well to remember that any such theory opens the door to the possibilities of an infinite beyond. Were Clifford's theory true, we must assert the existence of a space of four

---

[1] The term "laws of motion" in this lecture is used in a wider sense than that of dynamical text-books. It includes the *hows* of the fundamental motions, or what are usually termed the laws of gravitating, cohesive, magnetic or other force.

dimensions, for otherwise we could not conceive a bend in our own space, we throw back the problem of matter upon a universe outside our own of which we can know nothing— we can only assert its existence. Were Schopenhauer's theory true, we should be thrown back on the psychological problem of will, and might possibly have to assert universal consciousness. Luckily, science is not called upon at present to take any such leap into obscurity ; it contents itself with recognizing this vast unknown as a problem of the future, and steadily refuses to accept any solution, whether based upon a mechanical, a metaphysical, or a theological dogma.

If I have in any way placed before you the true scientific view of the universe, I think you will agree with me that the popular conception of matter, as a hard, dead something, is merely a superstition. The very essence of matter is motion, and motion of such a kind that although we can describe *how* it takes place, we in no single case have yet discovered *why*. We do not say that the motion induced by two particles of the ether in each other is *really*, but at least it *appears* spontaneous. We do not say, when we see a man raising his arm, that the motion is *really*, but at least it *appears* spontaneous,—the outcome of what we term his *will*. We are accustomed to associate *apparently* spontaneous motion with life. Is there not, then, something extremely absurd in terming matter dead ?

Let us take the most primitive organism possible, a simple organic cell—what do we find in it at first sight ? A combination of apparently spontaneous motions ; we believe those motions to be possibly not spontaneous, but we can only say that we cannot at present explain them. Let us take the ultimate form of matter—if gross matter is going to be explained by the ether, then a particle of the ether— what do we find ? Why, that this particle has motion, and is capable in some way of influencing the motion of other particles. Where is it possible to draw the line between the ultimate germ of life and the ultimate element of matter ? Some of you may feel inclined to answer : But the ultimate

germ of life can reproduce itself. What does this exactly
mean? It means that, if placed under favourable conditions,
it can collect other particles of matter and endow them with
movements similar to its own. But is there anything more
wonderful in this, more a sign of life, than atoms collecting
to form molecules, molecules to form chemical compounds,
and chemical compounds to form nebulæ and eventually new
planets? Why is one more a process of reproduction than the
other?

All life is matter, say some. This statement may mean
anything or nothing, according as to the dogma held with
regard to matter. But I venture to assert that the converse
means just as much, or just as little:—*all matter is life*, is not
a whit more absurd or dogmatic than: *all life is matter*. Our
ultimate element of matter has certain motions and
capacities for influencing motion, which we have not explained, so has our ultimate germ of life. What then?
Shall we explain life by mechanism? Certainly, if we find
that dogma satisfactory, but remember that we have still to
explain in what mechanism consists. On the other hand,
why not explain mechanism by life? Certainly, if we find
that dogma more satisfactory than the first, but remember
that no one has yet discovered what life is!

But I fancy one of you objecting: This may be very true,
but it neglects the fundamental distinction between matter
and life, namely the phenomenon of consciousness. Very
good, my dear sir, let us endeavour to analyze this phenomenon of consciousness, and see whether denying consciousness to matter may not be just as dogmatic as asserting that
matter possesses it. Now let me ask you a question: Do you
think I am a conscious being, and why? The only answer
you can give to that question will be agnostic. You really
do not know whether I am conscious or not. Each individual *ego* can assert of itself that it is conscious, but to
assert that that group of sensations which you term me is
conscious, is an assumption, however reasonable it may
appear. For you, sir, I and the rest of the external world
are automata, pure bits of mechanism; it may be practically

advisable for you to endow us with consciousness, but how can you prove it? You will reply, I see spontaneous actions on your part, similar to those I can produce myself. I am compelled by analogy to endow you with will and consciousness. Good! you argue by analogy that I have consciousness; you will doubtless grant it to the animal world; now you cannot break the chain of analogy anywhere till you have descended through the whole plant world to the simple cell, there you find apparently spontaneous motion and argue life—consciousness. Now I carry your argument a step further and tell you that I find in the ultimate atom of matter most complex phases of motion and capacity for influencing the motion of others. All these things are to me inexplicable. They *appear* spontaneous motion; *ergo* by analogy, dear sir, matter is conscious.

Now the only thing, which I am certain is conscious, is my own individual *ego*; I find nothing, however, more absurd in the assertion that matter is conscious, than in the assertion that the simple cell is conscious, or working upwards that *you* are conscious. They are all at present unproven assertions. That matter is conscious is no more nonsense than that life is mechanism; possibly some day, as the human intellect developes with the centuries, we may be able to show that one or other of these statements, or more probably both, are true.

Those of you who have followed what I have said as to force and matter will recognize that to consider the universe capable of explanation on the basis of matter and force is to endeavour to explain it by obscure terms, and is therefore utterly unscientific. To the man of science, force is the description of *how* a motion changes, and tells him nothing of the *why*. To the man of science, matter is something which is behind mechanism; if he knew its nature he could explain why motions are changed, but he does not know. For aught science can say, matter may be something as spiritual as life, as mental as consciousness. How absurd, then, is the cry of the theologian and the theologically minded, that modern science would reduce the universe to a

dead mechanism, to 'little bits of matter exerting force on
each other.' Modern science has been striving to render the
universe intelligible, to replace the dead mechanism of the
old creation-tales by a rational, an intelligible process of
evolution. What, then, if she at present halts at the
empirical laws of motion ? Is she not quite sure that if she
can but discover the nature of matter, mechanism will be an
intelligible and rational result of that nature ? I admit a
certain danger here; so long as there was no physical
science, theologian and metaphysician rushed in, and
'explained' on dogma and on obscure idea the whole
physical universe. If men of science once clearly assert that
they are at present quite ignorant as to the nature of matter,
that the one thing they are sure of is that it is not
mechanism, but explains mechanism, then will not the
retreating band of theologians and metaphysicians take
refuge in this unknown land, and offer great opposition to the
true discoverers, the true colonists of the unknown, when
they finally approach its shores ? Something of this kind is
very likely to happen, but I do not apprehend much danger.
So long as the human intellect is in its present state of
development there will be theologians, and metaphysicians
will come into being, and it is perhaps as well they should
have some out-of-the-way corner to spin their cobwebs in.
Matter is perhaps as good a spot for them as soul, and might
keep them well occupied for some time. Further, the possibility of resistance in this sort of folk to the progress of knowledge is now not very great ; its back has been broken in the
contest wherein scientific thought won for itself the physical
universe. The theologians of Galilei's era were all-powerful,
they could be aggressive and force him to recant ; the theologians of to-day in congress assembled mourn over the progress
of knowledge, but they cannot resist it. Let them make
what they will of matter ; science can only say : At present I
am ignorant, but I will not accept your dogma. If the day
comes, as I believe it will, when I shall know, then you and
your cobwebs will be promptly swept out. Not by inspiration, not by myth, is the problem of matter to be solved, but

by the patient investigation and thought of trained minds spread over years, possibly over centuries. What is impossible to the human intellect of to-day, may be easy for the human intellect of the future. Each problem solved, not only marks a step in the sum of human knowledge, but in general connotes a corresponding widening in the capacity of the human mind. The greater the mass of knowledge acquired, the more developed will be the function which has been employed in acquiring such knowledge. We can look fearlessly to the future, if we but fully cultivate and employ our intellectual faculties in the present.

Let us now turn from matter to soul, and inquire how far we can make any definite assertions with regard to it. I have used the word 'soul' in my lecture, although *mind* would have better suited my purpose, because had I spoken only of mind you might have been led to imagine I admitted the existence of a soul in the theological sense behind mind. Now as we are trying to discover *facts* as apart from imaginings, we must dismiss from our thoughts at once all theological or metaphysical dogma with regard to the soul. It may be matter of myth, or of revelation, or of belief in any form, that the soul is immortal, but it is not a matter of science—that is, of knowledge; on the whole it is a delusive, if not a dangerous hypothesis. Aristotle, in his great work on the soul, practically identifies it with life (*De Anima* ii. 3). So also does his disciple, the great Jewish philosopher, Maimonides, who even grants a soul to the plant world (*Eight Chapters. Chapter I.*). It remained for Christian theology with dogmatic purpose to distinguish soul from life. Hegel has defined the soul as the notion of life, and though we must accept the definition of a metaphysician with great caution, yet I do not think we shall go far wrong in following him, at least on this point. For, if we begin to inquire what we mean by the notion of life, we are inevitably thrown back on the phenomena of consciousness and will, shortly, upon those *apparently* spontaneous motions, which we have before referred to. Wherever we find the notion of life, there we postulate consciousness, or

the possibility of consciousness, and, except in the case of
our individual selves, we judge of consciousness only by
apparently spontaneous motions. If we accept the soul as
the notion of life, we cannot deny soul to any living thing,
it must exist in the most primitive organism; but, as we
have seen, it is mere dogmatism which asserts that there is
a qualitative difference between the simplest cell and the
ultimate vibrating atom. · We cannot say what is the ultimate element of matter; it is equally idle to say, in the
present state of our knowledge, 'matter is conscious,' or
'matter is unconscious.' If this be so, and the possibility
of consciousness be our notion of life, or of soul, then it is
nonsense for any one at the present time to assert either
that 'soul is matter,' or 'matter is soul.' We must on this
point be absolutely agnostic, *but* we must at the same time
remember that all persons who draw a distinction between
soul and stuff, between matter and mind, are pure dogmatists. There may be a distinction or there may not; we
certainly cannot assert that there is. So far, then, from
idealism and materialism being opposed methods of thought,
it is within the range of possibility that they represent an
idle distinction of the schools. To assert that mind is the
basis of the universe and to assert that matter is the basis
of the universe are not necessarily opposed propositions,
because for aught we can say to the contrary mind and
matter may be at the bottom one and the same thing, or at
least be only different manifestations of one and the same
thing. To assert that 'mind is matter,' or that 'matter is
mind,' is purely meaningless, so long as we remain in our
present complete ignorance of the nature of the ultimate
element of either. Both are dogmas which can only be
confirmed or refuted by the growth of positive knowledge.

If our consideration of matter and mind has been of any
value, it will have at least led us to admit the *possibility* of
the same element being at the basis alike of the physical
and of the mental universe. Let us inquire, in conclusion,
whether this possibility is in any way denied or confirmed
by our conceptions of physical and of mental law.

We may best reach our goal by a concrete example. The old Greek astronomers, by observations, as careful as the means then possible allowed, discovered something of the character of the motion of the sun, the earth, and the moon; this motion they represented with a certain degree of accuracy by a complex system of circles, by eccentric and epicycle. This was a result which satisfies the notion still widely current that a physical law is a mere statement of physical fact. Experiment and observation give us a class of facts which we can embrace under one general statement. We have before our experiment no reason for saying the statement will be of one kind rather than another, and after our experiment the only reason for the statement is the sensible fact on which we base it. Such a physical statement is termed an empirical law, its discovery depends not on reason, but on observation. Physical science abounds in such empirical laws, and their existence has led certain confused thinkers to look upon the physical universe as a complex of empirical law, not as an intelligible whole. At this point the mathematician steps in and says there is something behind your empirical laws, they are not independent statements, but flow rationally one from the other. Tell me the laws of motion and I will rationally deduce the physical universe; the physical universe no longer shall appear a complex of empirical law, you shall see it as an intelligible whole. If Newton's description of the manner in which sun, earth, and moon fall towards each other be the true one, then they must move in such and such a fashion. The Greek eccentric and epicycle are no longer empirical descriptions of motion, they have become intellectual necessities, the logical outcome of Newton's description of planetary motion. Grant for a moment that Newton's law of gravitation is the whole truth, then I say earth, sun, and moon *must* move in such and such a fashion. So great is our confidence in the power of the reason, that when it leads us to a result which has not been confirmed or discovered by physical observation, we say look more carefully, get better instruments, and you will find it *must* be so. There are several instances of reason discovering before observation the existence of a physical phenomenon.

Now in this process of rendering the universe an intelligible whole, a very important fact comes to light, to which I wish to draw your special attention. Let us grant for a moment that we have in Newton's law of gravitation the whole truth as to the way earth, sun, and moon are falling towards each other. We work out on our paper the whole of their most complex motions, and we find that the results agree completely with the physical phenomena. But why should they? Why should the intellectual, rational process on our paper coincide absolutely with the physical process outside? Why is it not possible for one empirical law of the universe to be contrary to another? I mean that, starting from one empirical law, we should by reason arrive at a result opposed to another? But you will answer: This is absurd, Nature cannot contradict herself. I can only say my *experience* teaches me she never *does* contradict herself, but that does not explain *why* she never does.

When we say that: Nature cannot contradict herself, we are really only asserting that experience teaches us that: Nature never contradicts, not herself, but our logic. In other words, the laws of the physical universe are logically related to each other, flow rationally the one from the other. This is really the greatest result of human experience, the greatest triumph of the human mind. *The laws of the physical universe follow the logical processes of the human mind.* The intellect—the human mind—is the keynote to the physical universe. To contrast a law of matter and a law of mind, is as dogmatic as to contrast matter and mind. It is true that we are a long way yet from that glorious epoch when empirical laws will be dismissed from science. Even if we deduced all such laws from the simplest laws of motion, we should have still to show how those laws of motion are a rational result of the nature of matter; we have still to discover what matter is, before we render the whole physical universe intelligible. But did we know the nature of matter, there is little doubt that we could rationally create the whole

universe ; every step would be a logical, a mental process.
It is a strong argument for the possible identity of matter
and mind, if from one and from the other alike the whole
physical universe can be deduced. Externally, matter appears
as the basis of a world, every process of which is in logical
sequence; internally, mind pictures a similar world following
exactly the same sequence. It is difficult to deny the *possibility* of both having their ultimate element of a like quality.
This identity of the physical and the rational processes is
the greatest truth mankind has learnt from experience. So
great is our confidence in this truth, that we reject any statement of a physical fact which opposes our clear reasoning.
To state that a physical fact is opposed to reason, is, nowadays, to destroy the possibility of thought. We argue at
once that our senses have deceived us, that the fact is a
delusion, a misstatement of what took place. Any physical
fact which is opposed to a physical law is opposed to a
mental law ; we cannot think it,—it is impossible.

That is all the man of science means when he says that for
a dead man to arise out of his tomb and talk is nonsense ; he
would have to cease thinking, were such things possible.
My law of thought is to me a greater truth, a greater necessity of my being than the God of the theologian. If that
God, according to the theologian, does something which is
contrary to my law of thought, I can only say I rate my
mind above his God. I prefer to treat the world as an intelligible whole, rather than to reduce it to what it seems to
me the theologian ought in his own language to term a
'blind mechanism.' To any one who tells me that he only
means by God the spiritual something which is at the basis
of physical phenomena, I reply : 'Very good, your God then
will never contradict my reason, and the best guide I can
adopt in life is my reason, which, when rightly applied, will
never be at variance with your God.' Nay, I might even
suggest a further possibility. What we call the external,
the phenomenal world, is for us but a succession of sensations ; of the ultimate cause of those sensations, if there be
one, we know nothing. All we can say is, that when we

analyze those sensations we find more than a barren succession, we find a logical sequence. This logical sequence is for us the external world as an intelligible whole. But what if it be the mind itself which gives this logical sequence to our sensations? What if our sensating faculty must receive its images in the logical order of mind? We know too well that when the mind fails the sensations no longer follow a logical order. To the madman and the idiot there is no real world, no intelligible universe as we know it. May it not be the human mind itself which brings the intelligible into phenomena? Then they who call the intelligible which they find in the laws of the physical universe God will be *but deifying the human mind*. It is but a possibility I have hinted at, but one full of the richest suggestions for our life and for our thought. The mind of man may be that which creates for him the intelligible world! At least it suggests a worship and a religion which cannot lead us away from the truth.

If for a moment we choose to use the old theological terms, hallowed as they are with all the feelings and emotions of the past, how rich they appear once more with these new and deeper meanings! Symbols which may raise in the men of the future an enthusiasm as great as those of Christianity have done in the past! Religious devotion would become the pursuit of knowledge, worship the contemplation of what the human mind has achieved and is achieving; the saints and priests of this faith would be those who have worked or are working for the discovery of truth. Theology, no longer a dogma, would develop with the thought, with the intellect of man. No room here for dissent, no room here for sect,— not belief variable as the human emotions, but knowledge single as the human reason would dictate our creed. Nothing assuming, neither fearing to confess our ignorance, nor hesitating to proclaim our knowledge, surely we all might worship in one church. Then, again, the Church might become national; nay, universal, for *one* Reason existeth in all men. Cultivate only that one God we are certain of, the mind in man; and then surely we may look forward in the future to a day when the churches shall be cleared of their cobwebs, when loud - tongued ignorance shall no longer brazen it in their pulpits, nor meaningless symbols be exposed upon their altars. Then will come the day when we may blot out from their portals: "He is dead and has arisen; I believe because it is impossible"; and may inscribe thereon (as Sir William Hamilton over his classroom): "On earth there's nothing great but man: in man there's nothing great but mind"—"I believe because I understand." Not to convert the world into a 'dead mechanism,' but to give to humanity in the future a religion worthy of its intellect, seems to me the mission which modern science has before it.

' NOTE TO PAGES 27 and 56.—The old idea of matter affords an excellent example of how it is impossible to think things other than they really are without coming to an 'unthought,'—a self-contradictory concept. 'Matter is that which exerts force and is characterized by extension.' 'Mass is the quantity of matter in a body.' 'An Atom is the ultimate indivisible element of Matter.' But the physicist endows his atom with mass ; hence the basis of material sensations itself possess matter, *i.e.,* is extended. We thus find it impossible to conceive it as indivisible or ultimate. Professor E. du Bois-Reymond, in his well-known lecture (*Ueber die Grenzen des Naturerkennens,* Leipzig, 1876, pp. 14, 15), finds here an *unlöslicher Widerspruch,* and despairing over this limit to our understanding, cries : *Ignorabimus !* But what can we expect but an intellectual chaos, if we start from the hypothesis that : 'the material world will be *scientifically intelligible* so soon as we have deduced it from atomic motions caused by the mutual action of *central atomic forces* ' ?

IV.

THE ETHIC OF RENUNCIATION.[1]

THAT 'man is born to trouble even as the sparks fly upwards;' that endowed by race-development with passions
and desires, he is yet placed in a phenomenal world where
their complete gratification is either impossible or attended
with more than a counterbalancing measure of misery,—
these are facts which age by age have puzzled alike philosopher and prophet. They have driven thinkers to seek
within themselves for some quiet haven, for some still waters
of peace, which they could by no means discover in that
stormy outer world of phenomena. The apparent slave of
his sensations, man in the world of sense seems ever subjective and suffering; only mentally, in the inner consciousness,
does there appear a field for free action, for objective creation. Here man may find a refuge from those irresistible
external forces which carry him with such abrupt transition
from the height of joy to the depth of sorrow. Is it not
possible for the mind to cut itself adrift from race-prejudice,
from clogging human passions, from the body's blind slavery
to phenomena, and thus, free from the bondage of outward
sensation, rejoice in its own objectivity? Cannot man base
his happiness on something else than the transitory forms of
the phenomenal world? By some rational process on the
one hand, or some transcendental rebirth on the other, cannot man render himself indifferent to the ever-changing
phases of phenomenal slavery, withdraw himself from the
world in which fate has placed him? The means to this
great end may be fitly termed, *Renunciation,*—renunciation of

[1] This essay was written in 1883, but is now published for the first
time.

human passions to avoid human slavery. At first sight, for a man to renounce human passions appears to be a process akin to that of 'jumping out of his own skin,' yet the great stress which the foremost thinkers of many ages have laid upon the need of renunciation justifies a closer investigation of its meaning. I propose to examine, under the title of 'Ethic of Renunciation,' a few of the more important theories.

The earliest and perhaps the greatest philosopher who has propounded a doctrine of renunciation is Gautama the Buddha. In considering his views I shall adopt a course which I shall endeavour to pursue throughout this paper, namely, to ascertain first, as clearly as possible, what it is that the philosopher wishes men to renounce, and secondly, what he supposes will be the result of this renunciation. In the Buddhist theory it is the 'sinful grasping condition of mind and heart' which has to be extinguished. This condition is variously described as Trishnā—eager yearning thirst—and Upādāna—the grasping state.[1] The origin of the Trishnā is to be found in the sensations which the individual experiences as a portion of the phenomenal world. When the individual is ignorant of the nature of these sensations, and does not subordinate them to his reasoned will, they act upon him as sensuous causes, and produce in him, as in a sensuous organism, sensuous effects, namely, sensuous passions and desires of all kinds. Beside present ignorance as a factor of desire, we have also to remember the existence of past ignorance; past ignorance either of the race or individual has created a *predisposition* to the Trishnā. The sources, then, of the 'sinful grasping condition of mind and heart' may be concisely described as ignorance and predisposition which have culminated in irrational desire. In order that the individual may free himself from this condition of slavery he must renounce his desires, his delusions; the only means to this end is the extermination of ignorance and predisposi-

---

[1] Here, as elsewhere, my description of the Buddhist doctrine is drawn almost entirely from Mr. Rhys Davids' well-known works on the subject.

tion. The Buddhist doctrine, then, by no means asserts that man can free himself from the sensational action of the phenomenal world, only that it is possible for him to renounce the delusive desires created by that action. It may be concisely defined as a rational renunciation of the mere sensuous desire which uncontrolled sensations tend to produce. The method of renunciation viewed as destructive of ignorance is termed self-culture, viewed as destructive of desire, self-control. From these combined standpoints the method is fitly described as ‘the noble path of self-culture and self-control.’ Let us consider, then, the desires or delusions which, according to the Buddha, form the elements of the ‘sinful grasping condition,’ and whose immediate cause is to be sought in ignorance and predisposition. The three principal delusions upon which corresponding desires are based are termed sensuality, individuality, and ritualism. These are the sources from which human sorrow springs. Sensuality may be supposed, for our present purpose, to include sensuousness, delight in all forms of pleasure produced by the influence of the phenomenal world upon the senses. The grosser kinds at least of sensuality are certainly irrational, and causes of a vast proportion of human misery. Gautama seems to have condemned all sensuality, all love of the present world, as a fetter to human freedom. In this point he was practically in agreement with the early and mediæval Christian ascetics. Both condemned the pleasures of sense—the Christian because he considered them to interfere with the ordering of his life as dictated by revelation ; the Buddha because he saw much sorrow arising from them, and could find no rational argument for their existence. Both were alike ignorant of their physiological value, and rushed from Scylla on Charybdis. The true *via media* seems in this case to have been taught by Maimonides, another philosopher of renunciation — namely, that the pleasures of sense, although renounced as *purpose*, are to be welcomed as *means*, means to maintain the body in health, and so the mind in full energy. Sensuality ceasing to be master was to do necessary work as a servant. The Egyptian physician had a truer grasp of the physiological origin and value of 'desire' than the Indian philosopher.

The second of the great delusions to which Gautama attributed human misery is Individuality. The belief in Attavāda,—the doctrine of self,—is a primary heresy or delusion; it is one of the chief Upādānas, which are the direct causes of sorrow in the world. Gautama compared the human individual to a chariot, which was only a chariot so long as it was a complex of seat, axle, wheels, pole, &c.; beneath or beyond there was no substratum which could be called chariot. So it is with the individual man, he is an ever-changing combination of material properties. At no instant can he say, 'This is I,' and to do so is a delusion fraught with endless pain. It follows that when a self is denied to the individual man, no such entity as soul can be admitted, and it is logical that all questions as to a future life should be termed a 'puppet-show' or 'walking in delusion.' That the doctrine of Attavāda has been productive of infinite human misery is indisputable. The belief in the immortality of the soul, and so in future state, has led men in the present to endure and inflict endless pain. To the Christian such pain appears justifiable, it is but a means to an end. Pushed to its logical outcome it might be a sin to render a poor man comfortable and well-to-do for fear of weakening his chances of heaven. It would be highly criminal to refuse sending one man to the stake in order to save the souls of a hundred others. The Buddhist finds in all this nothing but that misery which is the outcome of delusion. For him the man who believes in a future state is hindered in his spiritual growth by the most galling chain, the most fatal Upādāna. The Christian, on the one hand, trusting to revelation, does not demand a rational basis for his belief in the existence of the soul; the Buddhist, on the other, has been charged by Gautama to accept nothing which his reasoning powers do not commend to his belief. Experience teaches us that here reason can prove nothing. It is beyond the limits of the theoretical reason, and the assertions of the practical reason are at best but belief based upon

6

recognized, but unanalyzed, desire. So far Gautama's position seems to me to be correct, the Attavāda is the outcome of desire or of predisposition. But a far more important step has to be taken before it can be declared a delusion; the historical origin of the predisposition, the growth of the desire must be tracèd. It may be that the origin is as natural, and yet as irrational, as the origin of the mediæval belief that the sun goes round the earth. In that case the predisposition will probably disappear with the knowledge of its cause. It will be classed as a myth produced by misunderstood sensations, the seemingly objective action of the phenomenal world will have been misinterpreted by the subjective centre, and the error perpetuated have given rise to a predisposition. Such a necessary criticism was, of course, not undertaken by Gautama; it is doubtful whether anthropology and the science of comparative religion are even yet sufficiently advanced to enable us to trace the development of this predisposition to Attavāda. We may certainly lay it down that, at some stage in the evolution of life, organisms were not conscious of any belief in the existence of a soul; it is not, however, necessary to assert that the belief originated in man as we know him. Between that early stage and man as he now is the predisposition has arisen. Until every element of that ' between ' is mapped out it will be impossible to *prove* that a theory of instantaneous implantation is fallacious, however contrary it may be to our general experience of the growth of ideas. The argument that, as the predisposition exists, man must satisfy it in order that he may not be miserable, is by no means valid. Besides the fact that many individuals live happily after rational renunciation of the desire for immortality, and so afford a proof that education and self-culture can free men from the predisposition, we must also remark that the acceptation of a belief recognized intellectually as groundless cannot in the long run tend to intellectual happiness. Even if, for an instant, we grant that without belief in the immortality of the soul our views of life must be pessimistic, —nay, that life without such belief is insupportable—still this admission is no proof of immortality; it only shows that man, or at all events his present phase, is not well fitted to the phenomenal surroundings. With regard, then, to this second great factor of human pain, we notice that Gautama proceeds rather dogmatically than logically when he asserts that it is a delusion. It is true that the belief in individuality cannot be rationally deduced, but the existing predisposition to that belief cannot, on the other hand, be validly put aside until it has received critical and historical investigation. I must remark, however, that if Gautama had firmly convinced himself that the belief in individuality was a fetter on man's progress towards righteousness, he was justified in calling upon men to renounce that doctrine without demonstrating its absolute falsity. It is not impossible that the Buddha's conviction, that the belief in some personal happiness hereafter is destructive of true spiritual growth, was what led him to denounce the Attavāda as the most terrible of delusions. " However exalted the virtue, however clear the insight, however humble the faith, there is no arahatship if the mind be still darkened by any hankering after any kind of future life. The desire for a future life is one of the fetters of the mind, to have broken which constitutes 'the noble salvation of freedom.' Such a hope is an actual impediment in the way of the only object we ought to seek— the attainment in this world of the state of mental and ethical culture summed up in the word arahatship " (*Hibbert Lectures*). Obviously only a philosopher, who has had deep and bitter experience of the destruction of "mental and ethical culture " by the sacrifice of this life to some emotional process of preparation for the next, could give vent to such a strong condemnation of the belief in individuality.

If we compare Gautama's two first Upādānas we see that there is between them a qualitative difference; the one is a direct physical desire, the other a mental craving only indirectly the result of the influence of the phenomenal world on man. According to the Buddhist theory we ought to renounce both. We have shown above some reason why, following Maimonides, the first desire, renounced as an end, should be adopted as a means to physical health. While a man can admittedly control and to some extent mould his physical existence, he cannot without injury wholly subdue his physical wants nor leave unsatisfied his physical desires. Hence the renunciation of the first Upādāna in its broadest sense is impossible. On the other hand, it is possible to destroy belief, to eradicate mental cravings. The mind is in itself an exceedingly plastic organism, subject to endless variations as the result of education, and capable at every period of changing its desires under the influence of self-culture and rational thought. There is always a possibility, then, of renouncing a mental predisposition. Such a predisposition cannot, of course, be driven out by force, it can only be destroyed by a growth of knowledge. Only the mind replete with intelligence can free itself from the delusion of individuality. Knowledge is for Gautama the key to the higher life; it alone can free men from the delusions which produce their misery. Here his teaching is in perfect harmony with that of Maimonides and Spinoza. It is this which makes his theory of renunciation a rationalistic system, which raises him from a prophet to a philosopher. He strongly inculcates philosophical doubt; he holds that all which cannot be rationally deduced has no claim on belief. " I say unto all of you," he replied once to his disciples, " do not believe in what ye have heard; that is, when you have heard any one say this is especially good or extremely bad ; do not reason with yourselves that if it had not been true, it would not have been asserted, and so believe in its truth ; neither have faith in traditions, because they have been handed down for generations and in many places. Do not believe in anything because it is rumoured and spoken of by many ; do not think that that is a proof of its truth. Do not believe because the written statement of some old sage is produced : you cannot be sure that the writing has ever been revised by the said sage, or can be relied upon. Do not believe in what you have fancied, thinking that because it is extraordinary it must have been implanted by a Dewa or some wonderful being." [1]

[1] Alabaster, *Wheel of the Law*, p. 35.

The words quoted in the preceding paragraph show exactly Gautama's method of treating ideas. When no rational origin can be discovered, the idea is treated as a delusion. It is true that the philosopher himself strangely neglected to apply this test to the dogma of transmigration, and thus evolved from it his wondrous theory of Karma. But in the third delusion, that of ritualism, to which I now turn, the test has been rigorously applied, and the result deduced: that gods, if they exist, are things about which it is a delusion to trouble oneself. We may define ritualism as a formal worship rendered to a being supposed capable of influencing the lives of men. Gautama satisfied himself that such ritualism was a delusion without entering into any discussion as to the existence or non-existence of divine beings. Such a discussion ought of course to follow the same lines as that on the Attavāda. The impossibility of any rational proof of the existence of a deity would become manifest, and the whole question would then turn upon a critical investigation of the historical origin of the predisposition. The Buddha seems to have been so impressed with the absolute validity of the law of change, that for him the very gods under its influence sunk into insignificance; they were but as butterflies in the ever-growing, ever-decaying cosmos. Could there be any rational basis for the worship of such gods? Is it not a mere ignorant delusion to suppose them eternal? Shortly, the predisposition to ritualism is only a debasing superstition, the outcome of those misinterpreted sensations which the phenomenal world produces in ignorant man. Ritualism, like the belief in individuality, is a most fatal hindrance to man's mental and moral growth. Here, as in the previous case, we notice that the Buddha's proof is insufficient, and that he dogmatically asserts ritualism to be a delusion without critically examining the growth of the predisposition. After once settling his *summum bonum*, however, it is possible for him to condemn ritualism *à priori*, having regard to the enormous evil it has brought mankind; for all evil hampers the entrance on that noble path which ends in arahatship.

Let us endeavour to sum up the results of Gautama's theory of renunciation. It calls upon man to renounce three predispositions which have influenced, and in the majority of cases still do enormously influence, the course of men's actions in the phenomenal world. Without sensuous pleasure would life be endurable? Without belief in immortality can man be moral? Without worship of a god can man advance towards righteousness? Yes, replies Gautama; these ends can be attained, and only attained, by *knowledge*. Knowledge alone is the key to the higher path; the one thing worth pursuing in life. Sensuality, individuality, and ritualism are, like witchcraft and fetish-worship, solely the delusions of ignorance, and so must fetter man's progress towards knowledge. The pleasures of sense subject man to the phenomenal world and render him a slave to its evils. Morality is not dependent upon a belief in immortality; its progress is identical with the progress of knowledge. Righteousness is the outcome of self-culture and self-control, and ritualism only hinders its growth. Knowledge is that which brings calmness and peace to life, which renders man indifferent to the storms of the phenomenal world. It produces that state which alone can be called blessed:

> "Beneath the stroke of life's changes,
> The mind that shaketh not,
> Without grief or passion, and secure,
> This is the greatest blessing." [1]

The knowledge which Gautama thus makes so all-important is not to be obtained by a transcendental or miraculous process as that of the Christian mystics, it is purely the product of the rational and inquiring intellect. Such knowledge the Buddha, in precisely the same fashion as Maimonides, Averroes, and Spinoza, installs as the coping-stone of his theory of renunciation.

If we turn from the Buddhist to the early Christian doctrine, we find a no less marked, although extremely different conception of renunciation. It is a conception which is

[1] Mangala Sutta, quoted by Rhys Davids: *Buddhism*, p. 127.

by no means easily expressed as a philosophical system, for it claims revelation, not reason, as its basis. We must content ourselves here with a few desultory remarks, and leave for another occasion a more critical examination of the fuller form of the Christian theory as it is philosophically expressed in the writings of Meister Eckehart. The Christian, as decisively as the Buddhist doctrine proclaims sensuality a delusion. The phenomenal world is essentially a world of sin, it is the fetter which hinders man's approach to righteousness. Until the sensuous world has been renounced, until the 'flesh' with all its impulses and desires has been crucified, there can be no entry into the higher life. This renunciation is termed the 'rebirth.' The rebirth is the entrance to the new moral life, to the spiritual well-being, to that mystic union with god which is termed righteousness. The rebirth cannot be attained by human wisdom or knowledge, it is a transcendental act of divine grace for which man can only prepare himself by faith and by good works. Christianity made no more attempt than Buddhism to reconcile the sensuous and the spiritual in man. The early fathers looked upon the sensuous nature of humanity as the origin of universal sin, and went some way towards deadening moral feeling by bidding men fly from the very sphere where moral action is alone possible. They make, of course, no attempt to prove rationally that the sensuous desire is a delusion; when once it is admitted that the mystic rebirth requires renunciation, renunciation follows as a categorical imperative.

The position taken by the Christian with regard to the other two great delusions differs widely from that of Gautama. So far from their being delusions for him, they are the terms which regulate the whole conduct of his life; they are precisely what induces him to renounce the world of sense. The Christian desires no rational deduction of individuality and ritualism, he accepts them as postulated by revelation. The key to his path of righteousness is faith, not knowledge. If the human reason oppose the Christian revelation, this only shows that the human reason is corrupt. The early Christian looked upon all rational thought, as he did upon all sensuousness, as an extremely dangerous thing. Nay, he did not hesitate to assert' that Christianity was in contradiction with human wisdom and culture. *Et mortuus est dei filius; prorsus credibile est, quia ineptum est. Et sepultus resurrexit; certum est, quia impossibile est.* The philosophers are but the patriarchs of heretics, and their dialectic a snare. "There is no more curiosity for us, now that Christ has come, nor any occasion for further investigation, · since we have the gospel. We are to seek for nothing which is not contained in the doctrine of Christ." Shortly, the only true gnosis is based upon revelation. Spinoza, following Maimonides, has identified all knowledge with knowledge of god. To the early Christian god was incomprehensible, could not form the subject of human knowledge; and every attempt at rational investigation of his nature must lead to atheism. Human perception of god was only attained by a transcendental process in which god himself assisted.

That the reader may fully recognize how this view of Christian renunciation propounded by the early Latin fathers is essentially identical with that of mediæval theology, it may not be amiss to quote one or two passages from a writer whose teaching has met with the approval of nearly all shades of Christian thought. I refer to Thomas à Kempis.

"Restrain that extreme desire of increasing Learning, which at the same time does but increase Sorrow by involving the mind in much perplexity and false delusion. For such are fond of being thought men of Wisdom, and respected as such. And yet this boasted learning of theirs consists in many things, which a man's mind is very little, if at all, the better for the knowledge of. And sure, whatever they may think of the matter, he who bestows his Time and Pains upon things that are of no service for promoting the Happiness of his Soul, ought by no means to be esteemed a wise man" (B. i., chap. ii.).

"Why should we, then, with such eager Toil, strive to be Masters of Logical Definitions? Or what do our abstracted Speculations profit us? He whom the Divine Word instructs takes a much shorter cut to Truth; For from this Word alone all saving knowledge is derived, and without this no man understands or judges aright. But he, who reduces all his studies to, and governs himself by this Rule, may establish his mind in perfect Peace, and rest himself securely upon God " (B. i., chap. iii.).

For Thomas à Kempis as for Tertullian there is a 'shorter cut to truth' than knowledge and learning, there is a mystic or transcendental process of 'instruction by the Divine Word' which brings 'perfect peace.' The revelation is an all-sufficient basis for the act of renunciation. The phenomenal world is for Thomas just as destructive of human freedom as Gautama has painted it. The earth is a field of tribulation and anguish; we must daily renounce its pleasures and crucify the flesh with all its lusts (cf. B. ii., chap. xii.). He will hold no parley with the "strong tendencies to pleasures of sense;" "true peace and content are never to be had by obeying the appetites, but by an obstinate resistance to them " (B. i., chap. vi.). It will be seen that the writer of the *Imitatio* is on all essential points in agreement with the Latin father, and we may not unfairly take the like statements of two such diverse and distant writers as the real standpoint of Christian thought. With this assumption we are now to some extent in a position to formulate the Christian doctrine of renunciation.[1]

As in Buddhism, it is the sensuous desires which are to be renounced. This renunciation is not based on rational, but on emotional grounds. The Christian arahatship or rebirth cannot be attained by a purely intellectual process, but only by passing through a peculiar phase of emotion, transcendental in character. Herein it differs *toto cœlo* from the Buddhist conception. The object of renunciation is in both cases the same—to attain blessedness,—but in the one case the blessedness is mundane and temporal, in the other celestial and eternal. The Christian admits that by accepting his revelation—or, in other words, by believing in the Buddhist delu-

[1] The reader will find the Christian doctrine more fully discussed in the paper on Meister Eckehart.

sions—he reduces this world to a sphere of sorrow and trial—
a result foretold by Gautama ; yet, on the other hand, sure
of the after-life, he holds the sacrifice more than justified.
The Buddhist, finding no rational ground for the Christian's
belief in individuality, endeavours to attain his blessedness
in this world, and to free himself from the sorrow and pain
which the Christian willingly accepts on faith. The one
finds in knowledge, the other in the emotions, a road to salvation. Both renounce the same sensuous desires, but the
one on what he supposes to be rational grounds, the other on
what he considers the dictates of revelation. Such seem to
be the distinguishing features in the ethic of renunciation as
taught by the two great religious systems of the world.

From this Christian doctrine let us turn to a mediæval
Eastern doctrine of renunciation. Here we find ourselves
once more on rational as opposed to emotional ground ; here
Jewish thought stands contrasted with Christian. What
influence Indian philosophy may have had over Hebrew and
Arabian it is hardly possible at present to determine, yet the
Arabs were at least acquainted with more than that life of
Gautama which, received by Christianity, led to his canoni-
zation. Whatever the influence, there can be no doubt that
the Bo Tree, the tree of knowedge, rather than the Cross,
the tree of mystic redemption, has been the symbol of what
we may term Eastern philosophy. Indian, Arab, Jew alike,
have declared the fruit of the Bo Tree to be the fruit of the
tree of life ; that a knowledge of good and evil leadeth
to beatitude rather than sin. From this tree Gautama
went forth to give light to those who sit in darkness, to
prepare a way of salvation for men. The religion of the
philosopher, Averroes tells us, consists in the deepening
of his knowledge ; for man can offer to god no worthier
cultus than the knowledge of his works, through which we
attain to the knowledge of god himself in the fulness of
his essence. From the cognition of things *sub specie æternitatis*—from the knowledge of god—arises, in the opinion of
both Maimonides and Spinoza, the highest contentment of
mind, the beatitude of men. On the extent of men's wisdom

THE ETHIC OF RENUNCIATION.   91

depends their share in the life eternal.[1] Let it be noted that
this wisdom lays claim to no transcendental character ; occasionally it may have been obscured by mystical language or
the dogma of a particular revelation, but in the main it pretends to be nought but the creation of the active human
intellect.   At first it might be supposed that there must be
a broad distinction between a doctrine like the Buddhist,
wherein the name of god is only mentioned as forming the
basis of a delusion, and systems like those of Maimonides
and Spinoza, which take the conception of god for their keystone.   The distinction, however, exists rather in appearance
than reality, Spinoza's conception of the deity differing *toto
cœlo* from the personal gods of the Christian or the Brahmin,
and being quite incapable of giving rise to the delusion of
ritualism.   God is for him the sum of all things, and at the
same time their indwelling cause ; he is at once matter and
the laws of matter (*nescio, cur materia divinâ naturâ indigna
esset.   Ethica* i. 15, Schol.), not the ponderous matter of
the physicist, but that reality which must be recognized as
forming the basis of the phenomenal world ; not the mere
' law of nature,' as stated by the naturalist, but the law of
the phenomenon recognized as an absolute law of thought ;
shortly, the material world realized as existing by and
evolved from intellectual necessity.   Such a conception
must have been as necessary to Gautama as to Spinoza ;
the latter only has chosen to call it god.   The formal
worship of such a god is obviously impossible.   Spinoza
recognized as fully as the Buddha what evils spring from the
delusion of ritualism ; far more critically than the Buddha
he investigates the causes from which the predisposition
to ritualism arises.   Noting that there are many *præjudicia*

---

[1] Maimonides, *Yad Hackazakah*, Bernard, 1832, pp. 307-8. See
the essay on Maimonides and Spinoza, where the identity between
the views of both philosophers is pointed out.   The resemblance to
Eckehart is also noteworthy.   The immortality of the soul consists in
the eternity of its *vorgendezbild* in the mind of god.   By the higher
knowledge or union with god the soul becomes conscious of this reality,
or realizes its eternity.   Hell consists in an absence of this consciousness.

which impede men's knowledge of the truth, he adds: *Et quoniam omnia quæ hic indicare suspicio præjudicia pendent ab hoc uno, quod scilicet communiter supponant homines, omnes res naturales, ut ipsos, propter finem agere, imo ipsum Deum omnia ad certum aliquem finem dirigere, pro certo statuant: dicunt enim, Deum omnia propter hominem fecisse, hominem autem, ut ipsum coleret* (*Ethica* i., Appendix; Van Vloten, vol. i. p. 69). Very carefully does Spinoza endeavour to show the falseness of this fundamental prejudice; he points out *how* men have come to believe the world was created for them, and that god directs all for their use; *how* it arises: *ut unusquisque diversos Deum colendi modos ex suo ingenio excogitaverit, ut Deus eos supra reliquos diligeret, et totam Naturam in usum cæcæ illorum cupiditatis et insatiabilis avaritiæ dirigeret*. So has the prejudice turned into superstition, and struck its roots deep in the minds of men (Van Vloten, vol. i. p. 71). He paints blackly enough the resulting *communis vulgi persuasio*: the mob bears its religion as a burden, which after death, as the reward of its slavery, it trusts to throw aside; too often it is influenced in addition by the unhealthy fear of a terrible life in another world. These wretched men, worn out by the weight of their own piety, would, but for their belief in a future life, give free play to all their sensual passions (*Ethica* v. 41, Schol.). Gautama could not have better described the out-come of the superstition among ignorant men; he nowhere displays such critical acumen in endeavouring to show that all worship of god is a delusion (see especially the whole Appendix to *Ethica* i.). These remarks apply, though in a lesser extent, to Maimonides' conception of god. The philosophy of Maimonides is struggling at every point with his dogmatic faith, and he finds it impossible to hide the antagonism between his conceptions of god as the world intellect and as the personal Jehovah of his religion. The general impression one draws from his writings is, however, that he held with Averroes that the true worship of god is the attainment of wisdom, or the knowledge of his works. With regard, then, to the delusion of ritualism, we find that Spinoza, and at heart Maimonides, are in agreement with Gautama; the belief in the worship of the deity is a prejudice which must be renounced; it is chief cause of the ignorance which impedes men's knowledge of the true nature of god (*i.e.*, the intellectual basis of reality).

If we turn to the second Buddhist delusion, we find Maimonides and Spinoza in essential agreement with, although formally differing from, Gautama. Both Jewish philosophers base man's immortality on his possession of wisdom, his knowledge of the deity; the older with some obscurity,[1] the later with direct reference to a theory of ideal reality existing in god. The scholastic variation of the Platonic doctrine of ideas, which placed all things *secundum esse intelligibile* in the mind of god,[2] was not without great influence on the thought of Spinoza. He found in the *esse intelligibile* an indestructible element of the human soul; this idea in god, or the individual *sub specie æternitatis*, was the conception which led him to assert that *aliquid remanet, quod æternum est* (*Ethica* v. 22, 23). The realization by the mind of its own *esse intelligibile*, that is, its knowledge of god (v. 30), is laid down as the quantitative measure of the mind's immortality (cf. the passage: *Sapiens . . . sui et Dei . . . conscius nunquam esse definit, Ethica*, v. 42, Schol.). We may ask how far this possible eternity of the mind can affect men's actions. In the case of both Maimonides and Spinoza the *quantum* of eternity is based on the *quantum* of wisdom; not by any ritual, not by any particular line of conduct, not by any faith—solely by the possession of wisdom can the eternity of the mind be realized. Imagination, memory, personality, cease with death; no material duration belongs to the eternity of the mind (v. 23, Schol., and 34, Schol.). Surely this is with Gautama denouncing individuality as a delusion! Such eternity is no reward for virtue; we do not attain beatitude because we restrain our sensuality, but we realize our eternity in this world by the higher cognition; and it is

---

[1] A comparison of the doctrines of Spinoza and Maimonides on the immortality of the soul is given in the sixth paper of this volume.

[2] This form of the Platonic idealism is precisely that laid down by Wyclif in the first book of the *Trialogus*.

this knowledge, this beatitude, which enables us to control
our passions (v. 42).   Surely Spinoza's *beatitude* is but
another name for the Buddhist Nirvāna! What Spinozist
could ever be driven by a theory of reward hereafter to
religious persecution, to asceticism, or to that intellectual
nihilism which scorns reason? He rejects such evils, and
discards the Attavāda as decisively as Gautama himself.[1]

If we turn to the third great Buddhist delusion, the
pleasures of sense, we find the Jewish philosophers by no
means so unrestrictedly call for its renunciation as the
followers of Gautama and Jesus. The great goal of human
life, according to their philosophy, is the attainment of
wisdom, and renunciation is to be of those things only
which are a hindrance in the path of intellectual development.
Unsatisfied desire may be as real an obstacle as the same
desire converted into the rule of life; to make the renunciation of such desires the chief maxim of conduct is to raise
the secondary phenomenal above the primary intellectual.
Fitness of body is an essential condition for fitness of mind,
and the passage of life's span, *mente sana in corpore sano*, is
the requisite for human happiness (*Ethica* v. 39).   To
renounce, then, the gratification of certain sensuous desires,
which have a physiological value, is merely by an unfit
body to hamper the progress of the mind. To make these
sensuous desires the motive of human conduct is equally
reprehensible; the sole method of escape lies in the *via
media*.   Clearly enough does Maimonides reject ascetic
renunciation: " Perchance one will say: since jealousy, lust,
ambition, and the like passions are bad, and tend to put men
out of the world, I will part with them altogether, and
remove to the other extreme—and in this he might go so far
as even not to eat meat, not to drink wine, not to take a wife,

---

[1] I may cite a passage thoroughly Spinozist in character : " Buddhism
takes as its ultimate fact the existence of the material world and of
conscious beings living within it ; and it holds that everything is constantly, though imperceptibly, changing. There is no place where this
law does not operate ; no heaven or hell, therefore, in the ordinary sense"
(Rhys Davids : *Buddhism*, p. 87).

not to reside in a fine dwelling-house, and not to put on any
fine garments, but only sackcloth, or coarse wool or the like
stuff, just as the priests of the worshippers of idols do; this,
too, is a wicked way, and it is not lawful to walk in the same "
(*Yad Hackazahah*, Bernard, p. 170). The keynote to all
sensuous pleasure is to be found in its treatment as medicine,
whereby the body may be preserved in good health.[1] In
precisely similar fashion Spinoza tells us that only superstition can persuade us that what brings us sorrow is good,
and again, that what causes joy is evil. " Cum igitur res illæ
sint bonæ, quæ corporis partes juvant, ut suo officio fungantur,
et Lætitia in eo consistat, quod hominis potentia quatenus
Mente et Corpore constat juvat vel augetur; sunt ergo illa
omnia, quæ Lætitiam afferunt, bona. Attamen, quoniam
contra non eum in finem res agunt, ut nos Lætitia afficiant,
nec earum agendi potentia ex nostra utilitate temperatur,
et denique quoniam Lætitia plerumque ad unam Corporis
partem potissimum refertur; habent ergo plerumque Lætitiæ
affectus (*nisi Ratio et vigilantia adsit*), et consequenter Cupiditatis etiam, quæ ex iisdem generantur, excessum " (*Ethica* iv.,
Appendix, cc. 30, 31). These quotations must suffice to show
how different the Hebrew standpoint is to the Buddhist or
Christian; it approaches nearer the Greek. It consists in the
rational satisfaction (not renunciation) of sensuous desires as
a necessary step towards bodily health and consequent mental
fitness (see Maimonides, *Yad*, pp. 167–169; Spinoza,
Ethica iv. 38, 39, and Appendix, c. 27).

---

[1] The following passage is so characteristic of the Hebrew standpoint,
that it deserves to be cited : "When a man eats or drinks, or has sexual
intercourse, his purpose in doing these things ought to be not merely that
of enjoying himself, so that he should eat or drink that only which is
pleasant to the palate, or have sexual intercourse merely for the sake of
enjoyment ; but his purpose whilst eating or drinking ought to be solely
that of preserving his body and limbs in good health " (*Yad. B.* 173).
The position is thoroughly opposed to Christian asceticism, which
Maimonides probably had in his mind when speaking above of the
"priests of the worshippers of idols." It was doubtless in Spinoza's
thoughts, too, when he wrote: "Multi, præ nimia scilicet animi impatientia,
falsoque religionis studio, inter bruta potius quam inter homines vivere
maluerunt."

The reader may feel inclined to ask on what grounds we have classed Spinoza and Maimonides as philosophers of renunciation. What do they call upon their disciples to renounce, if they wish to be free from the slavery of the phenomenal world? Do they teach no rebirth by which men may approach beatitude? Most certainly. They call upon their disciples to renounce not individuality, ritualism, and sensuality, but obscure ideas on these as on all other matters. They teach how, by that higher knowledge which sees the true causes of things, man is born afresh, born from slavery to freedom. Such is the rebirth which Spinoza terms the idea of god making man free, and Maimonides the Holy Spirit coming to dwell with man (see the paper on Maimonides and Spinoza). We must content ourselves here with a short investigation of Spinoza's doctrine. What does that philosopher understand by obscure ideas? What by the 'idea of god making man free'? In his system, god, we have seen, is identified with the reality of things, not things regarded as phenomena, but as links in an infinite chain of intellectual causality. He is the λογος which dwells in and is all existence; 'laws of nature' are only the sensuous expression of the laws of the divine intellect; the story of the world is only the phenomenalizing of the successive steps in the logic of pure thought. Spinoza, then, *assumes* the thought attribute in the deity is qualitatively the same as that in the human mind.[1] From this it follows, since god's capacity for thinking and his causation are identical, that it is theoretically *possible* for the human mind to grasp things as they exist in their intellectual necessity. Such knowledge of things is fitly termed a knowledge of god or an understanding of things *sub specie æternitatis;* it is seeing phenomena

---

[1] Wyclif (who, by the bye, also identified the divine perception and creation) makes the same assumption : "Et sic intellectus divinus ac ejus notitia sunt paris ambitus, sicut intellectus creatus et ejus notitia ; et sic falsum assumis quod multa intelligis, quæ Deus non potest intelligere. Imo quamvis omne illud intelligis, quod Deus potest intelligere et e contra, tamen infinitum imperfectiori modo, quam Deus potest intelligere" (*Trialogus*, Ed. Lechler, p. 70).

as they exist in eternal necessity. Now, external objects
produce in the individual certain sensations, which excite
definite emotions followed by desires in the mind. These
emotions arise from causes 'external' to ourselves; with regard to them we are passive or suffer; they are what Spinoza
has termed passions. These are the causes of man's misery
in the phenomenal world, the fetters whence human slavery
arises (*Ethica* iii.; Def. 1, 2; iv. 2-5). By what means
may man free himself from the mastery of these passions?
They are harmful to him because they arise from causes external to him, he is not their adequate cause. But, argues
Spinoza, man is a part of nature, and can suffer no changes
except those which can be understood by his own nature, and
of which it is the adequate cause (*Ethica* iv. 4). In other
words, if a man only understands a thing clearly, he becomes
its adequate cause. The human mind, in so far as it perceives
things truly (*sub specie æternitatis*), is a part of the infinite
intelligence of god; the thing is dissevered from its external
cause and seen as a necessary outcome of the human (and
divine) intelligence. Henceforth the emotion ceases to be a
passion (ii. 11., v. 3, &c.). In replacing obscure ideas by clear
ideas we renounce our passions, and are reborn from human
slavery to human freedom by 'the idea of god'—that is, by
our knowledge of things *sub specie æternitatis*. Henceforth we
have the power *ordinandi et concatenandi corporis affectiones
secundum ordinem ad intellectum* (v. 10); we are no longer blind
suffering implements in the hands of phenomenal causality.
Here, then, we have the Spinozist renunciation and rebirth.
Like the Buddhist road to Arahatship, it is the destruction
of ignorance by knowledge, the replacing of confused, by clear
ideas. It is only to be attained by intellectual labour, and
not by a transcendental mystery. It sets the attainment of
wisdom as the goal of human existence, for by this alone can
humanity free itself from slavery to the phenomenal world.
Difficult is the path which leads to the Spinozist Arahatship,
yet the philosopher himself at least phenomenalized his
system, and taught us to appreciate *quantum sapiens polliat,
potiorque sit ignaro, qui sola libidine agitur.*

7

Since Spinoza there has been no great philosopher who has made a doctrine of renunciation the centre point of his system. The old difficulties as to the phenomenal world, the old consciousness of human slavery, have been ever present in the thoughts of men, but their attention has been directed more and more to a critical investigation of the relation of the human mind to the phenomenal world. This is a necessary preliminary to any theory of practical conduct whereby man may free himself from phenomenal subjectivity. The founder of the critical school has, however, enunciated a theory of rebirth which it is all the more interesting to examine, as it possesses marked analogies to Eckehart's, and is an attempted return from the intellectual Hebrew to the mystic or transcendental Christian standpoint. Before inquiring the meaning of the Kantian *Wiedergeburt*, it may not be without profit to mark a connecting link between the Spinozist and Kantian theories, which is to be found in the poet Goethe.[1] Like Spinoza, Goethe believed that god was the inner cause working and existing in all things (*Weltseele*), or, as he expresses it :

> " Was wär' 'ein Gott, der nur von aussen stiesse,
> . Im Kreis das All am Finger laufen liesse,
> Ihm ziemt's, die Welt im Innern zu bewegen,
> Natur in Sich, Sich in Natur zu hegen,
> So dass, wass in Ihm lebt und webt und ist,
> Nie seine Kraft, nie Seinen Geist vermisst."
> *Gott und Welt. Proemion.*

But this identification of god with the universe, like all forms of pantheism, renders it impossible for man to look upon the world as a mere field for his moral action, its pain and sorrow as mere means to his own *Willensläuterung*, and sensuous desires as mere material for that renunciation which leads to beatitude. The laws of god's nature cease to be either good or bad; it is impossible to assert a moral

[1] On the philosophy of Goethe, cf. E. Caro : *La philosophie de Goethe*, Paris, 1866. Especially for our present purpose, Chapitre vii., *Les conceptions sur la destinée humaine.*

principle as the basis of the world.[1]   How, then, is man to regard those sensuous impressions which alternately elevate and depress him ?   Shall he strive, as Buddha and Eckehart teach, to renounce all sensuous existence ?   By no means, replies Goethe ; the real freedom of men does not consist in asceticism, but in *rational* enjoyment of all the world produces.   Life is no valley of tears ; man shall not hate it and fly into the wilderness because he cannot realize all his dreams (*Prometheus* v. 6) ; there is room enough for happy, joyous existence :

> " Den Sinnen hast du dann zu trauen ;
> Kein Falsches lassen sie dich schauen,
> Wenn *dein Verstand dich wach erhält.*
> Mit frischem Blick bemerke freudig,
> Und wandle, sicher wie geschmeidig,
> Durch Auen reich begabter Welt.
> Geniesse mässig Füll' und Segen ;
> *Vernunft sey überall zugegen,*
> Wo Leben sich des Lebens freut.
> Dann ist Vergangenheit beständig,
> Das Künftige voraus lebendig,
> Der Augenblick ist Ewigkeit."
> > *Gott und Welt.   Vermächtniss.*

With true Greek spirit Goethe is yet practically taking the same view as Maimonides and Spinoza ; sensuality is *not* an unqualified delusion.   But the phenomenal world is not always so kind to man, it is not always possible for him to enjoy it : there is pain, there is grief, there is death.   In the moment of joy man is cast into the lowest depths of misery ; how shall man preserve his freedom when, in the midst of delight in the sensuous world, its great forces may turn and

[1]   " Denn unfühlend
Ist die Natur :
Es leuchtet die Sonne
Ueber Bös' und Gute,
Und dem Verbrecher
Glänzen, wie dem Besten,
Der Mond und die Sterne."
> *Das Göttliche.*

crush him?[1]   How can such a man free himself from the
slavery of the phenomenal?   Here Goethe adopts the
Spinozist doctrine of renunciation ; clear ideas of nature and
man's relation to it will render him immovable amidst the
storm of external circumstance.   Only let man recognize
the eternal necessity which rules all being—

> " Nach ewigen, ehrnen,
> Grossen Gesetzen
> Müssen wir alle
> Unseres Daseyns
> Kreise vollenden."
> > *Das Göttliche.*

and he will put aside all childlike grief, that the world is not
'as it ought to be.'   Let him only see things *sub specie
æternitatis* and he will recognize that all phenomena, including humanity itself, are but passing changes on the
surface of the eternal.   "When this deeper insight into the
eternal nature of things has firmly established itself in our
reason, what are those accidents which throw into despair
the thoughtless and the commonplace?   A necessary detail
of the order of the universe, wherein death is the nourishment
of life ; in which law, ever replete in change, destroys all to
renew all."[2]   Every step in growth is a stage in decay.

> " Und umzuschaffen das Geschaffne,
> Damit sich's nicht zum Starren waffne
> Wirkt ewiges, lebendiges Thun.
>
> .   .   .   .   .
>
> Es soll sich regen, schaffend handeln,
> Erst sich gestalten, dann verwandeln ;
> Nur scheinbar steht's Momente still.
> Das Ewige regt sich fort in allen ;
> Denn Alles muss in Nichts zerfallen,
> Wenn es im Seyn beharren will."
> > *Gott und Welt.   Eins und Alles.*

---

[1] Well expressed by Schleiermacher : " Der Mensch kenne nichts als
sein Dasein in der Zeit, und dessen gleitenden Wandel hinab von der
sonnigen Höhe des Genusses in die furchtbare Nacht der Vernichtung '"
(*Monologen* i., *Betrachtung*).

[2] Caro, p. 192.

In this knowledge of the eternal nature of things is to be found that contentment of mind which raises man above temporal sorrow, frees him from the bondage of the phenomenal.[1] Even as Spinoza deduced an eternity for those minds which had realized the eternal essence of things and of themselves, so Goethe supposed an immortality for those beings who by clearness of vision had approached spiritual perfection. Here in this nineteenth century Goethe we find, on the one hand, the strongest recognition of the Buddhist law of universal dissolution and composition; on the other, the fullest acceptation of the Spinozist doctrine that the knowledge of things in their eternal aspect is the true means to that peace of mind which constitutes the Arahatship of Indian and Jew alike.   Strange is this enunciation of the Eastern intellectual doctrine at the very time when Kant was busy reconstructing a transcendental Christian system!   Yet Goethe is in a certain sense nearer to Kant than Spinoza; his belief tends, it is true, rather to a scientific naturalism, than a transcendental idealism, but yet where his reason does not carry him, he finds it unnecessary to contest the rights of faith.   He is a poet, and finds no inconsistency between his rational pantheism and a semi-mystical acceptation of the Christian dogma.   It is here that Kant's position is logically stronger than Goethe's, and his reconciliation of reason and the Christian revelation of a more satisfactory character, because he has not by pantheistic premises previously denied the possibility of transcendental mystery.[2]

We must now turn to Kant's theory of the Christian *Wiedergeburt.*   Proceeding on the same lines as Meister

[1] The thought is again well expressed by Schleiermacher. He is referring to the crushing effect of the phenomenal on the absolutely insignificant individual, and then to the effect of the 'higher knowledge': "Erfass' ich nicht mit meiner Sinne Kraft die Aussenwelt? trag ich nicht die ewigen Formen der Dinge ewig in mir? und erkenn' ich sie nicht nur als den hellen Spiegel meines Innern" (*Monologen* i.).

[2] The 'reconciliation' is a noteworthy fact of the 'critical' philosophy. It might well be termed "transcendental scholasticism," if the name did not suggest an unfavourable comparison with the depth, logical consistency, and single-mindedness of Thomas Aquinas.

Eckehart, he separates a phenomenal world, or world as it appears in the sensuous perception of the human mind, from a world of reality, the so-called *Dinge an sich.* The latter he does not, like the mystic, identify with the intellect (or will) of god. He identifies it with the sphere of freedom or self-determined will. Let us endeavour to grasp by what process he arrives at this conclusion. Man is one of the phenomena of the sensuous world, and as such is subject to the causality of its empirical laws. He feels the influence of sensuous causes impelling him to act after a certain fashion; his *Wollen* is produced by physical causes over which he has no control. On the other hand, the man is conscious within himself, not by sensuous perception, but by mere apperception (*durch blosse Apperception*), of a certain power of self-determination, there is something in him of an 'intelligible' character. He finds in practical life that certain imperatives *appear* to rule his action as well as sensuous causes. There is a *Sollen* as well as a *Wollen.* The *Sollen*, according to Kant, expresses a necessity which exists nowhere else in the phenomenal world. "Es mögen noch so viel Naturgründe sein, die mich zum *Wollen* antreiben, noch so viel sinnliche Anreize, so können sie nicht das *Sollen* hervorbringen, sondern nur ein noch lange nicht nothwendiges, sondern jederzeit bedingtes Wollen, dem dagegen das Sollen, das die Vernunft ausspricht, Maass und Ziel, ja Verbot und Ansehen entgegen setzt."[1] The existence of this *Sollen* is not deduced by reason, it is a fact based upon the common consciousness of men. Here Kant and Goethe are in perfect accord :

> "Sofort nun wende dich nach innen,
> Das Centrum findest du da drinnen
> Woran kein Edler zweifeln mag.
> Wirst keine Regel da vermissen :
> Denn das selbstständige Gewissen
> Ist Sonne deinem Sittentag."
>
> *Gott und Welt. Vermächtniss.*

---

[1] *Kritik d. r. Vernunft.* Elementarlehre II., Th. ii., Abth. ii., Buch. 2 Hauptst. 9, Abschn. iii., *Möglichkeit der Causalität durch Freiheit.*

Kant makes no attempt to question whether this *Sollen* may
not be an innate *Wollen*, an hereditary predisposition, the
outcome of racial experience in the past ; one of the conditions by which the human type maintains its position in
the struggle for existence, and which it has consequently
impressed upon all its members.   Independent of the immediate phenomenal, he assumes its existence not to be due to
sensuous causes.   From the existence of this *Sollen*, this absolute *Sittengesetz*, Kant deduces the possibility of freedom ;
the *Sollen* denotes a *Können*.   In other words, the freedom of
the will, its causality, is asserted.   Now the conception of
causality carries with it the conception of law ; the empirical
causality connotes natural laws ; this intelligible causality
connotes laws also unchangeable ; but in order that the free
will may not be chimerical (*ein Unding*), it must be regarded
as self-determinative, as a law to itself.   " Der Satz aber: der
Wille ist in allen Handlungen sich selbst ein Gesetz, be-
zeichnet nur das Princip,nach keiner anderen Maxime zu han-
deln, als die sich selbst auch als ein allgemeines Gesetz zum
Gegenstande haben kann.   Dies ist aber gerade die Formel
des kategorischen Imperativs und das Princip der Sittlich-
keit ; *also ist ein freier Wille und ein Wille unter sittlichen Geset-
zen einerlei.*[1]   It will be seen that Kant identifies the idea of
freedom with the sphere of the moral law ; the will is only so
far free as it obeys the fundamental principle of morality,
and obeys it, not from any phenomenal desire, but solely because it is the fundamental principle.[2]   Accordingly we find
the world of intelligible causality identified with the moral
world; but this self-determining will, wherein freedom consists,
cannot exist in time and space ; it cannot be phenomenal, or
it were subject to empirical causality.   We are compelled

[1] *Grundlegung zur Metaphysik der Sitten*, Abschnitt. iii.   *Der Be-
griff der Freiheit* (Hartenstein, iv. pp. 294, 295).
[2] This fundamental principle is the well-known Kantian extension of
the Christian " Do unto others as you would that they should do to you,"
namely, " Handle nur nach derjenigen Maxime, durch die du zugleich
wollen kannst, dass sie ein allgemeines Gesetz werde " (Ibid. Abschn. ii.
Cf. especially the paragraphs *Die Autonomie* and *Die Heteronomie des
Willens*).

to identify it with the *Dinge an sich*. "Folglich, wenn man sie (die Freiheit) noch retten will, so bleibt kein Weg übrig, als das Dasein eines Dinges, sofern es in der Zeit bestimmbar ist, folglich auch die Causalität nach dem Gesetze der Natur-nothwendigkeit blos der. Erscheinungen, die Freiheit aber ebendemselben Wesen, als Dinge an sich selbst, beizulegen."[1] Such, then, is the *outline* of the process by which Kant identifies the *Dinge an sich* with the world as will, or the sphere of the moral law.

We have next to inquire what is the process of *Wiedergeburt* whereby man is enabled to disregard the pain and sorrow of the phenomenal world. Here we are concerned with a portion of the 'critical scholasticism,' *i.e.*, Kant's deduction of the Christian doctrine. In the disposition of the will, and in that alone, is to be found the basis upon which we may define good and evil. The good disposition is that which takes the moral maxim as its *sole* motive (*das Gesetz allein zur hinreichenden Triebfeder in sich aufgenommen hat*); the evil disposition is that which rejects this motive entirely, or is influenced by others in addition.[2] The passage, then, from evil to good denotes an entire change of disposition; it is an alteration in the very foundation of character; but an evil disposition can never will anything but evil. So (according to Kant) there can be no process of bettering, no passage from good to evil by a gradual *reform*. "Wie es nun möglich sei, dass ein natürlicher Weise böser Mensch sich selbst zum guten Menschen mache, das übersteigt alle unsere Begriffe, denn wie kann ein böser Baum gute Früchte bringen?"[3] But even as there exists an 'ought' to become good, so there must exist a means. Such means must accordingly be transcendental—quite beyond human comprehension. The change from good to evil disposition is termed the *Wiedergeburt*.[4] Man is alone conscious that it is impossible

---

[1] *Kritik der p. Vernunft*, i. Th. 1, B. iii., Hauptst. (Hartenstein, v. p. 100).
[2] *Religion innerh. d. Grenzen d. blossen Vernunft*. i. Stück. 2. *Von dem Hang zum Bösen* (Hartenstein, vi. p. 123, *et seq.*).
[3] Ibid. *Allg. Anm.* p. 139.
[4] Ibid. *Allg. Anm.* p. 141.

for him unaided to make the change; the change is to him incomprehensible. It needs some supersensuous aid, a mystery to accomplish it. This mystery must be the action of god. The moral law tells him that he *must*, and therefore *can*, become good; but without the assistance of god the mysterious process is impossible; it depends on the action of the divine grace.[1] Here is the limit to which the mere reason can go in matters of religion. The *Wiedergeburt* is, then, a transcendental change of disposition; as such it takes place not in the phenomenal, but in the intelligible. It is not a temporal act, but an act of the intelligible character. On the existence of this intelligible world (the *Dinge an sich*) depends the moral change in man and (according to Kant) the Christian doctrine of redemption.[2]

If we suppose the *Wiedergeburt* to have taken place, the question next arises, how the redemption can follow upon it? The *Wiedergeburt* has only effected a change in disposition, it has by no means wiped out the guilt consequent upon the old evil. This guilt can only be expiated by corresponding punishment; such is absolutely necessary to the conception of divine justice. In this form of punishment for moral evil, a primary condition for its being expiatory is the recognition that it is deserved. Hence there can be no such punishment so long as the disposition has not changed. The expiatory punishment must take place after the *Wiedergeburt*.[3] The new man must offer himself up as propitiation for the old. "Der Ausgang aus der verderbten Gesinnung in die gute ist als ("das Absterben am alten Menschen, Kreuzigung des Fleisches") an sich schon Aufopferung und Antretung einer langen Reihe von Uebeln des Lebens, die

---

[1] "Jeder, so viel als in seinen Kräften ist, thun müsse um ein besserer Mensch zu werden; . . . (er kann dann hoffen dass) was nicht in seinem Vermögen ist, werde durch höhere Mitwirkung ergänzt werden" (Ibid. *Allg. Anm.* p. 146).

[2] On this somewhat obscure point in Kant's treatise on Religion, cf. Kuno Fischer, *Geschichte d. n. Philosophie*, Bd. iv. p. 419, *et seq.*, 2 Ausg.

[3] *Religion innerh. d. Grenzen d. blossen Vernunft*, II., Stück. i., Absch. c. (Hartenstein, vi. p. 166, *et seq.*).

der neue Mensch in der Gesinnung des Sohnes Gottes, nämlich blos um des Guten willen übernimmt; die aber doch
eigentlich einem andern, nämlich dem alten (denn dieser ist
moralisch ein anderer), als *Strafe* gebührten." Shortly;
after the *Wiedergeburt*, all the pain and evil of life, all the
phenomenal subjectivity of man, recognized as merited punishment, are gladly endured because therein the new-born
man finds moral blessedness. The lasting consciousness that
they are merited is to him a proof of the strength and persistency of his disposition to the good; he endures them
gladly, because on them he bases his hope of final forgiveness for his sins. Thus Kant supposes man, by means of
the renunciation of the evil disposition in the mystic *Wiedergeburt*, to arrive at a position from which he can regard his
phenomenal slavery even as a cause of moral blessedness.[1]

We cannot now criticize this fantastic system of Kant's,
which supposes the whole phenomenal world produced as a
means whereby man may purify his will,—the goal of universal existence to be the production of morally perfect
humanity. It must suffice here to note its relation to the
doctrines of renunciation previously considered. In its general
lines it agrees with those Christian types we have had under
consideration; the state of blessedness, Arahatship, is reached
not by an intellectual, but by a supersensuous or mystical process. Kant, however, differs from Eckehart in that he does
not suppose the state of blessedness to be attained by even
a transcendental form of knowledge. It is not the 'higher
knowledge' of the real nature of things as they exist in the
mind of god, which brings peace, but that willing submission to punishment which follows on acknowledged moral

---

[1] The following statement is very suggestive of Kant's intensely anthropomorphic position: "Alle Uebel in der Welt im Allgemeinen als Strafen
für begangene Uebertretungen anzusehen ... liegt vermuthlich der mensch-
lichen Vernunft sehr nahe, welche geneigt ist, den Lauf der Natur an
die Gesetze der Moralität anzuknüpfen, und die daraus den Gedanken
sehr natürlich hervorbringt, dass wir zuvor bessere Menschen zu werden
suchen sollen, ehe wir verlangen können, von den Uebeln des Lebens
befreit zu werden, oder sie durch überwiegendes Wohl zu vergüten"
(Ibid., footnote, p. 168).

delinquency. If we turn to Spinoza's purely intellectual standpoint we find Kant is at the very opposite pole of thought. For Spinoza only the wise can attain blessedness, for Kant only the moral. Nor does the latter philosopher by any means suppose morality a mere component part of wisdom; it is based upon a universal moral apperception common to the ignorant as well as to the wise. Understanding, judgment, knowledge, do not tend to produce a 'good will,' and are not necessary: "um zu wissen, was man zu thun habe, um ehrlich und gut, ja sogar um weise und tugendhaft zu sein." [1] Could a greater gulf be well imagined than exists between these two philosophical systems? The one, Ptolemæan, causes the whole universe to revolve about man's moral nature; the other, Copernican, does not even allow that nature to be the sun of its own insignificant system. Only once, when both consider the freedom of god to consist not in indeterminism, but in absolute spontaneity, do they seem for an instant to approach. But even here Kant is regarding the inner moral necessity, Spinoza the inner intellectual necessity of god's action. [2] Needless is it to compare the Buddhist with the critical philosophy. So far from Gautama and Kant being at opposite poles of thought, they do not even think on the same planet!

With Kant we must draw to a conclusion this brief review of the various doctrines of renunciation which have been propounded with the aim of relieving man from his phenomenal slavery. Hitherto we have contented ourselves by endeavouring to put them clearly before the reader, and leaving him as a rule to judge of their logical consistency. Apart from this, however, there is a deeper question as to their practical value. In how far is the Buddhist, the Christian, or the Spinozist really superior to the

[1] Cf. the *Erster Abschnitt* of the *Grundlegung zur Metaphysik der Sitten* (Hartenstein, vi. p. 241), which treats especially of this point.

[2] *Religion innerhalb der Grenzen der blossen Vernunft*, Stück. i., *Allg. Anm.* (Hartenstein, vi. p. 144, footnote). Cf. Spinoza, *Ethica* i. 17, and Defn. 7.

sorrow, the pain, above all to the passion of the sensuous world ? The lives of Buddhist monks, of Christian ascetics and pietists, of the lens-polisher of Amsterdam, prove sufficiently that men can render themselves more or less indifferent to the storm of outward sensation.[1] Is such, however, the result of any phase of theory, or rather an emotional state peculiar to certain individuals ? Again, may we not question whether the renunciant obtains the greatest joy from life ? May not he who drinks deeper from the cup of existence find in greater joy more than sufficient recompense for greater pain ? Nay, may we not ask with Herder, whether man has any 'right' to remove himself into this blessed indifference, whether it must not destroy that sympathy for his fellows which can only arise from like passions, whether it does not 'rob the world of one of its most beautiful phenomena—man in his natural and moral grandeur'?[2] We cannot now enter upon any analysis of these doubts ; we refer merely to those philosophers, who do not absolutely renounce sensuous pleasures, as giving at least a *partial* solution, and shall conclude our ethic by a short investigation of the term 'phenomenal slavery,' which will perhaps serve as a basis for criticising any future doctrine of renunciation which may lay claim to logical consistency.

Phenomena in a variety of ways are capable of holding

[1] It is hardly necessary to argue with those who would deny the *possibility* of man freeing himself from the intensity of outward sensation. It is matter of common experience. "Der Mensch vergisst sich selbst : er verliert das Maass der Zeit und seiner sinnlichen Kräfte, wenn ihn ein hoher Gedanke aufruft, und er denselben verfolgt. Die scheusslichsten Qualen des Körpers haben durch eine einzige lebendige Idee unterdrückt werden können, die damals in der Seele herrschte. Menschen die von einem Affekt, insonderheit von dem lebhaftesten reinsten Affekt unter allen, der Liebe Gottes, ergriffen wurden, haben Leben und Tod nicht geachtet und sich in diesen Abgründe aller Ideen wir im Himmel gefühlt " (Herder: *Philosophie der Geschichte der Menschheit*, i., Buch. v., Absch. iv.).

[2] If any form of Arahatship became common we should cease to meet in practical life those Hamlets and Fausts which add so much to its richness and depth. The pious and the resigned are the most uninteresting of mortals.

in bondage the individual man. All we understand by
'phenomenal slavery' is, that phenomena directly or
indirectly produce certain effects in man which he is
apparently incapable of controlling. So long as these effects.
tend to preserve his existence or favour his growth, he finds
them causes of happiness, and does not recognize them as
slavery. (In the normal state no one objects to being *subject*
to the sun's light and heat.) When, however, these effects
tend to destroy existence or check human growth, then they
become sources of pain, and are at once recognized as limit-.
ing human freedom. (The heat of the sun may be so great as.
to produce sunstroke.) Besides this direct pain and pleasure,
phenomena, either immediately or by continuous repetition,.
are capable of producing in man certain desires, predispositions, and prejudices. These are not the cause of any
direct pain or pleasure, but become a standard according to.
which future sensations will be judged as pleasurable or.
painful. To the first kind of phenomenal slavery, that which
favours man's growth, only the extreme and of course
irrational ascetic can raise any objection. The extent of
these pleasurable phenomena is to the theologian 'the argument from design'; to the evolutionist, evidence of the
extent to which mankind and his surroundings have in the
course of their development mutually adapted themselves.
The direct pain-producing sensations, however, are those
which peculiarly convince man of his absolute subjectivity to.
the phenomenal world. The theologian, regarding man as.
the centre of the universe, finds his rationale for pain in the
supersensuous,—it is a means to *Willensläuterung;* the.
evolutionist considers that it merely marks the limit to which
the present human type has adapted itself to its surroundings. Here the evolutionist can bring less comfort than the
theologian, for the latter teaches the individual that he is
bearing pain for a purpose, *i.e.*, with a view to future
pleasure. Can the philosopher of renunciation here offer·
any remedy? A painful sensation is not like a sensuous.
desire; there can be no possibility of directly renouncing it.
If we turn to the theories of most of the thinkers we have

examined, we find them asserting that a knowledge of the
real nature and cause of the painful sensation—the broader
view which recognizes man's true relation to the universe
wherein he is placed—will make him indifferent to his
personal discomfort, free him from this phenomenal slavery.
This is the practically identical view of Eckehart, Spinoza,
and Goethe.   The intellect ceases to chafe against what it
recognizes as an absolute necessity.   To the vulgar mind it
might appear that an earthquake would be none the less crushing a phenomenon, were its causes calculable, and the catastrophe recognized as an absolutely necessary step in the
cosmic development; nor, again, is it apparent how a tooth-
ache is the less painful because its origin and pathology are
exactly understood.   Nevertheless there can be small doubt
that the mental condition has a great influence over the
manner in which pain is endured.   Not only is illness often
cured by mental excitement, but, what is more to our purpose,
consciousness of pain is lost.   Where faith, where superstition
are recognized as influencing factors, it is perhaps not inconceivable that knowledge too may have its value.   Such at least
has been the opinion of more than one weighty thinker, and
the subject is even on this account the more worthy of
investigation by the scientific psychologist.

   If we turn to the last type of phenomenal influence we
have referred to, that which is busied in the creation of
desires and predispositions, whereby a standard of individual
pleasure and pain is produced—we find ourselves in the
peculiar sphere of the renunciant.   Here it seems perfectly
possible that the renunciation of a predisposition or desire
may diminish pain, and so lessen the positive or hostile side
of phenomenal slavery.   In order to ascertain how renunciation is possible we must examine somewhat the origin of
such predispositions and desires.   These affections arise
from the peculiar 'set' of either mind or body.   Under the
term 'set' I refer to a process, such as race-development,
or physical influences, wherein the individual is to a great
extent purely subjective.   In so far as the mind comes to
any conclusions of its own, and by these conclusions guides

the body or itself,—in so far as it adopts a reasoned system
of life and belief—it cannot be called subjective. Here there
is no question of phenomenal slavery. What we have to
consider is the tendency of the phenomenal world to form
affections in the individual. For the sake of brevity we
shall term such mental set, a predisposition; such bodily set,
a desire. First, with regard to the desire: as a general
rule, it is the outcome of the past development of the race.
To this extent it is almost beyond the power of the individual
to renounce it. His body and the desire are the outcome of
a common growth—the desire is a physiological need. It is
impossible to renounce the desire to sleep or to eat, or to
have sexual intercourse. On the one hand, these 'racial'
desires may to a certain extent be varied—diminished or
exaggerated. This variation in the desire is capable of
becoming as 'confirmed habit' a standard of pleasure or pain.
Here in the variation is the sphere of the renunciant. To him
the question of which variations he shall foster, which he shall
repress, becomes all-important. The answer to this question
can only be ascertained by investigating the nature of the
particular desire, it becomes a matter of physiological knowledge; a clear insight into the causes of the desire will
point out what gratification is physiologically useful, what
is harmful. The man is freed from 'phenomenal slavery'
by *that renunciation which is based on knowledge*. The term
'harmful' must be understood to refer not only to direct injury
to the individual, but to that which is indirectly harmful to
him by producing injury to his fellows. It will indeed be
found on investigation that as the human type has been
chiefly persistent in the struggle for existence by its development of the social instinct, so that variation which is
harmful to others is in general checked by the fact that it
brings direct injury to the varying individual.

Finally, let us turn to the predisposition. The field for
inquiry is here so extensive, that it must suffice to note one
or two aspects of the subject. Predispositions exercise an
enormous influence over the life and the thought of the human
race; it is within the bounds of possibility that the individual

actually comes into the world disposed to accept the beliefs
and modes of thought customary to his forefathers. But at
any rate long before he arrives at years when he can investigate for himself, the customary methods of thought and
belief have engrained themselves into his mind, his mind
has received a permanent set. Social and religious prejudices
are so grafted by youthful surroundings and early training
upon his nature that he does not stop to inquire whether they
have any rational bases, they have become predispositions,
and he treats them much as he does his innate physical
desires. As examples of such predispositions we may
mention the beliefs in the immortality of the 'soul' and in
the existence of a personal god—in short, the two Buddhist
delusions of individuality and ritualism. These predispositions
have led the theologian to assert the truth of the belief owing
to the universality of its existence; the anthropologist to inquire whether man will not always arrive at the same mental
conceptions under the influence of similar forces of development; and the evolutionist to suggest that something in these
predispositions may tend to preserve the groups that possess
them in the struggle for existence. For example, the tribe
which has evolved in some manner the conception of immortality may be more fearless in battle than its neighbours, and
thus be the more likely to predominate; or, again, a second
tribe which has attained to a strong belief in the existence of a
personal god, and thus possesses a centre for common worship
and a symbol for united action, may thereby be placed in a
position of advantage with regard to other groups having a
less definite religion, or no religion at all. We thus see how
possibly a tribe with a prejudice may tend to be a surviving
variation.[1]   A predisposition, or a prejudice having absolutely
no rational basis, may have a social value and tend to preserve
an individual or group of individuals in the struggle for
existence. Do we not here catch a glimpse of how a nigh

[1] There is little doubt in my own mind, that the survival of the Jewish
race has been largely due to two irrational beliefs, the one in the
special efficacy of their tribal god, and the other in the value of circum-
cision.

universal predisposition may exist without our being able to give it a rational basis? We can perhaps trace its historical growth, we may see how it took root, and the mode in which it has developed; but the utmost we can assert is, that its origin and permanence are due to the assistance it gives the human race in the struggle for life. What is true of such pre-dispositions, and the resulting prejudices or beliefs in the mind of mankind as a whole, applies equally well to the customary beliefs of smaller sections of human society. Such beliefs may have absolutely no rational basis, may indeed be demonstrably false, but the race, the tribe, the society may in the long run force them upon all or the majority of its members,—those who do not accept the belief being destroyed, expelled, or ostracised. The deeper knowledge, the clearer insight may show the individual that many beliefs are due only to racial predispositions; that they are intellectually false and productive of pain and misery to the individual. *He* may go so far as to renounce for himself all the Buddhist delusions, but can such renunciation become a general rule? May not the non-renouncing sections of humanity ultimately survive? Will the race always force its predispositions as factors of permanence upon the great mass of its members? For the sake of race-survival may not the individual be com-pelled to believe what is intellectually absurd? We can free ourselves by study from our predispositions, but may we not thus be opposing the interests of the race by eliminating cer-tain factors of its permanency? As in the days early Chris-tianity, mankind may again come to look upon intellect as prejudicial to its welfare. A movement akin to the Salvation Army may carry society over a critical period when its very existence hangs in the balance, and humanity may again believe with Luther that intellect is the devil's archwhore. Herein lies one of the deepest and most momentous prob-lems of renunciation, and one which the philosophers of renunciation have but lightly touched upon. This is the secret of our modern pessimism and optimism,—they are involved in the impossibility or the possibility of permanent intellectual progress for all classes. The answer given to this problem will determine the value to be placed upon a life of intellectual activity and the wisdom or folly of those who attempt to enlarge the sphere of human knowledge. Does the human mind, as the centuries roll by, tend to free itself from irrational belief, and grasp things in their true relation to their surroundings? Does it more and more succeed in casting off phenomenal slavery by reducing its sensations to an intelligible sequence? Do human predispositions tend to take the firmer basis of intellect, or must the individual ever be ultimately sacrificed to all which may, regardless of its intellectual truth or falsehood, contribute to the preservation of the race? Does or does not surviving belief approximate more and more to rational law? On the answers which are given to these questions must largely depend the possibility of man's freedom from 'phenomenal slavery.' We shall not have long to wait for those answers so far as concerns our own folk. In the great social and religious changes, which are looming so largely in the near future, will intellect or market-place rhetoric guide our people?

V.

THE ENTHUSIASM OF THE MARKET-PLACE AND OF THE STUDY.[1]

'Who will absolve you bad Christians?' 'Study,' I replied, 'and Knowledge.'—*Conrad Muth in a letter to Peter Eberbach, circa* 1510.

THERE are two types of human character which must have impressed themselves even upon those least observant of the phases of life which surround us. Nor is it only in observing the present, but also in studying the past, that we find the same two types influencing, each in its own peculiar fashion, the growth of human thought and the forms of human society. By 'studying the past' I do not mean reading a popular historical work, but taking a hundred, or better fifty, years in the life of a nation, and studying thoroughly that period. Each one of us is capable of such a study, although it may require the leisure moments, not of weeks, but of years. It means understanding, not only the politics of that nation during those years ; not only what its thinkers wrote ; not only how the educated classes thought and lived ; but in addition how the mass of the folk struggled, and what aroused their feeling or stirred them to action. In this latter respect more may often be learnt from folk-songs and broadsheets than from a whole round of foreign campaigns. Any one, who has made some such study as I have suggested, will not only have recognized these two opposing types of human character, but be better able to judge of the parts

[1] This lecture was delivered at South Place Institute, on Sunday, November 29, 1885, and afterwards printed as a pamphlet, dedicated to H. B., a genuine 'man of the study.'

which they have played in human development. Without
asserting that one of these types is thoroughly harmful, and
that the other is alone of real social value, we may still inquire
whether the one be not of more service to humanity than the
other, and whether we ought not to try and repress the one
and cultivate the other. If, on examining longer periods of
human history, we find that in the more developed extant
societies the first type is tending to recede before the second,
we shall be considerably aided in arriving at a judgment of
their relative social value.

The two types which I am desirous of placing before
you this morning I term the " Man of the Market-Place," and
the " Man of the Study."   Let me endeavour to explain to
you what meanings I attach to these names.

In the earlier forms of human society, impulses to certain
lines of social conduct are transmitted from generation to
generation, either by direct contact between old and young,
or possibly by some hereditary principle.   Upon these impulses the stability of the society depends ; they have been
evolved in the race-struggle for existence.   Looked at from
an outside point of view, they form the social custom and
the current morality of that stage of society.   Without them
the society would decay, and yet no man in that primitive
state understands how they have arisen.   Viewed on the one
side as indispensable to the race, and on the other appearing
to have no origin in human reason or human power, it is not to
be wondered at if we find morality and custom in these early
forms of civilization associated with the superhuman. To give
the strongest possible sanction to morality—for on that sanction race-existence depends—it is associated with the supersensuous, it becomes part of a religious cult.   Immorality,
the only rational meaning of which is something anti-
social, becomes *sin ;* it plays a part in the relation of each
individual to the supernatural.   Nor is it hard to understand how such a superstition might be a valuable factor in
race-preservation.   On the scientific and historical basis
there is no difficulty whatever in explaining how morality
has come to have a supernatural value, nor why the belief in

a supernatural sanction should be so widespread. You may be inclined to object : But every reasoning person considers immorality as another term for what is anti-social! This may be quite true, but reasoning persons are not to be met with on every Sabbath day's journey; and I find vast numbers of those with whom I come in contact still talk of morality, justice, good and evil, as if they had at least an abstract value, and were not synonymous with what is social or anti-social. When a great modern thinker like Kant can lay down the absurd proposition that the world exists in order that man may have a field for moral action; when from thousands of voices in this land, from the platform and the press, we hear cries of justice and morality, and human right, and divine retribution, then indeed we become conscious how widespread is the delusion that there is an absolute code of morality or justice which is hidden somewhere in the inner consciousness of each individual. In judging of Christianity, not as a revelation, but as a system of morality, we are often apt to give it too high praise, forgetting that to the teaching of Jesus the Christ, carried to its legitimate outcome in the Latin Fathers, modern Europe owes the superstition that life is created for morality, not morality created for life. I assert, that life exists for wider purposes than mere morality ; morality is only a condition which renders social life possible. I am moral, not because such is the object of my life, but because by being so I gratify the social impulses impressed upon me by early education, and by hereditary instinct. Gratification of impulse brings pleasure, and pleasure in life is one of the conditions necessary to our grasping it and working it to the full extent of its rich possibilities.

If we agree, then, that morality is what is social, and immorality what is anti-social, that neither have an absolute or supernatural value, we shall be led to inquire of any course of action how it affects the welfare of society ; that is, not only of those towards whom the action may be directed, but of him who is its source, for both alike belong to society. To judge whether an action be moral or not we must investi-

gate its effects, not only on *others*, but on *self*. Now if the
only actions which came before us were such as murder or
brute-sensuality, there would be no difficulty in judging their
effect on others or on self,—in determining their anti-social
character.   But most of the actions required in human life
are far more difficult of analysis, far more complex in their
bearings on others and on self.   In addition they often require
an immediate decision.   When a man decides rapidly on
his course of action, we say he is a man of *character*; when
his decisions generally prove in the sequel to have been
correct, we attribute to him insight or wisdom.   We look
upon him as a wise man, and endeavour to imitate him, or
to learn from him.   The insight or wisdom we have thus
spoken of, and which is so intimately connected with
character, is the result of training, of mental discipline, or of
what in the broad sense of the word we may term *education*.
It is not only experience of men, but still more a knowledge
of the laws which govern human society, of the effects of
certain courses of action as manifested in history, nay even
of natural laws, whether mechanical or physiological, which
govern man because he is a part of nature; it is all this which
makes up education. But more, this knowledge, this education,
in itself is not sufficient to form what we term a wise man;
each truth learnt from science or history must have become
a part of man's existence; the theoretical truth must form
such a part of his very being, that it influences almost
unconsciously every practical action; the comparatively
trivial doings of each day must all be consistent with, I will
even say dictated by, those general laws which have been
deduced from a study of history and from a study of science.
Then and then only a man's actions become certain, har-
monious and definite in purpose; then we recognize that we
have to deal with a man of character; with a man whose
morality is something more than a superstition—it is an integral part of his thinking being. If a theory of life is worth
studying, let its propounder give evidence that it has
moulded his own character, that it has been the mainspring
of his actions.   There is no truer touchstone of the value

of a philosophical system. Examine the lives of the great German metaphysicians, Kant, Hegel, Schopenhauer, you will find them men petulant, irritable, even cowardly in action. Examine the life of a Spinoza and you will for the first time understand his philosophy; it was an element of his being.

Lecturing from this platform nearly three years ago, I described freethought not merely as the shaking off of dogmatism, but as the single-minded devotion to the pursuit of truth. Deep thought, patient study, even the labour of a whole life, might be needed before a man obtained the right to call himself a freethinker. Some of my audience, in the discussion which followed, strongly objected to such a system as leaving no place for morality, for the play of the emotions. I was much struck by the objections at the time, as it showed me what a gulf separated my conception of morality from that of some of my audience. Morality was then, and is still, to me the gratification of the social passion in one's actions. But in what fashion must this gratification take place? On the basis of those principles of human conduct which we have deduced *by study* from history and from science. As I said then, the ignorant and uneducated cannot be freethinkers; so I say now, the ignorant and the uneducated cannot be moral. As I said then, freethought is an ideal to which we can only approximate, an ideal which expands with every advance of our positive knowledge; so I say now, that morality is an ideal of human action to which we can only approximate—an ideal which expands with every advance of our positive knowledge. As the true freethinker must be in possession of the highest knowledge of his time, so he will be in possession of all that is known of the laws of human development. He, and he only, is capable of fulfilling his social instinct in accordance with those laws. He, and he only, seems to me capable of being really moral. Morality is not the blind following of a social impulse, but a habit of action based upon character—character moulded by that knowledge of truth which must become an integral part of our being.

Let me give you one or two examples of what I mean by the relation of morality to knowledge. The question of compulsory vaccination is one which can only be answered by investigation of general laws and particular statistics, not always easily accessible or easily intelligible when accessible; yet, notwithstanding this, the question has been dragged on to the hustings, made a matter of 'human right,' 'individual liberty,' and those other vague generalities which abound on the market-place. Another good example is that of sexual morality; here the most difficult questions arise, which are intimately connected with almost every phase of our modern social life. These questions are extremely hard to answer; they involve not only a wide study of comparative history, but frequently of the most complex problems in physiology; often problems which that science, only in its infancy, has not yet solved. Such questions we ought to approach with the most cautious, the most impartial, the most earnest minds, because their very nature tends to excite our preju- dices, to thrust aside our intellectual rule, and so, to warp our judgment. But what do we find in actual life? These questions are brought on to the market-place; they are made the subject of appeal on the one side to the supernatural, or to some absolute code of morality,—on the other side to strong emotions, which, utterly untutored, are the natural outcome of our strong social impulses. Where we might expect a calm appeal to the results of science and the facts of human history, we are confronted with the deity, absolute justice, the moral rights of man, and other terms which are calcu- lated to excite strong feeling, while they successfully screen the yawning void of ignorance.

As a last example, let me point to a problem which is becoming all-important to our age—the great social change, the economic reorganization, which is pressing upon us. We none of us know exactly what is coming; we are only conscious of a vast feeling of unrest, of discontent with our present social organism, which manifests itself, not in one or two little groups of men, but throughout all the strata of society. The socialistic movement in England would have

little meaning if we were to weigh its importance by the
existing socialist societies or their organs in the press. It is
because we find throughout all classes a decay of the old
conceptions of social justice and of the old principles of
social action—a growing disbelief in once accepted economic
laws—a tendency to question the very foundations of our
social system—it is because of these manifestations that we
can speak of a great social problem before us. This problem
is one of the hardest which a nation can have to work out ;
one which requires all its energy, and all its intellect ; it is
fraught with the highest possibilities and the most terrible
dangers. Human society cannot be changed in a year,
scarcely in a hundred years ; its organism is as complex as
that of the most differentiated type of physical life ; you can
ruin that organism as you can destroy life, but remould it
you cannot without the patient labour of generations, even of
centuries. That labour itself must be directed by knowledge,
knowledge of the laws which have dictated the rise and decay
of human societies, and of those physical influences which
manifest themselves in humanity as temperament, impulse,
and passion. No single man, no single group of men, no
generation of men can remodel human society ; their influence
when measured in the future will be found wondrously
insignificant. They may, if they are strong men of the
market-place, produce a German Reformation or a French
Revolution ; but when the historian, not of the outside, but
of the inside, comes to investigate that phase of society
before and after the movement, what does he find ? A great
deal of human pain, a great deal of destruction. And of
human creation ? The veriest little ; new forms here and
there perhaps, but under them the old slave turning the old
wheel ; humanity toiling on under the old yoke ; the same
round of human selfishness, of human misery, of human
ignorance—touched here and there, as of old, by the same
human beauty, the same human greatness.

It is because the man of the study recognizes how little is
the all which even extended insight will enable him to do for
social change that he condemns the man of the market-place,

who not only thinks he understands the terms of the social problem, but has even found its solution. The man of the study is convinced that to *really* change human society requires long generations of educative labour. Human progress, like Nature, never leaps; this is the most certain of all laws deduced from the study of human development. If this be formulated in the somewhat obscure phase : " Social growth takes place by evolution not by revolution," the man of the market-place declares in one breath that his revolution is an evolution, and in the next either sings some glorious chant, a blind appeal to force, or informs you that he can shoulder a rifle, and could render our present society impossible by the use of dynamite with the properties of which he is well acquainted. Poor fellow ! would that he were as well acquainted with the properties of human nature !

The examples I have placed before you may be sufficient to show how much morality is a question not of feeling but of knowledge and study. In a speech at the recent Church Congress a theologian, a man of the market-place, declared that he considered questions of ethics as lying outside the field of the intellect ; that is one of the most immoral statements I have ever come across. It causes one almost to despair of one's country and its people, when it is possible for the holders of such views to be raised to positions of great social and educative influence !

You will feel, I know, that it is a very hard saying : *The ignorant cannot be moral.* It is so opposed to all the Christian conceptions of morality in which we ourselves have been reared, and which have been impressed upon our forefathers for generations. Morality with the Christian is a matter of feeling ; obedience to a code revealed by a transcendental manifestation of the deity. The hundreds of appeals made weekly from the pulpits of this country, urging mankind to a moral course of life, are appeals to the emotions, not to the reason. In my sense of the words, they are made by men of the market-place, not by men of the study. The Christian movement, as Mark Pattison has well pointed out, arose entirely outside the sphere of educated thought. Un-

like modern freethought, it was not the outcome of the
knowledge and culture of its age.   In its neglect of the great
Greek systems of philosophy, it was a return to blind
emotion, even to barbarism.   This opposition of Christianity
and Reason reached its climax in the second century, possibly
with Tertullian.   " What," writes this Father, " have the
philosopher and Christian in common ?   The disciple of
Greece and the disciple of heaven ?   What have Athens
and Jerusalem, the Church and the Academy, heretics and
Christians, in common ?   There is no more curiosity for us,
now that Christ has come, nor any occasion for further
investigation, since we have the Gospel. . . . The Son of
God is dead ; it is right credible, because it is absurd ; being
buried, he has arisen; it is certain, because it is impossible."

Although there have been periods of history when Christianity has stood in the van of intellectual progress, we must
yet hold that she has on the whole, and perhaps not unnaturally, exhibited a suspicion of human reason.   She has
preferred the methods of the market-place to those of the
study ; men of words, prophets, and orators may be picked
up at every street corner ; the scholar, the man of thought
requires a lifetime in the making, and, being made, will he
any longer be a Christian ?   If, and if only, he finds Christianity to be one with the highest knowledge of his age.

I have endeavoured to emphasize this relation of Christianity to intellect, because our current morality is essentially
Christian—is essentially a matter of blind feeling—and hence
it comes about that we find the statement : *The ignorant cannot
be moral,* such a very hard saying.   The freethinker, placing
on one side the supernatural, finding an all-sufficient religion
in the pursuit of truth, in the investigation of law, will
surely not be content to accept the old Christian conception
of morality ?   To leave his reason on this point out of
account, and to appeal to feeling as a test of truth ?   Let him
remember what other teachers, in their way as great or
greater than Jesus—greater if we measure them by intellectual power—have taught.   With Gautama the Buddha,
knowledge was the key to higher life ; right living the out-

come of self-culture. Moses the son of Maimon, chief of Jewish philosophers, tells us that evil is the work of infirm souls, and that infirm souls shall seek *the wise*, the physicians of soul. Averroes, the greatest of mediæval freethinkers, whom Christian art depicted with Judas crushed in the jaws of Satan, asserted that knowledge is the only key to perfect living. That Spinoza taught that all evil arises from confused ideas, from ignorance, is generally known. If the philosophers, as Tertullian has declaimed, are the patriarchs and prophets of heretics, then surely we freethinkers should attend to what they have taught! But I can give you a still more striking instance of how the men of the study have based morality upon knowledge. I refer to that little band of real workers, to the Humanists of the early sixteenth century. Men like Erasmus, Sebastian Brant, and Conrad Muth were working for a real reformation of the German people on the basis of education, of knowledge, of that progress which alone is sure, because it is based on the reason. These men, one and all, identified immorality with ignorance; the immoral man with the fool. Feared on the one side by the monks, abused on the other by the Lutherans, they were asked: 'Who will absolve you bad Christians?' 'Study,' they replied, 'and Knowledge.' It were instructive, had we time, to see how the labour of these men of the study was swept away by the popular passion roused by the men of the market-place. Suffice it to say that Luther described evil-doing as disobedience to a supernatural code; sin as a want of belief in Jesus the Christ; and reason as the 'archwhore' and 'devil's bride.' Appealing to popular ignorance and blind emotion, he re-imposed upon half Europe the Christian conception of morality; and we freethinkers of to-day have again to start from the standpoint of the Humanists: Study and Knowledge alone absolve from sin; morality is impossible to the ignorant.

If you will agree with me, at least for the purposes of my present lecture, that the ideal moral nature is a character moulded by study and knowledge—a mind which is not only in possession of facts, but in which the laws drawn from

these facts have become modes of thought inexplicably
wound up in its being, then we may proceed further and
inquire: How can this ideal be approached? What is the
motive force behind it? How does it affect our practical
conduct?

How can this ideal be approached? If immorality be one
with ignorance, this question is not hard to answer. The
moral life to the freethinker is like the religious life, it is a
growth—a growth in knowledge. As the freethinker's religion
is the pursuit of truth and his sole guide the reason, so his
morality consists in the application of that truth to the
practical side of life. His morality is a part of his religious
being, even as much a part as the Christian's. More than
once a Christian has said to me: "I do not deny that you
present freethinkers may be moral. You have been brought
up in the Christian faith, and its morality still influences
your lives. How will it be, however, with your children and
your children's children, who have never felt that influence?"
"Never felt that influence?" I reply. "No! but the
influence of something more human, something which is
matter not of belief, but of knowledge; something which
can guide their life infinitely more surely than a supernatural
code. The morality which springs from the human, the
rational guidance of the social impulse, is ten times more
stable than the morality which is based upon the emotional
appeals of a dogmatic faith." When the Christian comes to
me and prates of his morality, I feel like Hamlet scorning
Laertes' love for Ophelia—

> Why I will fight with him upon this theme
> Until my eyelids will no longer wag.

> * * * *

> Swounds, show me what thou'lt do:
> Woo't weep? woo't fight? woo't fast? woo't tear thyself?
> Woo't drink up eisel? eat a crocodile?
> I'll do it. Dost thou come here to whine?
> To outface me with leaping in her grave?
> Be buried quick with her and so will I;
> And, if thou prate of mountains, let them throw

Millions of acres on us, till our ground,
Singeing his pate against the burning zone,
Make Ossa like a wart ! Nay, an thou'lt mouth,
I'll rant as well as thou.

That we freethinkers have no moral code, or only the
remnants of an antique faith—prejudices gained from a
Christian education which cling like limpets to the rock of
our intellectual being—is the libel of ignorance. We *have*
a morality, and those who hold it assert that it stands above
the Christian dispensation, as the Christian above the Hebrew.
Like the Hebrew, however, it is a matter of law, and the lawgiver is Reason. Reason is the only lawgiver, by whom the
intellectual forces of the nineteenth century can be ordered
and disciplined. The only practical method of making
society as a whole approach the freethinker's ideal of
morality is to educate it, to teach it to use its reason in
guiding the race instincts or social impulses. Understand
what I mean by education. I do not mean mere knowledge
of scientific or historic facts; but these facts co-ordinated
into laws, and these laws made so much a mode of thought,
that they are the received rules of human action. The *learned*
man may be in no sense of the word *educated*, and is thus frequently immoral. Often what we are accustomed to call education is merely the means to its attainment. You must give
your folk—if you wish it to be moral, to have social stability—
not only the means of education, but the leisure to pursue that
means to its end. Let us put this statement in a more
concise form. Society depends for its stability on the
morality of the individual. The morality of the individual
is co-ordinate with his education. It is therefore a primary
function of society to educate its members.

It may even seem to some of you a platitude when I say
that to improve the morality of society you must improve its
education. Yet how far is this principle carried into practice
by our would-be moral reformers? Do they set themselves
down to the life-long task of slowly but surely educating
their fellows? Or do they rush out into the market-place,
proclaim that God bids men do this or that; that this or

that course of action is virtuous, is righteous, is moral, without once troubling to define their words?   How many such
moral reformers have made that study of science and history,
have gained that knowledge of social and physical law which
would enable them to be moral themselves, to say nothing of
guiding their fellows?   In many of the complex problems of
modern life, we freethinkers can only say, that we are
struggling towards the light, that we are endeavouring to
gain that knowledge which will lead us to their solution.
And yet how often does the man of the market-place rush
by us proclaiming what he thinks an obvious truth, appealing to the blind passions of the ignorant mass of humanity,
and drawing after him such a flood of popular energy that
those germs of intellectual life and rational action which for
years we may have been laboriously implanting disappear
in the torrent!   After the flood has subsided, when human
life has returned, as history shows us it invariably does, to
its old channels, the men of the study come back to what
may be left of their old labours and begin afresh their endless
process of education.   Some few will be disheartened, quite
hopeless, but the many know that the work in which they
are engaged requires the slow evolution of centuries,—not to
accomplish, because there is no end to human knowledge, no
end to the discovery of truth, but even—to manifest itself in
its results.   The man of the study has no desire to leave a
name as the propounder of an idea; he is content to have
enjoyed the fulness of life—to have passed a life religious,
because it is rational,—because it has been spent in accordance with the highest knowledge of his day,—and moral,
because it has been directed to social ends, to the purposes
of education, to the discovery and spread of truth.

It is easy to see how the man who has time for education,
for self-culture, may strive towards the freethinker's standard
of morality.   But what about the toiler, the man whose days
are spent in the hard round of purely mechanical labour?   I
can only reply that so long as such a man has no time for
the development of his intellectual nature he cannot be
moral in my sense of the word.   He may follow instinctively

a certain course of action, which may not in ordinary matters be directly anti-social, but in the complex problems of life he will as often go wrong as go right. The existence of large masses of men in our present society incapable of moral action is one of the gravest questions of the time; it indicates the instability of our social forms. It places at the disposal of the men of the market-place a power of stirring up popular passion, the danger of which it is hard to exaggerate. That education is now a privilege of class, is the strongest argument which our socialistic friends could adopt if they knew how to use it aright, but it is not one with which they can appeal to the blind feeling of the masses. If all social reform be, as I am convinced it is, the outcome alone of increased morality, and if morality be a matter of education and of knowledge, then all real social reform can only proceed step by step with the slow, often hardly perceptible, process of popular education. What a field of social action lies here for all who wish to enjoy the fulness of life! Here the freethinker's mission is at once religious and moral! His morality—not perhaps in the sense of the market-place, but at least in that of the study —is socialism, his religious cult is that pursuit of truth, which, when obtained, directs his moral, his social action. Would that more men of learning were so educated as to recognize this new code of social action! We want education for the masses, not that the workman may make ten good screws where he formerly made nine bad ones, but that every member of society may be capable of moral, that is, of social action. Men of science proclaim the need of technical education for the English artizan, if he is to survive in the battle for existence with German and French rivals. A more pitiable plea for technical education could hardly be imagined. We, freethinkers, demand technical education for the workman, because we believe that it enables him to replace a mechanical routine by a series of intelligent acts; we believe that when he is accustomed to intelligent, rather than to mechanical action in handicraft, he will no longer be content with a mechanical code of social action; he will begin to inquire and to investigate;—his morality also will become a matter of thought and of knowledge, no longer of faith or of custom. That would indeed be a great step towards social reform, a great advance in social stability. To the freethinkers of the old school, who fancy their sole mission is to destroy Christianity, we of the new school cry: 'Go and study Christianity; learn what it, as a purely human institution, has in 1,800 years done and failed to do, then only will you be in a position in destroying to *create;*—to create that religion which is alone foreshadowed in the future.' To the socialists of the old school, who think that revolutionary agitation, paper schemes of social reconstruction, and manifestoes appealing to class passion, are the only possible modes of action, we of the new school cry: 'Go out and educate, create a new morality, the basis of which shall be knowledge, and socialism will come, although in a shape which none of us have imagined. It may need the labour of centuries, but it is the one method of action, which at each step gives us sure foothold. To the firm ground of reason trusts the man who would build for posterity.'

So much, then, in answer to our first question of the method by which we can approach the moral ideal.

Our second question: *What is the motive force behind this morality?* leads me to a point, which has given the title to this lecture, and presents undoubted difficulty to those who have thrown aside all appeal to the emotions as the motive force in conduct. The energy which enables a man of the market-place to carry out his projects, may be measured by the amount of *enthusiasm* he is capable of raising among his fellow men. To create enthusiasm by an appeal to the emotions, and direct it to a definite goal, is essentially the method of the man of the market-place. He does not try to move men through their reasons, he does not try to educate them, but he strives to influence their feelings, to excite their passions, and, in so doing, to raise their enthusiasm for the cause he has at heart. Party passion, superstition, religious hatred, national prejudices, class-feeling, every phase of individual desire or of race-impulse, is made use of by the man of the market-place to raise the excitement necessary for the accomplishment of his purpose. Where can the man of the study find a motive force, an enthusiasm like this? How can his calm appeal to the reason, his slow process of education, ever produce the enthusiasm needful for the achievement of a great end? Is there no enthusiasm of the study which can be compared with the enthusiasm of the market-place? This is the question we have to answer. Here is the void which so many have felt in the freethinker's faith, in that morality which is based on knowledge. What is there in the calm pursuit of truth to call forth enthusiasm, what great social heroism can be based on a study of the laws of human life?

I do not know whether any of you ever read the sermons of Christian divines, but for me they form a frequent source of amusement and instruction. They afford an insight into human character, human ignorance, and human striving, such as hardly manifests itself elsewhere. A theologian, preaching before the University of Cambridge a few years since, made use of the following words :—

" But what is enthusiasm, but, as the term imports, the state of one who is habitually ἔνθεος, possessed by some power of God ? "

The sentence is interesting, not only as bearing upon the character of the preacher, who could dismiss with a philological quibble, a possible enthusiasm among us freethinkers, but also as clearly marking the gulf which separates the enthusiasm of the market-place from that of the study. Perhaps, indeed, the gulf is so great that we ought not to call the two things by the same name, yet to do so is convenient if only for the sake of the contrast.

The enthusiasm of the market-place is, as our theologian expresses it, the state of one who is possessed (or rather imagines he is possessed) by some superhuman power. It is not a state of rational inspiration, but rather of frenzy— of religious, social, or political fanaticism. It is the state of excitement to which the ignorant may be aroused—on the one hand, by confused ideas taking possession of their fancy; or, on the other hand, by a rhetorical appeal to their pre-judice and to their passion. Enthusiasm of the market-place is so prevalent to-day that we have not to go far in search of samples. It is rampant in our political and social life. The politicians to whom we entrust the destinies of our country are essentially men of the market-place; men who have won their present positions by appeal to class prejudice and to passionate ignorance. The politician who discusses a bill with a view to its social value, who does not speak from a party standpoint, and who tries to reason in the House, is scarcely yet known. The present Prime Minister raises enthusiasm among a section of his countrymen by express-ing his horror at the 'wave of infidelity' he tells us is sweeping across the land; the late Prime Minister raises enthusiasm in another section of his countrymen by employ-ing his leisure in defending what he terms the 'majestic process' of creation described in the first chapter of Genesis. When a writer talks of "the detachment and collection of light, leaving in darkness as it proceeded the still chaotic mass from which it was detached,"—we recognize how hopelessly ignorant he is of the conceptions of modern science as to light. We demand what intellectual right he has to criticise, what he describes as the vain and boastful theories of modern thought. We cry: 'Understand, go into the school and learn, before you come in to the market-place and talk.' Mr. Gladstone, in his recent article in the *Nineteenth Century*, also writes that: "We do not hear the authority of Scripture impeached on the ground that it assigns to the Almighty eyes and ears, hands, arms, and feet; nay, even the emotions of the human being." Now, these are precisely the strongest arguments which free-thinkers at present use against Scripture, and which many great philosophers have used in the past: "The under-standing, will, and intelligence, ascribed to God," says Spinoza, "can have no more in common with our human faculties than the Dog a sign in the heavens has with the barking animal we call a dog on earth." Is Mr. Gladstone ignorant alike of past and present ? Those of you who wish to study enthusiasm of the market-place should read his article, notably the last two pages, wherein he tilts, like Don Quixote at the windmill, at the scientific doctrine of evolution. The language is magnificent, the rhetoric is unsurpassed, only there is an utter absence of logical thought, of the spirit of scholarly investigation. If our political leaders make such statements, what shall we say of them ? Are they intellectually inferior men, or are they intellectually dishonest ? Let us content ourselves by describing them as men of the market-place.

Such enthusiasm as we have described—an enthusiasm in the sense of the Cambridge theologian—based upon prejudice not upon reason, is an impossibility for the man of the study. If this is all enthusiasm means, then the ideal freethinker must be without it. But is there nothing which can take its place ? Nothing which can be termed enthusiasm of the study ? We think there is, although as its strength lies in calmness not in fanaticism, in persistence rather than petulance, it is not easy to make it manifest to those who have not experienced it as a motive power in action.

The enthusiasm of which I speak springs from the desire of knowledge. You cannot deny the existence of this desire, amounting in many cases to an absolute passion. Men have sacrificed everything, even their life, in the pursuit of truth. Nor was the spirit which moved all of them ambition : many neither sought nor knew anything of fame. Granting that knowledge plays a great part in the struggle for existence, it is not hard to understand how the pursuit of truth has become a passion in a portion of mankind. All life, which does not grasp the laws of the social and physical world which surrounds it, is of necessity cramped and suffering ; its sphere of action is limited, and it cannot enjoy existence to the full. Increasing knowledge brings with it increasing activity ; life becomes an intelligible whole, every physical law without is found to be one with a mental process within ; crude conceptions of a distinction between matter and spirit fade away. That process of science which Mr. Gladstone speaks bitterly of as converting the world into a huge mechanism, is grasped as the one process by which the world becomes intelligible—spiritual, if you will. Physical law and social law become as much facts of the intellect as any mental process. The truth gained by study becomes a part of a man's intellectual nature, and it is as impossible for him to contradict it in action as to destroy a part of his own body. The man of the study would as soon think of breaking through a social law, which he had discovered by historical research, as of acting contrary to a physical law; both would be alike destructive of a part of his intellectual nature. It is this consistency of action, this uniform obedience to rational law, which gives the man of the study *character*, raises his morality from a matter of feeling to a matter of reason. The steady persistency which arises when knowledge of truth, social and physical, has become a part of man's intellectual nature, is what I term the enthusiasm of the study. It is this enthusiasm of the study which, I believe, must be at the back of all really social action. Enthusiasm of the market-place may for the moment appear to move mountains, but it is appearance only. The reaction comes, and when the flood has subsided we find how little the religious, the social, or the political fanatic has in truth accomplished! The froth remains—the name, the institution, the form—but the real social good is too often what the mathematician terms a negative quantity. The long, scarcely perceptible swell of the sea may be more dangerous to an ironclad than the storm which breaks over it. So it is that the scarcely perceptible influence of enthusiasm of the study may with the centuries achieve more than all the strong eloquence of the market-place. It is faith in this one principle which makes us struggle towards the ideal of freethought, which makes us proclaim reason and knowledge as the sole factors of moral action; nay, which makes us believe that the future may bring a social regeneration for our folk, if in the social storms of the future it trusts for guidance to the enthusiasm of the study rather than to the enthusiasm of the market-place.

If I have made my meaning in the least clear to you, it would seem almost idle to attempt an answer to my third question : What effect should these doctrines have on our practical conduct ?   To cultivate in ourselves the persistent enthusiasm of the study; to endeavour by every means in our power to assist the education of others who have not the like means of intellectual development ; to insist that moral problems shall be solved not on the basis of customary morality or individual prejudice, but solely by a thorough investigation of physical and social law ; to repress so far as lies in our power those men of the market-place, who render our political life an apotheosis of ignorance, not a field for the display of a nation's wisdom; to recollect that inspiration and blind will, the prophet and the martyr, are not wanted in this our nineteenth century, they belong to the past ; should any man cry out that he has discovered a great truth, to listen to no emotional appeal, but demand the rational grounds of his faith, however great be his name or respected his authority ; to refuse belief to an opinion, although it be held by the many, until we find a rational basis for its existence ; shortly, to consider all things, which are not based on the firm ground of reason subject to the sacred right of doubt ; to treat all mere belief as delusion, and to reckon the unknown not as a field for dogma, but as a problem to be solved ;—to act thus and think thus, surely is to allow the doctrines of freethought to influence our practical conduct !   To convert the market-place into the study !   And if his life be spent in only struggling towards these ideals, in the long task of learning how to live, may we not at least place as an epitaph over our freethinker, Robert Browning's lines to the old Humanist who perished before he had satisfied his craving for knowledge :—

> Did not he magnify the mind, show clear
>   Just what it all meant?
>   ＊   ＊   ＊   ＊
> That low man seeks a little thing to do,
>   Sees it and does it :
> This high man, with a great thing to pursue,
>   Dies ere he knows it.

HISTORY.

Alle wahre Geschichte hat überall zuerst einen religiösen Zweck gehabt, und ist von religiösen Ideen ausgegangen.

Schleiermacher.

VI

MAIMONIDES AND SPINOZA.[1]

PROF. SCHAARSCHMIDT, in his excellent preface to Spinoza's *Korte Verhandeling van God*, &c. (Amsterdam, 1869), has drawn attention to the somewhat one-sided view usually taken of Spinoza's position in the evolution of thought : the importance attributed to the influence of Descartes, and the slight weight given to the Jewish writers. He concludes his considerations with the remark :—"Attamen in gravissimis rebus ab eo (Cartesio) differt et his ipsis cum Judæorum philosophia congruit, quorum quidem orthodoxiam repudiavit, ingenium ipsum et mentem retinuit." (Præfatio xxiv.)

The subject is all the more important because even an historian like Kuno Fischer (*Gesch. der neuern Philos.*, 3rd ed., 1880) still regards Spinoza as a mere link after Descartes in the chain of philosophical development, rejecting the view that he belongs rather to Jewish than Christian Philosophy. The hypothesis that Spinoza was very slightly influenced by Hebrew thought has become traditional, and is to be found in the most recent English works on Spinoza. Mr. Pollock writes that the influence of Maimonides on the pure philosophy of Spinoza was comparatively slight (p. 94). Dr. Martineau tells us somewhat dogmatically that "no stress can be laid on the evidence of Spinoza's indebtedness to Rabbinical philosophy" (p. 56). These opinions seem in part based on a perusal of Maimonides' *More Nebuchim* and of Joël's *Zur Genesis der Lehre Spinozas* (1871), taken in

---

[1] Reprinted from *Mind : a Quarterly Review of Psychology and Philosophy*. No. XXXI.

conjunction with Mr. W. R. Sorley's "Jewish Mediæval Philosophy and Spinoza" in *Mind* No. XIX. Neither Mr. Pollock nor Dr. Martineau seems acquainted with Maimonides' *Yad Hachazakah*. It is the relation of this work to Spinoza's *Ethica* to which I wish at present to refer.[1]

Maimonides (1135-1204) completed his *More Nebuchim* about 1190, its aim being to explain on the ground of reason the many obscure passages of Scripture and apparently irrational rites instituted by Moses. Hence the book was termed the "Guide of the Perplexed," being intended to lighten the difficult path of Biblical study. As might easily be supposed it is only concerned in the second place with philosophical ethics. The influence of such a book on Spinoza is, as we might anticipate, most manifest in the *Tractatus Theologico-Politicus*. The *Yad Hachazakah*, however, or the "Mighty Hand," written some ten years previously, has far greater importance for the student of Spinoza's *Ethica*. Its author originally termed it "The Twofold Law," *i.e.*, the written and traditional law—Bible and Talmud,—and under fourteen headings or books considered some of the most important problems in theology and ethics. Portions of the *Yad* were in 1832 translated by Herman Hedwig Bernard, and published in Cambridge under the title:—*The Main Principles of the Creed and Ethics of the Jews exhibited in selections from the Yad Hachazakah of Maimonides*. Of this book I propose to make use in the following remarks on the thought-resemblance between Spinoza and Maimonides.[2] I shall omit all matter which

---

[1] While on the subject of works concerning Spinoza and Jewish Philosophy I may give the following titles :—E. Saisset : "Maimonide et Spinoza," *Revue des deux Mondes*, 1862; Salomo Rubinus : *Spinoza und Maimonides*, Vienna, 1868.

[2] Two other translations of the First Book of the *Yad* may be mentioned, both "edited" by the Polish Rabbi, Elias Soloweyczik. The first—into German (Königsberg, 1846)—omits the last or fifth part of the First Book containing : "The Precepts of Repentance." The second—into English (Nicholson, 1863)—nominally contains all five parts, but really omits many of their most interesting sub-chapters (*e.g.*, Part III., c. v.-vii., on the relation of a scholar to his teacher and on respect for the

has no direct bearing on Spinoza's *Ethica*, however interesting it may otherwise be, and endeavour to make allowance
for the age and theologico-philosophical language in which
Maimonides wrote. We have rather to consider the spirit
in which Spinoza read the *Yad* than that in which it was
composed.

Let us first of all consider Maimonides' conception of
God. This is contained in the "Precepts relating to the
Foundations of the Law," and the "Precepts relating to
Repentance," especially in the chapters entitled by Bernard

wise). This English edition, too, loses much of its scientific value owing
to the omission or perversion of many paragraphs where the editor has
with a very false modesty thought Maimonides too outspoken for modern
readers. On the title-page stand the words : "Translated from the
Hebrew into English by several Learned Writers." The chief of these
"Learned Writers" is Bernard, who has been freely used without apparent
acknowledgment. Portions of the remainder appear to be translated
from the German, and not directly from the Hebrew. Appended to this
English edition is a translation of the fifth Chapter of Book xiv. of the
Yad: or "Laws concerning Kings and their Wars." Whatever may
have been the causes which gave rise to this so-called English translation, it must be noted that Soloweyczik's German translation is an
independent work, suffering from none of these faults, and of considerable
value to the student of Maimonides.

Before entering upon a comparison of the intellectual relation of Maimonides to Spinoza, I may refer to a close connexion between Spinoza's
method of life and Maimonides' theory of how a wise man should earn
his livelihood. It seems to me the keynote of Spinoza's life at the optical
bench,—his refusal of the professorial chair. " Let," writes Maimonides,
"thy fixed occupation be the study of the Law" (*i.e.*, divine wisdom),
" and thy worldly pursuits be of secondary consideration." After stating
that all business is only a means to study, in that it provides the necessities of life, he continues : " He who resolves upon occupying himself
solely with the study of the Law, not attending to any work or trade, but
living on charity, defiles the sacred name and heaps up contumely upon
the Law. Study must have active labour joined with it, or it is worthless,
produces sin, and leads the man to injure his neighbour." . . . " It is a
cardinal virtue to live by the work of one's hands, and it is one of the
great characteristics of the pious of yore, even that whereby one attains
to all respect and felicity in this and the future world." (After *Soloweyczik*, Part III., Chap. iii. 5–11.) Why does Spinoza's life stand in
such contrast to that of all other modern philosophers? Because his life
at least, if not his philosophy, was Hebrew!

"On the Deity and the Angels" (p. 71), and "On the Love of God and the true way of serving Him" (p. 314), which correspond roughly to *Ethica* i. and v. of Spinoza. Maimonides, to start with, sweeps away all human attributes and affections from the Godhead. God has neither body nor frame, nor *limit* of any kind; He has none of the accidental qualities of bodies—"neither composition nor decomposition; neither place nor measure; neither ascent nor descent; neither right nor left; neither before nor behind; neither sitting nor standing; neither does He exist in time, so that He should have a beginning or an end or a number of years; nor is He liable to change, since in Him there is nothing which can cause a change in Him" (B. 78). Add to this, God is *one*, but this unity is not that of an *individual* or a material body, "but such an One that there is no other Unity like His in the Universe" (B. 73). That God has similitude or form in the Scripture is due only to an "apparition of prophecy"; while the assertion that God created man in His own image refers only to the soul or intellectual element in man. It has no reference to *shape* or to manner of life, but to that knowledge which constitutes the "quality" of the soul (B. 106). The "pillar of wisdom" is to know that this first Being exists, and "that He has called all other beings into existence, and that all things existing, heaven, earth, and whatever is between them, exist only through the truth of His existence, so that if we were to suppose that He did not exist, no other thing could exist" (B. 71). Among the propositions which Spinoza, in the Appendix to *Ethica* i., tells us that he has sought to prove are these :—that God exists necessarily; "quod sit unicus; . . . quod sit omnium rerum causa libera, et quomodo; quod omnia in Deo sint, et ab ipso ita pendeant, ut sine ipso nec esse nec concipi possint,"—words which might almost stand as a translation of Maimonides. Compare also *Ethica* i. 14 and Corollary, and 15.

That God is not divisible (B. 73) Spinoza proves, i. 13; that He is without limit, i. 19, or better, *Principia Cartesii*, 19; that God is incapable of change, i. 20, Coroll. 2; the notion that God has body or form is termed a "childish fancy," i. 15, Scholium; while the infinite and eternal nature of God is asserted at the very commencement of the *Ethica*. Add to this that Maimonides' conception of the Deity, without being professedly pantheistic, is yet extremely anti-personal and diffused. Still more striking is the coincidence when we turn to the denial of human affections. Maimonides tells us that with God "there is neither death nor life like the life of a living body: neither folly nor wisdom, like the wisdom of a wise man; neither sleep nor waking; neither anger nor laughter; *neither joy nor sorrow;* neither silence nor speech, like the speech of the sons of men" (B. 79). Compare with this Spinoza's assertions that the intellect of God differs *toto cælo* from human intellect (i. 17, Schol.), and that "God is without passions, and is not affected by any emotion *of joy or sorrow*"—"He neither loves nor hates any one" (v. 17 and Coroll.).

Curiously enough, while both Maimonides and Spinoza strip God of all conceivable human characteristics, they yet hold it possible for the mind of man to attain to some, if an imperfect, *knowledge* of God, and make the attainment of such knowledge the highest good of life. There would be some danger of self-contradiction in this matter, if their conception of the Deity had not ceased to be a personal one, and become rather the recognition of an intellectual cause or law running through all phenomena—which, showing beneath a material succession an intellectual sequence or mental necessity, is for them the Highest Wisdom, to be acquainted with which becomes the end of human life. This intellectual relation of man to God forms an all-important feature in the ethics of both Maimonides and Spinoza; it is in fact a vein of mystic gold which runs through the great mass of Hebrew thought.[1]

---

[1] The Talmudic picture of the world to come, where "the righteous sit with their crowns on their heads delighting in the shining glory of the Shechinah" is thus interpreted: their crowns denote intelligence or wisdom, while "delighting in the glory of the Shechinah" signifies that they know more of the truth of God than while in this dark and abject

Before entering upon Maimonides' conception of the
relation of God to man, it may be as well to premise what
he understands by *intelligence*.   The Rabbinical writers
oppose the term *quality* (or *property*) to the term *matter* (B.
Note, p. 82); most frequently, and in the *Yad* invariably,
when these terms are opposed, the former signifies intelligence or thought; so that in the language of Spinoza we
may very well call them *thought* and *extension*.   If we leave
out of account the angels, to whom Maimonides, rather on
doctrinal and theological than on philosophical grounds,
assigned an anomalous position, we find that all things in
the universe are composed of matter and quality (*i.e.*, extension and thought), though possessing these attributes in
different degrees.   These degrees form the basis of all
classification and individuality (B. 82–84).   We now arrive
at a proposition which may be said to form the very foundation of Spinoza's *Ethica* : " You can never see matter without quality, nor quality without matter, and it is only the
understanding of man which abstractedly parts the existing
body and knows that it is composed of matter and quality "
(B. 105).   This coexistence of matter and quality, or extension and thought, is carried, as in Spinoza's case, throughout all being.   Even " all the planets and orbs are beings
possessed of soul, mind, and understanding " (B. 97).
Spinoza, in the Scholium to *Ethica* ii. 13, remarking on the
union of thought and extension in man, continues—" nam
ea, quæ hucusque ostendimus, admodum communia sunt,
nec magis ad homines quam *ad reliqua Individua pertinent*,
quæ omnia, *quamvis diversis gradibus*, animata tamen sunt."
The parallelism is all the more striking in that in this very
Scholium a classification is suggested based on the *degrees*
wherein the two artributes are present in individuals.   Dr.

body. The attainment of wisdom as the self-sufficient end of life is one of
the highest and most emphasized lessons of the Talmud and its commentators. The strong reaction against a merely formal knowledge at the
beginning of our era led the founder of Christianity and his earlier followers to a somewhat one-sided view of life which neglected this all-
important truth.

Martineau, in a note on this passage (p. 190), remarks on a
superficial resemblance between Giordano Bruno and
Spinoza : " Bruno animates things to get them into action ;
Spinoza to fetch them into the sphere of *intelligence*." It
will be seen at once how Spinoza coincides on this point
with Maimonides, who wished to explain how it is that all
things in their degree know the wisdom of the Creator and
glorify Him. Each intelligence, according to the latter
philosopher, can in its degree know God ; yet none know
God as he knows himself. From this it follows that the
measure of man's knowledge of God is his intelligence.
With regard to this intelligence Maimonides—speaking of
it as that " more excellent knowledge which is found in the
soul of man "—identifies it with the " quality " of man,
i.e., his thought-attribute ; this " quality " of man, indeed, is
for him identical with the soul itself (B. 105). The bearing
of all this on Spinoza's theosophical conceptions must be
apparent ; yet it is but a stage to a far more important
coincidence, which lies in the principle :—that the *knowledge of God is always associated in an equal degree with the
love of God.* This is what Spinoza termed the " *Amor Dei
intellectualis.*" Understanding the work of God is " an
opening to the *intelligent* man to love God," writes Maimonides (B. 82). Further, " a man, however, can love the
Holy One, blessed be He ! only by the knowledge which he
has of Him ; so that his love will be in proportion to his
knowledge : if this latter be slight, the former will also be
slight ; but if the latter be great, the former also will be
great. And therefore a man ought solely and entirely to
devote himself to the acquisition of knowledge and understanding, by applying himself to those sciences and doctrines
which are calculated to give such an idea of his Creator as it
is in the power of the intellect of man to conceive " (B. 321).
This intellectual love of God is for Maimonides the highest
good ; the bliss of the world to come will consist in the
knowledge of the truth of the Shechinah ; the greatest
worldly happiness is to have time and opportunity to learn
wisdom (*i.e.*, knowledge of God), and this maximum of

earthly peace will be reached when the Messiah comes, for
his government will give the required opportunities (B. 308,
311, &c.).   Furthermore, the intensity of this intellectual
love of God, of this pursuit of wisdom, is often insisted
upon ; the whole soul of the man must be absorbed in it—
"it cannot be made fast in the heart of a man unless he be
constantly and duly absorbed in the same, and unless he
renounce everything in the world except this love " (B. 320).
It will be seen at once how closely this approaches Spinoza's
" Ex his clare intelligimus, qua in re nostra salus, seu
Beatitudo, seu Libertas consistit ; nempe in constanti et
æterno erga Deum Amore " (v. 36, Schol.), and " Hic erga
Deum Amor summum bonum est, quod ex dictamine
Rationis appetere possumus" (v. 20).   Spinoza's " third
kind of intellection," his knowledge of God, is associated
with the renunciation of all worldly passions, all temporal
strivings and fleshly appetites ; it is the replacing of the
obscure by clear ideas, the seeing things under the aspect of
eternity,—in their relation to God.   There is in fact in
Spinoza's system a strong notion of a ' renunciation ' or
' rebirth,' by means of which a man becomes *free,* thence-
forth to be led " by the Spirit of Christ, that is, *by the idea of
God,* which alone is capable of making man free " (iv. 68,
Schol.).   This notion of rebirth or renunciation has very
characteristic analogues in the ' Nirvana ' of Buddha and
the ' Ewige Geburt ' of Meister Eckehart.   It is, however,
peculiarly strong in the theosophy of Maimonides.   First
recalling to the reader's mind that the contemplation of the
highest truths of the Godhead has been figuratively termed
by Rabbinical writers, " walking in the garden," I proceed
to quote the *Yad* :—

" The man who is replete with such virtues, and whose
bodily constitution, too, is in a perfect state on his entering
into the garden and on his being carried away by those great
and extensive matters, if he have a correct knowledge so as
to understand and comprehend them—if he continue to keep
himself in holiness—*if he depart from the general manner of
people, who walk in the darkness of temporary things*—if he con-

tinue to be solicitous about himself, and to train his mind so that it should *not think at all of any of those perishable things, or of the vanities of time and its devices*, but should have its thoughts constantly turned on high, and fastened to the Throne so as to comprehend those holy and pure intelligences and to meditate on the wisdom of the Holy One ; . . . and if by these means he come to know His excellency—*then the Holy Spirit immediately dwells with him ;* and at the time when the spirit rests on him, his soul mixes with the degree of those angels called Ishim, so that he is changed into another man. Moreover he himself perceives from the state of his knowledge that he is not as he was " (B. 112).

Separate the notions of this paragraph from their Talmudic language and they contain almost the exact thoughts of Spinoza—the passage from obscure to clear ideas, and the consequent attainment to a knowledge of God. Maimonides' assertion that the man himself perceives that he has attained this higher knowledge is perfectly parallel with Spinoza's proposition, that the man who has a true idea is conscious that he has a true idea, and cannot doubt its truth (ii. 43). The parallel between this mediæval Jewish Philosophy and Christian Theology is of course evident, and probably due to the fact that both had a common origin in antient Jewish Philosophy,—if the analogy of Buddhism does not point to a still wider foundation in human nature.

Still one point in the relation of God and man, wherein Maimonides and Spinoza follow the same groove of thought. With the former the "cleaving to the Shechinah," the striving after God, is identified with the pursuit of wisdom. The attainment of wisdom is in itself the highest bliss—it is as well the goal as the course of true human life ; wisdom is not to be desired for an end beyond itself—for the sake of private advantage or from fear of evil, above all not owing to dread of future punishment or hope of future reward—but only in and for itself because it is truth, because it is wisdom. Only "rude folk" are virtuous out of fear (B. 314). Spinoza expresses the same thought in somewhat different words: he tells us that the man who is virtuous owing to fear does not act reasonably. The perfect state is not the reward or goal of virtue, but is identical with virtue itself. The perfect state is one wherein there is a clear knowledge and consequent intellectual love of God; and this is in itself the end and not the means (iv. 63 and v. 42, &c.).

We may now pass to a subject which, in the case of both philosophers, is beset with grave difficulties—namely, God's knowledge and love of Himself. We have seen that in both systems the knowledge of God is always accompanied by a corresponding love of God; we should expect therefore to find God's knowledge of Himself accompanied by a love of Himself. This inference, however, as to God's intellectual love of Himself seems only to have been drawn by Spinoza; Maimonides is, on the other hand, particularly busied with God's knowledge of Himself. To begin with, we are told: *that God, because He knows Himself, knows everything.* This assertion is brought into close connection with another: all existing things, from the first degree of intelligences to the smallest insect which may be found in the centre of the earth, exist by the power of God's truth (B. 87). Some light will perhaps be cast on the meaning of these propositions by a remark previously made as to Maimonides' conception of the Deity as an intellectual cause or law. Behind the succession of material phenomena is a succession of ideas following logically the one on the other. This thought-logic is the only *form* wherein the mind can co-ordinate phenomena because it is itself a thinking entity, and so subject to the logic of thought. The 'pure thought' which has a logic of its own inner necessity is thus the cause, and an intellectual one, of all phenomena. That system which identifies this 'pure thought' with the Godhead may be fitly termed an intellectual pantheism or a pantheistic idealism. It is obvious how in such a pantheistic idealism the propositions—that God in knowing Himself knows everything, and that all things exist by the power of God's truth—can easily arise. Such a passage as the following, too, becomes

replete with very deep truth :—" The Holy One . . . perceives His own truth and knows it just as it really is.
And he does *not know with a knowledge distinct from Himself*
as we know; because we and our knowledge are not one;
but . . . *His knowledge and His life are one* in every possible
respect, and in every mode of unity. . . . Hence you may
say *that He is the knower, the known, and knowledge itself* all at
once. . . . Therefore He does not perceive creatures and
know them by means of the creatures as we know them ;
but He knows them by means of Himself ; so that, by dint
of His knowing Himself, He knows everything; because
everything is supported by its existing through Him "
(B. 87). What fruit such conceptions bore in the mind of
Spinoza must be at once recognized by every student of the
Ethica.

Let us compare these conceptions with their Spinozistic
equivalents. "All things exist by the power of God's truth."
To this *Ethica* i. 15 corresponds—"Quicquid est, in Deo est,
et nihil sine Deo esse neque concipi potest."

"God in knowing Himself knows everything." I am not
aware of any passage in the *Ethica* where this proposition is
distinctly stated, yet it follows immediately from Spinoza's
fundamental principles, and is implied in i. 25, Schol. and
Coroll., and elsewhere (ii. 3, &c.). It is of course involved
in God's *infinite* intellectual love of Himself (v. 35).

"God does not know with a knowledge distinct from Himself." "His knowledge and His life are one." " He is the
knower, the known, and knowledge itself." "His perception
differs from that of creatures." Compare the following statements of Spinoza. " Si intellectus ad divinam naturam
pertinet, non poterit, uti noster intellectus, posterior (ut
plerisque placet), vel simul naturâ esse cum rebus intellectis,
quandoquidem Deus omnibus rebus prior est causalitate; sed
contra veritas et formalis rerum essentia ideo talis est, quia
talis in Dei intellectu existit objective. Quare Dei intellectus,
quatenus Dei essentiam constituere concipitur, est re vera
causa rerum, tam earum essentiæ quam earum existentiæ "
(i. 17, Schol.). These words are followed by the remark

that this is the opinion of those " who hold the knowledge, will, and power of God to be identical," which probably refers to Maimonides. "Omnia quæ sub intellectum infinitum cadere possunt necessario sequi debent " (i. 16). " Sicuti ex necessitate divinæ naturæ sequitur, ut Deus seipsum intelligat, eadem etiam necessitate sequitur, ut Deus infinita infinitis modis agat. Deinde, i. 34, ostendimus Dei potentiam nihil esse, præterquam Dei actuosam essentiam " · (ii. 3, Schol.). Such expressions sufficiently show that God's knowledge, *i.c.*, His " intellectus," and His action—*i.c.*, His life, are one and the same. " Nam intellectus et voluntas, qui Dei essentiam constituerent, a nostro intellectu et voluntate toto cœlo differre deberent" (i. 17, Schol.) ; this sufficiently marks the difference between the divine and human intellect. Shortly, although in certain formal assertions of the *Ethica* this view is somewhat obscured, yet I venture to suggest that the only consistent interpretation of Spinoza's system is summed up in the following words :— That the intellect of God is *all ;* His thought is the existence of things ; to be real is to exist in the divine thought ; that very intellect is itself existence ; it does not understand things like the creature-intellect because *it is one with them.*[1] This is the equivalent of Maimonides' proposition that God is " the knower, the known, and knowledge itself."

As a step from theology to anthropology we may compare the views of the two philosophers on the immortality of the soul. We have seen that Maimonides identifies the soul with the "quality," *i.c.*, the thought-attribute in man. This quality not being composed of material elements cannot be decomposed with them ; it stands in no need of the breath of life, of the body, but it proceeds from God (the infinite intellect). This quality is not destroyed with the body, but continues to know and comprehend those intelligences that are distinct from all matter (*i.e.*, it no longer has knowledge of material things, and therefore must lose all trace of its former individuality), and it lasts for ever and ever (B..

---

[1] Cf. also Kuno Fischer's identification of Spinoza's Substance with Causality.

106). A certain crude resemblance to *Ethica* v. 23 and Schol. will hardly be denied to this view of immortality; but a still closer link may be discovered in the question whether this immortality is shared by all men alike. From the above it would seem that for Maimonides this question must be answered in the affirmative, but when we come to examine his notion of future life we shall find this by no means the case. For him goodness and wisdom—wickedness and ignorance—are synonymous terms.[1] He classifies all beings from the supreme intelligence down to the smallest insect according to their wisdom, the degree of " quality " in them. The wise man who has renounced all clogging passions, and received the Holy Spirit, is classed even with a peculiar rank of angel—" the man-angel." On the other hand, the fool, the evil man, may be in possession of no " quality," and therefore incapable of immortality. The future life of the soul of the wise is a purely *intellectual* one; it consists in that state of bliss which Spinoza would describe as perceiving things by the " third kind of intellection " : it lies in perceiving more of the truth of God than was possible while in the dark and abject body; it is increased knowledge of the Shechinah; or again, to use Spinoza's words, a more perfect " Amor Dei intellectualis " (B. 296). On the other hand, the reward of the evil man is, that his soul is cut off from this life; *it is that destruction after which there is no existence;* " the retribution which awaits the wicked consists in this, that they do not attain unto that life, but that they are cut off and die " (B. 294). Shortly, Hell and Tophet are the destruction and end of all life; there is no immortality. I will only place for comparison by the side of this a portion of the very remarkable Scholium with which Spinoza concludes the *Ethica* :—" Ignarus enim, præterquam a causis externis multis modis agitatur, nec unquam vera animi acquiescentia potitur, vivit præterea sui et Dei et rerum

---

[1] Many passages might be quoted from the *Yad* to prove this. A somewhat similar though not quite identical distinction of good and evil occurs in the *More Nebuchim* (b. i., c. 1), where they are held equivalent to true and false respectively.

quasi inscius, et simul ac pati desinit, *simul etiam esse desinit.* Cum contra sapiens, quatenus ut talis consideratur, vix animo movetur, sed sui et Dei et rerum æterna quadam necessitate conscius, *nunquam esse desinit,* sed semper vera animi acquiescentia potitur." Obviously Spinoza recognized some form of immortality in the wise man, which the ignorant could not share; the one ceased, the other never could cease to be.[1]

The influence of Maimonides on Spinoza becomes far less obvious when we turn to his doctrine of the human affections. On the one hand, this is perhaps the most thought-out, finished portion of Spinoza's work; on the other hand, Maimonides' somewhat crude "Precepts relating to the Government of the Temper" are an unsystematic mass of moral precepts, exegesis, and interpretation of the Talmud; added to which only certain portions are yet available in translation.   Nevertheless, we may find several points of contact and even double contact.

According to Spinoza the great end of life—the bliss which is nothing less than repose of the soul—springs from the knowledge of God. The more perfect the intellect is, the greater is the knowledge of God. The great aim, then, of the reasoning man is to regulate all other impulses to the end that he may truly understand himself and his surroundings —that is, know God (iv. Appendix, c. 4).   All things, there-

---

[1] It is a curious fact that the *last* words of the *Ethica* are very closely related to a paragraph in the *last* chapter of the *More Nebuchim,* wherein we are told that it is knowledge of God only which gives immortality. The soul is only so far immortal as it possesses knowledge of God, *i.e.,* wisdom.   To perceive things under their intelligible aspect is the great aim of every human individual, it gives him true perfection and renders his soul immortal.   In striking correspondence with this is Chap. 23 of the 2nd part of the *Korte Verhandeling van God,* &c.   We are told that the soul can only continue to exist in so far as it is united to the body or God.   (1) When it is united only to the body it must perish with the body.   (2) In so far as it is united with an unchangeable object, it must in itself be unchangeable.   That is, in so far as it is united to God, it cannot perish.   This "union with God" is what Spinoza afterwards termed the "knowledge of God."   The coincidence has been noted by Joël (*Zur Genesis der Lehre Spinozas*).

fore, all passions, are to be made subservient to this one end
—the attainment of wisdom. Following up this conception
Spinoza proves that all external objects, all natural affections,
are to be so treated or encouraged, that the body may be
maintained in a state fit to discharge its functions, for by
this means the mind will be best able to form conceptions of
many things (iv. Appendix, c. 27, taken in conjunction with
iv. 38 and 39). For this reason laughter and jest are good
in moderation ; so also eating and drinking, &c. ; music and
games are all good so far as they serve this end; "quo
majori Lætitia afficimur, eo ad majorem perfectionem
transimus, hoc est, eo nos magis de *natura divina participare*
necesse est " (iv. 45, Schol.). Nay, even marriage is consistent with reason, if the love arises not from externals only,
but has for its cause the " libertas animi " (iv. App., c. 20).
Shortly, Spinoza makes the gratification of the so-called
natural passions reasonable in so far as it tends to the health
of the body, and hence to the great end of life—the perfecting
of the understanding or the knowing of God. We may
gather a somewhat similar idea from Maimonides. I have
already pointed out that in the terminology of the latter's
philosophy "to be wise," to "delight in the Shechinah" or
" to serve the Lord " are synonymous. Remembering this,
the following passage is very suggestive :—" He who lives
according to rule, if his object be merely that of preserving
his body and his limbs whole, or that of having children to
do his work, and to toil for his wants—his is not the right
way ; but his object ought to be that of preserving his body
whole and strong, to the end that his soul may be fit to know
the Lord, . . . it being impossible for him to become intelligent or to acquire wisdom by studying the sciences whilst he
is hungry or ill, or whilst any one of his limbs is ailing. . . .
And consequently he who walks in this way all his days will
be serving the Lord continually even at the time when he
trades, or even at the time when he has sexual intercourse ;
because his purpose in all this is to obtain that which is
necessary for him to the end that his mind may be perfect to
serve the Lord " (B. 174). Elsewhere Maimonides tells us

that a man should direct all his doings—trading, eating,
drinking, marrying a wife—so that his body may be in perfect health, and his mind thus capable of directing its energies
to knowledge of God (B. 172).

Other points of coincidence may be noted. Spinoza attributes all evil to confused ideas, to ignorance. Maimonides
states that desire for evil arises from an *infirm* soul (here it
must be remembered that soul is the "quality" of a man,
his thinking attribute). "Now what remedy is there for
those that have infirm souls? *They shall go to the wise*, who
are the physicians of soul" (B. 159). Here evil is brought
into close connection with ignorance as its cause.[1] The
characteristic of the wise man is that he avoids all opposite
extremes, and takes that middle state which is found in all
the dispositions of man; the rational man calculates his dispositions (*i.e.*, his affections or emotions) and directs the
same "in the intermediate way to the end that he may preserve a perfect harmony in his bodily constitution" (B. 152).
There is an echo of this in Spinoza's "Cupiditas quæ ex
Ratione oritur, excessum habere nequit" (iv. 61). Maimonides holds haughtiness and humility extremes; the wise
man will steer a middle course between them (B. 154).
Spinoza tells us: "Humilitas virtus non est, sive ex Ratione
non oritur" (iv. 53). In the *Yad* we read, when a man is
in a country where the inhabitants are wicked (*i.e.*, ignorant),
"he ought to abide quite solitarily by himself" (B. 176).
In the *Ethica*: "Homo liber, qui inter ignaros vivit, eorum,
quantum potest beneficia declinare studet" (iv. 70). According to Spinoza all the emotions of hate, for example
vengeance, can only arise from confused ideas, they have no

---

[1] It may be worth while remarking how the keynote to the moral
Reformers who preceded the so-called Reformation is the conception that
the wicked man and the fool are one and the same person. In woodcuts
(cf. those in the *Narrenschiff*, 1494, and the recently discovered Block-
book c. 1470) and in words (cf. Sebastian Brand, Geiler von Kaiserberg,
and Thomas Murner) it is the ever-inculcated lesson. It is curious that
this re-establishment of morality on a higher *intellectual* basis in preference to the old penal theory has ever—from Solomon to Spinoza—
found such strong support in Hebrew philosophy.

existence for the rational man who marks the true causes of things. Maimonides writes of vengeance that it shows an evil mind, " for with *intelligent* men all worldly concerns are but vain and idle things, such as are not enough to call forth vengeance " (B. 197). Spinoza terms the passions obscure ideas (iii. final paragraph), and in so far as the mind has obscure or inadequate ideas its power of acting or *existing* is decreased. Curiously enough Maimonides, speaking of the passion anger, says: " Passionate men cannot be said to live " (B. 164).

Taken individually these coincidences might not be of much weight, yet taken in union, I think, they show that Spinoza was even in his doctrine of the human affections not uninfluenced by Maimonides, albeit to a lesser degree than in his theosophy.

. It may not be uninteresting to note one point of divergence, namely, on the insoluble problem of free-will. Spinoza reduces man's free-will to an intellectual recognition of, and hence a free submission to, necessity. Maimonides, on the other hand, tells us distinctly that "free-will is granted to every man "; that there is no predestination ; every man can choose whether he will be righteous or wicked, a wise man or a fool (B. 263). With regard to the question of God's pre-knowledge, and whether this must not be a predestination, Maimonides writes: " Know ye that with regard to the discussion of this problem, the measure thereof is longer than the earth and broader than the sea." He hints, however, that its solution must probably be sought in the fact that God's knowledge is not distinct from himself, but that he and his knowledge are one ("the knower, the known, and and the knowledge itself are identical "). Maimonides cautiously adds that it is impossible for man fully to grasp the truth regarding the nature of God's knowledge ; and, while granting God pre-knowledge, still concludes: " But yet it is known so as not to admit of any doubt that the actions of a man are in his own power, and that the Holy One, blessed be He! neither attracts him nor decrees that he should do so and so" (B. 270). Perhaps the ordinary workaday mortal will find Maimonides' evasion of the problem as useful as Spinoza's attempted solution!

In the above remarks I have considered only the *Yad Hachazakah*, because hitherto attention seems to have been entirely directed to the *More Nebuchim* (cf. Joël, Sorley, and others). It is not impossible that in the intervening ten years Maimonides somewhat altered his views. I should not be surprised to hear that the *More* was held more 'orthodox' than the *Yad*. The latter, despite much Talmudic verbiage and scriptural exegesis, notwithstanding many faults and inconsistencies, yet contains the germs of a truly grand philosophical system, quite capable of powerfully influencing the mind even of a Spinoza. Such a reader would, while rejecting the exegesis, recognize the elements of truth in the pure theosophy (cf. Joël, *Zur Genesis*, p. 9), and this is the point wherein the two philosophers approach most closely. In the second place, I have confined myself entirely to the influence of the *Yad* on the *Ethica*. Greater agreement would have been found with the *Korte Verhandeling van God, &c.*, while Spinoza's views of Biblical criticism (especially his conceptions of prophets and prophecy as developed in the *Tractatus Theologico-Politicus*) owe undoubtedly much to the *Yad*. But I wished to show that the study of Maimonides was traceable even in Spinoza's most finished exposition of his philosophy. Those who assert that Spinoza was influenced by Hebrew thought have not seldom been treated as though they were accusing Spinoza of a crime. Yet no great work ever sprung from the head of its creator like Athena from the head of Zeus; it has slowly developed within him, influenced and moulded by all that has influenced and moulded its shaper's own character. Had we but knowledge and critical insight enough, every idea might be traced to the germ from which it has developed. While recognizing many other influences at work forming Spinoza's method of thought, it is only scientific to allow a certain place to the Jewish predecessors with whom he was acquainted. Critical comparison must show how great that influence was. We naturally expect to find considerable divergences between any

individual Jewish philosopher and Spinoza; these divergences have been carefully pointed out by Mr. Sorley, but
they are insufficient to prove that Spinoza was not very
greatly influenced by Hebrew thought.   My aim has been to
call in question the traditional view of Spinoza's relation to
Jewish philosophy, *i.e.*, that he learnt enough of it to throw
it off entirely.   I cannot help holding that, while Spinoza's
form and language were a mixture of mediæval scholasticism
and the Cartesian philosophy, yet the ideas which they
clothed were not seldom Hebrew in their origin.   He might
be cast out by his co-religionists, but that could not deprive
him of the mental birthright of his people—those deep moral
and theosophical truths which have raised the Hebrews to a
place hardly second to the Greeks in the history of thought.

Hebrew philosophy seems to have a history and a development more or less unique and apart from that of other
nations; once in the course of many centuries it will produce
a giant-thinker; one who, not satisfied by the narrow limits
of his own nation, strives for a freer, wider field of action,
and grafts on to his Hebrew ideas a catholic language and a
broader mental horizon.   He becomes a world-prophet, but
is rejected of his own folk.   Such an one of a truth was
Spinoza, and another perhaps, albeit in a lesser degree,
Moses, the son of Maimon.[1]

---

[1] When the *More Nebuchim* became generally known, its author was
looked upon by a large section of the Jews as a heretic of the worst type,
who had "contaminated the religion of the Bible with the vile alloy of
human reason"!

VII

MEISTER ECKEHART, THE MYSTIC.[1]

Diz ist Meister Eckehart
Dem Got nie niht verbarc.
—Old Scribe.

STUDENTS of mediæval philosophy must often have been struck by the unexpected occurrence of phases of thought, even in Christian writers, which are utterly out of keeping with the framework of scholastic theology within which they are usually mounted. M. Renan has done excellent service in showing how many of these eccentricities may be attributed to the influence—the fascination—of the arch-sinner Averroes. There is, however, one field of Averroistic influence to which M. Renan has only referred without entering on any lengthened discussion; this is the extremely interesting, but undoubtedly obscure subject of fourteenth century mysticism. I purpose in the following paper to present the English reader with a slight sketch of the philosophical (or rather theosophical) system of Meister Eckehart, the Mystic,[2] who may be accepted as the chief exponent of the school. There are two points which ought peculiarly to attract the student of modern philosophy to

[1] Reprinted from *Mind:* a Quarterly Review of Psychology and Philosophy, vol. xi. No. 41.

[2] The Germans possess an excellent book on Eckehart from the pen of Prof. Lasson, but, for the purposes of this essay, I have made use only of Eckehart's own writings in the second volume of Pfeiffer's *Deutsche Mystiker.* That my results differ so often from those of Prof. Lasson is due principally to his strong Hegelian standpoint; at the same time I have to acknowledge the debt which I owe, not so much to his book, as to the charm of his personal teaching. English readers will find a short account of Eckehart due to Prof. Lasson in Ueberweg's *History of Philosophy.*

Eckehart : the first lies in a possible (and by no means improbable) influence which his ideas may have exercised over
Kant; the second consists in a peculiar spiritual relation to
Spinoza. This latter can be in no way due to direct contact,
but has to be sought in a common spiritual ancestry. Nor
is this link in the past by any means difficult to find. The
parallelism of ideas in the writings of Averroes and Maimonides has led some authors hastily to conclude an adoption
by the latter of the ideas of the former. The real relation is
a like education under the influences of the same Arabian
school. On the one hand, Maimonides was the spiritual
progenitor of Spinoza; on the other, Averroes was the
master from whom fourteenth century German mysticism
drew its most striking ideas. During this century Averroism was the ruling philosophical system at both the leading
European universities—at Paris and at Oxford. It was
the result of Averroistic teaching which produced two of
the most characteristic thinkers of the age. The theologico-philosophical system which John Wyclif, the Oxford
professor, develops in his *Trialogus* is unintelligible without a
knowledge of Averroistic ideas. The mysticism of Eckehart,
the far-famed Paris lecturer, owes its leading characteristics
to a like source. In 1317 the then Bishop of Strasburg
condemned Eckehart's doctrines; in 1327 the Archbishop
and Inquisitors of Cologne renewed the condemnation, and
Eckehart recanted; in 1329, a year after Eckehart's death,
a papal bull cited 28 theses of the master and rejected them
as heretical. What a parallel does this offer to the proceed-
ings of the hierarchy against Wyclif, culminating in his post-
humous condemnation by the Council of Constance! Yet
what more natural, when both men were deeply influenced
by the ideas of the arch-sinner Averroes, whom later Christian art was to place alongside Judas and Mahomet in the
darkest shades of hell ? [1]

[1] A further link between Eckehart and Wyclif is perhaps to be found
in the pseudo-Dionysius with his commentator Grossetête. Eckehart was
acquainted with "Lincolniensis" (*Deutsche Mystiker* ii. 363), whom
Wyclif regarded as peculiarly his own precursor.

Wyclif and Eckehart each in their individual fashion represent the Averroistic ideas under the garb of Christian scholasticism; in strange contrast with these thinkers we find in Spinoza the like ideas treated with a rationalism which, however, has not yet quite freed itself from the idealistic influence of Hebrew theosophy. The contrast is one possibly as interesting and instructive as could well be found in the whole history of the development of human thought.

Before entering upon a discussion of Eckehart's ideas, it may not be out of place to recall those features of Averroism with which we shall be principally concerned, and at the same time to prove by citations from a remarkable tractate of an anonymous writer of the fourteenth century the direct connection of Averroistic thought with German mysticism.

Aristotle in his *De Anima* (III. v. 1) distinguishes in man a double form of reason, the active and the passive ; the first is separated from the body, eternal, and passionless : the second begins and ends with the body and shares all its varied states. Unfortunately Aristotle has nowhere clearly explained what he understands by the relationship of these two reasons, and, as Zeller remarks (*Die Philos. der Griechen*, ii. Abth., 2 Theil, p. 572), it is not possible to reconcile his various statements by any consistent theory. Alexander of Aphrodisias endeavoured to obtain such a consistent theory by seeking the active reason, not in the human soul, but in the divine spirit. This view, although probably not the interpretation Aristotle would have given of his own statements, is yet eagerly adopted by the Arabian commentators, and the comparatively insignificant distinction made by Aristotle becomes with Averroes the basis of all that is original in his ideas.

While Alexander identifies the active reason or intellect, which brings the images ($\phi\alpha\nu\tau\acute{\alpha}\sigma\mu\alpha\tau\alpha$) before the passive intellect, with the divine spirit, Averroes looks upon it as emanating from the last celestial intelligence. He considers, however, with Alexander, that it is possible for the human or passive intellect to unite itself to the purely active intellect.

This union takes place, this perfection or blessedness is attained, by long study, deep thought, and renunciation of material pleasures. This process, consisting in the widening of human knowledge, is the *religion* of the philosopher. For what worthier cult can man offer to God than the knowledge of his works, through which alone he can attain to a knowledge of God himself in the fulness of his essence ? [1]

But to recognize fully what is original in Eckehart we must examine Averroes' views somewhat closer.

Averroes holds that things perceived by the understanding (*intelligibilia*) stand in the same relation to the material intellect (passive reason) as things perceived by sensation bear to the faculty of sensation. This faculty is purely receptive, and pure receptivity belongs also to the material intellect. Its nature is only *in potentia*,—it is a capacity for intellectual perception. At this point Averroes introduces a statement which disagrees with Aristotle and brings obscurity into his theory ; he holds that, as this passive reason exists only *in potentia*, it can neither come into being nor perish. Alexander's view, that the material intellect is perishable, is described as utterly false.[2] This statement was probably introduced to quiet the scruples of the theologians, which would be excited by anything appearing to destroy individual immortality. The like inconsistency recurs with Eckehart. Three premisses of Alexander are stated by Averroes to prove how in the course of time it is possible for the material to attain perfection through the separate intellect. In accordance with these premisses (which are based on the analogy mentioned above of the intellective and sensitive faculties) we ought to conclude that some portion of mankind can really contemplate the separate intellect, and these men are they who by the speculative sciences have perfected themselves. Perfection of the spirit is thus to be obtained by Knowledge, nor can it ever again be lost. Often, however,

[1] Cf. *Drei Abhandlungen über die Conjunction des separaten Intellects mit dem Menschen von Averroes,* herausgegeben von T. Hercz, Berlin, 1869.
[2] Ibid. p. 23.

it comes only in the moment of death, since it is opposed to
bodily (material) perfection.

The separate intellect (active reason) exercises two activities. The one, because it is separate, consists in self-
contemplation or self-perception. This self-perception is the
manner of all separate intellects, because it is characteristic
of them that the intellectual and the intelligible are absolutely one. The second activity is the perception of the
intelligibilia which are in the material intellect, that is, the
transition of the material intellect from possibility to
actuality. Thus the active intellect attaches itself to man
and is at the same time his *form*, and the man becomes by
means of it active—that is, he thinks. These statements
can hardly be said to be free from obscurity, but they receive
considerable light from Eckehart, who identifies the active
reason with the Deity, and explains the life of the universe
by his two activities : self-contemplation, wherein to think is
to create or act, and human contemplation which is the
" bearing of the Son."

The question now arises as to what follows upon the
complete union of the separate and individual intellects.
What happens to the man for whom there no longer remains any *intelligibile in potentia* to convert into an *intelligibile in actu ?* Such an individual intellect then becomes
in character like to the separate intellect ; its nature becomes
pure activity; its self-consciousness is like that of the separate intellect, in which existence is identified with its purpose
—uninterrupted activity. This statement Averroes holds to
be the most important that can be made concerning the
intellect.

While Eckehart himself makes no direct reference to
Averroes, a remarkable tractate written by one of his school
does not hesitate to cite the Arabian commentator as an
authority.[1] A short sketch of the views contained in this

[1] *Philosophischer Tractat von der wirklichen und möglichen Vernunft
aus dem vierzehnten Jahrhundert.* This was printed by B. J. Docen in
his *Miscellaneen zur Geschichte der teutschen Literatur* München, 1809 :
vol. i. p. 138.

tractate will serve to link more clearly the preceding statement of Averroes's theory with our sketch of Eckehart's
theosophy.

The writer quotes Meister Eckehart to the effect that
when two things are united one must suffer and the other
act. For this reason human understanding must suffer
the "moulding of God" (*uberformvnge Gotz*). Since God's
existence is his activity, the blessedness of this union can
only arise from the human understanding remaining in a
purely passive, receptive state. Only a spirit free from all
working of its own can suffer the "reasonable working" of
God (*daz vernunftige werch Gotz*). The writer, after describing the soul as a spark of the divine spirit, declares that
the union of this spark with God is possible, and that the
process of union is "God confessing himself, God loving
himself, God using himself"—a phraseology which is
characteristic of Eckehart and suggestive of Spinoza. After
these theosophical considerations, the tractate passes to the
more psychological side of the subject. There are two kinds
of reason, an active reason and a potential reason (*ein wur-
chende vernunft* and *ein moglich vernunft*). The latter is
possessed by the spirit at the instant when it reaches the
body. If the potential reason would simply subject itself
to the active reason, the man would be as blessed in this
world as in the eternal life, for "the blessedness of man
consists in his recognition of his own existence under the
form of the active reason." That is, it consists in contemplation of the individual essence in its connection with
and origin in the universal reason. The complete capacity
for understanding all things which this implies is not possible to the potential reason. The potential reason has only
the capacity for receiving the moulding of the active reason.

There are certain beings whose existence is their activity,
and whose activity is their understanding. In other words,
to be, to act, and to think are one and the same process
with them—(their *wesen*, *wurken*, and *verstan* are one). These
beings are termed intelligences, and are nobler than the
angels; they flow reasonably (*vernunftichlich*) and incessantly

from and to God, the uncreated substance. They belong,
as it were, to the divine flow of thought (which is at the
same time active creation), and so are not substances like
the angels. Such an intelligence is the active reason (pp.
146, 147). As proof that this particular intelligence is no
substance, but its existence is its activity, Averroes's commentary on *De Anima* iii. is quoted as authority. The
potential reason is filled with images (*bilde*) which are for
it externality and temporality. So soon as by the grace of
God the potential reason is freed from these images, it is
supplanted or moulded by the active reason. Whereas the
potential reason takes things only from the senses as they
appear to exist, the active reason goes to the origin of things
and sees them as they are in reality—that is, in God. But our
writer is again hampered by the current theological conceptions, although he twists them to his own theories; he asks:
if the active reason is ever present, ready to be united to the
potential reason, when once it is freed of the images, must
it not also be present in hell? The answer must necessarily
be affirmative; but hell in truth is not what the vulgar
(*grobe lvte*) believe it—fire; the agony of hell consists in the
sufferer's unconsciousness of his own reason (*irre aigen
vernunft*); that is, he cannot contemplate himself as he
appears to the active reason, or as he exists in the divine
mind. This spiritual pain is the greatest of all pains. Hell
is thus identified with the absence of the higher insight.
Finally we may note that the author of the tractate seems
uncertain whether the potential reason can ever arrive at
perfect union with the active reason before it is separated
from all material things.

Distorted as are the ideas of Averroes in this work, we
cannot doubt that it is those ideas which are influencing its
author. A far more complete attempt to reconcile Averroism
with Christian theology is to be found in the system of
Eckehart, to which we now proceed. Many difficulties and
obscurities will arise, but some elucidation they will undoubtedly receive from a brief examination of the relationship of Averroes to mediæval mysticism.

We shall be the better able to enter into Meister Eckehart's system, if we first note a few leading characteristics
of his intellectual standpoint.   Running throughout his
writings two strangely different theosophical currents may
be discerned—two currents which he fails entirely to
harmonize, and which account, for the most part, for those
inconsistencies wherein he abounds.   On the one hand, his
mental predilection is towards a pantheistic idealism; on
the other, his heart makes him a gospel, his education a
scholastic Christian.   He speaks of God almost in the
terms of Spinoza, and describes the phenomenal world in
the language of Kant; his theory of the *esse intelligibile*
is identical with Wyclif's, but he states the doctrines of
renunciation and of the futility of human knowledge in the
form at least of primitive Christianity.   Is it to be wondered
at that the deepest thinker among the German mystics is
the least intelligible?   He is the focus from which spread
the ever-diverging rays of many mediæval and modern philosophical systems.   For our purpose it is first of all necessary
to obtain some conception of the relation which Eckehart
supposed to exist between the phenomenal world and God.
According to our philosopher the active reason (*diu wirkende
vernunft*) receives the impressions from external objects
(*ûzewendikeit*) and places them before the passive reason (*diu
lidende vernunft*).   These impressions or perceptions as presented by the active reason are formulated in space and
time, have a 'here and a now' (*hie unde nû*).   Man's knowledge of objects in the ordinary sense is obtained solely by
means of these impressions (*bilde*), he perceives things only
in time and space (Pfeiffer, *Deutsche Mystiker*, ii. 17, 19,
143, &c.).   Of an entirely different character from human
knowledge is the divine knowledge.   While the active
reason must separate its perceptions in time and space, the
Deity comprehends all things independently of these perceptional frameworks.   The divine mind does not pass from
one object to another, like the human mind, which can only
concentrate itself on one object at a time to the exclusion of
all others.   It grasps all things in one instant and in one

point (*alle mitenander in eime blicke und in eime punte.—Ib.
20, cp. 14, 15*). Shortly, in the language of Kant, while the
human intellect reaches only the world of sense, the divine
is busied with the *Dinge an sich*. This higher knowledge is
of course absolutely unintelligible to the human reason. "All
the truth which any master ever taught with his own
reason and understanding, or ever can teach till the last day,
will not in the least explain this knowledge and its nature "
(*Ib.* 10). Shortly, the *Dinge an sich* form the limit of the
human understanding.[1]   But, just as Kant causes the
practical reason to transcend this limit, so Meister Eckehart
allows a mystical revelation or implantation of this higher
knowledge ; this process he terms the eternal birth (*diu
êwige gebûrt*). The soul ceasing to see things under the
forms of time and space grasps them as they exist in the
mind of God, and finds therein the ultimate truth, the *reality*,
which cannot be reached in the phenomenal world (*Ib.* 12).
The world as reality is thus the world as it exists in God's
perception ; but, since God's will and its production are
absolutely identical (there being no distinction between the
moulding and the moulded—*entgiezunge und entgozzenheit*), we
arrive at the result that the world as reality is the world as
will. Thus both Eckehart and Kant find it necessary to
transcend the 'limit of the human understanding'; both
find reality in the world as will.[2]   The critical philosopher
is desirous of finding an absolute basis for morality in the
supersensuous, and accordingly links phenomena and the
Dinge an sich by a transcendental causality, which somehow
bridges the gulf. The fourteenth century mystic, desirous
of raising the idea of God from the contradictions of a
sensuous existence, places the Deity entirely beyond the
field of ordinary human reason. In order to restore God

---

[1] Cp. *Kritik der reinen Vernunft*, Elementarlehre, ii. Th., 1 Abth.,
2 Buch., 3 Hauptst.

[2] This principle, usually identified with the *Grober Philosoph*, is clearly
expressed in the *Kritik der praktischen Vernunft*, i. Theil., 1 B., 3
Hauptst. The will, however, with Kant and Eckehart is very different
in character.

again to man, he postulates a transcendental knowledge ; in
order to show God as ultimate cause even of the phenomenal,
he is reduced to interpreting in a remarkable manner the
chief Christian dogma. We shall see the meaning of this
more clearly if we examine somewhat closer the conception
Eckehart had formed of God and his relation to the *Dinge
an sich* (*vorgéndiu bilde*, or 'prototypes' as we may perhaps
translate the expression).

Things-in-themselves are things as they exist free from
space and time in God's perception (*D. M.* ii. 325, &c.).
Thus the prototype (*vorgéndez bild*) of Eckehart corresponds
to the *esse intelligibile* of Wyclif, who in like manner identifies
God's conception and his causation (*Omne quod habet esse
intelligibile, est in Deo*, and *Deus est æque intellectivus, ut est
causativus, &c. Trialogus*, ed. Lechler, pp. 46–48).[1] This
form in God is evidently quite independent of creature-exist-
ence, and, not bound by time or space, cannot be said to
have been created, or indeed to come into or go out of
existence. The form *is* in an 'eternal now' (*daz éwige nú*).
To describe a temporal creation of the world is folly to the
intelligent man ; Moses only made use of such a description
to aid the ignorant. God creates all things in an 'ever-
present now' (*in cime gegenwürtigen nú. D. M.* ii. 266, and
267).[2] The soul, then, which has attained to the higher
knowledge grasps things in an 'eternal now,' or, as we may
express it, *sub specie æternitatis*. We can thus grasp more
clearly Eckehart's pantheistic idealism. By placing all
reality in the supersensuous, and identifying that supersensuous reality with God, he avoids many of the contradictions of pantheistic materialism. God is the substance
of all things (*Ib.* 163) and in all things, but as the reality of
things has not existence in space or time there can be no

[1] This is absolutely identical with Spinoza, *Ethica* i. 16, *Omnia quæ
sub intellectum infinitum cadere possunt, necessario sequi debent.* Cp.
Prop. 17, Scholium.
[2] Cp. Wyclif's *Omne quod fuit vel erit, est,* which is based upon the
conception that things *secundum esse intelligibile* are ever in the time- and
space-free cognition of the Deity. (*Trialogus,* ed. Lechler, p. 53.)

question as to how the unchangeable can exist in the phenomenal (*Ib.* 389).   Since all things are what they are owing to the peculiarity of God's nature, it follows that the individual though a work of God is yet an essential element of God's nature, and may be looked upon as productive with God of all being (*Ib.* 581).   The soul, then, which has attained the higher knowledge, sees itself in its reality as an element of the divine nature ; it obtains a clear perception of its own uncreated form (or *vorgêndez bild*), which is in reality its life ; it becomes one with God.   The will of the individual henceforth is identical with the will of God, and the Holy Ghost receives his essence or proceeds from the individual as from God (*dâ enpfâhet der Heilig Geist sîn wesen unde sîn werk unde sîn werden von mir als von Gote. Ib.* 55).   The soul stands to God in precisely the same relation as Christ does ; nay, it attains to "the essence, and the nature, and the substance, and the wisdom, and the joy, and all that God has" (*Ib.* 41, 204).   "Have I attained this blessedness, so are all things in me and in God (*secundum esse intelligibile ?*), and where I am, there is God" (*Ib.* 32).   From this it follows that the 'higher knowledge' of the soul and God's knowledge are one.[1]   It is scarcely necessary to remark that Eckehart defines this state of 'higher know-

---

[1] The whole of this may be most instructively compared with Spinoza's *Ethica* v. Prop. 22 :   In Deo tamen datur necessario idea (Eckehart's *vorgêndez bild*), quæ hujus et illius corporis humani essentiam (Eckehart's *ûzewendiges ding*) sub æternitatis specie exprimit.

Prop. 23 : Mens humana non potest cum corpore absolute destrui ; sed ejus aliquid remanet, quod æternum est (the *vorgêndez bild* exists in an *êwige nû*).

Prop. 29 : Quicquid mens sub specie æternitatis intelligit, id ex eo non intelligit, quod corporis præsentem actualem existentiam concipit ; sed ex eo, quod corporis essentiam concipit sub specie æternitatis.   (The 'higher knowledge' of the soul is concerned with the *vorgêndez bild* and not with the phenomenal world.)

Prop. 30 : Mens nostra, quatenus se et corpus sub æternitatis specie cognoscit, eatenus Dei cognitionem necessario habet, scitque se in Deo esse et per Deum concipi—(a proposition agreeing entirely with Eckehart's).

After this it is hard to deny a link somewhere between these two philosophers !

ledge' as blessedness. Thus both Spinoza and Eckehart base their beatitude on the knowledge of God, but in how different a sense ! Eckehart's knowledge is a kind of transcendental instinct of the soul steeped in religious emotion ; Spinoza's knowledge is the result of an adequate cognition of the essence of things—it is a purely intellectual (non-transcendental) process. A striking corollary to this similarity may be found in the two philosophers' doctrines of God's love. The love of the mind towards God, writes Spinoza (*Ethica* v. 36 and Cor.), is part of the love where-with God loves himself, and conversely God, in so far as he loves himself, loves mankind. The love of God towards men, says Meister Eckehart, is a portion of the love with which he loves himself (*D. M.* ii. 145-146, 180).

In both cases God's self-love is intellectual—it arises from the contemplation of his own perfection.[1] Eckehart perhaps even more strongly than Spinoza endeavours to free God from anthropomorphical qualities. His God, placed in the sphere of *Dinge an sich*, is freed from extension, but this by no means satisfies him—God must have no human at-tributes ; he is not lovable, because that is a sensuous quality—he is to be loved because he is not lovable. Nor does he possess any of the spiritual powers such as men speak of in the phenomenal world—nothing like to human will, memory or intellect ; in this sense he is not a spirit. He is nothing that the human understanding can approach. One attribute only can be asserted of him and of him only —namely, unity. Otherwise he may be termed the nothing of nothing, and existing in nothing. Alone in him the prototypes or uncreated forms (*vorgéndiu bilde*) can be said to exist, but these are beyond the human understanding and can only be reached by the higher transcendental knowledge. " How shall I love God then ?   Thou shalt love him as he is, a non-god, a non-spirit, a non-person, a non-form ; more, as he is an absolute pure clear *one*." (*Wie sol ich in denne*

---

[1] Wyclif, *Trialogus*, 56 : *Cognoscit et amat se ipsum.* Wyclif's whole theory of the divine intellect as the sphere of reality, and cognition by God as the test of possible existence, has strong analogy with Eckehart's.

minnen? Dû solt in minnen als er ist, ein nihtgot, ein nihtgeist, ein nihtpersône, ein nihtbild : mêr als er ein lûter pûr klar ein ist, &c. Ib. 320 ; cp. 319, 500, 506, &c.). Into this inconceivable nothing the soul finds its highest beatitude in sinking. How is this to be accomplished ? What is the phenomenal world, and how can the passage be made to the world of reality ? What is the price to be paid for this surpassing joy ? These are the questions which now rise before us, and which Eckehart endeavours to solve in his theory of renunciation.

All important is it first to note how the philosopher deduces the phenomenal from the real—the externality (*ûzewendikeit*) from the prototypes (*diu vorgêndiu bilde*). The solution of this apparent impossibility is found in a singular interpretation of the Christian mystery—' The Word became flesh '; the idea in God passing into phenomenal being is the incarnation of the divine λόγος. God's self-introspection, his " speaking " of the ideas in him produces the phenomenal world. " What is God's speaking ? The Father regards himself with a pure cognition, and looks into the pure oneness of his own essence. Therein he perceives the forms of all creation (*i.e., diu vorgêndiu bilde*), then he speaks himself. The Word is pure (self-)cognition, and that is the Son. God speaking is God giving " birth." The real world in the divine mind is " non-natured nature " (*diu ungenâtûrte nâtûre*) ; the sensuous world which arises from this by God's self-introspection is "natured nature " (*diu genâtûrte nâtûre*).[1] In the former we find only the Father, in the latter we first recognize the Son (*D. M.* ii., 591, 537, 250). Of course this process of " speaking the word " or giving birth to the Son is not temporal but in an eternal now; but we had better let Eckehart speak for himself :—" Of necessity God must work all his works. God is ever working in one eternal now, and his working is giving birth to his Son; he bears him at every instant. From this birth all things proceed, and God has such joy therein, that he consumes all his power in giving birth (*daz*

---

[1] These are in close agreement with Spinoza's *natura naturans* and *natura naturata.* Cp. *Ethica* i., Prop. 29, Schol.

er alle sine maht in ir verzert). God bears himself out of himself into himself; the more perfect the birth, the more is born. I say: God is at all times one, he takes cognition of nothing beyond himself. Yet God, in taking cognition of himself, must take cognition of all creatures. God bears himself ever in his Son; in him he speaks all things" (*Ib.* 254). Eckehart in identifying God's self-introspection with the birth of the Son, and the "phenomenalizing" of the real, has rendered it extremely difficult to reconcile this divine process in the *ewige nû* with the historical fact of Christianity. The difficulty is still further increased when we remember that the converse process by which the individual soul passes from the phenomenal to the higher or divine knowledge is also termed by Eckehart "God bearing the Son." The difficulty is lightened, though not removed, by uniting the two processes. The soul may be compared to a mirror which reflects the light of the sun back to the sun. In God's self-introspection the real is "phenomenalized" (as the light passes from the sun to the mirror); but the soul in its higher knowledge passes again back to God, the phenomenal is realized (as the light is reflected back to the sun). The whole process is divine—"God bears himself out of himself into himself" (*Ib.* 180–181). Logically, the process ought to occur with every conscious individual, for all have a like phenomenal existence. In order, however, to save at least the moral, if not the historical side of Christianity, Eckehart causes only certain souls to attain the higher knowledge; the Son is only born in certain individuals destined for salvation. Thus Eckehart's phenomenology is shattered upon his practical theology; it is but the recurrence of an old truth, that all forms of pantheism (idealistic or materialistic) are inconsistent with the assertion of an absolute morality as fundamental principle of the world. The pantheist must boldy proclaim that morality is the creation of humanity, not humanity the outcome of any moral causality.[1]

[1] That the world was created for the moral perfecting of mankind is a dogma alike with Kant and Averroes (*Drei Abhandlungen*, p. 63). It has been wisely repudiated by Spinoza and Maimonides.

Let us now observe how the soul is to pass from the world of phenomena to the world of reality. So long as the active reason continues to present external objects to the soul, the soul cannot possibly grasp those objects *sub æternitatis specie*. The human understanding which can only perceive things in time and space is useless in this matter, nay, it is even harmful ; the soul must try to attain absolute ignorance and darkness (*ein dunsterniisse und ein unwizzen*, *D. M.* ii. 26). Eckehart's contempt for the creature-intellect is almost on a par with Tertullian's, and is in marked contrast with the fashion in which Gautama, Maimonides, and Spinoza make it the guiding star through renunciation to beatitude. The first step to the eternal birth (*ewige gebûrt*) is the total renunciation of creature-perception and creature-reason. The soul must pass through a period of absolute unconsciousness as to the phenomenal world ; all its powers must be concentrated on one object, on the mystical contemplation of the supersensuous deity,—the 'nothing of nothing,' of which the soul, if it seeks for true union, cannot and *must not* form any idea (*Ib.* 13–15). Not by an intellectual development, but by sheer passivity, by waiting for the transcendental action of God, can the soul attain the higher knowledge, pass through the eternal birth. This intellectual nihilism, this ignorance, is not a fault, but the highest perfection ; it is the only step the mind can take towards its union with God (*Ib.* 16). The soul must, so far as in it lies, separate itself from the phenomenal world, renounce all sensuous action, even cease to think under the old forms. Then, when all the powers of the soul are withdrawn from their works and conceptions (*von allen irn werken und bilden*), when all creature-emotions are discarded, God will speak his word, the Son will be born in the soul (*Ib.* 6–9). This renunciation of all sensational existence (*alle ûzewendikeit der creaturen*) is an absolutely necessary prelude to the rebirth (*ewige gebûrt, Ib.* 14). Memory, understanding, will, sensation, must be thrown aside ; the soul must free itself from here and from now, from matter and from manifoldness (*liplichkeit unde manicvaltikeit*). Poor in spirit, and having nothing, willing nothing, and knowing nothing, even ·renouncing all outward religious works and observances, the soul awaits the coming of God (*Ib*. 24-25, 143, 296, 309, 280).   Then arrives the instant when by a transcendental process the higher knowledge is conveyed to the soul, it attains its freedom by union with God.   Henceforth God takes the place of the active reason, and is the source whence the passive reason draws its conceptions. The soul is no longer bound by matter and time; it has transcended these limits and grasped the reality beyond. Everywhere the soul sees God, as one who has long gazed on the sun sees it in whatever direction he turns his glance (*Ib*. 19, 28-29).   Such is the beatitude which follows the rebirth (*êwige gebûrt*).   "Holy and all holy are they, who are thus placed in the eternal now beyond time and place and form and matter, unmoved by body and by pain and by riches and by poverty" (*Ib*. 75).   Strange is this emotional Nirvāna of the German mystic, though it is a religious phenomenon not unknown to the psychologist.   This seclusion (*Abgeschiedenheit*, *Ib*. 486-487), as Eckehart calls it, is pronounced to have exactly the same results as the intellectual beatitude of Gautama and Spinoza.   The soul has returned to the state in which it was before entering the phenomenal world; it has recognized itself as idea in God and thrown off all creature-attributes (*crêatûrlichkeit*), the remaining in which is what Eckehart understands by hell; it sees everything *sub specie æternitatis*.   Secluded from men, free from all external objects, from all chance, distraction, trouble, it sees only reality.   To all sensuous matters it is indifferent.   "Is it sick?   It is as fain sick as sound; as fain sound as sick. Should a friend die?   In the name of God.   Is an eye knocked out?   In the name of God."   It is complete submission to the will of God, absolute indifferentism to heaven or hell, if they but come as the result of that will (*Ib*. 59-60, 203, &c.).   This is the state of grace wherein no joyous thing gives pleasure and no painful thing can bring sadness.   It is the extreme to which Christian asceticism—Christian renunciation of the world of sense—can well be pushed.[1]

---

[1] Meister Eckehart even goes so far as to assert that pain ought to be received, not only willingly, but even *eagerly*.' (*D. M.* ii. 599.)

Putting aside the antinomy between Eckehart's phenomenology and practical theology, let us endeavour to see the
exact meaning of his theory of renunciation. He asserts
that it is possible by a certain transcendental process to
attain a " higher knowledge "; that this higher knowledge
consists of an union with God, whereby the individual soul
is able to recognize and thus absolutely submit to the will of
God. The will and conception of God are identical. His conceptions are the prototypes (*vorgêndiu bilde*) or reality. Hence
we might well interpret Eckehart's mystical higher knowledge to refer to a knowledge of the reality which exists
behind the phenomenal, and consequently the submission of
the individual will to the laws of that reality. Such a theory
possesses a certain degree of logical consistency, and is
strikingly similar to Spinoza's doctrine of the beatitude
which flows from the higher cognition of God. Spinoza's
cognition, however, leads to joy and peace in this world, while
Eckehart's produces only a pure indifferentism. Still more
striking is the contrast when we examine the methods by
which the cognition is supposed to be attained. Spinoza's
is only to be reached by a renunciation of obscure ideas, by
a casting forth of blind passion, by a laborious intellectual
process. Eckehart declares, on the other hand, that all
knowledge of reality is only to be gained by a transcendental
act of the divine will; the act itself must occur during an emotional trance, wherein the mind endeavours to free itself from
all external impressions, to disregard the action of all human
faculties. Seclusion from mankind, renunciation of all sensuous pleasure, the rejection of all human knowledge and all
human means of investigating truth, are the preparations for
the trance and the consequent eternal birth (*êwige gebûrt*).
Physiologically there can be small doubt that such overwrought emotions as this trance denotes cannot be conducive of physical health.[1] To this, of course, the mystic

---

[1] That great excitement might produce the trance can hardly be doubted.
The mystics seem at least to have been acquainted with such ecstatical
phases. Cp. the curious tale of *Swester Katrei Meister Ekehartes Tohter*
(*D. M.* ii. 465). Numerous instances occur also in the Life of Tauler.

may reply that health is only a secondary consideration in matters of religious welfare. A greater evil than that of danger to health is the social danger which may arise from ignorant fanatics, who suppose themselves to have attained the " higher knowledge " by divine inspiration. *They* are acquainted with absolute truth and are acting according to the will of God. More than once in the world's history the cry has gone up from such men that all human knowledge is vain, and the populace believing them have destroyed the weapons of intellect and checked for a time human progress. What test have we, when once we discard reason and appeal to emotion, of the truth of our own or others' assertions ? To borrow the language of theology, who shall be sure that God and not the Devil has been born afresh into the soul ? Harmless perhaps to the educated, whom it calls upon to renounce their knowledge, Eckehart's doctrine becomes in the hands of the ignorant a most dangerous weapon. In the place of laborious toil, by which truth alone can be won, it allows the individual consciousness to claim inspired insight ; the emotions of the individual alone tell him whether he is in possession of the " higher knowledge," and there ceases to be a standard of truth outside individual caprice. Brilliant as are portions of Eckehart's phenomenology, and powerful as his language often is when expatiating on the goal of his practical theology, there hangs over the whole a strangely oppressive atmosphere of possible fanaticism which warns the thinker against trusting in any such version of Christianity,[1] in any such perversion of the ideas of Averroes.

[1] On the effects of an extreme form of 'rebirth' under the influence of strong emotional excitement, cp. Döllinger, *Kirche und Kirchen*, 333, 340, &c. : " The whole intellectual and moral character is ruined."

VIII.

HUMANISM IN GERMANY.[1]

Sancte Socrates, ora pro nobis!

THE forty years which preceded the Reformation have long been recognized as a period of intense intellectual activity, as an age alike of conscious and unconscious protestation. Everybody was protesting; claiming for themselves freedom of thought and freedom of action. Much of this protest, it is true, was of a blind, clumsy character, yet the revolt against established forms was none the less real. In every conceivable phase of life there was a rebellion of the individual against the old religious socialism and its failing institutions. The old method of teaching, the old theological philosophy, the old legendary history, the old magical natural science—these, one and all, with a myriad other matters, were to be rudely bundled out of the way; they were so many restrictions to freedom of learning, freedom of investigation, and freedom of thought, which formed the goal towards which the new spirit of individualism was, albeit unconsciously, striving.

The mediæval theory and system of education were entirely subservient to religious ends. All forms of knowledge were ultimately to lead to the great mother of all learning— Theology. So long as the Church was a progressive body, so long as her theology was not definitely fixed, nor her dogma thoroughly crystallized out, so long as monk and priest were the best educated men in the community, and, as such, the great teachers of the folk—so long this system was productive of good. For a time philosophy might well

[1] Reprinted from the *Westminster Review*, April 1, 1883.

submit to be handmaiden to theology; while the latter was herself developing, there was nothing to absolutely check philosophy's own growth. Philosophy, as the handmaiden of theology, is usually termed Scholasticism. All that seems meant by this name is that philosophy must submit to the control of theology in all points of possible variance between the two. The gain to Christian culture of early Scholasticism can hardly be overrated; Greek philosophy was adopted and preserved for future generations, and was doubtless not without its influence in moulding and expanding Catholic theology. Such men as John Scotus, Anselm, and Abelard represented the foremost thought of their day; and the assertion that true philosophy and true religion are one and the same was, historically, not so very preposterous, even when by true religion mediæval Christianity was understood. As the theology of the Church took a more and more concrete and fixed form, owing to consecutive heresies and the need for a sharply defined dogma, more drastic measures had to be adopted to make philosophy dovetail with theology. The teaching of Aristotle must be somewhat forcibly modified, that it might give support to the doctrines of the Church. Still there was a vast amount of genuine thought (nowadays sadly neglected!) in the later Scholastics, such as Albert the Great, the so-called " Universal Doctor," Thomas Aquinas, the "Angelic Doctor," Duns Scotus, the "Subtle Doctor," and William of Occam, the "Invincible Doctor." These men did probably all that was possible to harmonize natural and revealed religion; to preserve the peace between reason and faith. With them Scholasticism wrote itself out. Philosophy could go no further till she was free of theology.

As the general knowledge of man develops, his formulated system of thought—his philosophy—must develop too; but in this case his philosophy was choked beneath a stagnant theology. As Carlyle would express it, mankind was outgrowing these youthful clothes. Yet the Church would not give up her theology—that, in her eyes, was a fixed and eternal truth. Accordingly, these old thinkers, these universal, angelic, subtle, and invincible doctors, were brandished

about by monk-learning, and used as a means of crushing
any spark of new truth which did not quite dovetail with a
crystallized theology. "You do not believe the Angelic
Doctor ? You say the Subtle Doctor is in error ? You have
doubts as to the incontestability of the Invincible Doctor ?
You are a heretic—this deserves to be purged with fire ! "
Shortly, although the theologians might themselves squabble
over the merits of their various learned and holy doctors, yet
each group gave their favourite a position of far greater importance and authority than they were inclined to allow even
to one of the Evangelists.   It is easy to note how the whole
of learning must, under such a system, fall into a dead
formalism, there was no place left for individual thought ;
all ingenuity was consumed in composing commentaries on
the various great Scholastics. On the small book of sentences
of Peter the Lombard alone, innumerable folios in the form
of commentaries were written—sufficient to stock a fair-sized
library. All intellectual power was frittered away in gloss
and comment ; all freedom of thought crushed beneath this
scholastic bondage. To speak lightly of the Angelic Doctor,
or to laugh at Peter the Lombard's sentences, was a crime
worse than blasphemy. What wonder that the intellect of
man rose in revolt against such a system ?—that a race of
men grew up protesting against this slavery, declaring that
this dead formalism should no longer obscure the light ?
What wonder that, as this new spirit grew stronger and
stronger, and became more and more conscious of its power,
it waxed intolerant and even abusive of the old monkish
learning ; held up its supporters to the world's ridicule as
"obscure men," and mocked the childish petticoats which it
had itself only just laid aside ? This new spirit which is
to shake off the old bondage and divide Germany into two
hostile camps is the so-called *Humanism ;* its adherents are
the so-called *Humanists,* or, from their proficiency in the
classical languages, *poets.* Their opponents are the monks or
scholastic teachers, the "obscure men," or the "propagators
of sophistry and barbarism."

Such is the spiritual origin of Humanism ; its outward

or historical birth has been usually associated with the capture of Constantinople by the Turks in 1453, whereby great numbers of Greeks were scattered over Southern Europe, especially Italy. These men endeavoured to earn a livelihood by teaching their language, and thus gave rise to a considerable number of Greek students. The Greek tongue, with its all-valuable literature, was new life to the souls of men cramped in the old formal thought. The intellect of man began to breathe afresh, taking in long draughts of this new atmosphere. It found in this classic literature a truth and a freedom which mediæval Scholasticism no longer presented. It discovered something which was worth studying for itself; the end of which was not a barren theology—nay, which in the end might be opposed to theology, for it would lead to a new system of Biblical criticism and a new system of Biblical exegesis, which would refuse to submit themselves to Catholic dogma. The monks were not slow to recognize this feature of Humanism. "He is a poet and speaks Greek, therefore he is a bad Christian," cried the more ignorant of their number. "The monk is a cowl-bearing monster," retorted the Humanist.

To Italy, however, those who would trace the outward growth of German Humanism must turn. Rudolf Agricola, the pupil of Thomas à Kempis and Father of German Humanism, spends seven years in Italy, studying the classical languages. "In autumn," writes Erasmus, "I shall, if possible, visit Italy, and take my doctor's degree; see you, in whom is my hope, that I am provided with the means. I have been giving my whole mind to the study of Greek, and as soon as I get money I shall buy first Greek books, and then clothes."

Reuchlin, afterwards the great champion of German Humanism, learns Greek from two exiles, the one in Basel and the other in Paris. "To the Latin was then added the Greek," he writes, "the knowledge of which is absolutely necessary for a finer education. Thereby we are led back to the philosophy of Aristotle, which can first be really grasped when its language is understood. In this way we so won the mind of all those who, not yet wholly saturated with the foolish old doctrines, longed for a purer knowledge, that they streamed to us and deserted the trifling of the schools. The old dried-up sophists, however, were enraged ; they said, that what we taught was far from Romish purity, it was forbidden to instruct anybody in the learning of the Greeks, who had fallen away from the Church.".

Such opinions sufficiently mark the connection between the Humanists and the study of Greek. They show, too, how the new culture must ultimately step into open antagonism with the old Scholasticism. These Humanists will soon discover a truth in classical literature which cannot be subordinated to Catholic theology. For the first time in the history of culture, Hebraism and Hellenism will step out as conflicting truths. Men will for the first time become dimly conscious that they owe as much to the Greek as to the Jew. They will begin to feel with Erasmus that many saints are not in the catalogue, and scarce forbear to cry with him, " Holy Socrates, pray for us ! " They will hesitate to believe that the souls of Horace and Virgil are not among the blest.

" Whatsoever is pious and conduces to good manners," writes Erasmus, " ought not to be called profane. The first place must indeed be given to the authority of the Scriptures ; but, nevertheless, I sometimes find some things said or written by the antients, nay, even by the heathens, nay, by the poets themselves, so chastely, so holily, and so divinely, that I cannot persuade myself but that, when they wrote them, they were divinely inspired, and perhaps the spirit of Christ diffuses itself farther than we imagine; and that there are more saints than we have in our catalogue. To confess freely among friends, I can't read Cicero on Old Age, on Friendship, his Offices, or his Tusculan Questions without kissing the book, without veneration of that divine soul. And, on the contrary, when I read some of our modern authors, treating of Politics, Economics, and Ethics, good God ! how cold they are in comparison with these ! Nay, how do they seem to be insensible of what they write themselves ! So that I had rather lose Scotus and twenty more such as he (fancy twenty subtle doctors!) than one Cicero or Plutarch. Not that I am wholly against them either; but because, by the reading of the one, I find myself become better, whereas I rise from the other, I know not how coldly affected to virtue, but most violently inclined to cavil and contention."

No words could paint better than these the protest of the Humanists.

Whilst the revival of classical learning came to satisfy man's growing desire for fresh fields of thought, it must be noted that this revival would have been impossible had it not been at first encouraged by the Church, had not its first promoters been stout supporters of her dogma and her forms. The theologians were not at once aware of their danger, they were unconscious of what was involved in this new spirit of individual investigation. They did not perceive that the final outcome of an Agricola or a Wimpfeling would be a Crotus Rubianus or an Ulrich von Hutten. Only experience taught them that "the egg hatched by Luther had been laid by Erasmus;" that all forms of Humanism and all types of anti-popedom were alike phases of one great revolt, one great protest which was the necessary outcome of the birth of individualism. The relation of the Humanists to the Church supplies us, however, with a basis upon which we may divide the whole movement into successive schools. We have first the so-called *Older Humanists*. These men worked for the revival of classical learning and a new system of education, but they remained staunch supporters of the Church, and never allowed their culture to lead them beyond the limits of Catholic dogma. Secondly, there was a school of Humanists, whom I shall term the *Rational Humanists*. They protested strongly against the old Scholasticism; they protested against the external abuses of the Church; they took a rationalistic view of Christianity and its creed; but they either did not support Luther, or soon deserted him, being conscious that his movement would lead to the destruction of all true culture. These men were the most conscious workers for freedom of thought among all the sixteenth-century Reformers. The majority of them still professed themselves members of the Catholic Church; rightly or wrongly, they held it possible to reform that institution from within, and so to modify its doctrines that they should embrace the natural expansion of man's thought. The leaders of the Rational Humanists were Reuchlin and Erasmus. Their party and its true work of culture were shipwrecked by the Reformation storm. Lastly, we have the so-called *Younger Humanists*. A body of younger men of great talent, but much smaller learning, who were ready to "protest" against all things. The wild genius of many of them hated any form of restraint, and their love of freedom not infrequently degenerated into license. Some of them were, in their fiery enthusiasm, self-destructive; others with age became either Rational Humanists or supporters of Luther. The presiding spirit of this Younger Humanism was Ulrich von Hutten.

In order to trace more clearly the bearings of these three schools it may not be amiss to refer briefly to a few of their members. Of the Older Humanists, first of all must be noted the three pupils of Thomas à Kempis, namely, Rudolf Agricola, Rudolf von Langen, and Alexander Hegius, afterwards Rector of the Deventer School, these men have been not inappropiately termed the Fathers of German Humanism. To them we may add the names of Wimpfeling, the " Preceptor of Germany," who may be said to have revolutionized the schools of Southern Germany; and of Abbot Tritheim, who helped to found the first German learned society—the Rhenish Society of Literature—and whose biographical dictionary of ecclesiastical writers is still a very useful book. These men, one and all, worked for the revival of learning, not only in the matter of the classical tongues, but in all branches of knowledge. To them is in a great measure due those few years of intense intellectual activity which preceded the Reformation, and caused Ulrich von Hutten to exclaim : " O century ! O literature ! it is a joy to live, though not yet to rest. Study flourishes, the intellect bestirs itself. Thou, O Barbarism, take a halter, or make up thy mind to banishment ! " But while the Older Humanists insisted on the importance, and worked for the spread, of the new learning, they did not hold human culture to be the end of their studies, but the means to a religious life. They in no wise saw any innate opposition in classical literature to the dogma of the Catholic Church. "All learning," writes Hegius, "is pernicious which is attained with loss of piety." "The final end of study," says Murmellius, another of their number, "must be no other than the knowledge and honour of God." In like spirit, Rudolf Agricola recommends the study of the old philosophy and literature, but "one must not content oneself with the study of the antients, since the antients either were utterly ignorant of the true aim of life, or guessed it only darkly, as seeing through a cloud, so that they speak, rather than are convinced, of it." Therefore one must go higher, to the Holy Scriptures, which scatter all darkness, and preserve from all deception and error ; according to their doctrines we must guide our life. "The study of the classics shall be applied to a proper understanding of the Holy Scriptures." Wimpfeling tells us that the true greatness of Agricola consisted in this : " that all literature and learning only served him as aids to purify himself from all passions and to work by faith and prayer on the great building of which God is the architect." When we note that Hegius, by "piety," meant a child-like belief in the Catholic faith ; that Murmellius, by "a knowledge of God," meant an acquaintance with Catholic dogma, and that Wimpfeling understood, by the "great building of which God is the architect," the Catholic Church ; when we note these things, we may be sure that the Older Humanists were very far from throwing off the old Scholastic bondage. The new learning was to be for them subservient to the old theology ; they attempted to put new wine into the old skins. Perhaps the inconsistency of their standpoint might be best expressed by terming them *Scholastic Humanists*.

One of the most remarkable of these Scholastic Humanists, a man whose immense learning almost made his scholasticism a caricature, was the famous, much-abused opponent of Luther—Dr. Johann Eck. This man, we are told by the

Protestants, was vain, ambitious, and wanting in all religious
principles: the sole aim of his life, according to D'Aubigné,
was to "make a sensation." On the other hand, the
Catholics tell us that he was a man of unusual talent,
possessing a rare freshness and elasticity of mind, and with
deep inner conviction of the truth of the Catholic Church.
How are we to judge the man whom Luther termed the
"organ of the devil," and Carlstadt the "father of asses,"
but upon whose gravestone stands written that "great in
doctrine, great in intellect, he fought boldly in the army of
Christ," and whose University for long years preserved his
desk, his hood and cap, as valued relics of an honoured
master? If there is anything which makes us inclined to
doubt the Protestant assertions, it is the abuse that party
poured upon him in the grave. Luther writes that the
impious man has died of four of the most terrible diseases,
including among them raving madness; while the polished
Melanchthon does not scorn to mock the great opponent with
the epitaph:—

> " Multa vorans et multa bibens, mala plurima dicens,
>   Eccius hac posuit putre cadaver humo."

Let us at least be as just to the peasant's son of
Ottobeuern as we are to the peasant's son of Eisleben. In
Eck's writings there is, as a rule, a moderation of language
and a depth of research, from which Luther might have learnt
a lesson. That he employed a vast learning and no little
talent in defending a narrow dogma is a charge which may
be brought against any professional theologian — certainly
against Luther. He was not unconscious of the abuses of the
Church; but he believed in reformation from within: above
all, he held that her doctrines and her abuses were matters
to be kept distinct, and respect for the one did not involve
approval of the other. We, who naturally fail to sympathize
with this supporter of the old theological bondage, may at
least allow that he acted honestly, and fought for his real
convictions. The man who, in his youth, was the friend of
Brant, Reuchlin, and Wimpfeling, the leaders of German

thought; who, in early manhood, helped to humanize the
University of Ingoldstadt, and who raised himself, by a life
of study, from the peasant ranks to the foremost place among
Catholic theologians, deserves at least our respect, though
he applied his talents in a forlorn cause. If we find in him
a certain pride of his own learning, which nowadays might
have earned him the title of " prig," the cause is obvious
when we read the account he himself gives us of his own
education :—

" After I had learnt the elements, Cato was explained to
me together with the Latin Idioms of Paul Niavis, Æsop's
Fables, the Comedy of Aretin, the Elegy of Alda (?), and
Seneca's Treatise on Virtue; then the letters of Gasparinus,
the Josephinus of Gerson, St. Jerome's prologue to the Bible ;
Boethius on discipline, Seneca's Ad Lucilium, the whole of
Terence, the first six books of Virgil's Ænead, and Boethius
on the Consolation of Philosophy. I was practised also in
the five treatises of Isidore on Dialectic. In the afternoons
my uncle read with me the legal and historical books of the
Old Testament, the four Gospels, and the Acts of the Apostles;
I read also a work on the four last things, one on the soul, a
part of Augustine's speeches to the Hermits, Augustine of
Ancona on the Power of the Church, an introduction to the
study of law, the four chapters of the third book of the de-
cretals with the glosses. Panormitanus' Rules of Law in
alphabetical order I learnt by heart. Over and above this
I heard in school the Bucolics of Virgil, Theodulus, and the
six tractates of Isidore. The curate of my uncle explained
to me the Gospels, Cicero's work on Friendship, St. Basil's
introduction to the study of literature, and Homer's Trojan
War. Of my own accord I read the whole History of Lom-
bardy, the greater part of the Fortress of the Faith, and
many other scholastic and German books, although at that
time the study of literature was not in its bloom." [1]

Having accomplished all this, Eck went at *twelve years*
old to the University of Heidelberg, and in his *fifteenth year*

---

[1] *Seneca de Virtutibus* and *Cato* are the well-known mediæval
apocryphal classics.

was made Master of Arts by the University of Tübingen.
Such an education must necessarily have a prig-creating
tendency. It may very profitably be compared with that
of Melanchthon some few years later, and that of John Stuart
Mill in our own day.

Those who will take the trouble to investigate the course
of Eck's boyish studies will see at once why he combined
Scholasticism and Humanism. That he was a Scholastic,
subordinated all his culture to theology, his works sufficiently
prove ; that he was a Humanist the following quotation will
evidence. It is not unworthy of Ulrich von Hutten :—" I
praise our century wherein, after we have given barbarism
notice to quit, the youth is instructed in the best fashion ;
throughout Germany the most excellent speakers of the
Latin and Greek languages are to be found. How many
restorers of the fine arts now flourish, who, removing the
superfluous and unneedful from the old authors, make all
more brilliant, purer, and more attractive ; men who bring
the great authors of the past again to light, who translate
afresh the Greek and Hebrew. Truly we may hold ourselves
fortunate that we live in such a century ! "

Other types of the Older Humanists, who present us with
instructive pictures, are the Abbot Tritheim and Rudolf Agricola. The worthy abbot seems to have been an " all-round "
genius, who corresponded with the learned of Europe upon
all topics, and was never tired of collecting information of
every kind. Well versed in Hebrew and Greek, he did not
neglect to cultivate the natural sciences just bursting into life,
and he did it in no slavish way. Of astrology, to which men
of greater name than he have fallen prey (Melanchthon's
belief in the stars was a source of constant annoyance
to Luther), he would hear nothing. " The stars," said
he, " have no mastery over us." " The spirit is free, not
subject to the stars, it is neither influenced by them nor follows their motions." In his library at Sponheim, the collection of valuable books and manuscripts was the admiration
of the learned world. Visitors from all parts of Europe,
doctors, masters of arts, nay, even princes, prelates, and the

nobility came to study therein, and were put up, even for
months, free of expense by the genial abbot. Round him, too,
under their president Dalberg, gathered the distinguished
members of the Rhenish Society of Literature, Conrad
Celtes, Reuchlin, Wimpfeling, Zasius, Peutinger, and Pirkheimer, the two latter representatives respectively of the culture of the citizens of Augsburg and Nürnberg. These men
met together in a sort of discussion club to criticize each
other's writings and theories in all fields of knowledge. For
Tritheim, however, the authority of the Church is to be
decisive on all points, and the highest study is theology.
Strangely enough, he teaches that theology must busy itself
more with the Holy Scriptures; he does not see how, in so
doing, he is raising the question whether the Bible and
Catholic theology are in perfect agreement—how he is pre-
paring the way for Luther with his: " I will believe no human
institution, no human tradition, unless you can prove it in
the Bible." No, for Tritheim the Catholic Church and the
Bible confirm one another, and he tells us that the Church
alone, on doubtful points, must interpret Scripture, and he
who dares to reject her interpretation has denied the gospel
of Christ. The worthy abbot is clearly very far from protesting; he cannot see that the ultimate outcome of the
studies he fosters will be to make each man *think* for himself;
to make each man pope, church, and priest of his own faith.
Shortly, he is unconscious of freedom of thought.

Rudolf Agricola, termed by his contemporaries a second
Virgil, and whose services to German Humanism have been
compared with those of Petrarca to Italian, was one of the
kindliest figures of the whole movement; to spread culture in
his fatherland was the aim of his life; not only the educated,
but the great mass of the folk should be made to feel the
influence of the classical spirit. The great classics should be
brought before the masses in German translations and with
German footnotes.[1] He recognized the need of cultivating
the language of the folk, for only through it could the folk be

[1] Thucydides, Homer, Livy, Ovid, &c., appeared in German translations soon after 1500, adorned with copious woodcuts.

made to participate in the newly acquired fields of knowledge.
While many of the later Humanists were scarce able to speak
their native tongue, Agricola found time to compose German
songs, and loved to sing them to his zither. To him is probably due the impulse to the study of German history and
antiquity, which brought such rich fruits in Strassburg, under
the guiding hands of Wimpfeling and Brant. Perhaps thus
indirectly may be attributed to him the fact that Brant wrote
his *Ship of Fools*, the greatest German literary work of the
sixteenth century in the vulgar tongue. Such men must
suffice as types of the Older Humanists.

Their enthusiasm rapidly spread throughout Germany;
everywhere sprung up new centres of intellectual activity;
the men of all ranks and all occupations were beginning to
think, to demand a *why* for everything. Within fifty years
from 1456 new universities appeared at Greifswald, Basel,
Freiburg, Ingoldstadt, Trier, Tübingen, Mainz, Wittenberg,
and Frankfurt-on-the-Oder, while a great impulse was given
to the development of the old. Nor did this spirit reach the
universities alone, the imperial towns became centres for the
spread of the new culture. Round Pirkheimer in Nürnberg,
who, though a Rational Humanist, was in friendly communication with men of the old type, gathered an unsurpassed
group of men : Regiomontanus, the greatest astronomer of
the time, Hartmann Schedel, the historian and antiquary,
and a host of lesser men of science and literature ; these men
were assisted in their work by a noteworthy band of artists :
Wolgemuth and his apprentices prepared the woodcuts for
Schedel's great historical work, and Dürer engraved charts of
the heavens for Regiomontanus. On all sides there was real
intellectual activity. From Nürnberg there was a constant
interchange of letters with the whole Humanistic world ; not
the least pleasing are those of Pirkheimer's sister, the Abbess
Charitas, with the great men of her brother's circle. This
Humanistic nun seems to have been a woman of surpassing
power, and to have almost justified the extravagant praise
of Conrad Celtes. Her memoirs present us with a most remarkable picture of womanly courage and perseverance under

the brutal persecutions which befell her cloister in the Reformation days. In all branches of art and technical construction—nay, even in pure Humanism—Nürnberg stood second to none of the German towns or universities. A similar, if not quite so famous, activity developed itself in Augsburg, round Conrad Peutinger, who worked especially for the study of German antiquity; he edited the old German historians, and by his *Sermones convivales de mirandis Germaniæ anti-quitatibus* created an interest for the national past. A lasting witness to Peutinger's historical spirit is the monument in the Franciscan church at Innsbruck to Kaiser Maximilian, the patron of these Nürnberg and Augsburg Humanists.

These few remarks must suggest rather than fully picture the extreme mental activity which was created throughout Germany by the Older Humanists. We must, however, remember that these men were firm Catholics, and that this intellectual movement was entirely in the hands of the Church. The universities (Erfurt alone, perhaps, excepted) were under her thumb, and the new thought was only allowed in so far as it did not conflict with the old theology. All knowledge might be pursued so far as it was conducive to faith, but it must be at once suppressed if it proclaimed a new truth beyond the old crystallized belief of past centuries. This especially is the view of the leaders of the Strassburg school of Older Humanists; of Wimpfeling (see later pp. 198–209); of Geiler von Kaiserberg, the folk-preacher; and of Sebastian Brant, the author of the *Ship of Fools*. "Don't," they cried to the folk, for such is the audience to which they appealed, "be led away from the faith if dispute arises concerning it, but believe in all simplicity what the Holy Church teaches. Don't let your reason meddle with things it cannot grasp. Go home and cure your own sins, your idleness, drunkenness, luxury, love of dancing, dress, and gambling; when you have done that, which, however, is no light matter, then go and fight for the unity and purity of the faith; go and fight for the defence of the Empire. Battle for Kaiser and Church! Restore again the all-embracing Empire, and the all-embracing Church to their old grandeur!

Study by all means, if you can, but always remember the end
of your study is the understanding of Holy Scripture, the
refutation of heresy; in all this you will have need of the
unerring rules of the Catholic faith." Such preaching shows
us at once that for these men the old socialistic notions were
still sufficient guide in life; they still believed in Kaiser and
Pope, and tied culture to the apron-strings of theology.
They still believed it possible to vivify the old institutions.
They were unconscious of the movement they had themselves
set going. They knew nothing of the protest, the revolt man's
reason was about to make against all the old forms of belief;
they did not see that religion is a thing which, like all
thought, grows and develops, and that the Christianity of
yesterday will no more suit the man of to-day than the clothes
of his grandfather; that the very culture they were themselves propagating must ultimately oppose a theology which
had ceased to keep pace with the progress of thought. For
this reason we may term them Scholastic Humanists, not
from any contempt, because they did good and true work, but
since they remained in the old bondage, and did not grasp
the coming struggle between the new culture and the formulated religion.

Herein is the distinguishing mark between the Older and
Rational Humanists—the latter declined to accept the old
theological tutelage. "We are going," said the Rationalists,
"to think over these matters for ourselves. We are not going
to submit our studies to any antiquated formalism." And,
after thinking over these matters, they ceased to have any
very great respect for the old institutions. For themselves
they threw off entirely the old mental yoke, but that did not
mean that they proposed the destruction of the Catholic
Church. No! they held it possible that its framework might
be modified to suit the new state of affairs. They did not
preach to the folk, who were incapable yet of thinking:
"These old forms are nonsense; shake them off and destroy
their supporters." That sort of work was left to Wittenberg.
The Rational Humanists merely said: "Our first business
is to spread culture, to educate the folk, to tell them the

truths we have discovered; then it will be time enough for a vast public opinion to react on the Catholic Church. All we insist upon at present is the right to teach, to clear away ignorance of all sorts, even that of monk and priest. The 'obscure men' shall not silence us, but we do not term them a 'devil's litter,' to be destroyed by force. We are going to educate them, we are going to educate the folk to understand something better; our labour is not that of a day, but of long years. Some abuses, however, are so obvious, and strike so deeply at all national life, that we shall insist upon their removal at once. We must have the misuse of indulgences, pluralities, simony, the misapplication of the Church's temporal power, seen to immediately, please." Such is the teaching of the Rational Humanists, varying, of course, in the individual from active propaganda to quiet disbelief in the Catholic dogma. Of the two leaders of this party, Reuchlin and Erasmus, it is needless to say anything now. We have already mentioned the names of Pirkheimer and Celtes. One of the most remarkable Rational Humanists, however, Conrad Muth, is less generally known, and may be taken here as a type of the class. Like so many of the first men of his time, Muth was educated under Hegius at Deventer, and afterwards completed his studies in Italy. He finally retired to Gotha, where he had been presented to a small canonry, and devoted his life to study. Attracted by his personal influence and the charm of his character, a group of young men, whose names were soon to be resounding throughout Germany, gathered round the genial Canon. He may truly be termed the "Preceptor of Younger Humanism." From the Canon's house, behind the church at Gotha, spread the fiery youths who were to subvert all things, and protest against all forms of discipline. Here might have been found Eoban Hesse, who tried most things, but proved alone faithful to poetry; Crotus Rubianus, the deviser of that immortal satire, the *Epistolæ Obscurorum Virorum;* Justus Jonas, later secretary to Martin Luther; Spalatin, afterwards most respectable of Reformers, and last, but

greatest, we may mention Ulrich von Hutten, the glowing
prophet of Revolution.   There this little band gathered
round the older Canon, were fired by his eloquent talk, and
adopted his radical and rationalistic notions without temper-
ing them by his learning.   From this centre was directed
the battle of Humanism against Scholasticism; from thence
went forth the biting satires in aid of the Humanistic champion, Reuchlin, in his contest with obscurity; from thence
the youthful Humanistic evangelists spread through the German Universities; calling upon the students to protest
against the so-called "barbarism" and "obscurity" of the
theologians and monkish teachers. The University of Erfurt,
close at hand, was soon won for the good cause, Heidelberg
and Wittenberg followed; everywhere, where a "poet"
commenced to lecture on the classics, his lecture-room was
crowded with students, and the theologians had to expound
the works of subtle and invincible doctors to empty benches.
Satirical dialogues, Latin epigrams, street mocking, and even
ill-usage, were cast in a perfect torrent upon the old teachers.
Youth, ever ready for something fresh and dimly conscious
of the barrenness of the old, seized upon this new culture
without fully grasping its meaning or penetrating to its
calmer delights. Students no longer desired to be bachelor or
master, but to be "poet," a skilful composer of Latin verse,
and ready in the wit of Horace and Juvenal. These "Latin
cohorts" despised everything savouring of German as barbarism, even to their names, so that a Schneider became a
Sartorius, a Königsberger a Regiomontanus, and a Wacher a
Vigilius.[1] In this youthful party Humanism degenerated,
and while Erasmus, Reuchlin, and Muth viewed Luther's
propaganda with distrust, the younger Humanists flocked to
the new standard of protest and revolt, and so doing brought
culture into disgrace and shipwrecked the revival of learning

[1] It is often extremely difficult to conceive how some of the poets
arrived at their classical names. Thus plain Johann Jäger of Dornsheim
became Crotus Rubianus, and Theodorici, Ceratinus! Perhaps the most
ingenious adaptation was that of the Erfurt printer Knapp, who styled
himself Cn. Appius.

in Germany. It was a foretaste of the future, when in 1510, as the outcome of an anti-scholastic riot of the Erfurt students, the mob destroyed the University buildings, the colleges and bursaries, and, worst of all, the fine library with all its old documents and charters! It is only party bigotry which induces Catholic historians to attribute these disasters to the teaching of Erasmus and Muth; they were the outcome of that spirit of protest and revolt which accompanied the birth of individualism. The Rational Humanists, while working for freedom of thought, strove, so far as lay in their power, that that freedom should be achieved by a gradual evolution; the more violent religious party produced a revolution. Nothing will show more strongly the spirit of Rational Humanism than a few quotations from the letters of the Canon of Gotha to his youthful friends :—

"I will not lay before you a riddle out of Holy Scripture," he writes to Spalatin, "but an open question, which may be solved by profane studies. If Christ is the way, the truth, and the life, what have men done for so many centuries before his birth? Have they gone astray, wrapt in the heavy darkness of ignorance, or did they share salvation and truth? I will to thy help with my own view of the matter. The religion of Christ did not commence with his becoming man, but has existed for all time, even at Christ's first birth. Since what is the true Christ, what the peculiar son of God, if it be not, as St. Paul says, the wisdom of God? which, not only the Jews in a narrow corner of Syria, but even the Greeks, Italians, and Germans possessed, although they had different religious customs." "The command of God which lights up the soul has two chief principles: love God and thy neighbour as thyself. This law gives us the kingdom of heaven; it is the law of Nature, not hewn in stone as that of Moses, not graven in brass as the Roman, nor written upon parchment or paper, but moulded in our hearts by the highest teacher. Who enjoys with pious mind this memorable and holy Eucharist does something divine, since the true body of Christ is peace and unity, and no holier host exists than reciprocal love."

In a letter to Urban [1] he writes :—

"Who is our redeemer? Justice, peace, and joy, that is the Christ which has descended from heaven. If the food of God is to obey the divine commandments, if the highest commandment is to love God and our neighbour, so consider, my Urban, if those fools rightly enjoy the food of the Lord, who swallow holy wafers and yet against the Sacrament of Christian love disturb the peace and spread discord. The true Christ is soul and spirit, which can neither be touched with the hands nor yet seen. Socrates said to a youth, 'Speak, that I may see thee.' Now note, my Urban, that we only reveal by our speech the spirit and the God which dwells in us. Therefore we only share heaven, if we live spiritually, philosophically, or in a Christian manner, obeying the reason more than our desires."

In this letter Muth goes so far as to say the Mahomedans are not so wrong, when they say that the real Christ was not crucified. Another time he writes to Urban :—

"New clothes, new ceremonies are introduced, as if God could be honoured by clothes or attire. In the Koran we read : 'Who serves the eternal God and lives virtuously, whether he be Jew, Christian, or Saracen, wins the grace of God and salvation.' So God is pleased by an upright course of life, not by new clothes; since the only true worship of God consists in not being evil. He is religious who is upright; he is pious who is of a pure heart. All the rest is smoke."

Yet again we read :—

"There is only one god and one goddess, but there are many forms and many names—Jupiter, Sol, Apollo, Moses, Christ, Luna, Ceres, Proserpine, Tellus, Mary. But be cautious not to spread that. We must bury it in silence like the Eleusinian mysteries. In matters of religion we must use the cloak of fable and riddle. Do you with Jupiter's grace, that is, with the grace of the best and greatest god, silently despise all little gods. If I say Jupiter I mean

[1] Not the better known Urbanus Rhegius, but Heinrich Urbanus, a very interesting personality of the Gotha circle.

Christ and the true God. Yet enough of these all too high matters."

Muth had need of caution; the "godless painters" were exiled even by the Protestants for much less than this! A man who cast aside confession, neglected the services of the Church, and laughed at fasting, had reason, even in the neighbourhood of Erfurt, to be very careful. Another interesting letter is almost as venturesome :—

"Only the stupid seek their salvation in fasting. I am tired and stupid. That is due to the food of stupidity, to say nothing more severe. Donkeys, forsooth donkeys they are, who don't take their usual meals and feed on cabbage and salt fish." "I laughed heartily," Muth writes to Peter Eberbach, "when Benedict told me of your mother's lamentations because you so seldom went to church, would not fast, and eat eggs contrary to the usual custom. I excused this unheard-of and horrible crime in the following fashion : Peter does wisely not to go to church, since the building might fall in, or the images tumble down ; much danger is always at hand. But he hates fasting for this reason, because he knows what happened to his father, who fasted and died. Had he eaten, as he was formerly accustomed to do, he would not have died. As my hearer continued to knit his brows and asked : ' Who will absolve you bad Christians ? ' I answered : *Study and Knowledge.*"

Still a last quotation :—

"Where reason guides, we want no doctors. The school is the grammarian's field of action; theologians are of no use there. Nowadays the theologians, the donkeys, seize the whole school and introduce no end of nonsense. In a university it were enough to have one sophist, two mathematicians, three theologians, four jurists, five medical men, six orators, seven Hebrew scholars, eight Greek scholars, nine philologists, and ten right-minded philosophers as presidents and governors of the entire learned body."

These extracts will perhaps convey some notion of the man who gave the tone to Younger Humanism. With his ridicule of fasting, saint-worship, and outward religion, we might on first thoughts suppose he would support Luther. But, like Erasmus, he saw that the 'Reformer's' movement would destroy all true freedom of thought, and he remained formally in the Catholic Church. Luther's journey to Worms was followed by the so-called "priest-riots," in which the Lutheran mob stormed the house of the Canon of Gotha. From this time Muth's circumstances grew worse and worse ; a few years afterwards he appealed for a little bread and money for necessaries to the Elector Friedrich, but no aid came. Yet a little struggle with bitter poverty, and he passed calmly away with the words, "Thy will be done," amidst the turmoil of the Peasant Rebellion—that first out-come of the Reformation. He found at last the "Beata tranquillitas," which he had in vain inscribed over his door at Gotha. His death is very typical of the disregarded death of culture amid the noise of mob-protestation and the bray-ing of rival theological trumpets.

But though this nigh-forgotten Canon of Gotha was the preceptor, he was by no means the parent of Younger Humanism. Strangely enough its spirit has a far longer history than the renascence of the fifteenth century. The Younger Humanists were the direct descendants of the stroll-ing scholars, who, from the twelfth century onward, con-tinued to protest in life and writings against the Catholic hierarchy in particular, and the habits of respectable society in general. These strolling scholars are the material out of which the 'Latin cohort' was formed. It preserved their traditions, their wild method of life, and later, in its battle with monkdom and Rome, even adopted their satires and poems. It is impossible now to consider at any length this most interesting phenomenon of European history. A few remarks may serve to show its relation to Younger Humanism. We find these strolling scholars at home in England, France, Italy, and Germany; they were banded together into societies, as those of the Goliards and the 'Ordo Vagorum.' They wandered about from school to school all over Europe. Latin was their common language, and the capacity for drinking and song-making the sole qualifications for admission to the order.

At first all were clerks, but later they became less exclusive, and their numbers were recruited from every class. They led a wild, careless life, an open protest against all forms of social order. A monk, a long-beard, a jealous husband, were the favourite subjects for their satire; a good tavern, jovial company, and a merry-eyed damsel their idols. Their hatred for the Church was intense; not so much for her dogma as for the greed and stupidity of her priesthood. They poured out line upon line of bitter satire against Rome and the temporal power of the Pope; they were in the field centuries before Wyclif, and yet did much fo. the propagation of his opinions: traces of them may be found throughout the fifteenth century, and Luther shows knowledge of their songs. Their numerous songs against the dominion of Rome are a curious memento of protestation and individualism struggling in dark corners for more than three centuries before the Reformation. There is a genuine ring of true poetry about some of these verses which makes them one of the most valuable literary productions of mediæval Latinity. Strolling scholars, too, had their 'poets' and 'archpoets' long before Humanism was thought of. The Church in council and synod in vain issued decrees against them; that they should not be given charity; that they should be excluded from Mass; that they should be imprisoned and punished. They flourished all the same, they continued to make satires on the Church, to lie about on the public benches, to drink in the taverns, and make love to the burghers' daughters. They read their Horace and Juvenal, and filled themselves with the classical spirit, long before the days of Humanism. They parodied the songs of the Church in drinking songs; they parodied the words of Scripture: "In those days were many multitudes of players of one soul and with no tunic;" or, again, "In the spring-time the wine-bibbers were saying to one another, Let us cross over even to the tavern;" or, "What is to be done that we may gain money? The Pope replied: It is written in the law which I teach you: Love gold and silver with all thy heart and with all thy soul and riches as thyself; do this and live."

For these strolling scholars, as for Wyclif, Huss, and Luther, the heads of the Catholic Church are the disciples of Antichrist. More pleasing than their Church and monk satires are their love and drinking songs; some of the former possess surpassing grace, and the humour of the latter is undeniable.[1] There is no want of genius, but it is genius which has sunk to the tavern, has joined the order of vagabonds, and delights in roving over the face of the earth and protest-ing against all forms of established order. Such is the heritage of the Younger Humanists; they are the strolling scholars coming again into prominence. No one can truly appreciate the spirit or understand the origin of the *Epistolæ Obscurorum Virorum* who has not read the satires of the strol-ling scholars; the one was a natural outcome of the other. Such men as Ulrich von Hutten and Hermann von dem Busche were really strolling scholars under a new name. They led a restless, wild life, now listening in the halls of the universities, now serving as soldiers, or even the day after playing the highwaymen. There is a charm about their life which it is difficult to cast aside; there is the stamp of genius, though it be too often saturated in wine or openly dragged through the mire. If, in modern times, breaches of social custom have been on more than one occasion cast into the shade by the greatness of a poet's talent, we shall not find it hard to forgive Ulrich von Hutten lesser offences for a wider and more enthusiastic genius. Such, then, is the spirit of Younger Humanism—of the men who will by satire, wit, and even violence destroy the old scholastic theology; they will be among the first to protest, to revolt. They will join Luther, they will join Sickingen; they will eagerly deform and up-set, but, unlike the Rational Humanists, they are incapable of reconstructing. What the effect of such a party gaining the mastery of the universities must be, is too obvious. The old learning toppled over and carried the new cul-ture with it. Such was the end of Humanism and the

[1] Since the above was written, Mr. J. A. Symonds has, in *Wine, Women, and Song* (1884), translated some of these songs into English verse.

beginning of Protestantism — the meeting of Ulrich von Hutten and Martin Luther. All energies, all intellectual vigour were turned into theological channels. Culture in the higher sense understood by an Erasmus or Muth, disappeared.

" All learned studies lie despised in the dust," writes the Rector of Erfurt in 1523, " the academic distinctions are scorned, and all discipline has vanished from among the students." " So deep are we sunk," moans even Eoban Hesse himself, " that only the memory of our former power remains for us ; the hope of again renewing it has vanished for ever. Our university is desolate and we are despised."

In a like melancholy tone Melanchthon writes of the state of affairs in Wittenberg : " I see that you feel the same pain as I over the decay of our studies, which so recently raised their heads for the first time, yet now begin to decline." Surrounded by narrow uncultured spirits, Melanchthon declares Wittenberg a desert without a congenial soul.

Not only utter dissoluteness and disorder ruled among the students, but their numbers at all the universities rapidly decreased. In the fourteen years before the Reformation (1522), 6,000 students matriculated at Leipzig, in the fourteen following years less than a third that number. In Basel, after 1524, we are told the University lay as if it were dead and buried, the chairs of the teachers and benches of the students were alike empty. In Heidelberg, in 1528, there were more teachers than students. In Freiburg the famous jurist, Zasius, must content himself (1523) with six hearers, and these French! The University of Vienna, which formerly numbered its 7,000 students, was frequented only by a few dozens, and some of the faculties were entirely closed. Everywhere the same complaint—no students, or useless students. The old scholastic system was destroyed, but the study of the ancients, which was to replace it, had disappeared likewise ; the minds of men were directed into one channel only. Youth had no thought of study, but was eager for religious disputation, for theological wrangling. The rival trumpets were resounding throughout the schools, and their

noise was rendering dumb all honest workers.   Luther had
brought back a flood of theology on Europe, and men could
and would no longer delight in the sages of Greece and Rome.
We grasp now what Erasmus meant when he declared that,
" Wherever Lutheranism reigns, there learning perishes."

\

NOTE ON JACOB WIMPFELING.[1]

IT is impossible to appreciate the work of a reformer without
some conception of the state of affairs he set himself to
remedy.   I shall, therefore, describe briefly the type of
school-books in existence before 1500.   We have seen that
the chief aim of the schools was to teach Latin, and that
Latin was learnt principally for theological ends.   In the
twelfth century the generally accepted Latin grammar was
that of Donatus ; at the commencement of the thirteenth
rules from Priscian were turned into hexameter-verse by
Alexander de Villa Dei.   Both these books were somewhat
miserable productions; still it was possible to learn some Latin
out of them, and for centuries they remained the standard
school grammars.   Now, when Scholasticism lost its early
vigour, and degenerated into a mere drag on human thought,
it not only produced enormous folios on every line of the great
' doctors,' but even these poor school-books, Donatus and
Alexander, were absolutely buried beneath a mountain of
commentary and gloss.   This was especially prevalent towards
the end of the fifteenth century.   The unfortunate scholars
were not only compelled to learn their Donatus by heart, but
the whole of the commentary in which he was imbedded !
The absolute nonsense and idiocy of the commentaries can
nowadays hardly be conceived.   All their absurdities the
children had to learn by heart, so that, as Luther said, " a boy
might spend twenty to thirty years over Donatus and Alexander and yet have learnt nothing."   For example, a certain

---

[1] This Note was printed for students attending a course of lectures on
mediæval Germany, given in 1882.

commentary entitled: *Exposition of Donatus, with certain new and beautiful notes according to the manner of the Holy Doctor* (Thomas Aquinas), 1492, commences with ten considerable paragraphs as to what Donatus meant by his title: *The Dialogue of Donatus concerning the Eight Parts of Speech*. Thus the expression *of Donatus* is said to show that Donatus was the *cause* of the grammar; but then the poor schoolboy must distinguish whether Donatus as the cause of the grammar was an efficient moving cause, or an efficient moved cause, or a material cause, or a second cause, or an efficient first and ultimate cause; also the relation between God and Donatus as to the creation of the book and its ultimate end and approximate end. A like flood of nonsense accompanied every word of the grammar; a still worse muddle was made of Alexander. Long paragraphs were written on the nature of the man who first wrote a grammar, wherein it appeared that the first grammarian must have been a natural philosopher with a knowledge of metaphysics. It is argued: "Before the invention of grammar there was no grammar, therefore the first inventor of the grammatic science was not a grammarian. That is to say, the first inventor of the grammatic science had an imperfect grammar by nature; this he perfected by study and labour through his sense of memory and experiment." What wonder that if boys learnt anything at all from such a method of education, it was to quibble, wrangle, and play with words! School and university tended to the same results; argumentations and discussions were the order of the day. In these discussions the great end was to catch your opponent in a word-trap—to make him contradict himself even by the use of a double-meaning phrase or the like. To wrangle was the great end of university education; and a public wrangling would precede the conferring of all degrees. Such a method has given the name to the Cambridge mathematical honoursmen; such a method of public dispute, the theological wrangle, forms a marked feature in the Reformation. Catholic and Protestant held disputations. Luther, Eck, Melanchthon, Carlstadt, Murner, publicly *wrangled* over the various dogmas of their respective faiths.

So hot did the wranglers often grow, that in the Sorbonne a wooden barricade was erected between the contending parties to prevent them appealing to physical argument. Books were written to assist the student in "wrangling"—as for example: *The Incontestable Art; teaching how to dispute indifferently concerning all things knowable* (1490). Let us examine some incontestable cases out of this latter book. The two wranglers are termed the opponent and respondent.

Granted, the respondent will give something to drink to any one who tells him the truth, and to no other. The opponent says to the respondent: "You will not give me anything to drink." The question is whether the respondent ought to give anything to drink to the opponent or not ? If he does give, then opponent has spoken falsely—in which case he ought not to give. If he does not give, then opponent has spoken the truth, and consequently the respondent ought to give.

Suppose that Peter always runs till he meets some one telling a lie ; and first, Paul meets Peter, and says: "Peter, you do not run." The question is whether Paul has spoken truly or falsely ?

Granted that Plato says: "Sortes is cursed if he has cursed me ; " and Sortes says: "Plato is cursed if he has not cursed me." The question is whether Plato has cursed Sortes or not ?

Such are the quibbles which the schools taught and wherein the universities delighted in the fifteenth century.[1] The first to attack this method of education was Laurentius Valla ; but the man who, working on his lines, did the most for educational reform in Germany was Jacob Wimpfeling, while Erasmus put the finishing touch to his labours. Wimpfeling cut away the commentaries on Donatus and Alexander, and prepared a practical reading book and grammar for schoolboys. "It is madness," he writes, "to teach such superfluities while life is so brief." Now I think we can grasp that it was no commonplace when Wimpfeling,

[1] My guide is Zarncke : see his edition of the *Narrenschiff*, p. 346.

in his epoch-making book, the *Adolescentia*, commenced
with the chapter: "To the preceptors of boys, that they
teach them useful matters." Far from being a commonplace,
it is the *protest* of the educational reformer of Germany.

In this chapter he bids schoolmasters and instructors of
boys not to devote great time and much study to obscure and
difficult matters, which are not necessary, but to care rather
for straightforward things worthy of knowledge : not only for
those which strain the intellect, as the subtle knots of
dialectic, syllogisms with their first and second premises.
Parents and friends wish children educated so that their
studies may lead them to the salvation of their souls, the
honour of God, and the glory of the commonweal. The
ready minds of the young are to be excited to virtue, to
honesty, to fear of God, to remembrance of death and judgment, not to subtleties of logic. Do not encumber their
tender years with speculations, unproductive opinions, quibbles
of words, with genera, species, and other universals. These
very universals are taught as though the Christian religion
grew out of them, as though the worship of God, our reverence, the enthusiasm of the soul, had their foundation in
universals—as though the knowledge of all arts and sciences
flowed from them ! " Just as if the use of body and soul,
the government of kingdoms and all principalities, the happy
rule of all lands, the extension of the commonweal, the
defence of states, the excellence of the clergy, the honour
of the orders, the reformation of the Catholic Church, the
safety of the Roman Church, the strength of virtue, the
destruction of vice, the glory of peace, the escape from war,
the concord of Christian princes, the vindication of Christian
blood, the repulse of the Turks and the foes of our religion,
the end of human life, and the whole machine even of the
world would break down did it not depend on, consist in,
turn about universals ! "

Such is Wimpfeling's protest against Scholasticism in
education !

Let us consider his theory of education. Many of its
precepts will not seem new ; but they were new to the

fifteenth century; and not a few of our public schools could study them with advantage to-day.

Children at an early age are to be handed over to discipline, as they are then most susceptible. Parents and preceptors are always to ascertain what is the nature of the child's capacity; the mind of the child is to be measured and examined in order to ascertain for what study it seems best fitted. This method of varying education with the individuality of a child is too often neglected to-day; whatever its peculiar bent may be, it is treated as uniform raw material, which is all passed into the same educational machine; and the result is too often disastrous. Next, Wimpfeling tells us that children of high birth and position must especially be educated in order that they may set a good example to others. (He is thinking peculiarly of the children of the robber nobility of his own time; but the remark still applies.) They are not to be left to idleness, to give themselves up to boorish and violent amusements—here, as elsewhere, he is particularly bitter against those who spend their time in hunting—but to devote themselves to those studies wherein they may excel their own subjects. Why should these nobles despise all the labours and exercises of the mind? They ought rather to study the customs of the antients, the usages of their own lands and history, so that they may act wisely at home and in war.

Then we are told the various signs by means of which the existence of talent may be detected in a child. These are: (1) its being excited to study by praise; (2) its striving at the highest things in hope of glory; (3) promptness in working and shunning idleness; (4) fear of scolding and the rod, or rather looking upon them as a disgrace, so that on reproof the child blushes, and on being birched grows better; (5) the love of teachers and no hatred of instruction; and lastly (6) obedience freely given, an absence of obstinacy.

Since youth is an age lightly given to sinning, and unless held in check by the example and authority of elders, rapidly slips from bad to worse, Wimpfeling gives us a list of the

six good and the six bad qualities of the youthful disposition,
and suggests methods of encouraging the one set and repress-
ing the other.   Thus the six good qualities are: generosity,
cheerfulness, high-spiritedness, open-heartedness—that is,
not being readily suspicious, fulness of pity, the lightly feeling
ashamed.   The six bad qualities are: sensuality, instability,
lightly believing all things, stubbornness, lying, and want
of moderation.[1]

It will be seen at once how Wimpfeling makes the keynote
of education, not the knowledge of Latin, but the inculcating
of morality, or, as he himself expresses it, the teaching of
good conduct and morality.   He belongs essentially to the
Strassburg School of Religious Humanists, who hoped to
reform religion by laying less stress on dogma and striving
for a new and purer morality.   Such was the object of
Sebastian Brant in his *Ship of Fools*, of Geiler von
Kaisersberg in his sermons, and Wimpfeling in his pedagogic
works.   This makes the following passage of the *Adolescentia* peculiarly characteristic; it might stand for a manifesto of the whole school :—" The instruction of boys and the
young in good morals is of the utmost importance for the
Christian religion and for the reformation of the Church. The
reformation of the Catholic Church by a return to its primitive
pure morals ought to begin with the young, because its *deformation began with their evil and worthless instruction*."   Strange to
find in 1500 a strong Catholic recognizing the *deformation* of
the Church, and its cause; seeing also that its true reformation
can only be brought about by a process of genuine education !
Well, if Luther, seventeen years afterwards, had understood
this fact !

Wimpfeling's four means of correction do not show much
originality, yet they prove that even here he had thought and
classified.   They are as follows : Public attendance to hear
the divine word, a private talking to, corporeal correction
where verbal has failed, and that peculiar to the Christian
faith, namely, confession.

The old Scholastic system made Latin the chief subject

[1] Aristotle ?

of education with a view to theology. Wimpfeling, giving
morality the first place, introduced something beyond theology: " The instruction of youth in good morals is highly
conducive to the welfare of the civic and political community."
This apparent commonplace was a veritable battering-ram
against the old Scholastic education.

Wimpfeling's so-called *Laws for the Young* possess perhaps
more value for the history of culture than for that of pedagogic ; but they are not without interest for the latter.   They
run :—(1) To fear and reverence God. (2) Not to swear.
(3) To honour parents. (4) To respect the aged, and seek
their friendship and society. (5) To respect the clergy (here
the attention of the young is especially drawn to the state of
Bohemia, owing to disobedience to this law). (6) Not to
speak ill of men, especially those in authority (evil merits
our compassion rather than abuse,—Wimpfeling refers particularly to the Pope, and quotes St. Paul about resisting the
" powers ordained,"—the very text which Luther was afterwards to use as argument for implicit obedience to the princes
in their opposition to Popedom!). (7) Bad society to be fled.
(8) Also covetousness. (9) To be cautious against talkative-
ness. (10) To show modesty,—especially in matters of dress.
The dress of the students must often have been very improper
to need the rebukes here administered. Elsewhere in the
book Wimpfeling makes propriety in dress a point of religion;
long close-fitting tunics ought to be worn. Other forms of
dress are due to a total want of devotion and religion, or at
least to a desire to please shameless women. An improper
dress denotes improper morals; the dress, no less than the
tongue, belongs to the inner man. Many years afterward
Melanchthon, in an oration on dress to the students of Wittenberg, harps on the same theme.[1] (11) To avoid idleness
and seek honest work. The famous Dalberg is here quoted as
example of such work; his occupation, among other matters,
being the study of the ' vulgar tongue.' (It was from the
Strassburg circle that the first impulse was given to the study
of the German language and history.) (12) To be frugal. (13)

[1] 1480–1580 is the Dress-Deformation.

There are three virtues peculiarly necessary for the young, both towards themselves and others,—namely, that they should have firm guard over themselves; that they should be an example to others; and, lastly, that they should be loved sincerely and in Christian fashion by all, especially the good. (14) We have a law as to the means of increasing virtue and as to the efficacy of habit in a child. The keynote here is an expression of sympathy in all its doings. We must accustom ourselves to be moved by childish grief and childish pleasure, so that from the beginning even to the end of life children may hate what ought to be hated, and love what is worthy of love. Even as when we wish a boy to be an architect we show pleasure in his building toy-houses, so play is to be made use of to create and confirm good habits in children. "We ought to strive in all matters, even in playing, that we may turn the inclination and desire of children towards those things of which we wish them to attain knowledge." This precept itself was epoch-making in the fifteenth century, yet even to this day has hardly been generally accepted as a leading principle of education. (15) Against luxury; especially against children feeding and drinking too extravagantly. (16) Against foppery in general, but particularly against the curling of the hair. We are told it offends God, injures the brain, disfigures the head, creates a "sylva pediculorum," deforms the face, ultimately makes the countenance hideous, shows that the youth loves his hair more than his head, cultivates his curls rather than his intellect; and the saying of one Diether, an honest and valiant knight, is quoted to the effect, that a curler will be excluded from the kingdom of heaven, because the great and best God will not deem him worthy of the kingdom of the saints, who, not content with His image, His face, and His curls, with which He had endowed him, has not blushed to create these spurious things for himself—a despiser and hater of the divine gifts, and one who longs for strange matters. The just Judge, on the Day of Judgment, will not be able to upbraid the curler severely enough: "We did not fashion this man; we did not give these features; these are not the

natural locks with which we furnished him!" (17) Youth is
to avoid all perturbations of the mind, violent passions of all
kinds, great hate, desire, anger. The child should be taught
to bridle itself in great and little matters alike. (18) Life is
to be corrected by others' example; yet the child must not
argue that what others do is permitted to it. (19) The end
of study: this is to learn the best mode of life (*optima ratio
vivendi*), and consists in the true performance of the duties of
social and civic life in this world and in the preparation for the
next.   (20) And lastly, there must be willing submission to
correction. A list of the vices to which youth is inclined follows, but it presents no very great originality or merit. Five
things to be observed by a child when in the presence of its
elders or superiors may be noted : " When you stand before
your master you must observe these five things—Fold the
hands ; place the feet together ; hold the head erect ; do
not stare about ; and speak few words without being bid."

  Much of the rest of the book is filled with quotations,
proverbs, or letters from friends and admirers; these extend
over such a wide field as Horace, Seneca, Jerome, Gerson,
Petrarca, Solomon, Æneas Sylvius, Hermann von dem
Busche, Sebastian Brant, homely satirist of human folly,
and the folk-preacher of Strassburg, Geiler von Kaisersberg.
The letter of the latter is peculiarly characteristic of this
new didactic school. He mourns that the age produces few
poets [1] like Jerome and Augustine, but a host of Ovids
and Catullusses. Geiler finds in his own land an army of
theologians, but few theophils. It is the letter of a man of
deep, earnest, moral purpose, but of somewhat narrow power.
He is weary of the Scholastic philosophy which is choking
religion ; but his only alternative seems to be the reduction
of religion to mere morality. Wimpfeling caused this letter
of Geiler's to be read before the assembled University of
Heidelberg; and the reading resulted in the professors and students setting to work to write epigrams on the various virtues
and vices, which epigrams are inserted in Wimpfeling's book.
It is obvious that thus a great deal of padding is introduced

  [1] Plato was termed ' poet' by the Humanists.

which has very little to do with education. Perhaps the
only other matter which possesses any particular interest
are certain short sentences of Wimpfeling's own, containing
maxims for children. These were first inserted in later editions of the book. I translate some of them which seem to
have more general value for folk-history :—Love God ; honour
your parents ; rise early in the morning ; make the sign of
the cross in the name of the Father, the Son, and the Holy
Ghost ; put on your clothes; wash and dry your hands;
rinse the mouth, the water being not too cold, as it injures
the teeth ; comb the hair, particularly with an ivory comb
(if you have one) ; rub the back of the head with a hard and
coarse cloth ; say, with bended knees, the prayer Christ
taught his disciples; repeat the salutation which Gabriel bore
to the Virgin Mary ; repeat the same to your own guardian
angel, or say this distich : "Angel, who by the grace of
heaven art my guardian, save, defend, guide me, who am
committed to thy charge." (This notion of a guardian
angel was very prevalent in the fifteenth and sixteenth centuries, and possesses real poetic beauty. In Geiler von
Kaisersberg's *How to Act with a Dying Man* there is
an invocation to the angels, with special reference to the
"good angel, my guardian." The good and bad angels
accompanied a man through life, the one assisting, the other
tempting ; they may be seen in the woodcuts of the old law
books on either side of the prisoner, and they stand beside the
dying man in the well-known block-book, the *Art of Dying*.
What is now a poet's fancy was, in the fifteenth century, an
article of faith.) After prayer gird thyself to study, because
"the fear of the Lord is the beginning of wisdom ; " if there
is time, look through your next lesson before going to school;
pay great attention to your master; do not be ashamed to
inquire of him or of another wiser than yourself; practise the
Latin tongue frequently ; love Christ who redeemed you on
the Cross ; do not say, "by God, 'pon my soul, on my oath,
i' my faith ; " on Sunday and holy days read the lessons
appointed concerning the Lord ; in knocking do not violently
shake the door or bell, lest you be judged mad or a fool ;

beware of horses and water; never carry a candle without a
candlestick; carrying a candle for the purpose of showing
the way, go first although a worthier follow you; do not
place your hands upon the hips; do not examine the letter,
purse, or table of another; being called to meals, do not be
late, content yourself with the seat your host appoints, and
do not bring a dog with you; meeting your superior, take
his left side and leave his right free, do not change this side;
passing the cup among those at meals, do not give it into
their hands, but place it upon the table; do not enter unbid
into the kitchen of a prince (I suppose this means, do not go
where you are not bid, or you will be punished for it; it
may be connected with the mediæval German proverb: "At
court every seven years a kitchen knave is devoured"); do
not place on the plate bread you have touched with your
teeth; pour wine rather into another's belly than your own;
put all your things in their appointed and proper places;
avoid hot food; do not touch the teeth with your knife;
wash after cake, honey, &c.; who lends money to a friend
loses friend and money; the blood of princes does not make
good sausages,—with which enigmatical proverb we will
leave Wimpfeling's short sentences.

Of the other educational works of Wimpfeling, I may
mention: the *Isidoneus* (1497), a vigorous criticism of the
then usual methods of teaching,—the *Germania* (1501), with a
description of an improved gymnasium as well as general hints
on the education of boys and girls,—and lastly, the earlier
Elegantiarum Medulla (1490). This latter is a Latin reading
and exercise-book for boys, and was at that time a revolutionary step in school-books. On the title-page is a woodcut
of a schoolmaster seated on a large carved chair; in his
right hand a birch; below him, on low stools, are seated
three pupils—one to the extreme left is apparently constru-
ing from a book.

The slight sketch which I have given of Wimpfeling's
educational theories will, perhaps, be sufficient to indicate
the excellent work he did for German education.[1] He may

[1] Within twenty years 30,000 copies of his pedagogic works were sold.

be said to have humanized the schools; and his *Youth* may be fitly termed the first great German—perhaps the first great modern—book on education. His contemporaries, with just admiration, termed him the "Preceptor of Germany," the "Father of German Pedagogic."

His true value has hardly yet been recognized, partly owing to his having been a Catholic, and thus passed over by Protestant historians; partly to the extreme scarcity of his works, several of which are wanting even in a library like that of the British Museum.

For the present I must content myself with having indicated the magnitude of Wimpfeling's educational labours. Germany, at least, owes to its 'Preceptor' a complete reprint of his pedagogic works.

NOTE.—The reader will find excellent material for the study of German Humanism in the following works :—

J. Janssen : *Geschichte des deutschen Volkes*, vol. i. pp. 54-134 ; vol. ii. pp. 1-128. (Catholic bias.)

K. Hagen : *Deutschlands literarische und religiöse Verhältnisse im Reformationszeitalter.* (Protestant bias.)

L. Geiger : *Johann Reuchlin.* (Without bias.)

Th. Wiedemann : *Dr. Johann Eck.* (Catholic bias.)

D. F. Strauss : *Ulrich von Hutten.* (Slight Protestant bias.)

F. W. Kampschulte : *Die Universität Erfurt.* (Without bias.)

C. Krause : *Der Briefwechsel des Mutianus Rufus.*

B. Schwarz : *Jacob Wimpfeling, der Altvater des deutschen Schulwesens.*

IX

MARTIN LUTHER.[1]

Vernunft ist des Teufels höchste Hure.

DURING the past year there has been so much talking and so much writing concerning Luther that we might suppose the majority of people, for whom direct historical research is impossible, to have been provided with sufficient material for arriving at a true judgment of the man and of the movement wherein he was the principal actor. Probably more books have been written about the Reformation than about any other period of history. Yet since the time when history emerged from the mist of legend, such a mass of myth has never grown up to obscure all true examination of fact. Not only is this myth the predominant element in popular lives of Luther, but its influence may be continually traced in works having far greater claims on the consideration of scholars. The origin and growth of this myth are perhaps not hard to explain; the upholders of a particular phase of religion invariably invest its originator with a legendary perfection— all the great achievements of mankind during his century, and often those of an even more distant date, are attributed to him; all human errors, all sins of the age, are thrust upon his opponents. To the sect its founder becomes the saviour of mankind, and his adversaries a generation of vipers. So it has arisen that numerous well-meaning folk look upon Luther as almost a second St. Paul, and upon the Pope as undoubted Antichrist. It is impossible to escape the dilemma: the orthodox Christian must regard Luther either as nigh inspired of God, or else as a child of the Devil. There

[1] Reprinted from the *Westminster Review*, January, 1884.

can be no reconciliation of Lutheranism and Catholicism ; if the teaching of the one is true, the doctrine of the other is false. An " Interim " would be no more successful to-day than it was in 1548. It may perhaps be suggested that the contradiction is to be found in the Apostolic writings themselves, yet the orthodox Christian is hardly likely to make an admission which would certainly deprive those writings of all claim to inspiration. To be consistent, he must adopt one view or the other ; and having done so, Luther at once appears to him either as a prophet or a heretic—the discoverer of a long forgotten truth, or the perverter of the teaching of Christ. So long as there is a shred of dogma left about Christianity, there is small chance that Christendom will not divide itself into two hostile parties—the admirers and contemners of Luther. When we consider this fundamental distinction, and the proverbial intensity of theological hatred, it is no wonder that myth should survive and persistently obscure even the most prominent facts of Reformation history. Again and again scholars have shown that Luther's Bible-translation was neither the first, nor immeasurably superior to its predecessors ; that vernacular hymns and sermons were common long before the Reformation; that Luther's methods were entirely opposed to the spirit of Humanism ; that the German Reformation was by no means a great folk-movement—yet these and innumerable other facts have been persistently contradicted in the flood of magazine and newspaper articles which the centenary has brought into existence. Myths, which were first invented to blacken the character of opponents, and found a fitting receptacle in the scurrilous tracts of the sixteenth century, are still dealt out to the public by journalists and pseudo-historians as facts of the Reformation. We are told that toleration was a part of the programme of the German Reformers, a statement absolutely opposed to all critical investigation; we are told that Luther's coarseness and violence were only typical of his age, without the least attempt to inquire whether the nobler thinkers of the age were really coarse and violent; we are told that the Refor-

mation swept away intolerable abuses, yet we search in vain
for any scientific comparison of the moral and social conditions of the clergy and laity at the beginning and at the
middle of the sixteenth century ; we are told that
literature and learning were fostered by the Reformation,
and yet we find absolute ignorance as to the intellectual
collapse of Germany in the sixteenth century ; lastly, we are
told, on the one hand, that the thought of to-day owes its
freedom to Luther, while the theologians insist, on the other,
that Luther was by no means the father of modern Rationalism.   Here, the theologians, for the most part guided by
instinct rather than by research, are undoubtedly right.   The
whole history of Rationalism is as much opposed to Lutheranism as to Catholicism.   Rationalists ought never to forget
that thought could express itself far more freely in Basel and
Erfurt in 1500 than it could anywhere in Europe by the
middle of the century.   Not from the doctrines of Lutheranism, but from the want of unity among theologians, has
intellect again won for itself unlimited freedom.   To the
Protestant, who asserts that all our nineteenth-century culture is the outcome of Luther and his followers, the Ration-
alist must reply : " Yes, but not to their teaching, only to
that squabbling which rendered them impotent to suppress."
It is sectarian prejudice which has hitherto obscured the
history of the Reformation, and has led a distinguished
German critic thus to conclude his review of the literature
on the subject :—

"The field of history must be thoroughly cleared of all
such theological tendencies, whether they come from the
right or the left or the middle.   A true history of the
Reformation must fundamentally and completely reject all
theological and ecclesiastical party considerations and party
aims of whatever character.   A history of Luther is only
possible for him who contents himself with writing history,
and without the smallest reservation despises making propaganda for any theological conception." [1]

[1] Maurenbrecher: *Studien und Skizzen zur Geschichte der Reforma-
tionszeit*, p. 237, 1874.

The object of the present essay is neither to write a history of Luther, nor to endeavour to dispel all the myths which obscure our view of the Reformation. It will entirely avoid theological discussion as to the truth or falsehood of any particular dogma, or as to the degree of sacrifice of intellectual and moral progress which ought to be made in order to attain a phase of doctrine asserted to be most in accordance with divine revelation. This essay will confine itself solely to the effect of Luther's teaching on the social and intellectual condition of the German people. It will endeavour to raise the question : whether any progress can ever be made by a violent reformation, or must not always be the outcome of a slow educational evolution ? It will ask whether the folk as a body can ever be elevated by a vehement appeal to their passions, or whether all advance does not depend on a gradual intellectual development ?

Let us endeavour to describe, as briefly as clearness will permit, the position of affairs in the Catholic Church towards the close of the fifteenth century. It must never be forgotten that throughout the Middle Ages the Church was by no means an institution concerned only with the spiritual element of man's nature, it was besides the basis of the entire mediæval social system, and the keynote to the whole of mediæval intellectual life. All social combinations, whether for labour, for trade, or for good fellowship—trade unions, mercantile guilds, and convivial fraternities—were part of the Church system. A higher spiritual side was thus given to the most every-day transactions of both business and pleasure. It was the Church which formed a link between man and man, between class and class, between nation and nation. The Church produced a unity of feeling between all men, a certain mediæval cosmopolitanism, which it is hard for us to conceive in these days of individualism and strongly marked nationalism. So long as the Church was powerful, so long as it could make its law respected, it stood between workman and master, between peasant and lord, dealing out equity and hindering oppression. The battle which arose in Germany in the latter half of the fifteenth century between

the Canon and Roman laws was not a mere contest between
Church and State for supremacy, between ambitious ecclesiastic and grasping lay ruler. It involved the far more important
question whether the peasant should be a free man or a serf.
The Roman Law had been created for a slave State; the
Canon Law, Roman in form, was yet Christian in spirit, and
infinitely more in accord with the Christianized folk-law of
the German people. The supporters of the " Reception of
the Roman Law " were the German princes, for it increased
immensely their power and importance; each became a
petty Roman Emperor within the boundaries of his own
dominions. The opponents of the Reception were first and
foremost the leading Catholic preachers and theologians.
Wimpfeling recognized in the contest of the two laws " the
most fruitful mother of future revolutions."

    " That among the heathen slavery was at home, and the
greater part of humanity was reduced to an almost brute
service is, alas ! " writes the Abbot Tritheim, " only too true.
The light of Christendom had to shine for a long time before
it was able to scatter the heathen darkness, godlessness,
and tyranny. But what shall we say of Christians, who,
appealing to a heathen system of law, wish to introduce
a new slavery, and flatter the powerful of the earth, that they,
since they possess the might, have also all right, and can
measure out to their subjects at will justice and freedom !
Surely this is a hideous doctrine !   Its application has
already given rise to rebellion and rioting in many places,
and in the near future great folk-destroying wars will
break out, unless an end be put to it, and the old law of
the Christian folk, the old freedom and judicial security of
the peasants and other labouring men, be again restored."

    That freedom was never restored; the Roman law was
" received " throughout Germany, notwithstanding the advice
of Popes, the protests of the Catholic clergy and the murmurs
of the people. All who were interested in oppressing the
masses became eager workers for the introduction and spread
of Roman Law. As the Catholic Church lost power, the
advance was more and more rapid, till it became all-victorious.

in the Reformation, culminating in Luther's doctrines of the divine right of princes, and the duty of implicit obedience.[1] Thus Tritheim's prophecy was fulfilled, and that "great folk-destroying war," the Peasants' Rebellion, broke out. Only one other point can be noted here with regard to the Reception : the Roman Emperor had been head of the heathen religion; the new Jurists said to the German prince-lets :—"You, too, have a right to be Pope in your own land!" Such teaching was not long in bearing fruit.

These few remarks may suffice to show that apart from religious teaching pure and simple, the Catholic Church was the foundation of mediæval society. Any violent attempt to destroy that Church would in all probability be perilous to the established social life—it would lead to the triumph of might over all forms of right. Such, purely apart from dogmatic considerations, was the effect of the German Re-formation; it consummated the degradation of the free peasant to the serf; it destroyed or reduced to a mere shadow of their former selves the innumerable guilds, partly by decrying them as "Papist institutions," partly by re-moving the old Church influence, the old moral restraints which prevented their becoming selfish trade monopolies; above all, by suddenly weakening the old religious beliefs, it brought about what might almost be described as a break-up of German society—the immorality and dissoluteness of the German people in the middle and second half of the sixteenth century is almost indescribable. It only finds its parallel in the almost complete disappearance of all true intellectual and artistic activity. Such is no overdrawn description of what Mr. Pattison has fitly termed "the narrowing influence of Lutheran bigotry." The reader must not suppose that we at all blind ourselves to the abuses which had grown up in the Catholic Church in the fifteenth century ; we recognize them to the full; but in return we ask': Did the Lutheran Church produce a purer and more enlightened clergy; did it increase the moral and social welfare of the people; was it

---

[1] It is a significant fact that Luther burnt, with the papal bull, a copy of the Canon Law.

foremost in the support of literature and art; was it more
tolerant, more charitable, nay, even more Christian, than
that which it attempted to replace? Shortly, did it reform
more evil than it destroyed good? To none of these questions can we give an affirmative answer. The Catholic
Church needed reform urgently enough, but the reform which
it needed was that of Erasmus, not that of Luther. Had
the labours of Erasmus not been blighted by the passionate
appeals of Wittenberg, at first to the ignorance of the masses,
and then to the greed of the princes, we believe that the
Catholic Church would have developed with the intellectual
development of mankind, would have become the universal
instrument of moral progress and mental culture, and—
dogmas gradually slipping into forgetfulness—we should now
be enjoying the blessings of a universal church, embracing
all that is best of the intellect of our time. If the Church
in 1500 could contain an Erasmus, a Reuchlin, and a Muth,
who shall say that in our days Professor Huxley and Mr.
Arnold might not have been numbered among its members?
Luther, by insisting on details of dogma, dragged Europe
into a flood of theological controversy, and forced the Church
into a process of doctrinal crystallization, from which it can
now never recover. This is probably what was passing through
the mind of the great German poet when he declared that
Luther threw back by centuries the civilization of Europe.

Let us, however, examine still more closely the condition
of the Roman Church at the beginning of the sixteenth
century. What were the particular failings which pressed so
peculiarly for reform? We may note first the ignorance of
both monks and clergy. It is quite true that the typical
monk was by no means that combination of stupidity and
bestiality which the *Epistolæ Obscurorum Virorum* paints
for us. There were monasteries which preserved something
of the old literary spirit, and whose schools were not to be
utterly despised; there were still convents of both sexes
where the old earnest religious spirit was very far from dead,
and which were only broken up by the most violent methods
of "reform." Still the Church had ceased to represent the

foremost culture, the deeper knowledge of her time. She was no longer the intellectual giantess she had been in earlier centuries—a certain spiritual sloth had grown upon her, while wealth and power had deadened her mental activity. She was behind the current knowledge of her age and wanting in sympathy for its methods. A second failing—almost more grave, but yet closely linked with the former—was the moral collapse of the spiritual members of the Church. Clergy, monks, and nuns had lost consciousness of the meaning of their vows, and the spiritual calling had become merely a means of obtaining an easy subsistence. Let us grasp fully the very worst that can be said on this point. Many monasteries were little better than taverns; occasionally nunneries approached something still more repulsive. In an order of the Regensburg administrator of 1508, we read of the clergy seated at night in the public taverns, consuming wine to drunkenness, playing at dice and cards, brawling with their neighbours, and even fighting with knives or other weapons; the dress, too, of these tavern clergy, we are told, was luxurious and improper. Erasmus bears faithful witness to the condition of many of the monks and clergy in his day: "I know," he says through one of his characters, "some monks so superstitious that they think themselves in the jaws of the Devil, if by chance they are without their sacred vestments; but they are not at all afraid of his claws, while they are lying, slandering, drunken, and acting maliciously." Yet Erasmus does not indiscriminately abuse clergy and monks; he points out pious and worthy examples of both, and such undoubtedly existed in far greater numbers than Protestant polemic would allow us to believe, even when Luther was pouring out his most violent anathemas against the monastic life. Insults, threats, bribes were often insufficient to break up the convents in Saxony and elsewhere. The reforming Church Visitors frequently found a passive resistance, which could only be the outcome of a deep religious conviction, and which to the modern investigator throws all charges of intolerance and bigotry upon the shoulders of the reforming party. Noteworthy in this

respect was the system of insult and petty tyranny, which
the high-minded Abbess Charitas Pirkheimer and her convent
had to endure at the hands of the coarse and fanatic Osiander.   Her diary of these events is one of the most interesting
records extant of the methods of Lutheran reformation.[1]
Yet her experience was by no means unique; we possess
other records of a like kind which show how unfounded were
Luther's charges: that in no nunnery was there daily reading
of the Bible; and that among a thousand nuns scarce one went
with pleasure to divine service, or wore, except under com-
pulsion, the dress of her Order.   Such assertions as these,
however, have, on the authority of Luther, been handed down
from writer to writer till they are quoted as facts in modern
history books.   That the cloister-life of the early part of the
sixteenth century needed reform is indisputable ; but that
any real good was effected by absolutely forbidding the
members of the Orders to wear their distinctive dress, by
bribing the more worldly-minded to leave their convents, by
forcing the remainder to listen to Lutheran preachers abusing
the Catholic faith and the ascetic life in the coarsest fashion,
and finally by the appropriation as soon as possible of the
convent revenues, may very reasonably be doubted.   Considering how small a portion of those revenues was ultimately devoted to educational or charitable purposes,
Cobbett's charge against the Reformation—that it was a
plundering of the heritage of the poor—is not without foundation.   The doctrine of salvation by faith alone may perhaps
be most in accordance with St. Paul's teaching, yet it is
perfectly certain that the belief that works are of assistance, not only saved pre-Reformation Germany from a State
pauper system, but adorned her churches with the noblest
works of Christian art.   Luther's doctrine, misunderstood
if you please to term it so, was immediately destructive of
charity, and endless were the lamentations of the Reformers
that people had ceased to give as they did in the dark ages
of Popery.

[1] Charitas Pirkheimer : *Denkwürdigkeiten aus dem Reformationszeitalter.* Bamberger Hist. Verein, Bd. iv. Edited by Höfler, 1852.

The third great evil under which the Church laboured was the worldly aims of the hierarchy. The Church had become not only a spiritual but a great social and even political authority. The princes of the Church had power equal to or greater than the lay rulers, and they needed a princely revenue to support their state. Still more excessive were the wants of the Papal Court, and the means by which those wants were supplied was not at all calculated to make Rome acceptable to the German people. The national unity of France and Spain had enabled those countries to resist successfully the Papal extortions, and to establish a fairly equitable *modus vivendi* with the head of the Church. But national unity was the very thing wanted in Germany. Her princes were eager for self-aggrandizement, and there was no security for that permanent union which alone could dictate terms to the Pope; one and all of them were always open to the conviction of a bribe. This disunion of the German princes rendered a solution of the question after the French fashion impossible. The same grievances were expressed time after time at successive Reichstage, but no genuine attempt at self-help ever seems to have been made. The pocket has usually far greater influence than the idea, hence it came to pass that the mass of the people at first welcomed Luther as their champion against the Roman imposition; they by no means grasped that his enterprise would ultimately shake the very foundations of their social life. The grievances of the German nation against the Pope are very clearly expressed in a document presented in 1518 by the then Catholic Germany to Kaiser Maximilian.[1] The Pope, euphonistically described as "pious father, lover of his children, and faithful and wise pastor," is warned to give heed to Germany's grievances, or else there may be a rising against the priests of Christ, a falling away from the Roman Church even as in Bohemia. The grievances are endless, the archbishops and bishops exact terrible sums from their flocks to pay the Pope for the *pallium*, the sign of his

[1] *Gravamina Germanicæ Nationis cum remediis et avisamentis ad Cæsaream majestatem*, 1518.

sanction to their appointment; the income from German fields, mines, and tolls, which might be used for administering justice, exterminating robbers, and for war against infidels, all goes to Rome. So-called "courtesans"—that is, the Pope's courtiers, his cardinals, notaries, and officers—hold the best benefices in Germany, a land many of them have never seen. The money of pious founders, which should be used not only for the repair of churches and monasteries, but for hospitals, schools, paupers, widows, and orphans, is grasped by avaricious Italians. These and other ignorant priests add living to living. Learned and earnest clergy, of whom Germany provides a sufficiency, can find no fitting posts. The begging friars, mere agents of the Pope, need to be sternly held within bounds. If Maximilian will only remedy these, and a good many other ecclesiastical griev-ances, he shall be hailed as the deliverer of Germany, the restorer of her liberty, the true father of his country! It will be noted that these grievances are not in the least matters of dogma, they are precisely the difficulties which national unity enabled France and Spain to conquer.

On the other hand, it is well to mark the character of the men into whose hands these ill-gotten revenues passed. They were the patrons, the enthusiastic patrons of literature and art; they were by no means particular as to dogma, and looked upon the Church rather as a means of social than religious government. An anecdote of Benvenuto Cellini is peculiarly characteristic of their conception of the relation between religion and art. Notwithstanding that Cellini had just committed what can only be termed a murder, the new Pope, Paul, sent for him, and prepared at once a letter of pardon. One of the courtiers present remarked that it was hardly advisable in the first days of office to pardon such an offence. Then the Pope turned sharply to him and said:— "You do not understand this as well as I. Know that men like Benvenuto, who are unique in their skill, are not bound by the law." The Pope then signed the letter of pardon, and Cellini was received into the highest favour.[1] Cellini's

[1] *Vita di Benvenuto Cellini;* Colonia, p. 99.

autobiography presents us with no edifying picture of sixteenth-century Popes, when we look upon them merely as spiritual authorities. It is singular to mark the Pope jesting over the power of the keys at the very time when Luther is forging iron bands of dogma for Northern Germany. But these are the Popes who built St. Peter's, and were the patrons of Raphael and Michael Angelo, and the character of their religion is essentially reflected in the works of those artists. They were not insensible to the need of reformation in the Church ; the Lateran Council shows sufficiently that it was the ignorance of the monks and greed of the clergy rather than the will of the Popes which hindered reform. Yet they looked for improvement rather by education and culture in the spirit of Erasmus, than by a sweeping destruction after the fashion of Luther. They were as a rule tolerant even to excess, and only the progress of Protestantism forced the Roman See again into the path of bigotry, again to lay stress upon phases of dogma.

What the Popes were to Italy, such were the spiritual princes in Germany. Cardinal Albrecht of Mainz, whom Luther thought fit to class with Cain and Absalom, was one of the most cultivated men of his time. His Court, under the direction of Ulrich's cousin, Frowin von Hutten, may be described as the centre of German art and literature. Here men like Reuchlin, Ulrich von Hutten,[1] Erasmus, Georg Sabinus, Dürer, Grünewald, and Cranach, met with support and sympathy. Albrecht was probably neither an exceedingly moral nor a deeply religious ecclesiastic. There are several pictures by Grünewald of St. Erasmus and the Magdalene, which are portraits of the Cardinal and, as is supposed, of the fair daughter of one Rüdinger of Mainz. It is not so many years ago since certain narrow zealots in Halle wished to have Cranach's grand altar-piece removed from the Market-Church, because they thought they recognized in the face of the Virgin a portrait of the same lady. The table also, now in the Louvre, which " the godless painter," Hans Sebald Beham, prepared for Albrecht,

[1] Hutten's *Panegyricus* on Albrecht will be found in the *Opera*, Ed. Böcking, iii., p. 353.

breathes anything but a religious spirit.[1]   The leaders of
the Church, both in Italy and Germany, were what we
should nowadays term 'emancipated'; they were enthusiastic encouragers of the fine arts and of all forms of
humanistic culture.   Is it to be wondered at that they could
not sympathize with a movement which re-introduced
doctrinal subtleties; which completely checked the spread of
of Humanism; which in Augsburg,[2] Braunschweig, Hamburg,
Frankfurt, Basel, Zürich, everywhere north and south,
handed over the noblest works of art to the fire and to the
hammer; or which, as in Wurzen, by the direct orders of
Luther's patron, Johann Friedrich, the "Great-hearted,"
caused the works of art, "so far as they were not inlaid with
gold, or represented serious subjects (*ernstliche Historien*), to
be chopped up, and the rest laid by in the crypt"?   These
are matters which must influence the cultured mind of to-
day when judging the Reformation, however indifferent or
even justifiable they may have seemed or seem to the iconoclastic zealots either of the past or present.

Granting, then, the existence of serious evils in the state
of the Church, we may ask, whether these evils were
unrecognized by the more thoughtful Catholics of the time;
was there no attempt at reform, which might have avoided
that break-up of moral, intellectual, and artistic life which
followed upon the violent destruction of the mediæval church
system?   We reply that there was such a recognition and
such an attempt—a reform constructed on a far broader basis
than Luther was capable of conceiving; this attempt at
reform has been not inappropriately named after its most
zealous supporter, the Erasmian Reformation.   A comparison
of the standpoints of Luther and Erasmus is of peculiar

---

[1] Cf. Förster und Kugler's Kunstblatt: *Der Kardinal Albrecht als
Kunstbejörderer*, 1846, Nos. 32 and 33.   Also Hefner Alteneck: *Trachten
des christlichen Mittelalters*.   Description to Plate 136, Bd. iii.

[2] "We have never either prayed to the saints or worshipped their
images," writes the Bishop of Augsburg.   "These monuments and pictures might at least have been preserved from destruction for the sake of
their age and artistic merit."

importance at the present time, when we are so frequently told that, apart from all theological questions, we owe our modern intellectual freedom to Luther. The plans of Erasmus were shipwrecked by the violence of the Lutheran movement. We have to inquire whether our modern thought has not been the outcome of a gradual return to the principles of Erasmus, a continuous rejection one by one of every doctrine and every conception of Luther. Mr. Beard, in his Hibbert Lectures, remarks, with great truth, that while the Reformation of the past has been Luther's, that of the future will be Erasmus's; we venture to remind Mr. Beard that but for Luther the Reformation of Erasmus would have been the Reformation of the past as well as of the future. It is impossible to reverse the course of history, but it is not idle to point out the failures of mankind; they form all-important lessons for our conduct in the future. What was the means then that the Humanistic party adopted to cure those two great evils—the ignorance and the immorality of clergy and monks? It may be shortly described as the revival of the religious spirit by inoculating the Church with the humanistic enthusiasm, by identifying Catholicism with the newly won scholarship and its progressive culture. Ecclesiastical ignorance could only be conquered by a gradual process of education, not by driving monk and priest into stubborn opposition, but by teaching them to appreciate at their true value the higher intellectual pursuits. It required above all a reform in the teaching of the schools and universities with their theological faculties. When we look back now at the forty years which preceded the so-called Reformation, we are astonished at the amount of improvement which the party of educational progress had in that time achieved. It must be stated at once that the Erasmian Reformation was essentially rational rather than emotional, it appealed to men's reason not to their passions. On this ground it is interesting to mark the great emphasis laid by the Humanistic moralists on the identification of sin and folly. It is folly, stupidity, ignorance which are the causes of immorality and crime, not the activity of the Devil, or any theological conception

of an inherited impulse to evil.   Once make men wise and
they will cease to commit sin.   This is the keynote to
Sebastian Brant's *Ship of Fools* (1494), to Wimpfeling's
pedagogic labours, but above all to Erasmus's *Praise of*
Folly.   Like the great folk-preacher, Geiler von Kaisersberg,
these men do not discard religion, but they lay stress upon
its ethical side in preference to the dogmatical.   They see
well enough the abuses in the Church, but they do not
therefore cry out for its destruction ; they lay ignorance and
folly bare with the most biting of satire.   If we open the
sermons of Geiler on Brant's *Ship of Fools*, and mark
how he turns its satire into the deepest religious feeling, we
are convinced that the highest moral purpose is at the bottom
of these satirical productions.   They are not written for the
reader's amusement, but to teach him the deepest moral
truths.   There is an intense earnestness about these men,
they are imbued with the one idea of reforming the Church,
of purifying and elevating both clergy and laity, and the
keynote of their method is education.   Humanistic culture,
combined with a higher moral conception, shall bring back
vitality to the old ecclesiastical institutions.   The spirit of
Geiler, Wimpfeling, and Brant was in the main the spirit of
Erasmus.   He, too, satirises ignorance and folly; he, too,
preaches a practical Christianity.   The *Enchiridion Militis*
Christiani, he tells us, was written "as a remedy against
the error which makes religion depend on ceremonies and an
observance almost more than Judaic of bodily acts, while
strangely neglecting all that relates to true piety."   Yet
Erasmus in this very work recognizes throughout man's
capacity for good, and expresses his belief in the guidance of
the reason.   The whole scope of life is to be Christ, but
Christ is not an empty name, he is charity, simplicity,
patience, purity—shortly, whatever Christ taught.   Not of
food or drink but of mutual love was Christ's talk.   While
rejecting merely formal works, Erasmus still places man's
salvation in the practice of Christian virtue ; he is very far
from accepting Luther's doctrine of justification by faith
alone.   The book is full of practical piety, not a trace of

theological dogma, nor any regard to theories of redemption and original sin. Nevertheless it does not hesitate to attack superstition, the common abuses of the Church, and the ignorance and stupidity of the monks. "To be a Christian is not to be anointed or baptized, nor is it to attend mass but to lay hold of Christ in one's inmost heart, and show forth his spirit in one's life." Such is the keynote to the religion of Erasmus, and it is precisely identical with what Christianity means to the best minds of to-day.

The proposal of these Humanistic moralists was to reform the Church by educating her. They believed that the more the intellectual side of a man is developed, the less likely he is to be selfish and bestial. They put faith in human reason. In what a totally different fashion does Luther regard this safeguard of human action! Without the pre-existence of faith reason, according to Luther, is the most complete vanity; it is blind in spiritual matters, and cannot point out the way of life. "In itself it is the most dangerous thing, especially when it touches matters concerning the soul and God." Luther saw in the reason the "arch-enemy of faith," because it led men to believe in salvation by works; nay, he went further, and asserted that whoever trusted to his reason must reject the dogmas of Christianity. In another passage he describes the natural reason as the "arch-whore and devil's bride, who can only scoff and blaspheme all that God says and does." Elsewhere, Luther declares that the reason can only recognize in Christ the teacher and holy man, but not the son of the living God; and on this account he pours out his wrath upon it. "Reason or human wisdom and the devil can dispute wondrous well, so that one might believe it were wisdom, and yet it is not." "Since the beginning of the world reason has been possessed by the devil, and bred unbelief." This particular dislike of Luther for human reason even found expression in his translation of the Bible, and he has in several passages introduced the word reason, where nothing of the kind is referred to in the original text, notably in Colossians ii. 4, where he replaces "enticing words" by

15

"vernünftige Reden." [1]   It will be seen at once, then, that
the theologians are right in asserting that Luther was not
the father of modern rationalism.   He considered reason as
the chief instrument of the devil, unless its application had
been preceded by the mystical process of redemption, the
transcendental attainment of perfect faith.   It is obvious
that such a condition destroys the only ground upon which
reason can be treated as a basis for truth common to all
mankind.   Nothing marks more strikingly than this contempt of human intellect the difference between Luther and
Erasmus; it expresses exactly the difference of the methods
they proposed for the reformation of the Church.

Let us consider how this fundamental difference between
the Humanists of Erasmus's school and the Lutherans
expresses itself in their teaching.   We have already noted
what a great step had been taken by the Humanistic moralists
in the identification of sin with folly ; it at once suggested a
rational method—namely, education—by which sin might be
diminished.   What the Humanists, however, attributed to
folly, the Lutherans asserted to be the direct action of
the devil ; not by education, but only by divine grace was
man enabled to resist sin.   It was the perpetuation, if not
the re-establishment, of the temporal government of a
personal devil and his assistants.   Those human errors
which in the *Praise of Folly* and the *Ship of Fools* were
attributed to stupidity and ignorance, were as a result of
the Lutheran doctrine distributed to individual devils.   The
Lutheran preachers wrote books on the Devil of Usury, the
Devil of Greed, the Devil of Pride, the Drink-Devil, the
Devil of Cursing, the Devil of Gambling, the Devil of
Witchcraft, nay, even of the Devils which make wives
bad-tempered and induce men to wear inordinately large
breeches.[2]   The Lutherans held that among them Satan was

---

[1] Cf. 2 Cor. x. 5 ; Eph. ii. 3 ; Col. i. 21, &c.

[2] In the second half of the sixteenth century appeared a mass of
works under such titles as :—*Geytz-und Wucherteüfel, Hoffteuffel, Sauff-
teuffel, Hurenteuffel, Zauberteuffel, Fluchteuffel, Spielteuffel, Hausteuffel,
Hosenteuffel,* &c.

particularly active, because they were the only hindrance to his absolute rule. It was not a mere allegorical representation of evil, but a belief in an active set of personal devils, who walked the face of the earth, and could do bodily as well as spiritual harm to mankind. Not only were the people taught from the pulpit that Catholic clergy and laity were possessed of the devil,—"every German Bishop," preached Luther, "who went to the Augsburg Reichstag, took more devils with him than a dog carries fleas"—but we know of more than one instance where the stake or the sword was the result of this supposed intercourse between anti-Protestants and the devil. Children were taught, even in Luther's catechism, that the devil not only brought about quarrelling, murder, rebellion, and war, but by his instigation came storm and hail, destruction of crops and cattle, poisoning of the atmosphere. "Shortly, it annoys him that any one should have a bit of bread from God, and if he had it in his power, he would not leave a blade in the field, a farthing in the house, not even an hour of man's life." Luther's writings and his Table-Talk teem with reference to this active personal Devil. The hazel-nut tale and the ink-pot tale of the Wartburg are common property; but many other anecdotes of how his friends and he put the devil to flight have been expurgated from modern editions of his works. There is no obscurity about his doctrine of demons. Satan, he tells us, lays changelings and urchins in the place of true children, in order to annoy people. "Since magic is a shameful defection, wherein a man deserts God to whom he is dedicated, and betakes himself to the Devil, God's foe, so it is only reasonable that it should be punished with body and life." "There are many devils in forests, waters, wastes, and damp marshy places, in order to damage wayfarers. Some are also in black and thick clouds; they raise storms, hail, and thunder, and poison the air. When this happens the philosophers and doctors say it is Nature or the stars! The doctors consider diseases to arise only from natural causes, and attempt to cure them with medicines and that rightly, but they forget that the Devil originates the natural causes of these diseases. I believe that my sicknesses were not all natural, but that Squire Satan by magic practised his roguery upon me. God, however, rescues his elect from such evils." Again, in the year 1538, there was much talk of witches who stole eggs from the hens' nests and milk and butter from the dairy. Luther said, " No one should show mercy to such people ; I would myself burn them, even as it is written in the Bible, that the priests commenced stoning offenders." We shall be told that all this was merely the current superstition of Luther's age.[1] We allow that such beliefs were very general, but we must, at the same time, point out that the Humanists were, if perhaps not quite free, yet distinctly far more emancipated on this point than Luther. Very strong is Brant against those " fools " who believe in days good for buying, for building, for war, for marrying, and so forth. Great is the folly of all kinds of fortune-telling, belief in the cry of birds, in dreams, in seeking things by moonlight, and in all related to the black arts. The printers, who spread such stuff among the folk, are much to blame. Still more clearly does Erasmus speak out his mind in the colloquy of the *Exorcism* which, in the words of its argument, " detects the artifices of impostors, who impose upon the credulous and simple by framing stories of apparitions, of demons, and of ghosts and divine voices." Perhaps the dulness of Erasmus's orthodox opponents may be best shown by quoting the following satires which they have used to prove his belief in witchcraft. Once in Freiburg he was tormented with fleas, which were so small that it was impossible to catch them ; they bit his neck, filled his clothes and even his very shoes as he stood writing. These, he used to tell his friends in jest, were not fleas but evil spirits. " This," he added, " is really no joke, but a divination ; for some days ago a woman was burned who had carried on an intercourse with an evil spirit, and

---

[1] Osiander denied the existence of ghosts, but Luther remarked that the said O. must always have a crotchet. He himself *knew* that persons were possessed by devils, and that ghosts frightened people in their sleep.—*Tischreden*, Bd. iii. p. 337.

confessed, among other crimes, that she had sent some large bags of fleas to Freiburg." On another occasion Erasmus narrates with all gravity how in the town of Schiltach a demon carried off a woman into the air and placed her upon a chimney-top, then gave her a flask which by his command she upset, and within a short time the town was reduced to ashes. The following caustic remark is then added: " Whether all the reports about it are true I will not venture to affirm, but it is too true that the town was burned, and the woman executed after confessing."[1] We do not assert that the Humanists were free from superstition, but their rationalistic tendency was distinctly opposed to it. The resuscitation by Luther of an active personal devil brought back superstition in a flood upon Northern Europe. Nowhere were witches so prevalent, nowhere were faggots and torture so common as in the Protestant countries in the sixteenth and seventeenth centuries. It is not our present purpose to enter into comparative statistics of the growth and prevalence of witch-superstition. We recognize the curse of such books as the *Witch-Hammer*, but we note that it was the Humanists not the Lutherans who were struggling against such criminal ignorance. It must suffice here to quote the words of a distinguished Protestant literary critic with regard to one Protestant country—Braunschweig :—

" Religious fanaticism was revived by the introduction of Protestant doctrine and kept well alive by the representatives of the church. This the district has to thank not only for the increased severity of the laws against the Jews, but for the inconceivable number of witch-trials conducted without any regard to person. The devil appeared to be peculiarly active where the Gospel was preached in its greatest purity, and the contest against him more necessary than ever. . . . Duke Heinrich Julius looked at the matter

---

[1] It is worth noting that shrewd old Hans Sachs, who is always bringing witches and the Devil on to the stage, yet remarks :—

> " Devil's dames and devil's knights
> Are only dream- and fancy-sprites ;
> To ride a goat exceeds belief."

simply as a jurist and confined himself to what torture
brought forth. . . . During his rule ten or twelve witches
were often burnt in *one* day, so that on the place of execution,
before the Lechenholz, near Wolfenbüttel, the stakes stood
like a small forest." [1]

Closely related to witchcraft is heresy; it will be generally
found that superstition and intolerance are bred by the same
causes.   In the sixteenth century witches and heretics were
alike treated as devil-possessed.   Thus Erasmus tells us in
his *Praise of Folly*, how " an irrefragable and hair-
splitting theologian " had deduced from the Mosaic law—
" Thou shalt not suffer a witch to live "—the like law with
regard to a heretic, since " every *maleficus* or witch is to be
killed, but a heretic is *maleficus, ergo*, &c."   For those who
would know, even nowadays, what true toleration. means,
nothing can be more profitable than the study of Erasmus's
works.   The keynote to his position [2] is contained in that
wonderful bit of satire in the Divinity Disputation of the
Praise of Folly.   " Why should it be thought more proper
to silence all heretics by sword and faggot rather than correct
them by moderate and sober arguments ? "   Such was the
spirit of toleration which Erasmus would have impressed,
and, we may add, *was impressing* upon the Catholic Church
when the Lutheran movement destroyed his labours.   Noteworthy also is the contempt which the younger Humanists
poured upon the *Fortalitium Fidei*.   This remarkable
work, due to Alphonsus de Spina, may be looked upon as the
fortress of mediæval bigotry and ignorance.   Its first book
deals with the beauty of the Christian faith, its second with
the crime of heresy, its third and fourth are bitter tirades
against Jews and Saracens, while the last is concerned
with demons and witchcraft.   The whole is not a bit too
strongly described in the *Letters of the Obscure Men*, as *merd-*

[1] Tittmann : *Die Schauspiele des Herzogs Heinrich Julius.*   Ein-
leitung, S. xxvii.

[2] Concisely expressed in a letter to Cardinal Campeggio :—" Neminem
quidem conjeci in vincula, sed plus efficit qui medetur animo quam qui
corpus affligit."—*Monumenta Reformationis Lutheranæ*, p. 306.

osus liber, et non valet ; et quod nemo allegat istum librum nisi stultus et fatuus.[1] Yet its theory of witchcraft was accepted by the Protestant party, and its language with regard to the Jews can only be paralleled from the works of Luther !

We have now to answer an all-important question :— What were the views of Luther and his disciples with regard to toleration ? We have already stated that all Catholics who did not desert their Church were, in the opinion of Luther, children of the devil. Now, as such, they were deserving of no charity, and must be removed from those districts in which only 'pure gospel' might be preached. Had they been treated as heretics and burnt, the immediate result would have been war with the German Catholic States, in which the latter, during the earlier part of Luther's career the stronger, would probably have prevailed, and so Protestantism have been stamped out. Accordingly, in the early days of the Reformation, it was customary to banish Catholics, while Anabaptists, who were a weak body, were imprisoned and executed. When Protestantism was firmly established, then there was no hesitation in sending Catholics to the stake or to the block. There is nothing to choose in the matter of toleration between either theological party; Protestant and Catholic were alike intolerant, alike opposed to the spirit of Erasmus. It is simply ignorance of historical facts which attributes toleration to the Reformers. As early as the Saxon Church Visitation of 1527 does bigotry break out. In the Instructions we read that not only are the clergy, who do not follow the prescribed code of teaching and ceremonial, to lose their posts, but even the laity, who have given rise to any suspicion as to their conception of the Sacrament, or as to their faith generally, are to be questioned concerning the same, and instructed ; then if they do not reform their ways within a given time, they must sell their goods and leave the country. " For," remarked the Elector, " although it is not our intention to dictate to any one what

---

[1] *Fortalitium Fidei* is not the full title, but my early edition has no title-page. The book is thus quoted in the *Epistolæ Obscurorum Virorum*, I. Epist. xxii. : II. Epist. xiii.

he shall believe or hold, yet we will not allow any sect or
separation in our land, in order that there may be no riots
or other disturbances." Such was the mildest form of toleration to be found in any of the German Protestant countries,
and it soon changed to something considerably more severe.
But is not this a mere sarcasm on the name? This form of
"toleration" was supported by a noteworthy doctrine of
Luther's. Before the Peasants' War, when struggling to
assert himself, Luther taught that heresy could not be repressed by force, that no fire could burn it, and no water
drown it. Yet so soon as Luther saw other sectaries springing
up around him, and claiming the same privilege as himself,
he declared that as *rebels* to the State they deserved punishment, even banishment and death. This, then, is Luther's
doctrine:—The State is the head of religion, and all sectaries
are rebels to the State. Luther invariably associates his
opponents with murderers and rebels. Those sectaries who
meet in secret for their primitive service " have not only the
false doctrine, but meet for murder and riot, because such
folk are possessed of the devil. . . . Such knaves are to be
forbidden by the severest punishment, in order that every
subject may avoid such conventicles, even as all subjects are
in duty bound to do, unless they wish themselves to be guilty
of murder and riot."[1] Still further did Martin Butzer, afterwards distinguished as an English Reformer, carry this
Lutheran doctrine. If thieves, robbers, and murderers are
severely punished, how much more harshly ought the followers of a false religion to be treated, since the perversion
of religion is an infinitely graver offence than all the mis-
deeds of corporal offenders. Government has the right to
destroy with fire and sword the followers of a false religion,
aye, to strangle their wives and children, even as God has
ordered in the Old Testament. Is it surprising to find
after this another Lutheran, namely Melanchthon, approv-
ing of the burning of Servetus, and terming that hideous
deed of Calvin's "a pious and memorable example for all

---

[1] *Von den Schleichern und Winckelpredigern*, 1532. It should be noted
that at this time the Anabaptists were innocent of any political schemes.

posterity"? There are passages in Luther's works which can be cited against the execution of heretics; but the expulsion of those not believing in the State-creed was an essential characteristic of that system of State-churches which he founded. Those who will take the trouble to investigate the reports of the Church Visitors in the young Protestant States will have some conception of the extent and the accompanying misery of that system of banishment which it was no small portion of the Visitors' duty to organize. Nor was charity to each other any more a characteristic of the early Reformers than toleration of their opponents; the slightest divergence of view was sufficient to raise infinite hatred and abuse. Luther terms Butzer a "chatter-mouth, and his writings potwash," while Zwingli, Oecolampadius, and Schwenkfeld are "in and in, through and through, out and out, devil-possessed, blasphemous hearts, and impudent liars." Flacius terms Melanchthon "a papal brand of hell. . . . He and all his followers are nothing other than servants of Satan: since the time of the apostles there have been no such dangerous men in the church." Carlstadt, because he differs as to the sacrament, is termed, by his former Wittenberg colleagues, a "murderer, one who wishes only bloodshed and riot." Still more ignorant, still more violent and intolerant is Luther's judgment upon the Jews. We must search the writings of Alphonsus de Spina and of the renegade Pfefferkorn to find a parallel. That most delectable bigot, Herr Hofprediger Stöcker, has recently been republishing Luther's words as an incitement to further anti-Jewish riots. To begin with, Luther tells us that he will give us his true counsel:—

"First, that the Jewish synagogues and schools be set on fire, and what will not burn be covered with earth, that no man ever after may see stick or stone thereof. . . . Secondly, that their houses in like fashion be broken down and destroyed, since they only carry on in them what they carry on in their schools. Let them content themselves with a shed or a stall like the gipsies, that they may know they are not lords in our land. . . . Thirdly, all their prayer-books and Talmuds must be taken from them, since in them idolatry, lies, cursing, and blasphemy are taught. . . . Fourthly, that their Rabbis, on penalty of death, be forbidden to teach. . . . Fifthly, that safe conduct on the highways be denied to Jews entirely, since they have no business in the country, being neither lords, officials, nor traders, or the like; they ought to remain at home. . . . Sixthly, usury shall be forbidden them. All that they have is stolen, and therefore it is to be taken from them, and used for pensioning converts."

These are Luther's propositions for treating the Jews as he thinks they deserved, and which he tells us he would carry out in earnest, if he only had the power of the princes; nay, he works himself up to a stronger pitch of passion than this :—

These " impudent lying devils " ought not to be allowed to praise or pray to God, since " their praise, thanksgiving, prayer, and teaching is mere blasphemy and idolatry." The penalty for any act of worship on the part of a Jew should be loss of life. Not only all their books, but even " the Bible to its last leaf " shall be taken from them. Not only are their synagogues to be burnt, but " let him, who can, throw pitch and sulphur upon them ; if any one could throw hell-fire, it were good, so that God might see our earnestness, and the whole world such an example."[1]

In the face of such teaching we must solemnly protest against that ignorance which terms Luther tolerant, or which attributes to him the origin of our culture to-day. We refuse to recognize in him either the prophet or the great moral teacher. We could fill pages with infinitely harder sayings against the Catholics,[2] but we have chosen the Jews as a neutral sect, with whom Luther was not waging a life and

[1] *Von den Juden und ihren Lügen*, 1543. Sämmtl. Werke, Bd. xxxii.
[2] For example: " If we punish the thief with the rope, the robber with the sword, the heretic with fire, how much rather should we attack with every weapon these masters of perdition, these cardinals, these popes, this whole filth of the Roman Sodom, which corrupts without end God's church ; how much rather wash our hands in their blood ?"—*Opera Latina*, v. a., Frankfurt, ii. 107.

death battle. The effect of such teaching upon the people can easily be imagined, and, as example, we have already mentioned the increased severity of the laws against the Jews in Braunschweig. How strangely, too, it stands in contrast with the conduct of the Humanist Reuchlin—a man whose writings show a sympathetic study of Jewish literature,[1] and whose defence of the Hebrew books against Pfefferkorn's violent pleas for their destruction brought down upon him the wrath of the whole Dominican Order, and was the cause of that notable battle between the party of intellectual progress and the party of ignorance and bigotry—the "obscure men." Mr. Beard, in his Hibbert Lectures, writes:—

" Luther used the weapons of faith to slay reason, lest perchance reason should lure faith to her destruction. But who can tell what might have been the effect upon the Reformation, and the subsequent development of the intellectual life of Europe, had Luther put himself boldly at the head of the larger and freer thought of his time, instead of using all the force of his genius, all the weight of his authority to crush it ? " (p. 170.)

No truer words have ever been spoken with regard to Luther, and yet this same writer blames us, because we refuse to express any gratitude to the man who crushed all those influences which we believe tend most to the progress of humanity!

We must briefly touch upon one or two other points connected with intellectual development, before we consider the social effects of the Reformation. Under the influence of the Humanists, Germany had at the beginning of the sixteenth century attained to an unparalleled activity in art and literature.[2] Those who have not visited the galleries at München and Augsburg or the cathedral at Ulm, can form but a slight conception of the artistic perfection of that age. Innumerable art treasures perished in the iconoclastic storms of the sixteenth century, but enough remain to show the

[1] *De verbo mirifico,* 1494, and *De arte cabalistica,* 1517.
[2] See the previous essay on German Humanism.

wondrous activity, which was brought to such an abrupt conclusion. On the one hand, religious art almost ceased, and thus
a great source of occupation for the painter and the sculptor
disappeared ; on the other, wealth found baser demands upon
it in the religious wars which so soon devastated Germany.
Holbein cannot find a living in his fatherland [1] ; Cranach
and others are reduced to employing their genius on the
coarsest and most repulsive of theological caricatures;
Dürer laments that "in our country and time the art of
painting should by some be much despised and be asserted
to serve only idolatry." Luther himself, in his sermons
against the iconoclasts, blames only the manner of removing
the works of art from the churches, not the removal
itself. "It should have been preached," he said, "that the
pictures were nothing, and that it was no service to God to
put them up; if this had been done the pictures would have
disappeared of themselves." But others were far from being
so tolerant even as this: "It were ten thousand times
better," they cried, "that the pictures were in hell or in the
hottest oven rather than in the houses of God." And we
hear of the churches being stormed and the images and
pictures trodden under foot. Down in the south under the
influence of Zwingli the works of art in the churches of
Zürich, Bern, Basel, St. Gallen, and other towns, were committed to the flames or the melting-pot, in some cases by the
Protestant mob, in others by order of the authorities.
Honest Hans Sachs, too, bemoans the decay of art, though
he does not recognize its cause :—" Formerly art flourished,
all corners were full of learned men, skilful workers and
artists, and books enough and to spare. Now the arts are
neglected and despised, few are their disciples, and these
looked upon as dreamers ; the world runs after pleasure and
money; the Muses have deserted the Fatherland!" Still
more mournful is another follower of the new Gospel :—
"God has by the peculiar divine ordinance of His holy
word now in our time in the whole German nation brought

[1] Note the expressive sentence : "God has cursed all who make pictures."
—Woltmann's *Holbein*, p. 356.

about a noteworthy. contempt for all the fine and free arts."
Only just now in the nineteenth century are certain earnest
workers trying to rouse again among the masses that love
for the beautiful which gave art such a potent influence in
mediæval folk-education.

Equally destructive was the effect of the Wittenberg
movement on literature. All thought was directed into
theological channels, every pen was busied with doctrinal
controversy, the very printers refused to accept anything but
controversial and theological works, because those were what
found the greatest sale; the more violent, the more mud-
bespattering a tract was, the greater the number of authorized
or plagiarized editions. Even the stage itself was per-
verted to sectarian purposes, and a mass of plays concerned
with abuse of the Pope and the Catholic Church, checked
that advance which had been so marked under Hans Sachs
and his contemporaries. The remarkable didactic literature
and satire of folly ceased, or rather was transformed into
theological pasquinade, while, according to Gervinus, folk-
song and folk-book decayed rapidly with the sixteenth
century.[1] It has been occasionally stated that if the vernacular
literature of Germany was at a low ebb in the sixteenth
century, at least it produced one all-sufficing writer—Luther.
While recognizing Luther's enormous power of language, we
think that the oft-repeated statement, that Luther was the
founder of modern German literature, arises rather from
ignorance of preceding and coeval writings, than from any
careful comparison. Luther was distinctly a linguistic giant,
but he was only a step in a long development, and we are
not prepared to admit that controversial theology can ever
take rank as pure literature. That the Germans themselves
do not think so, may perhaps be judged from the tardy sale
of the last edition of his works. If we turn to the more
scholarly side of literature we find no one to replace Erasmus
and Reuchlin. Protestantism after a time produced the
plodding critic, and ultimately the independent investigator

---

[1] The decay, such as it is, may be marked by a comparison of Eulen-
spiegel and Dr. Faustus. We are not inclined to lay stress upon it.

and man of letters arose, but arose not infrequently to throw
off Christianity, or at least Protestantism, altogether. Some
will perhaps be inclined to cite Casaubon, but even if we
disregard the fact that Casaubon was a Calvinist, and
"Calvanism, intolerant as it was, was not so narrow, nor had
it so cramping an effect on the mind as the contemporary
Lutheranism,"[1] still it must be remembered that Casaubon
was no Humanist, he had none of the spirit of Erasmus.
He approved of the burning of Legatt, that "feeble imitation
by the English Church of the great crime of Calvin;" he
wished the body of Stapleton to be dug up and burnt, because
he had used extravagant expressions with regard to the
power of the Church. Shortly, he was narrow in the
extreme ;—a man who could believe that the Greek equivalents of Christ's Hebrew speeches were put directly into
the mouths of the Gospel writers by the Holy Ghost! But
even Casaubon was French, and Scaliger thoroughly expresses
the state of Germany in the words: "It is Germany, look
you, Germany, once the mother of learning and learned
men, that is now turning the service of letters into
brigandage."

Closely connected with literature comes the subject of
education. The work of the Humanists in this direction
cannot be overrated. How far was it adopted by the Reformers? The almost general reconstruction of the German
universities by the Humanists is too well known to need
comment here. One after another became centres for the
new culture, and their general intellectual activity is one of
the most pleasing characteristics of the age. Education was,
as we have before noted, the fundamental instrument by
which the Humanists hoped to reform the Church, and the
success of their educational schemes can hardly be questioned.
But they did not confine their endeavours to the universities.
Jacob Wimpfeling[2] was essentially a school-reformer. It
was he who broke down the old scholastic system, and declared
that grammar and dialectic were not the only or the best means

---

[1] Cf. Pattison's *Isaac Casaubon*, pp. 73, 244, 502, &c.
[2] See the Note upon Wimpfeling, pp. 198–209, above.

of expanding the youthful mind. He insisted on the need of inculcating reverence and morality, while special subjects of education were to be chosen suited to each individual child. Noteworthy for our purpose are his words in the *Adolescentia*:—"The instruction of boys and the young in good morals is of the utmost importance to the Christian religion and the reformation of the Church. The reformation of the Catholic Church to its primitive purity ought to begin with the young, because its deformation began with their evil and worthless instruction." Could the Humanistic conception be more clearly expressed? The *true* reformation can only be brought about by a *process of genuine education*. It would have been well if Luther had fully grasped this law of development! It is one of the most striking examples of theological bias, that the term "Preceptor of Germany" has been transferred from Wimpfeling to Melanchthon. It is true Melanchthon was one of the few cultured Lutheran teachers, and that he wrote certain school-books, but it is very doubtful whether even the titles of these works would have survived had not their author won a name for himself in other matters. How many have ever investigated Melanchthon's theory of education at first hand, and of those who have done so, what proportion have taken the trouble to compare his theory with Wimpfeling's?[1] Melanchthon's views as to the constitution of a "reformed" school are given in the *Instructions of the Saxon Church Visitors* (1528). One cannot help being startled by the barren formalism of his system; he has nothing to propose beyond the old Latin Trivial School, and he is years behind the Brethren of Deventer, and immeasurably behind Wimpfeling. In this respect Luther is far superior to Melanchthon; his book to "the Town Councillors of Germany upon the organizing of Christian Schools" (1524), contains many noble thoughts, and it was written before he had learnt to despise and fear human reason. But the main object even in this work was sectarian. Luther

[1] How theological bias reacts even on independent writers may be noted in Mr. O. Browning's recent *History of Educational Theories*, wherein we seek in vain for even the name of Wimpfeling!

had recognized the enormous power which the education of
the young confers on a church, and he was not slow in
endeavouring to avail himself of it.   His gospel and church
were to be the first to profit by the proposed educational
organization.   One of the greatest difficulties of the Reformers was to obtain men of any culture or learning as
evangelical preachers ; it is the constantly recurring dilemma
of the Church Visitors that they cannot dismiss the unfit or
even Catholic clergy, because they have no theologians to
replace them.   From Luther downwards we have constant
complaints that no one will study divinity *as a profession*, and
that the Protestant universities do not furnish the necessary
evangelical ministers. Praiseworthy as Luther's attempts in
1524 were, they by no means point to a great school reform.
The Reformers might have made the Humanistic education
their own ; they did not seize their opportunity.   Mr.
Browning has very truly observed, in his *History of Educational Theories*, that had the Protestants adopted the new
method of instruction, they might have advanced by a
hundred years the intelligence of modern Europe.   They not
only failed to adopt it, but by the turmoil of their movement
checked indefinitely the revival of learning in Germany.
Their universities and schools fell into decay, and it is
mournful to read their self-confessions, their consciousness
of the difference between past and present.

   The result of the Reformation, if not the later teaching of
Luther, was the handing over of reason bound and chained
to an emotional faith ; all learning was to be the outcome of
a " natural light."   Christians were taught immediately by
God ; the whole of the Aristotelian philosophy was a "creation
of the devil," and all speculative science sin and error.   In
Strassburg the Protestants proclaimed that no other languages
or studies beyond Hebrew were necessary ; others held that
there must be no study whatever but the Bible ; above all,
Latin and Greek were superfluous and harmful.   Preachers
declared from the pulpit that the inexperienced youth must
be warned from studying, and that all learning was a deceit
of the devil.   It is true that Melanchthon wrote that such

preachers ought to have their tongues cut out ; but were they not the natural result of Luther's doctrine of the blindness of the human reason ? Nay, had not Luther himself written: "The universities deserve to be pulverized ; nothing savouring more of hell or devil has come upon earth since the beginning of the world. . . . All the world thinks that they are the springs whence flow those who should teach the folk; that is a hopeless error, for no more abominable thing has arisen upon earth than the universities." What wonder that such words—sometimes the outcome of transient passion—should have been seized by the ignorant, and have led the folk to despise education ? What wonder that cobbler and tinker mounted the pulpit—too often quarrelling on the steps—and proclaimed a new age, when learning should not be the result of years of study, but a direct revelation of God to those of the true—their own—faith ? Erasmus, the apostle of culture, was bitter in his lamentations over the decay of all earnest study wherever the new *piety* appeared. Still later in the century Dresser, Protestant Professor of Greek in Erfurt, wrote : "There is no hope, no prospect of saving learning any longer; in this decrepit time its total decay and collapse approaches. Note how all learned occupations are laid aside, the schools stand empty, knowledge is despised." The Protestant Major loses all hope when he thinks of the glowing eagerness, the unrestrainable desire for knowledge in the old dark Catholic days of his youth, and compares it with the idleness and the neglect of study under the rays of the recently kindled light of Protestantism. From 1550 to 1600 we have endless complaints from the Protestants of the utter decay and callapse of their schools.[1] They could find (even as Luther in Wittenberg had found) no other cause to which they might attribute it than the direct interference of the devil, who must bear an intense hatred to men in possession of the true gospel !

[1] The evidence for this decay has been collected by Döllinger, *Die Reformation*, i. 420-545. Although his book, from its sectarian bias, must be read with great caution, my own investigations are on this point in material agreement with Döllinger's.

Thus much follows then from a comparison of the methods
of the Erasmian and Lutheran Reformations: that, differing
totally in their aims, the one proposed a gradual educational
change, the other proceeded to a violent destruction. Before
we can judge between the two, we must endeavour to answer
the following questions: Had Erasmus any chance of success?
And, secondly, admitting that some sacrifice of intellectual
progress may be justifiable, if it be accompanied by the
increased moral and social welfare of the masses, we have
still to ask:—Did the Reformation improve the moral and
social condition of the German people?

What chance of success had Erasmus? It should be
remembered that the Humanistic proposals were not of a
revolutionary character, at least not those of the older party,
which fell more directly under the influence of Erasmus.
They embraced an educational reform, which must from its
very nature be a gradual change. To say, then, that Erasmus
was unsuccessful in his attempts, because monkish abuses
still remained, is quite beside the point. The investigation
must turn on the progress which had been made, and the
probability of its advancing with increasing yet stable
rapidity. Neither a church nor a nation can be educated in
one man's lifetime; it is the labour of long years. Erasmus
wished to gradually revivify existing institutions, that they
might aid the intellectual development of mankind. Luther
pulled them down; but his attempt to reconstruct them
upon his own ideas was by no means a success. How far
did the older Humanists revivify ecclesiastical institutions?
We hold, to a far greater degree than is generally supposed.
The German schools and universities, with few exceptions,
had suffered a transformation, which, considering its magnitude and rapidity, can only be described as magical. There
was an unparalleled activity, and this of no narrow dogmatical kind, from Vienna to Strassburg, and from Erfurt to
Basel.[1] We have already pointed out how emancipated the

---

[1] A most characteristic picture of the rise of a German university under
the Humanists, and its collapse with the Reformation, is given in Kampschulte's *Die Universität Erfurt*, 1858–60.

Pope and the Princes of the Church had become, how they were the patrons of art and letters, and how thoroughly they were in sympathy with the Erasmian spirit. We have evidence enough that the Humanistic influence was beginning to make itself felt not only in the cloisters, but among the clergy. Great moral preachers arose among the people; theology itself could hardly be accused of sluggishness in an age which could lay claim to such men as Cusanus, Heynlin von Stein, Tritheim, Geiler von Kaisersberg, and Gabriel Biel. The consciousness of the spiritual leaders of the people was again aroused; special preachers were appointed for the folk throughout the various German towns. In vernacular sermons and didactic works increased stress was laid on the moral and practical side of Christianity. The press served for the popularizing of religious ideas; edition after edition of the Biblical books was offered to the public and eagerly bought up. Collections of sermons, religious contemplations, prayer and confessional books in the vernacular, followed each other in rapid succession, and marked a revival of the religious spirit both in the clergy and laity. A succession of cultured and high-minded bishops like Johann von Dalberg arose in the German Church at the close of the fifteenth century:

"We note how the bishops compete with one another in visiting the convents in their dioceses, in order to effect in them the re-establishment of the old discipline; we see them founding and extending educational establishments to forward theological and theologico-humanistic studies; we find that, according to the canons of the Church, they hold periodical synods to collect their clergy about them, and to issue detailed instructions for their guidance. We note how the leading spirits of the learned world are on terms of the most friendly and confidential intimacy with the Princes of the Church; how, in harmony as to the goal of their mission in life, they labour and strive together with united powers."[1]

Assuredly the reformation of Erasmus was a possible one,

[1] Cf. Maurenbrecher: *Geschichte der katholischen Reformation*, Bd. i. S. 80; also S. 60-80 generally.

and in 1517 had already made great progress. The union between the leaders of the Church and the leaders of thought was one of its most noteworthy features. But in the work for the education of the clergy and the elevation of the folk, the general progress of knowledge was not forgotten. Noteworthy was the battle between the Dominicans and the Humanists for the freedom of study, which occupied the early years of the sixteenth century. We cannot enter into the Pfeffer-korn-Reuchlin controversy here, but we may note two facts concerning it. The first is, that among the supporters of Reuchlin were men whom the Reformation was soon to convert into the bitterest foes ; Erasmus and Hutten, Luther and Eck, Melanchthon and Cochlæus, Spalatin and Carlstadt, all declare themselves Reuchlinists. The second fact, which is of extreme interest for our present purpose, is, that the first two judgments of the leaders of the Church were *in favour of the Humanists ;* only after Luther had commenced his battle against the Church did Rome pronounce a third judgment *against* Reuchlin. The revolt of Luther caused the Church to reject Humanism, and was the death-blow of the Erasmian Reformation. What else could the Church have done ? Had not Luther expressed his admiration of Reuchlin, and in Luther's rebellion did it not seem as if the whole body of Humanists were moving against the Church ? In an instant Luther was hailed as a deliverer by all classes of the people. The Humanists believed he had come as a new champion of learning, who would sweep away the ignorance and obstinacy of the "obscure men." Pirkheimer, Ulrich von Hutten, Crotus Rubianus, Muth, even Erasmus, wel-comed Luther as a new ally in their battle against monkish stupidity. Humanistic moralists like Brant and Wimpfeling waited anxiously for the result of what they thought only an attack on the immorality of the clergy. The denizens of the towns and the German people generally looked upon Luther as the giant who had come to free them from ecclesiastical extortions, to put an end to the "grievances of the German nation." The peasantry hoped in some mysterious fashion that Luther would free them from tithes and the growing oppression of Roman Law. The princes and nobles were not slow to recognize in Luther an instrument, whereby they might satisfy their own peculiar greeds. Lastly, there were some simple, homely folk, who imagined that Luther was about ·to teach a form of primitive Christianity, a general reign of brotherly love, some hitherto unrealized union of communism and pietism. This class was not infrequent among the peasantry ; it was the source of the various sects generally classed as Anabaptists, and driven alike by Catholic and Protestant persecution into fanaticism. Those who would understand the earlier writings of Luther must grasp clearly his relation to these various groups, and his endeavours to satisfy each of them. The Diet at Worms marks the extreme height of Luther's popularity. Eobanus Hesse, Pirkheimer, Hutten and other Humanists hailed his journey southwards. Franz von Sickingen promised him more material aid in case of need ; the Elector of Saxony was his protector ; the well-to-do burghers made his entries into Erfurt and Worms triumphal processions ; and on the very day after Luther's audience a threat to march with 8,ooo men against his Papal foes was found nailed to the door of the council house. It concluded with the cry of peasant insurrection :—" Bundschuh, Bundschuh, Bundschuh ! "

It is of peculiar moment, in judging the value of the Refor mation, to mark how one by one the various parties we have noted ceased to be supporters of Luther. Gradually the Humanists learned that the Reformation was not making for learning and culture; that it was destroying the schools, and introducing a race of theologians, who were as narrow and as bitter as their old enemies the monks; they saw the "obscure men" perpetuated in a new class of dogmatists, and ignorance and passion trampling knowledge under foot. Erasmus withdrew the approval he had once given to Luther, regretting that he had not exhibited the same zeal in avoiding violence and preaching morality as he had in defending dogma. Erasmus saw new tyrants, but not a spark of the gospel spirit. Above all, he noted the increasing immorality of the people and the collapse of true learning. Reuchlin,

once the great opponent of monkish bigotry, tried to recall
his nephew Melanchthon from Wittenberg, and, failing withdrew from him the promised legacy of his library. The author
of the *Augenspiel* died in the Catholic Church. To that Church
Pirkheimer also was reconciled—Pirkheimer, whose satire on
Dr. Eck had caused him to be included in the Papal Bull
against Luther. " I confess," he writes, " that at first I was
a good Lutheran, even as our late Albrecht (Dürer), since we
hoped that the Roman trickery, as well as the knavery of
monk and priest, would be bettered. But, as one sees, matters
have grown worse, so that these evangelical rogues make
the former appear pious. . . . I hoped, to begin with, for a
certain spiritual freedom, but all is now obviously turned to
pleasure of the flesh, so that these later things are far
worse than the first." In like spirit, Crotus Rubianus, the
Humanist, who had conceived the bitterest satire, ever
written against monkdom, who had hailed with his chosen
comrade Hutten the outbreak of the Reformation, returned
to the Catholic faith full of bitterness at the growing immorality and the destruction of culture.

"In most places," he writes, "where the anti-papists rule,
severe laws have already been published against the professors of the old religion. He who does not renounce all
intercourse with the papists must go to prison, or purchase
his freedom by a heavy fine. Woe to him who dares to
enter a papist Church, to hear a sermon there or attend
mass, to confess to a priest or perform any ecclesiastical
rite! The new dispensation, which came from Heaven
yesterday, has its watchful spies, with Argus eyes, ready to
denounce the offender to the judge. . . . O just law, so
wholly eye and ear with regard to observation of ecclesiastical routine, but with regard to the adulterer, the
blasphemer, struck with blindness, and sunk in the deepest
sleep! ' "

Do not these words of Rubianus lay out clearly before us
the cause why the Humanists deserted Luther? They had
wished for a " spiritual freedom," for a cessation of dogma,
for a new and broader view of life and thought; and they

found themselves treated to Augsburg Confessions and the pitiable tyranny of evangelical church regulations.

Still worse fared the simple folk who had hoped to find in the new gospel the foundation of a millennium of Christian love and charity. Their pious enthusiasm was the stumbling-block of the Lutherans ; they carried Luther's own gospel to its logical outcome, and claimed in their turn that freedom of belief which Luther had demanded from Rome for himself. but which he practically refused to others. Luther saw that the mass of the people were drawn rather to this primitive faith than to his own doctrines, and as Melanchthon and he were unable to convince these sectaries by argument, at first banishment, and then the sword and stake, became the chief weapons of Protestant logic.[1] In such a book as Luther's 1532 tract *Upon Sneaks and Hole-and-Corner Preachers* we have all the hatred of an established and privileged church against any trespassers on its domain. Closely related to the Anabaptists were the oppressed peasants, only these latter found out their delusion at a somewhat earlier date and suffered more complete discomfiture. In 1525 the brutal tyranny of princes and nobles reached its height, and the peasants broke into open rebellion. We have lying open before us now the original Twelve Articles printed and circulated by the peasant leaders. This curious tract tells its own tale of oppression and delusion. It appeals through-out to the " Holy Evangely," as Luther's teaching was then termed. Article 6 demands that all parsons and vicars shall be called upon to teach and preach the " Gospel," and on their refusal shall be dismissed from office. The claims of the peasants would appear to most modern readers very far from unreasonable. Noteworthy is the naming of umpires to decide between the peasants and their oppressors ; imme-diately following the Imperial Stathalter are placed Duke Friedrich of Saxony, together with Martin Luther, Philip

[1] Luther attributes the obstinacy of the early Anabaptists to the " in-fluence of the devil." The writings of Luther, Melanchthon, and other Protestants against these simple folk are the quintessence of bigotry and of the narrowest theological intolerance.

Melanchthon, and "Pomeran" (Bugenhagen). We have thus
the most complete evidence of how the peasants interpreted
Luther's teaching. From the purely historical standpoint
it is absolutely impossible to deny that the preaching of
Luther and his followers was the *immediate* cause of the
Peasant Rebellion. Doubtless Luther's doctrine of "evangelical freedom" was grasped by the peasants in a cruder
fashion than he understood it, yet it was most certainly the
spark which set on fire the inflammatory material collected
and heaped up by oppression.[1] A man who appeals to the
unlearned masses is responsible, not only for his direct statements, but for the results which may arise from his being
misinterpreted by his audience. Luther's position was at
the time of this outbreak an extremely difficult one. In his
first book on the Twelve Articles he endeavours to act the
part of umpire. He asserts that the peasants' demand
for the "pure gospel" is a most justifiable one, and he
does not hesitate to attribute the outbreak to the conduct of
the princes, nobles and—"more especially to you, ye blind
bishops, ye mad priests and monks." On the other hand, he
defends serfdom to the peasantry on Biblical grounds.
"There shall be no serf, since Christ has made us all free!
What is that? That is making Christian freedom purely
of the flesh. Had not Abraham and other patriarchs and
prophets serfs also? Read St. Paul what he teaches of
servants, who in his day were all serfs." "Therefore this
article is directly against the Gospel, and robbery, since each
takes from his lord that body which belongs to his lord." But
this position of umpire was impossible for Luther; it would
in all probability have led to the collapse of his Gospel
between the two parties. After a few weeks' consideration
Luther threw in his lot with the princes. His tract,
Against the Murderous and Rapacious Rabble of Peasants
(1525), is the most terrible appeal to bloodshed ever published by a minister of Christ's Church. It is the first
manifesto of the doctrine, afterwards generally adopted by

---

[1] This has been very strongly expressed by Maurenbrecher: *Die
katholische Reformation*, Bd. i. p. 257. Cf. also p. 275.

the Reformers, of the divine institution of all civil authority, and the duty of implicit obedience on the part of all subjects, alike in matters spiritual and temporal.[1]

"A rebel," he writes in this book, "is outlawed by God and Kaiser, therefore who can and will first slaughter such a man does right well; since upon such a common rebel every man is alike judge and executioner. Therefore who can, shall here openly or secretly smite, slaughter, and stab, and shall hold that there is nothing more harmful, more poisonous, more devilish than a rebellious man. . . . O Lord God, when such spirit is in the peasants, it is high time that they were slaughtered like mad dogs."

Luther tells the princes that they are commanded by the Gospel, so long as the blood flows in their veins, to slay such folk. Those who are killed in such attempt are true martyrs before God. Carlyle has described Luther's conduct in the matter of the Peasants' War as showing a "noble strength very different from spasmodic violence." The sober historian must agree with our opinion, "that it is the most terrible appeal to bloodshed ever published by a minister of Christ's Church." Nothing could excuse it, not even the news of the Weinsberg atrocities, had it reached Wittenberg before the publication of the book. It was the death-blow of Lutheranism as a popular movement; henceforth the Reformation was carried out by the order and force of the temporal powers, the folk being indifferent or even hostile; henceforth Luther depends for support on the greed of princes or the rapacity of town-councillors. Before 1530 he has lost the sympathy not only of the Humanists, the party of culture, but even of the mass of the folk. The tyranny of petty princes has received the sanction of the Reformers, and learning has been crushed under the heel of theological dogma. It remains for us to consider how a Reformation carried through under these auspices affected the social and moral condition of the people.

---

[1] See, however, Luther's *Von weltlicher Obrigkeit*, 1523. Luther himself declares that he was the first to state the divine origin of all civil power (Werke, Bd. xxxi. S. 24). See also Melanchthon's *Wider die Artikel der Bauernschaft*, where the argument is based on Rom. xiii. 1.

A comparison between the condition of the masses in 1500 and 1550 far exceeds anything which can possibly be attempted within the limits of an essay of the present kind. It is a question purely of statistics, and these often of the dullest nature. Hitherto the topic has been entirely neglected by Protestant historians, and we owe most of our information on the subject to Catholic authors writing with an obvious party-tendency. Notwithstanding this, however, we have evidence more than enough to show a remarkable breakdown in the social and moral welfare of the German people. How far this was due to the direct teaching of the Reformers is a matter of the utmost importance. If the Reformation only checked culture, if freedom of thought and the rational method have only grown up in spite of the Reformation—because the theologians were not sufficiently united to suppress them—then the influence of the Reformation upon the social and moral welfare of the people will be the crucial question which must settle our judgment on Luther and his movement. Mr. Beard has thought fit to refer only to this crucial question in a short note to his Fourth Hibbert Lecture. He there comes to the conclusion that "the Reformation did not at first carry with it much cleansing force of moral enthusiasm." If Mr. Beard is referring solely to Germany, we are compelled to add that neither "at first" nor "at last" did the Lutheran movement carry with it any force of moral enthusiasm. It reduced the parts of Germany it reached to a moral torpor; for almost the whole of the two following centuries Germany's social as well as literary life was "stale, flat, and unprofitable." Only the emancipation of thought, the reaction against all religious dogma in the eighteenth century, awoke Germany from her slumbers. What Mr. Beard relegates to a note is, we hold, the ground upon which the Reformation must ultimately be judged. We have before remarked that the Catholic Church was the basis of mediæval social life; we have drawn attention to the triumph of the Roman over the Canon Law, and the reduction of the peasant to a serf; we have noted how intimately the decay of the guild system was connected with the collapse of the Church; we have yet to place before the reader some evidence of the direct influence of the Lutheran doctrines upon the morality of the folk. We shall confine ourselves here to two of them : the one relating to redemption by faith alone, the other to the meaning of marriage. On both these points we must again-repeat a caution we have given above—namely, that it is not sufficient excuse for Luther to say that his doctrines were misunderstood. He did not publish them in a form intended only for scholars, he thrust them into the hands of the ignorant, and he must be held responsible for the results of misinterpretation.

The emphasis which Luther laid upon the doctrine of justification by faith alone has identified it for ever with the Reformation ; so greatly was he enamoured of it, that he introduced in the ardour of his passion the word "alone" into his translation of Romans iii. 28, a passage which certainly does not contain the word in the most corrupt of manuscripts. Any dogma which lays, or appears to lay, stress only on the inner faith of the individual, is liable to most dangerous misconceptions. It misses what nowadays would be so generally acknowledged as the chief function of religion—the insistence on an upright, neighbourly, pure life. Instead of making it the first concern of man to live well in this world, it occupies his time with some process whereby he secures a satisfactory life hereafter. The individual retires into himself, he is satisfied that his faith will save his own soul, he becomes almost, or quite, regardless of the material welfare of his neighbour. It is not surprising, then, to find that sects grew up—even as under similar circumstances they had done among the Mahomedans—who based upon this doctrine the theory, that to the believer all things (even the most immoral) are permitted. Luther, of course, would have rejected any such enormity ; still it was the logical outcome of his statement, that the works of the righteous, or rather elect, are all alike good ; the most unimportant actions, and the greatest self-sacrifice, have the same worth before God. Obviously, such a theory destroys the possibility of a moral ideal, towards which man can only approach

by a lifelong struggle. "God," said Luther, "does not
ask how many and how great are our works, but how
great is our faith? . . . Thou owest God naught but confession and belief. In all other matters thou art free to do
as thou wilt, without any danger of conscience." It is
perfectly true that, if real faith be defined as that which is
always followed by good works, such expressions are harmless. But the danger of emphasizing, as the key to salvation, a merely subjective state of the emotions instead of
a particular course of action, can hardly be overestimated in
treating of the moral value of a dogma. To the great
uncultured masses it is all-important to insist upon good
works, upon a pure, charitable life, as the means to redemption. Is it not easy to understand how teaching like the
following was misinterpreted by the folk? "The proposition
that good works are needful for salvation must be entirely
rejected, since it is a false and deceptive doctrine that good
works are needful either to justification or salvation." "There
is no law sanctioned by God Himself which demands a single
work from the believer as necessary for salvation." "Works
do nothing; only consider one thing as needful—to hear
God's Word and believe it—that suffices and nothing else."
How the folk understood these expressions was very soon
obvious. "Under Popery," Luther himself writes, "people
were charitable and generous, but now under the Gospel
nobody gives any longer; now every man skins his brother,
and each will alone have all. The longer the Gospel is
preached, the deeper people sink in pride, greed, and luxury."
What a strange confession of failure lies in this, though
Luther hardly recognized its cause! Such complaints as to
the absolute decay of charity are constantly repeated by the
Reformers; they can obtain no support either for the clergy,
the churches, or the schools. Luther tells us on another occasion, how every town once, according to its size, supported
several convents, to say nothing of mass-priests and charitable
foundations; but now, under the new dispensation, men refuse
to support two or three preachers and instructors of youth
in a town, even when it is not out of their own property,

but out of that which has been left from Popish times. It is a fact, which is no less true of Germany than of England, that of the property of the old Church, which passed into the hands of the princes and town-councillors, but very little was again applied to charitable or public purposes. Most pitiable are the lamentations of the Church Visitors over the decay of charity. The lower orders throughout Saxony refused not alone voluntary but even legal church dues. In 1525, Luther wrote that unless very stringent measures were taken there would soon be neither preachers nor parsonages, neither schools nor scholars. In some villages the religious spirit had entirely died out; three or four persons went to church, and the peasants marched about with drums during the service; in others, even the building itself had been converted into a sheepstall, or made a depository for Whitsun-beer; in further instances we read of the beer-cans being handed about during the sermon, or of the peasants threatening to stone their parsons. The clergy itself was terribly degraded. One minister had three wives living, another did not even know the Ten Commandments, a third earned his livelihood as a weaver, while in many cases two or more cures had to be thrown together in order to obtain support for one preacher. In several villages the Visitors declared that the only remedy was the " executioner and the stocks." The moral decay of both peasantry and clergy is extraordinary; both are given to drink, both to sexual vice. In one small village alone there were fifteen illegitimate children in one year. One parson is described as " tolerably good," but he does not receive unqualified praise, because of his passion for drinking. Most charitable foundations had disappeared, to a great extent appropriated by the nobility; the revenues of the parsons had melted away; the parsonages were tumbling down, and cattle fed in the open churchyards. The schools, where they continued to exist, were in a most pitiable condition, while monastic teaching had of course disappeared with the monks. Villages had sold their church ornaments and vessels to pay the commune debts, or appropriated church funds for a like purpose. Scarcely anywhere in the rural districts was there the faintest trace of enthusiasm for the new dispensation. In one town, however, we find a Lutheran Council had been elected; they had bought out the nuns, and shut up their convents; they had dismissed the eighteen monks with thirty gulden apiece, and their guardian with double that sum. All the provisions or movables of the convent had been given away or sold; the windows had been transferred to the "Kaufhaus"; innumerable persons had been found ready to take charge of the large stock of cheese and lard left by the monks. "One sees," as the historian of the events naïvely remarks, "in what a short time a town government, inclined to Luther's views, could accomplish an immense amount; it is the towns peculiarly that we have to thank for their great services in forwarding the Reformation."[1] Such was the state of the Saxon Church under Luther's very nose in 1528. We by no means propose to thrust all these failings upon his shoulders; some of them were undoubtedly a legacy from Papal times, others were a result of the Peasant War (and so indirectly due to the Reformation); but enough remains to show that the destruction of the Catholic Church involved a break-up of social life in Saxony. It is quite sufficient for our purpose if we can convince the reader that the so-called Reformation did not improve the condition of the people, neither of clergy nor laity; if it did not, it failed in its object. What we have here described, on the report of the Visitors in 1528, is very closely akin to what we learn from Church Visitations, even until the Thirty Years' War destroys all possibility of judging between cause and effect. It is quite true that the number of "stubborn Papists" with whom the Visitors met, became fewer and fewer, but as one of the chief functions of successive Visitations had been to get rid of them, this is scarcely to be wondered at. In 1539 we find the schools still in a miserable condition, and the people themselves quite indifferent to education. The general tendency of the time was, as Musa reports, against learned, but especially against

[1] Burkhardt: *Geschichte der sächsischen Kirchen- und Schulvisitationen*, 1879, p. 67, *et ante*.

clerical, occupations; above all, charity no longer provided for the poor strolling scholar. The Reformers found themselves in absolute need of men of the most moderate education for their Church. In 1532, in the second Visitation, we find the old complaints as to the unthankfulness of the people towards the new gospel. On the other hand, uniformity has become an absolute law. All who defend articles of belief, other than appear in the printed "Instruction of the Visitors," are to be banished from the country. The increasing moral decay of the folk is to be checked by stringent regulations; crime, swearing, gambling, drunkenness, adultery, and the "passionate discussion of the dogmas of religion in the taverns," are to be investigated and punished by ecclesiastical superintendents. We find the same difficulties as to the support of the clergy, the same complaints as to the concession of churches and church property; one church has become a granary, the property of another has been used to build a tavern, and so forth. Childish were the means the Visitors took to bring people into the church; for example, those who did not attend the baptismal service were not to partake of the baptismal feast, and irregular communicants were to be banished from the parish.[1] We note the beginning of a second and worse ecclesiastical tyranny.

At the same time in the Wittenberg district itself matters were still more deplorable. The laity were given not to charity but to dissoluteness in its widest meaning; many had quarrelled with the clergy, and for long years abstained from the sacrament. Parsonages were in ruins, the cattle frequented or were even driven to the churchyard. The villagers refused the preacher his dues, or met together to consume them in drink. In the lordship of Schwarzburg the Visitors found forty-six Protestant preachers and seven Catholic priests. Eight or nine Protestants, although permitted to marry, were living with concubines, as also five of their Catholic brethren. Not only are these early Church Visitations strong evidence of the want of a "force of moral enthusiasm" in the Lutheran movement, but they are the best record we have of

[1] Burkhardt, p. 140.

the method of the Reformers. Most strange is the picture of
the manner in which the evangelical faith was forced upon
the semi-dependent principalities and bishoprics ; they were
compelled to accept Lutheranism whether they would or
not ; monks and nuns were forbidden to wear the dress of
their Order, were pensioned off, or allowed to await their end
in a convent where the old religious routine was entirely prohibited. Many, who thus found themselves deprived of the
only advantages of the ascetic life, returned again into the
world, or wandered into Catholic countries, thus assisting
the rapid process of secularization. In 1535 we find much
the same condition of things ; the Visitors complain of an
increase of godlessness, contempt of the divine Word, small
attendance at church, and almost total refraining from
communion. Then we hear of most indecent behaviour
during divine service, increase of vices of all kinds in a
most marked degree, and, above all, of the *sad collapse of
conjugal relations.*[1] Even the conduct of the clergy calls for
the gravest reprobation. Everywhere there was a want of
that spiritual supervision which had ceased with the old
Church. So much must suffice to give the reader a conception of the Saxon clergy and laity under the influence of the
Reformation. There was most undoubtedly a break-up of social
and moral relations, and more than one Protestant of that
day was bold enough to attribute it directly to Luther's
doctrine of redemption. Noteworthy is the almost unanimous
rejection of this doctrine by the sects of primitive Christians,
which so rapidly grew up among the folk. They declared
that Christ had given a model for life, rather than a mere
matter for belief. To this "babble of faith" they attributed
the increase in adultery, greed, and drunkenness. We will
conclude this subject by a characteristic but by no means
unique passage from the writings of Schwenkfeld :—

"One may reasonably accuse the Lutherans of discarding
external matters as unnecessary for salvation, since they not
only teach that faith alone, *sola fides*, makes a man righteous
and holy, but with complete indiscretion write and have

[1] Ibid. pp. 198-9.

written so sharply and severely against the good works of faith that many have entirely discarded all good works and godliness, and thus an atrocious godless manner of existence has become frequent. Alas! it is everywhere obvious that the masses do not know what to make of good works. How can it be otherwise, since these men have taught and written from the beginning that good works, even the best, are sins : nay, even that a righteous man sins in all good works ! " [1]

Turning to our second point, the theory of marriage, we have first to note the historical fact, and then to search for its cause. The undoubted fact is the decay of sexual morality, the collapse of the sanctity of marriage in Germany during the sixteenth century. Not only do we find strange evidence of this in the reports of the Visitors, but both Protestants and Humanists bear witness to the same effect. In one Protestant university we hear of the moral conduct being such "as Bacchus and Venus might prescribe to their following." Luther himself is continually crying out against the moral collapse in Saxony itself, and even compares it unfavourably with the state of things under Popery. Weary of battling against this increasing mass of disorder, he exclaims in despair : " It would almost seem as if our Germany, after the great light of the Gospel, had become possessed of the devil." Melanchthon attributes the greater difficulties of government to the increasing immorality of the folk. Luxury, shamelessness, and riotousness are ever extending. Bugenhagen, Osiander, Mathesius, and other evangelical preachers bear evidence to the decay of chaste manners ; they attribute it, not to the collapse of the old religious sanctions, but to the singular activity of the devil. The growth of little communities and sects, who not only taught but practised polygamy and even promiscuous intercourse, is one of the peculiar features of the time. It is necessary to inquire whether any ground can be found for these results in the teaching of the Reformers. There has been much discussion recently with regard to Luther's sermons on marriage, and

[1] Many expressions in Luther's works quite justify what some might fancy to be an exaggeration of Schwenkfeld's.

it is necessary to say a few words about them here. These sermons bear dates varying from 1519 to 1545, and we may state generally that the same conception of marriage runs through all of them; they contain Luther's views as a Protestant, and are essentially opposed to the teaching of the Catholic Church. The most characteristic of these sermons were preached by Luther as an evangelical teacher from the Wittenberg pulpit. They were likewise preached to an audience mixed as to age and sex. We will say nothing here of their coarseness, allowing that to be peculiar at least to a certain section of his contemporaries ;[1] we have to con-sider only their doctrine. The Catholic Church has always taught that marriage is a sacrament. We should be the last to defend the truth of such a conception, but we must call attention to the fact that it emphasized something beyond the physical in the sexual relation, it endowed it with a *spiritual* side. The conception of marriage as a spiritual as well as physical union seems to us the essential condition of all permanent happiness between man and wife. The intellectual union superposed on the physical is precisely what raises human above brute intercourse. Those marriages which arise purely from instinctive impulse are notoriously the least stable. We believe that the spiritual side must be kept constantly in view, if the stability of the sexual rela-tionship is to be preserved. Here it is that Luther, rejecting the conception of marriage as a sacrament, rushes with his usual impetuosity into the opposite and more dangerous ex-treme. He lays entire stress upon the physiological origin of the sexual union. He teaches not only truly that chastity has no peculiar value in the eyes of God or man, but also that it is *impossible*, and directly contrary to the divine mandate. The

---

[1] Sebastian Brant set his face against all forms of coarseness. "A new saint has arisen," he writes, "called Grobian, whom now all men worship and honour on every side with coarse words and dissolute works." Of this passage, Gervinus writes, "There was something great in attempting to stem such a torrent as this then was, and this aim Brant had." If the author of the *Ship of Fools* could resist the tendency of his time, might we not demand the same of the *Hero as Priest?*

vows of monks and nuns are void because they have vowed an
impossibility. He repeatedly proclaims from the pulpit that
neither man nor woman can control the sexual impulses.
He tells boys and girls that they cannot, nor does God bid
them, resist their passions. They must either marry or do
worse. A boy at latest when he is twenty, a girl between
fifteen and eighteen, must marry, and "let God take care
how the children are to be supported." This revolutionary
doctrine of the impossibility of chastity Luther carries into
the sanctity of wedded life, and makes statements at which
the modern reader can only shudder.[1] What Luther taught
to the folk, old and young, man and woman, from the Wittenberg pulpit was repeated throughout the Protestant
churches of Germany. Is it not necessary to connect the
decay of sexual morality with the propagation of such doctrines as these ? We are quite willing to allow that Luther's
primary aim was to sweep away the mass of corruption
which undoubtedly existed in the cloisters, and for this
purpose it was needful to assert that the ascetic life was not
a peculiarly holy one. But Luther, with his usual love of
extreme dogma, propounded a doctrine which must be sub-
versive of moral order. He took the lowest conceivable
view of the relation of man and woman, and the masses of
the folk, ever ready to accept a physical impulse as a divine
commandment, did not hesitate to embrace his theory, and
carry it to most disastrous results.[2]

There is another point to which his purely physical conception of marriage led him—namely, to what we are really
justified in terming an approval of polygamy. It is a common, but quite erroneous, opinion to suppose that Luther
only expressed his views on this matter in relation to the
bigamy of Philip of Hesse. So early as 1524 Luther
declared that polygamy is not forbidden by the word of

[1] See the essay in this volume on the Relations of Sex in Germany.

[2] In 1518 Luther wrote from the Catholic standpoint. He remarks that
God grants grace to unfruitful marriages, and concludes :—"Hæc si quis
animadverteret, *facillime* concupiscentiam carnis refrenaret."—*De Matri-
monio. Conciones, Opera Latina.* Wittenberg, 1545, i., fol. xc.

God, but to avoid scandal and preserve decency, it is
necessary to reject some things which are permitted to
Christians. " It is well that the husband himself should be
firm and certain in his own conscience that by the word of
God this thing is allowable. . . . I must forsooth confess
that I cannot prohibit any man from taking several wives,
nor is it repugnant to the Scriptures." Melanchthon went
still further, and advised our Henry VIII. not to divorce his
first wife, but to take another, because polygamy was not
forbidden by the divine law. We by no means assert that
either Luther or Melanchthon *openly* taught polygamy ; but
they did not strongly oppose it, and the result was obvious
in their followers. Carlstadt was not the only Protestant who
plainly expressed approval of polygamy, and in the tragedy
of Münster the doctrine was carried to the most anti-social
extremes. It is precisely in the spirit of the above quotations
that in 1540 Luther and Melanchthon replied to the Landgrave
of Hesse on his proposal to take a second wife. A special
dispensation may be granted to him, if bigamy be the only
means of preserving him from worse vices. Such bigamy is
allowed in the law of Moses, and not forbidden in the Gospel.
At the same time, it would not be wise to allow polygamy to
the common folk on account of the scandal to which it would
give rise. On this ground it is necessary that the second
marriage be kept an absolute secret. There is no mention
whatever that a second marriage is null and void, or tears
up by the very roots the hitherto accepted Christian theory of
marriage. Other Protestant divines, such as Bugenhagen
and Butzer, gave their sanction to this pitiable quibble ; and
Philip's court chaplain preached after the ceremony on the
legitimacy of polygamy ! We cannot help seeing in the whole
matter that doctrine of marriage which, disregarding the
spiritual, lays all stress on the physical relation. The Protestant " sanction " did not arise merely from political necessity,
for we have seen, that Luther in 1524, and Melanchthon
in 1531, expressed opinions of an exactly similar kind. It
was not out of keeping with a movement which throughout appealed rather to the passions than to the intellect,

which at every turn sacrificed reason to the dictates of undisciplined emotion. With this slight reference to that which even Protestant theologians admit to be a black spot of the Reformation, we must close our consideration of the influence of that movement upon the moral condition of the German folk. That influence, as we have endeavoured to show, was not in favour of progress.

The facts which we have now laid before the reader will, we hope, enable him to form some judgment of how Luther must be considered in relation to modern culture. We are perfectly aware that it is possible to cite passages from his writings full of truth and piety; we leave to Catholic theologians the task of denouncing Luther as a knave, a sensualist, or a heretic; we decline entirely to discuss whether his dogmas were better or worse than those of the Catholic Church. We recognize to their full extent the abuses which that Church presented in the sixteenth century; we only ask: Did Luther give the world anything of greater purity? Is it a fact that there was nothing to choose between the immorality and bigotry of Catholic and of Protestant clergy in the second half of the sixteenth century? We ask bluntly: What have we to thank Luther for? For a particular set of dogmas? Dogmas are to us matters of perfect indifference. For our freedom of thought? We reply that freedom of thought was more possible in 1500 than a hundred years later, and that our present freedom is not the result of Luther's teaching any more than of Eck's. It arises merely from the fact that Luther, Eck, and their co-theologians could not agree. The Protestants banished the freethinking painters from Nürnberg, they burnt Conrad 'in der Gasse' in Basel, they executed Krauth, Moller, and other Anabaptists in Jena and elsewhere; they burnt Servetus in Geneva, they beheaded Hetzer in Constance (it is said on a charge of polygamy!). Shortly, their intolerance was, if possible, narrower than that of their Catholic brethren. We owe our freedom not to their doctrine, but to their impotence. Toleration has grown to be a leading factor of our modern faith, in the very teeth of Protestant, or at least

Lutheran opposition. Again, does any one ask us to be grateful to Luther for modern culture? We answer, that he checked the growth of culture; that literature, and art, and scholarship, decayed under the influence of the Lutheran Church. Nay, if we are told that we must sacrifice intellectual progress for the sake of the moral and social welfare of the masses, we reply: willingly; but the German Reformation was a moral catastrophe to the folk. We refuse entirely to fall down and worship this man; we do not recognize him as a hero, or mark in him a great moral teacher. We see a reformation attempted by an appeal to passion, where we allow only the gradual influence of education to be effectual. We note the frustration of Erasmus's attempt at rational reform by a violent conjuration of emotional ignorance. History, it is true, cannot be rewritten; but the reason why we separate myth from fact is that we may learn history's true lesson; and the lesson of the Reformation is that all true progress of the folk at large can only be attained by a gradual process of education. Appeal to popular passion, and scholarship, culture, and true morality will be dragged into contempt, while narrowness, intolerance, and ignorance will triumph. It is because we believe in the former as true essentials of human progress that we sympathize with Erasmus, and see in his methods the methods of the future. It is on this ground that we hail the recent refusal of the University of Oxford[1]—within whose walls Erasmus taught— to take any part in the glorification of Luther, as a manifesto of the modern historical spirit. We see in this decision no victory of High Church over Low Church, but the triumph of the party of progress over obscurity.

[1] This was written in the year 1883.

X.

THE KINGDOM OF GOD IN MÜNSTER.[1]

I.

SOME few years before the end of the first quarter of the sixteenth century the dawn of a brighter day seemed about to burst upon the dark night of the myriad toilers in Germany. A free peasantry had been forced into the most galling serfdom by a brutal and ignorant nobility, whose chivalry had degenerated into vulgar licence, and whose knightly spirit of adventure found profitable, if somewhat hazardous, employment in highway robbery. The spirit of selfishness growing rampant with the decay of the old religious influences had led the German princelets to the most detestable doctrines of petty autocracy, and they welcomed with delight the Roman jurists, who found no place in their system for primitive folk-customs, village jurisdiction, or the communal rights of a free peasantry. The peasant could no longer fetch his firewood from the forest, drive his cattle into the common meadow, or kill the game which destroyed his crops. His barns were burnt at night, he was carried off for a pitiable ransom even on his way to mass, and if he did not fulfil his legal or imposed obligations to the letter, he was punished in a most barbarous fashion, not infrequently culminating in death. On the other hand, the mad craving for wealth in the towns was destroying the old independence of the handicraftsman; the great extension of trade, the rise of commercial specula-

[1] Reprinted from the *Modern Review*, 1884.

tion, and the perversion of the old guild system were making him more and more a tool in the hands of the moneyed classes. The Church, which for long had held in check with its spiritual terrors the individual struggle for power, had fallen into a state of corruption, which called down upon it the contempt of the community. The poor and the helpless no longer found in the established religion that spiritual comfort, which might' have strengthened them to endure their material misery. The great ideas of mediæval Christianity were fast losing their influence over the minds of men ; the spiritual seemed dying out in the folk, which was rushing blindly along in its race for material prosperity, and with the usual result—the stronger arm, the stronger head went to the fore, but the weaker, the more ignorant were forced closer and closer to their hopeless grinding toil. The nobles hated the princelets, the towns detested both alike, while the peasantry was bitter in its denunciations of all who took refuge behind walls of stone. On every side were signs of the decay of the social spirit, of the rise of a new materialistic and selfish conception of life—irreligious in the truest sense of the word. Self-sacrifice—which can arise only from clearness of vision, or from a strong and fervid social consciousness—was to all appearances dead. Every man was hurrying along in the race for worldly prosperity, and a Church no longer conscious of its mission, nay, which scarce blushed at its own impurity, could not cry, " Halt !— remember thy neighbour ! "   In vain the poorer members of the community sought around them for the cause of this misery, they sat helplessly looking into the night and waiting for a prophet ! And then Luther came—Luther, the son of a peasant, boldly facing the indolent priest and the tyrannic prince—preaching a new gospel, a ' pure evangely,' full of comfort for men's souls.   What wonder that the dawn seemed breaking for the folk, that they fancied the national deliverer had arisen ?

For a short time peasant and craftsman, the humble toiler of all sorts, looked to Luther as to a god. What could this ' pure evangely ' mean—which proclaimed the Bible as sole

authority, and itself as the primitive Christian faith—if it did
not herald a return to brotherly love, mutual charity, and an
apostolic simplicity of life? What wonder that these poor
ignorant folk, when they read the fiery appeals which Luther
and his fellow-theologians cast abroad o'er the land, thought the
battle was not for a dogma, not for the letter, but for a total
change in men's habits of life. They did not want a new set
of doctrines, they did not want a new pope, they wanted a
richer life for the listless struggler in the city, a more joyous
home for the toiler on the land. They wanted the bread of
a new emotion in life, and they were given dogmatic stones.

Worn out by generations of oppression the peasants banded
themselves together, and took as their password the 'pure
evangely'; throughout the district of the league this, and this
only, should be proclaimed from the pulpit. Could the people,
could the princes once hear this divine word, there would be
no need of dispute, its very simplicity would bring conviction
to the minds of all. Poor simple peasants, the 'pure
evangely' was clear enough to you, but it was hardly what the
rulers of men were inclined to accept! Nevertheless you
drew up your twelve modest demands and based each one of
them on an appeal to Scripture and a plea of brotherly love.
Brotherly love indeed! Were you not rebels disobeying the
higher powers—or worse, disobeying God, by whom all the
powers that be are ordained? So Melanchthon told you, so
Luther told you. Nay, even if there were some shadow of
justice in your claims, you still deserved a fearful judgment
for the terrible sin of angering the powers that be. Even
if all your articles were in the 'pure evangely,' which
Wittenberg was not inclined to admit, still you must wait,
sit down and wait in your misery, till the 'pure evangely'
should develop itself. That was the only consolation the
new prophets had to offer you! [1]

It was little wonder that the peasants grew restless, that the
terrible wrongs of the past would be ever reminding the
present of its strength. Here and there the pent-up passion,
the blind brute impulse to revenge, broke its fetters, and an

---

[1] Melanchthon : *Wider die Artikel der Bauernschaft*, 1525.

awful judgment of blood fell upon the toilers' oppressors.
Then Luther gave tongue to words which shocked even his
own century :—"A rebel is outlawed of God and Kaiser,
therefore who can and will first slaughter such a man does
right well, since upon such a common rebel every man is
alike judge and executioner. Therefore who can shall here
openly or secretly smite, slaughter and stab, and hold that
there is nothing more poisonous, more harmful, more devilish
than a rebellious man." Those words were the funeral knell
of the 'pure evangely' in the hearts of the simple and
ignorant oppressed. The peasants were slaughtered by the
thousand, massacred as they stood nigh helpless with pitch-
fork and hoe—racked, flayed, burnt, one or all—ay, any other
refinement of agony the scared ruler of men could contrive
was eagerly adopted. But note, from that day forth Luther
might found churches, but they were built on the will of the
princes ; he might still be a prophet, but not of the masses—
he was a prophet of the *bourgeoisie.*

The peasant rebellion was repressed, and society breathed
again, conscious that it had got the turbulent stream once
more into its narrow bed, and, so long as it stayed there and
turned society's mill-wheels at the wonted pace, society remained quite regardless of its chafings and eddyings and foam-
ings. Not so, however, the toilers, not so many others, who
were weary of the round of theological disputation, the tossing
about of dogmas, the religion of the letter. The longings,
the almost heart-sick yearning of the weary for a new spiritual
guide was not utterly blunted, not yet quite reduced to a dull
mechanical feeling of the hopelessness of life. If they had
thrown off the yoke of Antichrist, rejected the Roman Sodom,
could they not likewise discard the 'new pope of Wittenberg,'
the priest of the letter ?—If the teachers had all gone astray,
could not the simple-minded build up a faith for themselves ;
and what better foundation than the Bible, the undoubted
word of God ? Here was a new world, a new light for the
folk—this Bible should be their priest and their Church—its
wondrous powers should illuminate the craftsman at his
bench and the peasant at his plough. Here was a theology

without need of learning, a faith without dogma. Each might draw pure religion from the one book, and none dreamt that much was unintelligible, or might be interpreted in a thousand different fashions. The Bible spoke directly to men in the voice of God ; nay, might not that voice itself speak once again to them as to the faithful of old ?   So arose afresh the conception of a strange mystic converse with God,—of the Divine Spirit within comforting the miserable and oppressed. Even their very misery, the toil and burden of life might be the origin of this strange union,—the very cause which carried men heavenwards.   How could those who held this creed believe in Luther's dogma of justification by faith *alone* ?   A life of suffering, of labour, of self-repression, was the key to their most spiritual emotions.   With the failure of the Peasant Rebellion they had given up all hopes of a social or political reconstruction; they awaited in patience all the future might bring forth ; they would willingly have separated themselves from the world, if the world had but left them, which it would not, in poverty and peace.

"O dear brothers and sisters, we know how false the Pope is, but from those who should teach us this we hear nought but quarrelling and abuse ; the whole world sees how they are divided against each other. O Almighty God, we appeal to thee!—I pray all men in God's name, who desire salvation, that they will not despise his message, since the times are very terrible !   Every day we hear those, who should teach the folk, say that he whom God has ordained to sin must sin, and he whom God has ordained to salvation must be saved. O most beloved sisters and brothers, let us fly from this error ! Has not Christ said : 'Come unto me, all ye that labour and are heavy laden'? And shall not each of us go and be saved ?   Our teachers have led us astray; it is time that we turn from them, and depart from this darkness.   We believe no longer in the mass, nor the pleading of saints. We believe no longer in the cloister, the priest, nor aught of popedom. We know they have long led us astray. We do not think long prayers are good, as prayer has been hitherto ; if one only says 'Our Father,' and

understands it, 'tis enough. We do not want pictures and
images, nor should God be worshipped in a temple built with
human hands; the only temple in which he will dwell is the
heart of man.   O dearest sisters and brothers throughout
the world, help me to pray fervently to God for safety from
these errors. Oh, how long we have been living in sin! But
what did the folk who, ignorant of the crucified One, had
been living in sin, say to the apostle? 'O dear friend, what
shall we do?' And Peter answered them : ' Repent, repent,
and let each one be baptized to the forgiveness of sins in the
name of Christ Jesus!' Then all men went and were gladly
baptized to the number of three thousand. Shall we not do
likewise ?   O dearest brothers and sisters, take this book
with patience and in fear of God, since in my whole life I
have not written a syllable against any man—I speak in the
truth which is God himself." [1]

Such is the simple spirit of these early Anabaptists ; there is
not a touch of the bitterness or abusive language of the current
theology ; there is an unmistakable, almost terrible earnestness about it, which carries no ring of falsehood. For such
men the Catholic Church had in earlier days found an outlet
in new monastic orders; this was now impossible. Still less
could the 'pope of Wittenberg' give them a place in his
new evangelical Church. His justification by faith alone and
his serfdom of the human will were to them unintelligible
doctrines; nay, the rapid spread of this simple-minded faith
threatened to destroy the ' pure evangely' altogether; the
oppressed of all parties turned to the new brotherhood.   The
enthusiasm which Luther had once evoked flowed into the
new channel; here was a simple-minded piety, a brotherly
love, an apostolic Christianity, which the masses had sought
for in vain in the 'pure evangely.' With Bible as guide the
members of this new community separate themselves from
the rest of the world ; rebaptism shall be the passage from
the old world of sin to the new world of love. Simple in the
extreme are their tenets—community of earthly goods and

[1] *Ein Göttlich vund gründtlich offenbarung; von den warhafftigen
widertcuffern: mit götlicher warhait angezaigt.* MDXXVII.

a future where there shall be no usury or tax. The brethren accept no office, and carry no sword ; patience is to be their sole weapon, and brotherly correction, followed, if necessary, by expulsion from the community, the only punishment. Besides baptism, their one ceremony is that of bread-breaking, a communion of love and a reminder that all are brothers and sisters in the Lord Christ. Simple, and yet almost grand, in its simplicity is this re-establishment of primitive Christianity among the first Anabaptists.

The evangelical leaders, however, grow alarmed for the safety of their own Churches :—Luther sees in it all the direct agency of hell; he has no sooner stopped one mouth than the Devil opens ten others. The Anabaptists are prophets of the Devil, and as heretics to the ' pure evangely ' are rebels to be punished by the authorities. He has done his duty in refuting them, and the blood of all who will not listen to his advice must be upon their own heads.[1] It is painful nowadays to note how Luther utterly failed to grasp the religious essence of this primitive faith. He saw neither the want which called it forth, nor the earnest truth of its followers. Had he been of a more tolerant, more broadly sympathetic mind, the history of German Protestantism might have had brighter chapters to record amidst its dreary waste of theological wrangling. Zwingli, too, began to fear for the safety of the Swiss Church. His toleration had drawn many of the religious radicals to Zürich, and at first he had condescended to dispute with them, leaving, as usual, the decision to the Town Council. Town Council, indeed ! What had these enthusiasts to do with such a body ? " God has long ago given judgment," they cried ; " it is not in the power of men to judge." Then Zwingli began to talk about heresy, and the need of extermination. " No one has a right," he said, " to leave the church or follow any other opinion than that of the majority—than that appointed by the legal representatives of the community." Whereupon the Anabaptists girded themselves about with rope, and, as if

[1] *Von der Wiedertaufe, an zwei Pfarrherrn,* 1528. *Von den Schleichern und Winkelpredigern,* 1532.

prepared for a journey, wandered through the streets of
Zürich.   In the market-place and in the open squares
they halted to preach, talked of the need of a better life, of
justice and of brotherly love.   " Woe, woe upon Zürich ! "
they cried, half threatening, half warning.   What was to be
done with these fiery enthusiasts—they were not criminals,
they were not rebels ?   Banishment, suggested Zwingli, and
banishment and repression followed throughout Switzerland.

Banishment scattered the sparks all over Southern Germany from Strassburg to the Tyrol.   The apostles of this
simple faith came like the early Christian teachers into the
homes of the poor.   They entered with the greeting of peace,
and taught in plain, homely words, bringing new light,
untold comfort unto many a weary heart.   The preacher
arrived, taught, aroused the listless spirit, baptized, took up
his staff and passed on.   So in a few hours he might plant a
little community of the new faith on a spot where he had
never been seen before, and never might come again.   The
little community chose its own head, who had the simple
duties of Bible-teaching, reproving, baptizing, and bread-
breaking.   The brethren and sisters would meet on Sundays
for Bible-reading, for mutual exhortation, and to celebrate
their primitive form of the Communion.   Their clothing was
simple and without ornament, they saluted one another with
a kiss and " Peace be with you," while each termed the
other brother or sister.   Their property was at the service of
all members who might need it, they prohibited the oath and
the sword.   None of them might engage in a law-suit or
take a place of authority, for all government to them was
the rod of God sent to chastise his folk ; the brethren should
obey it, paying rather too much than too little, patiently enduring suffering and persecution, awaiting the coming of the
Lord.[1]   These primitive Christians endeavoured to live
apart from the world, avoided the churches, the taverns, the
social gatherings of citizens and guilds, nay, even the greeting of unbelievers, for were they not God's own folk, men

---

[1] See Carl Alfred Cornelius : *Geschichte des Münsterischen Aufruhrs*, a
most excellent book, which unfortunately remains incomplete.

who had taken up Christ's cross and were determined to follow him? Justification by faith *alone*, indeed! Was not a life of suffering itself their justification? Persecuted, deprived of all means of subsistence, or hunted down like wild beasts, they had in truth a witness in their lives which passed all the power of words. There was something far beyond Luther here. There was a depth of earnest conviction about these Anabaptists which completely puzzled the Lutherans, for whom even the very courage with which they met a martyr's death was the work of the Devil, or an obstinacy born of passionate hatred to their persecutors! In Strassburg Capito saw the truth more clearly than Luther: "I testify before God," he writes, " that I cannot say their contempt of death arises from infatuation, much rather from a divine impulse. There is no passion, no excitement to be marked ; no, with deliberation and wondrous endurance they meet death as confessors of Christ's name."

Such was the material upon which persecution was brought to bear, and it is one of the most instructive, although one of the most terrible lessons of history to mark what persecution made out of it. First and foremost let us obtain some conception of what that persecution meant ; only then shall we be able to judge truly of the catastrophe which followed. Men are so apt to be shocked by the brutal outrages of a great folk-upheaval that they cannot grasp to the full the long years of oppression, the grinding torture, the bitter injustice, which at last causes the repressed passions to break forth in a torrent—as of molten lava—sweeping before it all the bonds of customary morality and every restraint which knits society together. Persecution first reached a head in the Catholic districts, where Anabaptism was held a capital offence. In the Tyrol we find in 1531 upwards of a thousand persons executed. At Linz alone, in six weeks, seventy-three. Duke William of Bavaria gave orders that those who recanted should be beheaded, those who would not were to be burnt. The Swabian Bund organized bands of soldiers to hunt down Anabaptists, and to kill on the spot, without trial, those captured! As soon as the Evangelicals felt strong

enough, they, too, joined in this human hunt. The Anabaptists had introduced a partial community of goods among
themselves; it was declared from the pulpit that they aimed
at the confiscation of all property; their prophecies as to
the end of the world were declared open rebellion ; the darkest
and most vile political and social motives were attributed
to them. Lutheran preachers poured out the foulest abuse
upon them, and encouraged the growth of a religious hatred
which sprang up with its wonted rapidity and its characteristic
bitterness. The Anabaptists were promptly declared political
offenders. They were beheaded in Saxony and drowned in
Zürich.   The blood of leaders and disciples flowed in
streams upon the land: Mantz was executed at Zürich;
at Rotenburg Michael Sattler was torn in pieces by red-hot
pincers and then burnt; Hubmaier, comforted by his faithful wife, was burnt at Vienna; Blaurock was burnt in the
Tyrol, Rinck was imprisoned for life in Hesse, Hätzer
beheaded at Constanz.   In Salzburg, however, the tide of
brutality seems to have reached its flood. Here a brotherhood had been founded which met on waste spots, worshipped in a primitive fashion, and shared their goods
together. The sign of membership was rebaptism. Thirty
of its members being captured, their preacher and two
others were burnt alive in the Fronhof, because they could
by no means be brought to confess their errors. A woman
and a 'bright maiden of sixteen years' refused to recant,
although told their lives would be spared ; the executioner
dragged them to the horse-pond, held them under the water
till they were drowned, and then burnt their bodies. Two
others, one even of noble birth, the other a wallet-maker,
were, on confessing their error beheaded and burnt.   A
button-maker and a belt-maker who remained obstinate were
burnt on the market place; we are told " they lived long and
cried with all their hearts to God ; it was pitiable to hear
them."   Ten women and several men who confessed were
banished.   "Upon the following Wednesday, a town notary,
a priest, and three others, among them a young and handsome belt-maker, were led out of the town to a house, where

they had held their services, and as they would not recant, but boldly defended their opinions and had no fear of martyrdom, they were placed inside the house, which was then set on fire; they lived for a long while, and cried piteously to one another. God help them and us according to His pleasure." Not content with destroying the persons of these poor folk, the very houses in the town where they had met, we are told, were burnt down for a memorial. " Forty-one persons still lie in gaol, no one knows what will be done with them. God settle it for the best." [1]

Needless, perhaps, to collect further evidence of this terrible baptism of blood! Men, women, and even children, went boldly singing psalms to the stake ; the very bonds which bound the community together seemed to grow stronger and stronger as the list of martyrs increased. Heart-rending are the songs which the poor suffering peasants and handicraftsmen sent up to God from their prison houses! Some breathe a quiet spirit of resignation : "O God, to thee I must appeal against the violence which in these evil days has befallen me. For Thy Word's sake I suffer greatly, lying in prison I am threatened with death. They led me bound before their rulers, but with Thy grace I was ready to confess Thy Name. They asked me of our faith, and I told them it was the Word of Christ. They asked me who was our leader, and I told them Christ and his teaching. He, our true Saviour, has promised us peace. To that I hold fast; that I will seal with my blood." " He, who first sang this song was named Johann Schütz, and to strengthen his comrades he sent it from the prison cell: Let man trust in God, however great his need let him put faith in no other. He can give life for death." Or again : " The world rages and palms off its falsehoods upon us ; it terrifies us with its burning and slaughter. We are scattered as the sheep who have lost their shepherd ; we wander through the forests; like the ravens we seek refuge in cave and cleft. We are pursued like the birds of the air, we are

[1] *Newe Zeyttung von den widderteuffern und yhrer Sect newlich erwachsen yhm stifft zu Salzburg vnd an andern enden.* MDXXVIII.

hunted down with dogs, and led like dumb lambs captive and in bonds. Through the agony and sorrow of death the bride of the Lord hastens to the marriage feast." Other songs again show a spirit which, like the worm, must turn at last. "O Lord, how long wilt thou be silent? Judge their pride, let the blood of thy saints ascend before thy throne." Painfully intense hymns, evidently written for congregational singing, call upon God for aid and, at last, for vengeance.[1] Ballads of their martyrs, as that of the Two Maidens of Beckum burnt by the tyrants of Burgundy, strengthened the faith in the hearts of the persecuted, and fanned their conviction almost to the fanaticism of despair.

In vain we seek a justification for this reign of terror; its only cause lay in the ignorant, nay, rather brutish, self-assertion of the powerful of earth. They never troubled themselves to examine the real beliefs of these simple-minded folk; they accepted every denunciation by their own narrow-minded theologians as based on fact; they saw rapidly spreading what they were taught to believe was a vast political conspiracy, and they stopped at no brutality which they fancied might check its growth, no bloodshed which could assist the work of extermination. Persecution brought, as it always does, a terrible retribution upon blind humanity. The Anabaptists driven wild with cruelty began to take a harsher view of their persecutors. Such horrors could only precede the day of judgment. They were surely among the terrors of the last days announced in the Book of the Revelation. God would surely come to avenge the blood of his saints:—"Await your Shepherd, since he is near who shall come at the end of the world." "Rejoice with all your heart and all your soul, thank God and praise him, since the Lord has revealed to us brothers the time wherein

---

[1] See *Auss Bundl, Etliche schöne christenliche Lieder*, 1583 (Reprint, 1838), and *Münsterische Geschichten und Legenden*, 1825. *Inter alia*, we may note the song beginning—

"In diesen letzten Zeiten,
"Wo wir auf beiden Seiten
"Mit falschen Schlangen streiten." (*i.e.*, Luther and the Pope!)

he will punish those who have persecuted and scattered you. Those, who have slain with the sword, shall be themselves slain with the sword; those, who have hanged the faithful, shall themselves be hanged; those, who have condemned the pious, shall meet with a like judgment. So shall they also be condemned without mercy according to the terrible anger of the Lord." Let the brethren be prepared to cross the Red Sea, girded to leave the land of Pharaoh. God is building a new Sion—a place of comfort for his people. The day of redemption is at hand.[1]

It is strange what very great influence the Book of Revelation has had in shaping many of the most characteristic religious movements. The notions of a coming destruction, a terrible retribution upon the oppressors of men, of the founding of a new and purer era—a kingdom of the good alone—of the millennium of joy and the coming of Christ have a wondrous attraction for the injured and the miserable; they form the channel into which the thought and hope of Franciscan dreamers, of Lollards and of Anabaptists alike drift. The allegory of some hysteric Jew becomes an immediate future to all those who feel strongly the need of a great reformation, a judgment on centuries of abuse and intolerance; they require a voice for their passionate protest, and they find it in the Apocalypse. In its wild demoniacal destruction of the past and its errors, in its prophecy of a brighter future, they hear expressed, even in the weird language of inspiration, the pent-up emotion of their own dumb souls. Such was the first thought to which persecution drove the Anabaptists :—the Divine Avenger would come and found a new Sion for his saints. But as the months rolled by, and the bloody baptism of fire continued, a new idea began to spread among the community :—the Avenger surely meant to use the righteous themselves as the sword of Gideon ; the saints should themselves arise and exterminate the worshippers of idols, then they might found the kingdom of righteousness and of love. The worm was

---

[1] *Zwen wunderseltzamen Sendbrieff zweyer Widertauffer an ire Rotten gen Augsburg gesandt. Verantwurtung: durch Urbanum Rhegium*, 1528.

beginning to turn at last ! Let him, who will, cast the first stone. He, who shuts his eyes to the misery of one half the human race, or he, who thinks their wretchedness is an eternal necessity of all forms of human society, may smile cynically when he marks the simple faith of these toilers rapidly developing into a self-destructive fanaticism. Ignorant, mis-guided people, why did ye not keep the hand to the plough, the foot to the treadle, and the body to its bench? Why did ye strive in your darkness to build up a faith for your-selves, to take that unfathomable Book for a basis? That was work better left to the priest, to the noisy theologian, to the professional twister of words. Get ye back to your toil, that the wheels of the social machine may run smoothly along! Your brotherly love and justice are absurd im-possibilities. Cannot you see that the Book and actual life are quite different matters, and society—at least, our civilized half of it—is by no means inclined for your fancies? As the ass must be beaten, or it will not move, so must the ruler drive, beat, hang, and burn the populace, *Sir Omnes*, or it will get the bridle between its teeth; the rough, ignorant *Sir Omnes* must be driven as one drives swine.[1] Crudely put, but that was still the view taken then, as it is now, by many a most worthy citizen of the "inevitable" darkness of the toiling myriads. Why should *he* be responsible for the outrages, grotesque and terrible, which spring from the ignorance and folly of these "dregs of the folk"?[2]

But the "dregs" do not always take the same view of matters, and in the last years of the third decade the blood of our Anabaptists began to approach boiling pitch. Their leaders were all slaughtered; their organization destroyed; they could not meet together to impart mutual advice or to seek mutual comfort. Each little community went on its own way, and often that way was a curious one. Nay, beyond the simple bread-breaking and adult baptism there was little in common among the various groups; persecution drove each to fanaticism in its own peculiar fashion. The ties of every-day morality were in some cases cast to the

---

[1] Luther.   [2] So Zwingli termed them.

winds. If Luther could find nothing forbidding polygamy
in the Bible, why should not Hätzer and a few followers
declare polygamy instituted by God?[1]   In other cases
madness broke out in its most extravagant forms. Some
grovelled upon the earth to free themselves from sin ; some
acted as little children, for the Gospel declared that to be a
stage to salvation ; Thomas Scheyger, at the command of
the Heavenly Father, beheaded his brother, with, indeed,
the brother's consent ; Magdalen Müllerin and her fellows
went about as Christ and the apostles ; some, believing
themselves divinely freed from all the curses of flesh,
made their liberty an excuse for every license ; prophets
arose, interpreting wondrous dreams, and proclaiming the
coming of the Lord. Isolated as such outbreaks of fanaticism
were, and steadily as the majority preserved their primitive
tenets of a simple and moral piety, it was evident that any
strong new impulse, any enthusiastic prophet, might rouse
the excited Anabaptists into an unbridled furor either of
religious fanaticism or of social license.

Nor had either to wait long for an efficient motor. Religious fanaticism found its prophet in Melchior Hofmann—
social license in his pupils the prophets of Leyden. These
men were the outward instruments, as persecution was the
inward cause, which changed the Anabaptists from passive
martyrs to ungovernable fanatics. While the process of
extermination had driven the Anabaptists out of Upper
Germany, some had found refuge in Moravia ; others, with
whom we are alone concerned, had fled to Strassburg, where
for a time toleration ruled. Here they and other religious
radicals had gathered in such numbers that the Lutherans
found comfort in the thought, that Providence, in order to
save the rest of the world, had allowed the dregs of heresy
to flow together into the sink of Strassburg. Here, soon
after 1530, Melchior Hofmann appeared on the scene.

[1] Luther's *Werke. Erlangen.* Bd. 33, p. 322. It is needless, perhaps,
to note that the views of Hätzer were not generally accepted by the Anabaptists. In their songs polygamy was repudiated as against the direct
teaching of Christ ; nor is it part even of the *Münsterische Apologie.*

This man was a native of Halle in Suabia, and a skinner
by trade. At first he was an eager disciple of Luther's, but his
Biblical studies and his keen sympathy with the sufferings of
his fellow-toilers soon led him beyond the 'pure evangely.'
For seven years he passed a strange, adventurous life, preaching in almost all the countries of Northern Europe, but still
earning his bread by the work of his hands. Driven from town
to town and country to country, persecuted by both Lutheran
and Zwinglian, he wandered with wife and child from trouble
to trouble, ever persisting in his self-appointed task.   Arriving at last in Strassburg we find him busy with the Apocalypse, and denouncing all evangelical doctrines as mere
faith of the letter ; true Christianity is a religion of the meek,
the humble, and the suffering. What wonder that the Anabaptists welcome him as their own ! From Strassburg he
passes as the prophet of Anabaptism into the Netherlands ;
but the faith he teaches is not the old brotherly love, not
primitive Christianity ; its leading doctrine is the immediate
coming of Christ. He appeals to an excited imagination, to
a fancy overwrought by persecution abroad and by suffering
at home. Surrounded by minor prophets, his life is half
mysticism, half madness. Strassburg is to be the New Sion,
the chosen city of the Lord, from which the 144,000 saints
shall march out to preach the Word of God. He himself
will then appear as Elias. Holland and Westphalia soon
become covered with a network of Anabaptist communities.
The poor, the handicraftsman, and the peasant, are carried
away by Melchior's enthusiasm. Louder and louder, more
and more earnest, grow his prophecies as the year 1533
approaches, which is to end the rule of unrighteousness and
witness the coming of God. Returning to Strassburg he
stirs up the folk almost to an outburst. He is imprisoned, but
preaches to the people in the town ditch through a window
in his tower. He is shut up in a cage, but he manages to
communicate with his disciples :—" The end of the world is
at hand, all the apocalyptic plagues are fulfilled except the
vengeance of the seventh angel. Babylon is tottering to its
fall, and Joseph and Solomon come to establish the kingdom

of God." [1] Wondrous are the reports of his doings which reach Holland, where the excitement is intense. A second prophet and witness, he who is to reveal himself as Enoch, arises,—Jan Mathys, baker of Haarlem, fanatic of a deeper dye even than Hofmann, who will lead the persecuted to break through all restraints. Mathys's creed is of a far more hostile character than Hofmann's. He teaches that the saints must themselves prepare the way of the Lord. He curses all brothers who will not hear his voice, and his fanaticism overpowers the scruples of the more fearful. He points out the lesson of those nine heads wagging on their poles over the harbour of Amsterdam. He sends out apostles to baptize, and proclaims that the blood of the innocent shall no longer be shed, that the tyrants and the godless will shortly be exterminated. Everywhere is endless commotion, unlimited fermentation among the Anabaptists. In Münster Mathys's disciple, the youthful Jan Bockelson, has won a strong foothold for the Anabaptist doctrines. The worm is beginning to turn in real earnest, it is grasping to the full the notion that God's people must separate themselves, that there may be a destruction of the godless. And then follows persecution renewed and bitter throughout Holland; the Anabaptists fly before it with one accord to Münster. Jan Mathys is with the fugitives, and he announces that God has chosen Münster for the New Sion, owing to the faithlessness of Strassburg. There towards the beginning of the year 1534 are gathered men, women, and children, from all quarters and of many classes, peasant, noble, trader, handicraftsman, monk and nun. The majority, it is true, are poor, miserable, and persecuted; the few, religious or political idealists; all are bent on establishing the rule of righteousness and love—the Kingdom of God in Münster.

Before entering into an account of this weird Kingdom of God—this grotesque and yet terrible drama—it will simplify matters to relate briefly the events which prepared the way for it in Münster. From the very first the Reformation took

[1] See Cornelius, vol. ii. chaps. iii. and ix. The best account of Hofmann is to be found in F. O. zur Linden's *Melchior Hofmann*, 1885.

in that town a strongly political character. On the one side we find a prince-bishop, Graf Franz von Waldeck, personally utterly indifferent alike to the old faith and the new 'evangely,' and ready to adopt either, as it may serve his purpose,—the maintenance of his autocratic authority; on the other side we have a populace who fancy that the 'pure evangely' means the abolition of the bishop and the triumph of self-government. We have the bishop, licentious, drunken, grasping after power in order to support his concubines and to enjoy his feastings to the full—the populace eager for freedom, ignorant, and full of contempt for the bishop and his underlings; between bishop and populace, the Town Council, composed for the most part of the patrician burghers, and by no means anxious for either bishop or democracy; the bishop supported by a corrupt chapter and an indolent, if not immoral clergy—the democratic element introducing the preachers of the 'pure evangely,' and the Council desirous of organizing them into a church, which while opposing the bishop shall yet remain under its own thumb. Such is the state of Münster. Among the preachers who found their way into the town was Bernard Rottmann—by no means a leader of men, incapable of really guiding or restraining the populace. His broad sympathy with the oppressed classes, unchecked by a clear and dispassionate reason, caused him to follow folk-opinion rather than direct it; while at the same time his power of language marked him out as a chief advocate of the popular cause. Carried along on the top of the stream he is the central object of attention till he dashes with it over the precipice. At first we find him preaching outside the gates of the city, as some say, with the connivance of the bishop. He adopts the Lutheran doctrine that faith alone can save mankind, all the rest—form and ceremony—is the devil's own handiwork. In spite of this, he has a large following in Münster, and the handicraftsmen and their wives flock out to hear him. His teaching is not without effect, and on Good Friday of the year 1531 the mob during the night storm the Church of St. Maurice outside the gates, and destroy the altars, pictures, and carving. Rottmann seems to have thought it better after this event to retire—not, however, without the suggestion of a bribe from the Catholic clergy.[1]   In the following year, notwithstanding, he returns once more to Münster, and although he is forbidden to preach, the folk erect a wooden pulpit for him in the church-yard of St. Lambert inside the city, and at last, to prevent a riot, the church itself is given up to him.   The 'pure evangely' having thus obtained a sure footing, Rottmann writes to Marburg for assistance, and we soon find six evangelical preachers in Münster battling to destroy the old faith.   The Town Council and the Syndic Van der Wieck favour the preachers, because with their assistance they hope to free themselves from the obnoxious chapter.   The six preachers prepare thirty articles, and, with the connivance of the Council, force the Catholic clergy to a disputation.   The Evangelicals are declared to have God and reason on their side, and the six parish churches are surrendered to their preachers.   Meanwhile the dean and chapter have left the town and appealed to the prince-bishop.   The bishop at first attempts to play one party off against the other, and even temporizes with democracy.   Finally, however, he holds a council at the little town of Telgte on the Ems, and deter-mines to starve his sheep out of their 'pure evangely.' Democracy laughs him to scorn, marches out guild-fashion to Telgte by night, and surprises the bishop's court, the council, and the dean and chapter—only unfortunately not his grace, who happens to have left a few days before.   The captives are brought into Münster, and handed over to the Town Council.   " Here we bring you the oxen ; hark how they bellow ! "   The bishop deprived of his ' oxen ' comes to terms ; the preachers shall be recognized in Münster, the cathedral alone reserved for the Catholics.   So the 'pure evangely' seems to be triumphantly established.

But democracy, having tasted ' evangelical freedom,' is by no means disposed to stop here, and where it drifts Rott-mann will follow.   As the Lutherans said : " The devil

[1] Dorpius : *Warhafftige historie wie das Evangelium zu Münster angefangen*, &c.

finding it impossible to crush the 'pure evangely' by
means of the priests, hunted up the Anabaptist prophets."
Already Rottmann, the idol of the populace, has begun to be
in bad odour at Wittenberg. Luther writes to the Town
Council: "God has given you, as I hear, fine preachers,
especial Master Bernhardt. Yet it is fitting that all
preachers be truly admonished and checked, since the
devil is a knave, and can well seduce even fine, pious,
and learned preachers." Master Bernhardt, it is true, had
been instituting somewhat curious ceremonies. The Holy
Supper, he argued, was only a feast of brotherly love, and
accordingly he broke bannocks in a pan, poured wine over
them, and invited all who would to partake. He preached
from the pulpit against the "bread and wine God" of the
Catholics and Evangelicals alike. He found that democracy was in perfect accord with Gospel teaching, and the
poor—the toilers—not only of Münster, but from far and
wide, gathered round him. "His doctrine is wonderful,"
wrote the Syndic Van der Wieck, "a miserable, depraved
mob gathers round him, none of whom, so far as I know,
could scrape together two hundred gulden to pay their
debts!" Still the Syndic and Council grow anxious, the
scum—the toiling oppressed—the persecuted and now
fanatical Anabaptists are gathering round "Bannock-Bernt"
in Münster. Forced on by his more radical following, he
begins to express doubts as to infant baptism. Hermann
Strapraede of Mörse declares from the pulpit that it is an
"abomination before God." The Council appeals to Luther
and Melanchthon, but these names have long lost all
authority among the masses. The Council orders that the
Anabaptist teachers shall be driven out of the gate of the
city, but the 'Spirit of the Lord' (or the Devil, as the
Evangelicals said,) moves them to march round the walls
and re-enter at the opposite gate. The Council, doubting
its own strength, appeals to reason in the shape of a disputation, and imports Hermann von dem Busche to combat
Bannock-Bernt. But Bannock-Bernt has by far and
away the glibbest tongue, and, after he has spoken for

several hours, the Council breaks up the disputation in despair. After a little further bickering, in which the power of the radical preachers becomes more and more evident, the Council shuts up all the churches. The preachers are even more effective outside their pulpits than in them, while Rottmann, with the working classes and an ever-increasing mob of Anabaptists at his back, scoffs at the Council. He will fulfil the duty laid upon him by God, however stiff-necked be the authorities. Then the Council try a new expedient; they introduce the Catholic orator, Dr. Mumpert. Mumpert preaches against Bannock-Bernt in the Cathedral, Bannock-Bernt against Mumpert in the Church of St. Servatius; this only leads to rioting and the banishment of Mumpert. In desperation the Council strives to establish an 'evangelical church order,' and imports Lutheran preachers from Hesse. Rottmann and his colleagues shall be banished. Crowds of women threaten the burgomasters, and demand· the restoration of their beloved preacher and the ejection of the Hessians. Again the mob triumphs; the Evangelicals are driven from the churches, even torn from the pulpit. Heinrich Rollius,[1] formerly a Lutheran, now a prophet, rushes through the town crying: "Repent! repent! and be baptized!" Many are baptized, some for fear of God, others for fear of their property. Suddenly the Anabaptists pour out of their holes and corners and seize the market-place, the Rathhaus and the town-cannon; Catholics and Evangelicals entrench themselves by the Church of 'Our Lady across the water.' Yet the 'party of order' is still the stronger; they march across the cathedral close, and plant cannon facing the approaches of the market-place. But then fear seizes them that the bishop will take the opportunity of falling upon the town. The Anabaptists find that they are still too few in numbers, a truce is made; all men shall hold what faith they please. "The day of the Lord has not yet come." Peace!

Peace in a seething mass of fanaticism like this? Nay!

[1] Shortly after Rollius was burnt as an Anabaptist at Maestricht.

Münster is to be the 'fortress of righteousness;' wait but a while, till more of the saints have arrived. From that day onward the saints continue to pour into Münster, and the 'party of order' dwindles away, flying with all its portable property out of the city. Bannock-Bernt declares he will preach only to the elect. Haggard-looking faces and people in strange garbs appear on the streets; families are broken up; wives speak of their husbands as the 'godless,' and even children leave their parents to become 'saints.' At midnight the gun booms over Münster, calling the Anabaptists to prayer; prophets rush with the mien of madmen, shrieking through the streets; the power of the Council vanishes in the whirlpool of fanaticism which, dark and terrible, is involving all things. On the 31st of February, 1534, the election of burgomasters falls entirely into the hands of the Anabaptists, and they appoint their own leaders, Knipperdollinch and Kibbenbroick. From that date the Kingdom of God commences in Münster.

Of the four principal actors in this terrible judgment of history we have marked the leading characteristics of Jan Mathys and Rottmann; it is necessary to say a few words of the other two, Knipperdollinch and Jan Bockelson of Leyden. Bernt Knipperdollinch was a draper of Münster, a favourite with the folk, probably on account of his burly figure and boisterous nature. Long before the outbreak he seems to have got into difficulties with the bishop; he had sung satirical songs against him in the streets, and won folk-applause by his somewhat ribald satires on the dean and chapter. At one time the bishop had put him in gaol, and the burly draper by no means forgave the insult; he determined "to burn the bishop's house about his head." Not in the least an enthusiast, he yet pinned his faith to democracy; desirous himself of power, he was yet not strong enough to be anything but the tool of others. His fanaticism when once aroused tended rather to sensual than spiritual manifestations. He represents the brute, almost devilish, element in the mad dance. He seems at times to have been conscious of the grim humour of this mock Kingdom

of God; and it is difficult to grasp whether his fanaticism
was a jest, or his jests the outcome of his fanaticism. Yet
when captured and examined under torture, he could only
say that he had done all from a feeling of right, all from
a consciousness of God's will![1] Of a far different nature
was Jan of Leyden. As the illegitimate son of a tailor in that
town—his mother being the maid of his father's wife—Jan's
early life was probably a harsh and bitter one. Very young
he wandered from home, impressed with the miseries of his
class and with a general feeling of much injustice in the world.
Four years he spent in England seeing the poor driven off
the land by the sheep; then we find him in Flanders,
married, but still in vague search of the Eldorado; again
roaming, he visits Lisbon and Lübeck as a sailor, ever seeking
and inquiring. Suddenly a new light breaks upon him from
the teaching of Melchior Hofmann; he fills himself with
dreams of a glorious kingdom on earth, the rule of justice
and of love. Still a little while and the prophet Mathys
crosses his path, and tells him of the new Sion and the
extermination of the godless. Full of hope for the future,
Jan sets out for Münster to join the saints. Still young,
handsome, imbued with a fiery enthusiasm, actor by nature
and even by choice, he has no small influence on the spread
of Anabaptism in that city. The youth of twenty-three
expounds to the followers of Rottmann the beauties of his
ideal kingdom of the good and the true. With his whole
soul he preaches to them the redemption of the oppressed,
the destruction of tyranny, the community of goods, and the
rule of justice and brotherly love. Women and maidens
slip away to the secret gatherings of the youthful enthusiast;
the glowing young prophet of Leyden becomes the centre
of interest in Münster. Dangerous, very dangerous ground,
when the pure of heart are not around him; when the
spirit "chosen by God" is to proclaim itself free of the
flesh. The world has judged Jan harshly, condemned him
to endless execration. It were better to have cursed the

---

[1] See *Die Geschichtsquellen des Bisthums Münster*, where the confession is given in full.

generations of oppression, the flood of persecution, which
forced the toiler to revolt, the Anabaptists to madness.
Under other circumstances the noble enthusiasm, with
other surroundings the strong will, of Jan of Leyden might
have left a different mark on the page of history. Dragged
down in this whirlpool of fanaticism, sensuality, and despair,
we can only look upon him as a factor of the historic judgment, a necessary actor in that tragedy of Münster, which
forms one of the most solemn chapters of the Greater Bible.

All is enthusiasm, ready self-sacrifice, and prophetic joy
in the New Sion during the first few days of its establishment. At every turn 'God be with you!' is heard in the
streets, and the cheery reply 'Amen, dear brother!' On
Saturday the new burgomasters had been elected; on the
following Monday they at once proceeded to take steps for
the defence of the town. With 1,500 saints they march out
from the St. Maurice Gate, and destroy the cloister of the
same name. The buildings and all their art treasures ascend
in flame to heaven, that they may not form a shelter for the
godless; meanwhile bands of women carry into the town all
the provisions that can be found in the neighbourhood.
Then precautions are taken for the safety of the walls
and protection against surprise. No sooner is the new
kingdom safe from the godless without, than it befits the
saints to destroy the godless within. What are these
pictures, these carvings, these coloured windows to the
chosen of God?   Symbols, which have long lost their
meaning, badges of a slavery which is past, signs of
a faith in the letter; they are but cursed idols in the
light of our new freedom. Let the stone prophets and
apostles come crashing from their niches; carry out these
painted semblances of God and his saints, and burn these
abominations on the market-place! Have we not prophets
and apostles of real flesh and blood, are not the saints
of New Sion better than these tawdry fictions, for God is
enshrined in their hearts? Away with this outward form,
these altar trappings, these gorgeous missals, these sacra-
mental cups! The Spirit of God works within us, why mask

it in idle display? Let us show our contempt for such devilish
delusions in the coarsest and most forcible fashion. But
further, these archives and documents, what need can there
be for such legal distinctions in Sion? Naught of the past
remains holy—what are these bones to us—bones of bishops
and saints, relics of men who lived in the age of sin? On
to the dunghill with them, for they cannot help us to the
light of day! So thought the Anabaptists, and stormed
the churches, cleared out the relics, the art treasures, and
the labour of many a generation; what for years men in
faith had been creating, the folk of New Sion in faith
and a night destroyed. Barbarous, fanatic, the world has
called it! Yet, while the Anabaptists cast down stone
images and burnt forms of canvas and paint, your prince-
bishop also played the iconoclast,—only his images were of
flesh and of blood. He drowned five Anabaptist women at
Wolbeck, he burnt five at Bevergem,—ten helpless, ignorant
souls, yet panting as all souls for life. What wonder the
saints in Münster grew mad in their fancies, and madder
in their deeds! Not only was ornament in the churches
grievous to the saints, but even the churches themselves.
God will not be worshipped in a temple made by human
hands. Let, then, these masses of stone be turned to
fitting purpose; the cathedral and its close becomes Mount
Sion, the gathering-place for God's elect; the Church of
St. Lambert becomes St. Lambert's stone quarry, whence
all may fetch stone for building their houses or repairing the
city walls. A like fate meets the other sacred buildings,
and over their portals are inscribed new names:—'Our
Lady's Quarry,' and so forth. Woe to the brother whose
unlucky tongue lets slip the old name! As penance he
shall be forced to drink "einen pot watter"![1] The
destruction, however, does not stop here; the innumerable
spires and towers of the city are not only dangerous as
marks for the enemy's cannon, but are also reminiscences of
an idolatry which has obscured the knowledge of God; so

[1] *Heinrich Gresbecks Bericht* in the *Geschichtsquellen des Bisthums Münster*, Bd. 2.

our children of the New Sion are "mighty to the pulling
down of strongholds, casting down imaginations, and every
high thing that exalteth itself against the knowledge of God."
The convents, too, can be turned to useful purposes, when
once the idols have been destroyed and the idolaters ejected ;
for a home can be found in them for the crowd of Anabaptist
strangers. Not that ejection is always necessary, since
the nuns of St. Ægidius soon flock to be baptized, and their
sisters of Overrat follow. The true spirit of asceticism
is long since dead, and in the New Sion the nuns hope to
unite holiness and the pleasures of sense. Nor are some
of the monks behindhand, for we hear at least of one old
convent guardian who, remaining, took unto himself in the
latter days of Sion four wives ! 'Tis a poor race of folk this,
with none of the noble aims of early Christian asceticism, a
very dangerous earthy element in the new kingdom of the
spirit. Nay, a stupid little abbess, who does even fly with
her nuns, can tell us but little of the doings of the saints.
She has no conception of the meaning of this great religious
fermentation. It is all very wicked, all very terrible, all
comes of a runaway Wittenberg monk saying mass in
German, and administering the communion in two forms.
So she fled with her nuns to Hiltorppe, and there on the
first night they found nothing to eat and drink, and some of
the sisters were so very thirsty that they were compelled
to drink—water ! [1] Both the saints and godless seem to have
had a horror of water. Still one more test follows of the
faith of the saints. On the night of Thursday, the 26th, the
prophet Mathys preaches against the letter, and calls upon
the folk to destroy all the books in Israel, all except the
Bible. Books, it is, that have led men astray, twisting with
words, and quibbling o'er phrases. The truth has been
strangled in a network of written lies, and God could not
reach the heart of man. Pile up the books in the market-
place, the kingdom of Sion is based on the spirit, not the
letter, and the wisdom of the past is idle delusion in the
light of our new day. Ascend in flame, ye vain strivings of

[1] *Chronik des Schwesterhauses Niesinck* in the *Geschichtsquellen.*

the human brain; Sion starts unhampered by your dark questionings; her knowledge springs directly from God; her wisdom is the outcome of inspiration; she has naught to do with the toiling, erring reason of the past!

But not even yet is Sion purified, not even yet are the godless separated from the saints.   On Friday, the last day of the first week of the establishment of God's kingdom in Münster, the prophets rush inspired through the streets with the cry, 'Repent, repent, ye godless! Out of the city of the blessed, ye idolaters! God is aroused to punish you!' On the same day the saints hunt the godless out of the town, all who will not be baptized must go.   The poor unfortunate Evangelicals escape from the fury of the Anabaptists only to fall into the hands of the bishop.   The Syndic Van der Wieck and two Lutheran preachers are promptly beheaded without trial.   What wonder that many remain and are baptized? For three days the cry of 'Out with the godless!' resounds through the streets, for three days the prophets stand baptizing in the market-place.   Before each prophet is placed a pitcher of water, and as the folk come up one by one and kneel before him, he exhorts the converts to brotherly love, to leave the evil and follow the good; then he baptizes them with three handfuls of water in the name of the Father, the Son, and the Holy Ghost.   Each new brother or sister is given a metal token with the letters D. W. W. F. inscribed upon it: "Das Wort ward Fleisch,"— the Word became flesh.   Even when the baptizing in the market-place is over, the prophets go round the town baptizing the old and feeble.   Every house is inspected, and if any godless are found, their property is seized for the benefit of the community, while the owners are driven from their homes.   So at last the new Sion is purified!   What is the value of such a purification?   It might purge the 'Kingdom of God' of human foes; could it reach the germs of disease within the hearts of the saints themselves?   We have yet to note how the 'rule of righteousness' prospered in Sion; how unchangeable are the laws of human development; how inexorable the judgments of historical evolution.

19

II.

The saints and the godless had been separated, but still the folk of New Sion were not quite one at heart. There were religious fanatics, who thought that all alike must share their enthusiasm for the kingdom of righteousness; there were knaves, who had joined it simply for plunder, and would not hesitate to convert it into an earthly hell; there were cowards, whom fear had impelled, and whose hands would fail when most needed; finally, there were the simpletons, who at first were stirred by words, the meaning of which they scarcely grasped, to join a fool's paradise, but whose spirit would die, when their material wants were not supplied, and who would in the end be butchered with small resistance —ignorant simple folk, conscious of some great injustice, easily guided by the stronger will, and then left to bear the brunt of outraged and relentless authority. It was not long before the lukewarm spirit showed itself, and called forth a terrible judgment. One Hubert, a smith, as he kept watch on the walls at night, ventured to say to some of his comrades that :—" The prophets will prophesy till they cost us our necks, for the devil is in them." [1]   Small wonder that the enthusiastic brethren of Sion were shocked to find the godless within their very ranks, a traitor within the purified city!   The saints gathered in the market-place, and the wretched smith—he, who had been the first to dim the bright hopes of the New Jerusalem—was led out into their midst. Then the prophets sat in judgment, and declared the poor trembling sinner worthy of death. " He had scorned the chosen of God—God whose will it was that there should be naught impure in the city. All sin must be rooted up, for the Lord wanted a holy folk." Let us try for an instant to feel as those prophets felt, to feel that if once a citizen of Sion could doubt their mission, nay, if once a shadow of doubt were allowed to settle in their own minds, if once the cold touch of reason should question their inspiration, then

---

[1] *Gresbecks Bericht.*   Dorpius has the more expressive " *Sie sind scheissende Propheten.*"

all the glorious hopes of this Kingdom of God would crumble into the dust. It was based solely on the saints' belief in the prophets, and on the prophets' belief in themselves ; they were the direct means of communication between God and his chosen folk. And here came one out of the very fold in the dawn of the new era, and ventured to doubt—to doubt where the very suspicion of doubt meant the madness of recognized self-delusion ! Nay, after the prophets had fallen, even when they were questioned under torture, they replied : We have failed, yet still were tools in God's hand. Awful is that first judgment in Sion, but not more awful than the maiden drowned in the horse-pond at Salzburg. In old Germanic days the priests had been the executioners, and now the prophets took upon themselves the dread office. The trembling smith was led to the cathedral—to the Mount of Sion ; there Jan, the prophet of Leyden, took a halberd and struck twice at him, but in vain ; Death grimly refused his prey. Back to prison the wounded man was taken, and a strange scene followed. God had deprived the arm of their prophet of strength, and the saints grovelling on their faces in the market-place shrieked that Sion had lost the grace of God ! Then the prophet Mathys orders the prisoner again to be brought out, and placed against the cathedral wall ; but he will not stand, falls crosswise on the ground, and begs for mercy. Mercy there is none in Sion, and Mathys takes a musket and shoots him through the back. And still he does not die. Then say the prophets : ' 'Tis the Lord's will that he live.' Live, however, he cannot, and he dies within the week. Such is the first blood shed in Sion, foretaste of the flood to come. Mad, raving mad, judged the world, when it heard of this and the like. ' Shoot them down like wild beasts ! ' it cried. And the world was right : 'twas the only way to cure the pest. But the world never learnt the lesson —will it ever ?—the judgment of history on the crimes of the past. It forgot the butchered Anabaptists of the decade before ; it forgot the ' laver of degeneration ' it had itsel administered in the baptism of ·blood.

But let us turn for a moment from the darker side of the

picture, which will soon enough demand all our attention, to
glance at what too often is forgotten—the social reconstruction in Sion.   So soon as the labour of separating the saints
from all taint of the godless was completed, the leaders
began to organize the new kingdom of righteousness according to their glowing ideals of human perfection.   First, a
community of goods was proclaimed.   "Dear brothers and
sisters, now that we are a united folk, it is God's will that
we bring together all our money, silver and gold; one shall
have as much as another.   Let each bring his money to
the exchequer in the council house.   There will the council
sit to receive it."   So the prophets and the preachers arise
and speak of the mercy of God, and of brotherly love, calling
upon all the saints, with terrible anathemas against defaulters,
to bring their wealth to the common stock.   In each parish
three deacons are appointed to collect all the food, which is
then stored in houses hard by the gates.   Here the common
meals are held—the women at one table and the men at
another—while some youth reads the weird and soul-stirring
prophecies of Isaiah or Daniel.   The deacons have the entire
domestic economy in their hands, particularly the charge of
the common food and property.   So great is at first the
enthusiasm for the commonweal, that even little children
run about pointing out hidden stores.[1]   The doors of the
houses are to be left open day and night, that all who will
may enter; only a hurdle is allowed to keep out the pigs.
Some half-dozen schools are founded for the children,
wherein they are taught to read and write, and to recite the
psalms; but above all they learn the doctrine of brotherly
love, and the glorious future in store for Sion.   Once a-week
the children march in pairs to the cathedral, hear one of the
preachers, sing one or two psalms, and return home in like
fashion.   Money, too, is coined in Sion, not, however, for its
inhabitants, but to bribe the men-at-arms who serve the godless.   Twelve elders are appointed, and they sit morning
and noon in the market-place to hear plaint and administer

---

[1] The Lutheran Dorpius terms them "maidens possessed of the Devil,
who betrayed what was hidden."—E. i.

justice. Terrible is the justice of the saints, for a thief is a traitor to the brotherhood, and even soldiers in Sion are shot for forcibly tapping a barrel of beer.

Not all, however, is stern earnest in the city ; in these first weeks the joy of the folk shows itself in coarse jest at the bishop's expense. An old broken-down mare is driven out of the city towards the bishop's camp, and tied to her tail is the treaty of peace with its great episcopal seal, whereby his grace had recovered the 'oxen' captured at Telgte. Then with ringing of bells a procession is formed, and a straw-stuffed dummy covered over and over with papal bulls and indulgences is conducted out of the gates and dispatched in like fashion towards the enemy's lines. Another time it is a huge tun which arrives on a waggon without driver ; great is the curiosity of the bishop and his court to know its contents,—being opened, they find themselves mocked with Anabaptist excrement pure and simple ! Nor do the saints content themselves merely with jests ; they make successful sorties, carry off gunpowder and spike guns even under the very nose of his episcopal grace. There is small discipline in the bishop's camp, and the appeal to his neighbours for aid is but slowly complied with. Later, during the siege, we hear of a mock mass in the cathedral ; fools dressed in priest's raiment officiate, while the folk offer rubbish, filth, and dead rats at the altar ; and the whole is concluded with a sham fight in the aisle. Upon another occasion the chancel is turned into a stage, and the play of the rich man and Lazarus is given. Merrily the three pipers play accompaniment, and the devil fetching the rich man to hell causes the building to ring with laughter. But this is in the latter days of Sion, when Sion has chosen a king, and suspicion stalks darkly amid the starving Anabaptists. The farce ends with tragedy. Sion's ruler has reason to suspect the queen's lacquey who acts the rich man ; and the rich man is dragged from hell to be hanged on a tree in the market-place. There was small room for jest in those latter days of Sion.

Yet at first even the most fanatical could unbend, and we hear that when the sternest Anabaptists were together

'they sat joyously over the table, and all their talk was
not of the Lord, of Paul, or of the holiness of life,'[1]   Shortly
before Easter we find the arch-prophet Mathys with his wife
Divara—the young and the beautiful, for whom he had
thrown off a union of the flesh—at a marriage feast.   Who
shall say what dark thoughts had entered the mind of the
austere prophet ?   Had he seen a glimpse of the spiritual
decay which was soon to fall over the new Sion ?   Had he
doubts as to the future, mistrust of himself ?   Did the shadow
of the butchered smith haunt his mind? Who shall say? We
know only, that in the midst of the general joy, Mathys was
suddenly moved by the Spirit, he raised his hands above his
head, his whole frame shook, and it appeared as if the hour of
death were upon him.   The bridal party sat in hushed fear.
Then the prophet arose and said with a sigh: 'O dear Father,
not as I will, but rather as thou wilt.'   Giving to each his
hand and a kiss, he added : ' God's peace be with you,' and
left the gathering.   A few hours after the saints in Münster
learnt that their chief prophet seizing a pike, and crying like
a madman : ' With the help of the heavenly Father I will
put the foe to flight and free Jerusalem,'—had rushed out of
the gates, and followed by a few fanatic enthusiasts had been
slaughtered by the bishop's troops.   So the first and chief
prophet of Münster, honest and true to his idea, died before
the moral decay of the saints.   He may have been a fanatic,
his idea may have been false ; still he fought and died for a
spiritual notion—his grace the bishop fought and triumphed
for *himself !*

Strange scenes follow the death of Mathys.   The prophets
and the folk gather in the market-place crying, ' O God, grant
us thy love !   O Father, give us thy grace !'   In the most
abject fashion the saints grovel on the ground.   Women and
maidens go dancing through the streets with wild cries.
With loosened hair and disordered dress they dance and
shriek till their faces grow pale as death, and they fall ex-
hausted to the ground.   There they strike their naked
breasts with clenched fists, tear out their hair in handfuls,

[1] *Gresbecks Bericht.*

and roll in the mud. But the youthful Jan of Leyden arises and proclaims that God will grant them a greater prophet even than Mathys. For long ago he saw a vision, wherein Mathys was bored through with a pike, and the voice of God bade him take the lost prophet's wife as his own.[1] So the folk cries, 'Grant it, Father, grant it!' and from this day Jan is the chief ruler in Sion. Unfortunately, however, the young prophet is already wed to a serving-maid of Knipperdollinch's, and how can he take in addition the beautiful Divara? For three days and three nights he remains in a state of trance, and then the power of evil triumphs, the floodgates of social license are thrown open, and Jan Bockelson awakes to preach the gospel of sense. In the one scale are the sensuous vigour of youth, the feeling of power, the animal will; in the other the hope of a new future for men, the rule of human love, the old moral restraints based on the experience of long generations. Sensuous pleasure and the toil of self-renunciation,—'tis an old struggle which has oft recurred in history, and is like to recur, till centuries of progress shall perchance harmonize the material and spiritual in man. And what remains to restrain the youthful tailor of Leyden, filled as he is with the consciousness of will and of power? There is no respect for the slowly acquired wisdom of the past, for the past is cursed with sin;—no appeal to the common sense of the folk is possible, for God dictates truth through the prophets only. Nay, there is this great danger in Sion—the women far outnumber the men—and in the hysterical religion of the female saints the sensuous impulse is strong. So it comes about that Jan preaches the gospel of sense. The preachers and the twelve elders declare that a man may have more wives than one. God has bid his chosen people 'be fruitful and multiply.' None shall remain single, but every Anabaptist bring up children to be saints in Sion. It is said that at first even some of the saints resisted this new license, but that the unmarried women themselves dragged

---

[1] Even in his confession under torture Jan maintained the truth of this vision, and his own wonder when it was fulfilled. *Geschichtsquellen des Bisthums Münster.*

the cannon to the market-place, and were mainly instrumental in destroying all opposition. Be this as it may, it is certain that on Good Friday, April 14th, the prophet Jan, amid the ringing of bells and the rejoicing of the folk, marries Divara, widow of the prophet of Haarlem. From that date onward the number of Jan's wives increases till they reach, besides their chief, Divara, the goodly total of fourteen. Rottmann had four wives, and Knipperdollinch and other leaders at least the same number. No woman might refuse marriage, though she might reject any proposed husband. Girls of tender age were given to the saints, and even the old women in Münster were distributed as wives among the folk, who had to look after them and see they fully grasped the great Anabaptist doctrines. ' Dear brothers and sisters,' said the preachers, ' all too long have ye lived in a heathen state, and there has been no true marriage.' Simple in the extreme was the new ceremony. The man went with a few friends to the home of the woman, and both taking hands in the presence of their friends proclaimed themselves husband and wife. But polygamy brings almost at once a grotesque judgment on the saints of Sion, for the wives quarrel endlessly with one another, and the saints have no peace at home. Daily cases of fighting and disorder among the women come before the twelve Elders, and imprisonment is found useless. So at last Bannock-Bernt declares that the sword will be tried, but the mere threat loses its force after awhile, and several women have to be executed. The leaders finding still that no punishment avails, bid all the women, who will, come to the Council House. There several hundred women, who have been forced into marriage or are tired of polygamy, give in their names. Summoned a few days afterwards before the Elders they are declared *free* from their husbands, and the preachers rising in the market-place proclaim them cursed of God, and body and soul the devil's ! The veil is best drawn over this plague-spot in Münster ; suffice it, if the reader remember, that 'tis ever at work undermining the kingdom of Sion, that it leads to terrible abuses, and ends, as that kingdom totters to its fall, in little short of sexual anarchy.

Even in Münster great social changes are not completed without rebellion. A less fanatical group, aided by the native saints, who by no means approve of the community of goods, suddenly rises, and, seizing the prophets and Knipperdollinch, imprisons them in the Council House cellar. The uxorious preacher Schlachtschap is torn from the midst of his wives, and placed in the pillory, where women, with old-fashioned ideas, pelt him with dung and stones, asking whether he wants more wives, or if he does not now think one enough ? The fate of Sion hangs in the balance, and a messenger is despatched to the bishop's camp. But before he is out of the town, the strangers from Holland and Friesland have seized the gates, and are marching six hundred strong upon the Council House. There is a short but severe fight, the defenders firing from the windows upon the strangers below; but alas! they have been spending the night in drinking from the stores in the town cellar, and the Dutchmen force their way in and make some 120 prisoners. Terrible is the vengeance of the enraged fanatics. Jan of Leyden, Knipperdollinch, the twelve Elders, and the prophets being released, cause the rioters to be brought out daily in batches of ten; then some are shot, some beheaded, some stabbed with daggers. Whoever desires to kill a traitor to Sion, may take one and slay him as he pleases. For four or five days the massacre lasts, the bodies being cast into two large pits in the cathedral close. Awful is this dance of death, this masquerade of loosened passion; but those who will learn its lesson must ever remember the ' baptism of blood.' At last the fury of the fanatics is glutted, the remaining prisoners are pardoned and taken into the cloister of St. George, where many-wived Schlachtschap, mounted on a high stool, preaches a sermon to them on their crime; how they have acted against the will of God, and must thank him that they have received grace. The preacher addresses each by name, and tells him how he has sinned against the brothers and sisters in Sion. They have been received into the fold again, may they duly appreciate such mercy.[1] There must have been many sore

[1] *Gresbecks Bericht.*

hearts in Sion, many weary and sick of this Kingdom of
God, and yet enthusiasm was not dead, it wanted but opportunity to show itself with all the force of old.

Since February the bishop had made but little progress,
and even within his camp he could not feel safe from the
fanaticism of these strange children of Sion.   A curious
incident had happened about Easter.   A maiden of the
Anabaptists, Hilla Feichen by name,[1] had heard the story
of Judith and Holofernes read aloud at the common meal.
Inspired by it, she determined to repeat the deed on the
shameless bishop in his camp at Telgte.   She announced
this as the will of God to his prophets, and they allowed
the damsel to go.   Dressed in her best and adorned with
gold rings, the present of Knipperdollinch, she arrived at
the hostile camp.   Only, poor deluded child, to fall into the
hands of the men-at-arms, to excite suspicion by her wondrous garb, to be tortured, to confess, and pay for the wild
vision with her life.   Why should her name not be remembered along with those whose bearers have planned nobler,
if less heroic deeds ?   There was power, there was genius in
Hilla, had the world brought it to fairer bloom, had it not
been poisoned in this slough of profanation at Münster !   By
the following Whitsuntide the bishop feels strong enough to
attack the town by storm ; and now an opportunity presents
itself to the inhabitants of Sion to show in mass the enthusiasm of Hilla.   Men, women, and children flock to the
walls on the first report ; only the aged and sick are left in
the town.   Out of every hole and corner, from every rampart
boiling oil and water, melted lead and glowing lime—a
perfect devil's broth, is poured upon the foe.   Blazing wreaths
of tar are thrown round the necks of the bishop's soldiers, a
hail of shot and stones greets them as they approach.   She-
devils on the wall batter with pitchforks the skulls of those
who mount scaling ladders.   The folk of Sion are mad in
their rage, as though the oppression of years, the whole

---

[1] See her confession in *Nieserts Münsterische Urkundensammlung*,
Bd. I., and also the confessions of Jan of Leyden and Knipperdollinch in
the *Geschichtsquellen*.

'baptism of blood' was to be avenged in this one day. "Are
ye come at last ? Three or four nights have we baked and
boiled for you ; the broth has long been ready, had ye but
come ! " Once, twice, thrice, the men-at-arms rushed to the
storm ; once, twice, thrice, a shattered remnant retired.
Theirs is the bull-love of fight, but not the enthusiasm which
springs from an idea. Their pluck fails and they retreat.
The defenders mockingly shout :—" Come again, come again,
will ye already fly ? surely the storm might last the whole
day ? " Then the Anabaptists fall upon their knees and sing:
" If the Lord himself had not been on our side when men
rose up against us, then they had swallowed us up quick."
Jan of Leyden and the minor prophets go dancing and
singing through the streets : " Dear brothers, have we not a
strong God ? He has helped us. It has not been done by
our own power. Let us rejoice, and thank the Father." The
inspired declare approaching deliverance ; Christ will come
at once and found the 1,000 years' kingdom of the saints.
There is new unity in Sion, fresh hope and fresh enthusiasm.
God has been but trying His saints. His grace the bishop
has also learnt a lesson, in future he will adopt the surer
method of blockade, he will shut these fanatics up till
starvation has won the battle for him. So, as aid comes in
from his allies, he completely cuts Münster off from the
outer world, and Sion becomes the centre of an impassable
circle of blockhouses.

The victory seems to have brought new inspiration to Jan
Bockelson. Were but the hand of one strong man to guide
these enthusiasts, surely the kingdom of Sion might even
now be established, even now the elements of decay might
be cut off, and the baser, selfish passions of the saints sub-
dued. The thought in the man becomes the will of God in
the prophet. A revelation comes to Jan that he is called to
be king of the New Jerusalem—nay, king over the whole
world, the viceroy of God on earth ; a lord of righteousness,
who shall punish all unrighteousness throughout the world.
Nor does the revelation come to Jan alone. On June 24th—
Johannistag, mysterious and holy sun-feast—Johann Dusent-

schuer, formerly a goldsmith of Warendorff, but now a prophet of the Lord, stumps, so fast as his lameness will allow, through the streets of Sion, crying to the folk to assemble in the market-place.   There the limping prophet throws himself upon the ground, and declares the will of heaven. God has ordained that Jan of Leyden, the holy prophet, shall be king over the whole world, over all emperors, kings, princes, lords, and potentates. He alone shall rule, and none above him.   He shall take the kingdom and the throne of David his father, till the Lord God requires it again of him. Then the folk look to their beloved prophet, and he, falling on his knees, tells them *his* revelation. " God has chosen me for a king over the whole earth.   Yet further I say to you, dear brothers and sisters, I would rather be a swineherd, rather take the plough, rather delve, than thus be a king.   What I do, I must do, since the Lord has chosen me."   Many another king has fancied himself appointed by heaven with as little justification ; few have been so successful in convincing their subjects of their divine right.   The bride Divara comes out among the people.   The limping prophet, taking a salve, anoints the new king, and presents him with a huge sword of battle ; the twelve Elders lay their weapons at his feet, and the tailor-monarch calls upon heaven to witness his promise to rule his people in the spirit of the Lord, and to judge them with the righteousness of heaven.   Then the excited folk dance round their king and queen, singing :—' Honour alone to God on high !'   Mock-majesty forsooth ; but the divinity which hedges a king has oft been more grotesque.   Sion, like Israel, has passed from a theocracy to an autocracy ; but there is no Nathan to check its ruler, because he is himself chief prophet.

The sovereign of Sion—although ' since the flesh is dead, gold to him is but as dung '—yet thinks fit to appear in all the pomp of earthly majesty.   He appoints a court, of which Knipperdollinch is chancellor, and wherein there are many officers from chamberlain to cook.   He forms a body-guard, whose members are dressed in silk.   Two pages wait upon the king, one of whom is a *son of his grace the bishop of*

Münster.[1] The great officers of state are somewhat wondrously attired, one breech red, the other grey, and on the
sleeves of their coats are embroidered the arms of Sion—
the earth-sphere pierced by two crossed swords, a sign of
universal sway and its instruments—while a golden finger
ring is token of their authority in Sion. The king himself
is magnificently arrayed in gold and purple, and as insignia
of his office, he causes sceptre and spurs of gold to be made.
Gold ducats are melted down to form crowns for the queen
and himself; and lastly a golden globe pierced by two
swords and surmounted by a cross with the words: " A
King of Righteousness o'er all " is borne before him. The
attendants of the Chancellor Knipperdollinch are dressed in
red with the crest, a hand raising aloft the sword of justice.
Nay, even the queen and the fourteen queenlets must have a
separate court and brilliant uniforms. Thrice a week the
king goes in glorious array to the market-place accompanied
by his body-guards and officers of state, while behind ride
the fifteen queens. On the market-place stands a magnificent throne with silken cushions and canopy, whereon the
tailor-monarch takes his seat, and alongside him sits his
chief queen. Knipperdollinch sits at his feet. A page on his
left bears the book of the law, the Old Testament ; another
on his right an unsheathed sword. The book denotes that
he sits on the throne of David ; the sword that he is king of
the just, who is appointed to exterminate all unrighteousness.
Bannock-Bernt is court - chaplain, and preaches in the
market-place before the king. The sermon over, justice
is administered, often of the most terrible kind ; and then
in like state the king and his court return home. On the
streets he is greeted with cries of : ' Hail in the name of
the Lord. God be praised ! ' There can be small doubt that
the show at first rouses the flagging spirits of the saints
in Sion.

The new government is more communistic even than the
old. To the limping prophet Dusentschuer God has re-

---

[1] *Newe Zeytung von den Widertäuffern zu Münster*, 1535. Usually
found with Luther's preface : *Auf die Newe Zeytung von Münster.*

vealed how much clothing a Christian brother or sister
ought to possess. A Christian brother shall not have more
than two coats, two pair of breeches, and three shirts—a
Christian sister not more than one frock, a jacket, a cloak,
two pair of sleeves, two collars, two 'par hosen und vehr
hemede;' while four pair of sheets shall suffice for each
bed. The deacons go around the town with wagons to
collect the surplus clothing : "God's peace be with you,
dear brothers and sisters. I come at the bidding of the
Lord, as his prophet has announced to you, and must see
what you have in your house. Have you more than is fitting,
that we must take from you in the name of the Lord, and
give it to those who have need. Have you want of aught,
that for the Lord's sake shall be given to you according to
your necessity ? " So the deacons return with wagon-loads
of clothes, which are distributed among the poorer brethren, or
stored for the use of the saints, whom God will soon lead
into Münster.[1] Then comes an order for the interchange of
houses, for no brother must look upon anything as his
own, and it is but right that all should share in turn
whatever accommodation Sion provides.

But difficulties are coming upon the Kingdom of God in
Münster, which no system of government will obviate, no
amount of show drive from the thoughts of the saints. Provisions are becoming scarcer, and though the prophets
announce the relief of the town before the New Year, yet
they permit the pavements to be pulled up, and the streets
sown with corn and vegetables. As want becomes more
urgent, despair begins to find more willing votaries, and
fanaticism takes darker and more gloomy forms. Fits of
inspiration become more frequent and more general among
the saints ; while at the same time social restraint becomes
weaker, and the grotesque yet terrible union of the gospels
of sense and of righteousness presents us with stranger and

[1] The chief authority for the above account is *Gresbeck*. His story
of the last days of Münster seems the fullest and least biassed. 'Two
pair sleeves,' *twe par mouwen*, would have been more intelligible two
centuries earlier, when ladies used their enormous sleeves as wrappers.

stranger phases of this human riddle.   Two maidens, eight
or nine years old, go about begging from all the brothers
whom they meet their coloured knee-ribbons; from the
sisters their ornamental tuckers; they pretend to be dumb,
and when they do not get what they want, they try to seize
it, or grow furious.   What they do get they burn.   The same
children are attacked by the 'spirit,' and in fits of inspiration require each four women to hold them.   The prophets
themselves, from the king downwards, are often 'possessed
of God,' and rush through the streets with the wildest
cries; or again they will give themselves up entirely to
pleasure, and throughout the night dance with their wives to
the sound of drum and pipe.   Soon, too, a new freak of
fanaticism seizes the limping prophet.   He declares that
after three trumpet blasts the Lord will relieve Sion, then
without clothes or treasure the saints shall march out of
Münster.   At the the third blast all shall assemble on Mount
Sion and take their last meal in the city.   Twice the still-
ness of the night is broken by the trumpet blast of the limper.
All wait the fortnight which must precede its last peal.
Again it is heard in Sion, and men, women, and children
collect in the cathedral close.   Two thousand armed men,
some nine thousand women with bundles containing the little
treasures they have preserved from the grasp of the deacons,
and twelve hundred children await the will of God on
Mount Sion.   Then the king comes in state with his queens,
and explains that 'tis only a trial of God to mark out the
faithful.   'Now, dear brothers, lay aside your arms, and let
each take his wives and sit at the tables, and be joyous in
the name of the Lord.'   Long lines of tables, and benches
have been arranged in the close, and here the disappointed
saints sit themselves down.   But the meal itself, though it
consists only of hard beef followed by cake—probably a rare
feast even in these days [1]—arouses the drooping spirits of
the Anabaptists.   The king and his court wait upon the
populace, and the preachers go about talking to the brothers
and sisters.   The limper proclaims that there are some on

[1] *Newe Zeytung, die Widerteuffer zu Münster belangende.* MDXXXV.

the Mount of Sion who before the clock strikes twelve shall
have been alive and dead.   Little notice is taken of the
prophecy, as the saints are cheered with the unwonted food
and drink.   'Tis true that Knipperdollinch desires to be
beheaded by the king, as he feels confident of resurrection
within three days, but the king will not comply with his request; Jan has some other fulfilment of the prophecy in view.
After the meal the king and queen break up wheat cakes and
distribute them among the populace, saying : ' Take, eat
and proclaim the death of the Lord.'   Then they bring a
can of wine and pass it round with the words :—' Take and
drink ye of it, and let every one proclaim the death of the Lord.'
So all break bread and drink together, and then the hymn
is sung :—' Honour alone to God on high.'   After this the
limping prophet mounts a stool, and announces a new revelation.   He has in his hand a list of nearly all the prophets
in Sion, divided into four groups :—' Dear brothers, I tell
you as the word of God, you shall before night leave this
city, and enter Warendorff, and shall there announce the
peace of the Lord.   If they will not receive your peace, so
shall the town be immediately swallowed up and consumed
with the fire of hell.'   Then he throws at the feet of the
prophets one-fourth of his list, with the names of eight
servants of God who are to proclaim the glory of Sion in
Warendorff.   In like words he bids three other groups of
prophets go to the 'three other quarters of the world '—
Ossenbrugge, Coisfelt, and Soist, he himself being among
the last.   All declare that they will carry out God's will.
Then Jan the king mounts the stool, and cries to the folk
that owing to the anger of God he renounces the sceptre in
Sion, but the prophet Dusentschuer promptly replaces him,
and bids him punish the unjust.   The king sets himself at
table with the twenty-four prophets who are about to depart
on their mission.   As it grows dark the regal fanatic stands
up, and bids his attendants bring up a trooper captured from
the bishop's army, and with him the sword of justice.   The
word of God has come to him, this trooper has been present
at the meal of the Lord.   He is Judas, and the king himself

will punish the unjust. In vain the trooper begs for mercy;
he is forced upon his knees, and the tailor-king beheads him,
so fulfilling the limper's prophecy. Thus ends in bloodshed,
in dire fanaticism, the Lord's supper among his saints. 'Tis
autumn now, and yet no relief; can God have forgotten his
chosen. folk in Münster?

What of the prophets that go forth? Some fall at once
into the hands of the bishop, others arrive at the four towns
to which they were despatched and begin preaching in the
streets : ' Repent, repent, for the Lord is angry, and will
punish mankind.' They are seized at once by the authorities, and examined under torture. They remain firm, and only
confess that since the time of the apostles there have been but
two true prophets, Mathys of Haarlem, and Bockelson of
Leyden, and two false prophets, Luther and the Pope—of
these *Luther is more harmful than the Pope*. So all the
twenty-four but one meet with a martyr's death. That one—
Prophet Heinrich—had been despatched with two hundred
gulden and a 'banner of the righteous.' He was to place
the banner upon the bridge at Deventer, and when the Anabaptists had flocked to his standard, he was to lead them to
the relief of Sion. So soon as the banner reappeared near the
blockhouses, the saints would flock out to meet it. Prophet
Heinrich, however, with his gulden and banner, goes straight
to the bishop, and writes to the town bidding the saints
surrender and receive the bishop's grace. But the saints
are not yet so hungry that they cannot scorn a traitor.
Bannock-Bernt preaches against the false prophet Heinrich :
" Dear brothers and sisters, let it not seem strange to you,
that false prophets should rise up amongst us. We are
warned thereof in Scripture. Such an one was Heinrich.
We have only lost two hundred gulden with him." But the
Anabaptists are not content with sending out prophets.
Bannock-Bernt writes a book, the *Restitution*, painting the
glories of Sion and the wrath of God; it is to be scattered
among the bishop's soldiers, in the hope that they may
desert. He writes another work also, the *Book of Vengeance*,
which is to be sent into Friesland and Holland. "Vengeance

20

shall be accomplished on the powerful of earth, and when accomplished, the new heaven and the new earth shall appear for the folk of God." "God will make iron claws and iron horns for his folk; the ploughshare and the axe shall be made into sword and pike. They will set up a leader, unfurl the banner, and blow upon the trumpet. A wild, unmerciful people will they stir up against Babylon; in all shall they requite Babylon for what she has done—yea doubly shall Babylon be requited." "Therefore, dear brothers, arm yourselves for battle, not only with the meek weapons of the apostle for suffering, but with the noble armour of David for vengeance, in order with God's strength and help to exterminate all the power of Babylon and all godlessness. Be undaunted, and hazard wealth, wife, child, and life." [1] Some thousand copies of this *Book of Vengeance* are smuggled through the bishop's lines. The Anabaptists in Holland and Friesland begin to stir, and gather together in various places, intending to march for the relief of Münster. Poor ignorant folk, ill-armed and undisciplined, they are shot down and massacred wherever found. In Amsterdam they seize the Council House, but are soon defeated and captured. While still living the prisoners have their hearts torn out and flung in their faces, then they are beheaded, quartered, and impaled. So a terrible sequel is added to Rottmann's *Book of Vengeance*, and all hope of outside relief vanishes.

Worse and worse grow matters in Sion; a new prophet of the future, noiseless and yet awfully explicit, replaces the twenty-four martyrs: Starvation begins to preach among the saints. As despair increases, madness and lust stride forward too. ' Let us enjoy while we can, for to-morrow we shall be slain'—becomes the watchword of a larger and larger party in Sion. At the New Year the king prophesies sure deliverance at Easter. "If salvation come not," he cries, "then hew off my head, as I now hew off the head of him who stands before me." Executions by the ' King of Righteousness ' are now commonplace to the saints. Everything is

[1] See Janssen's *Geschichte des deutschen Volkes*, iii. 313. There is a reprint of the *Bericht van der Wrake*, by Bouterwek, 1864.

done to keep the folk employed, to distract their attention from the grim prophet. All preparations are made for the relief which is impossible; a wagon-camp is constructed to be used on the march from Münster. A sham battle is held on the market-place; a battalion of female saints is formed to assist in the glorious campaign which approaches; the folk is summoned to the market-place and formed into two divisions, one of which is to be left to guard Münster. Twelve dukes are named, and the lands of the world distributed among them; tailors, cobblers, pedlars, sword-makers and what-not are appointed rulers of the world; for the present they must content themselves with small districts in the city, where they strive to keep the people quiet. Poor, miserably poor comfort this to the saints, who now are thinking the flesh of horse and dog luxuries, who are eating bark, roots, and dried grass! The gilt, too, is wearing off from royalty in Sion. One of the queenlets, Else Gewandscherer, grows sick of her life, throws her trinkets at the feet of the king, and asks to be allowed to leave Sion. Poor Jan! Is enthusiasm utterly dead among his nearest? Shall they be examples of cowardice and treachery to the lesser saints in Sion? On to the market-place with her and fetch the sword of righteousness! There let her bite the dust—the very corpse spurned by the foot of its lord— example of disloyalty, of faithlessness to the few who can take aught to heart in Münster. So the trembling wives of the king sing 'Honour alone to God on high,' as they stand round the headless form of their fellow.

At last Easter comes, and of course no relief. The king summons the folk to the market-place. He asks whether they will venture to fix a time for God? Not material relief had been prophesied, but only salvation from sin. He, Jan the prophet, has been laden with all their sins, and they in heart and spirit are now free. It cannot last very much longer, and not even a rule of terror will restrain for ever the starving folk. Execute twenty a day, and treat the suspected traitor with every horror you please—yet it must end at last. A wild demoniac dance are these latter days

of Sion.   Terror and jest trying to fight it out with starvation.   Day by day something new to keep the folk engaged.
First a religious fête.   Gaily attired their king *lies* at a
window in the market-place, reads from the Book of Kings
how David fought, and how an angel from heaven came
with a glowing sword and slew his foes.   'Dear brothers,
that can happen to us, 'tis the same God that still lives.'
'Still lives,' and yet makes no move to help you, poor
fanatics ?   What terrible doubt those words must have
raised in the souls of the starving saints of Münster !   'Still
lives,' and leaves you to perish, you misguided, mad, oppressed folk ! Peace,—you are judged and condemned. Then
the school-children come with their teachers, and sing psalms
—wan, pale little faces, it were best not to sing, for singing
only increases the void.   Finally Bannock-Bernt concludes
with a sermon from the window.   But religious nourishment
is a poor thing on an empty stomach, and Jan tries next a
more lively entertainment.   Another great folk-meal is held
in the market-place, but this time there is only bread and
beer.   After it is over, the king and his officers, midst
blowing of trumpets, ride with spears at a wreath stuck on
a pole, and marksmen fire at a popinjay.   Then the folk
play at ball and all this : because 'it is the will of God.'
Home again they go, chanting : ' Honour alone to God on
high.'   How hollow, how mockingly it sounds now, when
compared with the enthusiastic shout of the first weeks of
Sion !   The next day another section of the people is fed,
and afterwards there is a general dance on the market-place,
the king and queen leading off.   Picture the emaciated,
hunger-torn, lust-worn, and passionate faces of those despairing Anabaptists, as they danced before the Council House in
Münster.   Grimmest of jests—that dancing can stave off
starvation !   Bannock-Bernt preaches that 'it is God's will'
that who can shall dance and enjoy himself.   Every restraint
has long since vanished in Sion.   But will any such sensuous,
physical joy stand as a substitute for bread ?   'Tis a dance
of devils, not men—or rather, a dance of death where skeletons
only appear, to drag off *themselves* as prey.   What a strange

rôle to be playing in the world's drama; where shall we seek the answer to this weird riddle?

Yet another day and all the leaders of Sion seem themselves to enter into the dire humour of this very devil's jest. The starving folk are again gathered in the market-place. In vain the deacons have gone round searching every house, and finding naught beyond pitiable scraps hidden in the mattresses or under the eaves. Something must be done to occupy the minds of the people. Suddenly Knipperdollinch is moved by the spirit: 'Holy, holy, holy is the Lord!' he shouts,—'Holy is the Father, and we are a holy folk.' Then he begins to dance, and all the people wait in expectation, till he dances before the king, and cries to him: 'Sir King, a vision has come to me o'er night. I shall be your fool.' After a bit he continues:—'Sir King, good-day to you! Why do you sit here, Sir King?' Then Knipperdollinch turns to the king, sits down at his feet, and grins like a practised jester: 'Mark you well, Sir King, how we will march, when we leave Münster to punish the god-less.' The new prophet-fool now takes an axe, and struts about among the folk, mocking them. He tumbles over the benches; he proclaims this or that man or woman holy, and kisses them:—'Thou art holy, God has sanctified thee!' He refuses to 'sanctify' the old women, and one who comes forward is threatened with a cudgelling. He makes no attempt, however, to 'blow the spirit of holiness' into the king. But after awhile Jan himself is moved by the spirit; his sceptre falls from his hands, and he drops from his throne upon the ground. Now the women are all seized with inspiration, and shriek in chorus. Knipperdollinch comes and picks Jan up, replaces him upon the throne, and blows the spirit into him. Then the king arises and cries: 'Dear brothers and sisters, what great joy I see! The town goes round and round, and you all appear as angels. Each of you is more glorious than the other, so holy are you all at once become!' The women shriek: 'Father!' Again the spirit comes upon the king. He explains the fact of the 'town going round and round' to mean that the Anabaptists will march round the earth. In the midst of his explanations, however, he spies a man among the folk in a grey cap, and orders him to come up to the throne. All expect he will behead him, but instead he puts the trembling saint on his own seat, then he hugs him and blows the spirit into him. Placing a ring on his finger, he declares it all a revelation from God. Upon this the honoured saint begins to dance, and behaves as one possessed of the devil, till from sheer exhaustion he falls to the ground. So ends this wonderful day in Münster![1] These starving Anabaptists are nigh madmen now; religion has become an absolute mockery; morality is dead; yet immorality is dying too, and the starving man gazes wildly round on the half-dozen wives who would share his crust. The sooner his grace the bishop puts the epilogue to the tragic farce the better now. Let him come in and butcher what remains. Again we ask : What is the key to the riddle? The finger of philosophic history points unregarded to the generations of oppression, to the baptism of blood. Will the world ever learn to educate its toilers, and to redeem them from serfdom? Or must the old tale ever repeat itself—misery, dogmatic stones instead of bread, uprising, and bloody repression by a shocked 'society'? Are peasant rebellions, kingdoms of God, French revolutions, and Paris communes to be periodically recurring chapters of history? Is the development of man the evolution of fate, or can humanity shape its own rough edges, if perforce it must leave its final purpose to the mystery of futurity?

Scarce need to follow the story further; its lesson is written so that even they who run *might* read. Let us hasten through the last days of Sion. Knipperdollinch places himself on the throne of the King of Righteousness—in this mad dance, why should not a fool be king? Jan drags him off, and imprisons him for several days 'to do penance;' even yet the prophet of Leyden can influence the haggard saints in Münster. But the gaunt prophet Starvation has greater power than he! Closer and closer the

[1] *Gresbecks Bericht.*

siege-works creep. Hunger is lord of the saints. All grease
and oil are collected by the deacons; shoes, grass, rats, and
mice are the meagre fuel of life in Sion. Then come the
women and the weaker brethren, in whom not a shadow
of faith is left, who have not even the wild strength of
despair. 'Out, we must out,' is all they cry to the king.
And out they are sent stripped to a shirt, traitors, but who
has strength to punish them now—even the fourteen queenlets may go with the rest! Out from the gates and towards
the bishop's blockhouses, but what mercy is like to meet you
there? Poor starving shirted brothers, one and all of you,
are cut down. The women alone are driven back. Three
days and three nights they feed upon grass and roots between
blockhouses and gates, and then are allowed to pass. To
pass whither and to what? History has nought to tell us
of these wretched outcast women. Fancy in vain tries to
picture what became of the fourteen wives of the King of
Sion. The saints who are left determine to burn the city to
ashes and force their way through to Holland. But not
even so shall they die! Treachery shall at last be successful
in Sion. On St. John's Day, 1535—just one year after the
limping prophet had placed Jan of Leyden on the throne of
the New Jerusalem—Heinrich Gresbeck and Hensgin 'von
der langen Strasse' determine to introduce the bishop's
soldiers into Münster. In the night the former watchmaster
and the later historian of Sion lead three hundred of the
bishop's men-at-arms over a low part of the wall near the
Zwinger. Stealthily they creep on towards the Fish Market,
leaving St. Martin's Church on their right, onward through
the deserted streets to the very cathedral close. Then the
blast of trumpets tells the scared Anabaptists that Sion is
in the hands of the foe, and the bishop that the treachery is
successful. The saints rush to arms, the godless must be
forced out of Sion. Back they do force them, too, in bloodiest
of fights, back to St. Martin's Church—gaunt skeletons
struggling in the frenzy of despair. But the 'party of
order' is pouring in over the deserted walls, and the king
and Knipperdollinch already have fallen into the hands of

the bishop's men. Still the starving fanatics fight like demons round the walls of St. Martin's. A truce—some one sanctions a truce—the Anabaptists shall go to their homes and await the bishop's coming. Home they go, deceived to the last. No sooner scattered through the town, than the soldiers enter the houses, drag them out one by one, and hew them to pieces in the streets. Soon the whole town is strewn with the bodies of Anabaptists, or half-dead they crawl back to their holes, while their cries of agony rend the air. The butchery ceases at last; all that are captured shall be brought before the commander and then—beheaded! As for the women and children, drive them out of the city, but not before due notice is given throughout the surrounding district—notice put up on every church of God—that whoever shall succour these starving and helpless folk shall be held a cursed Anabaptist himself and punished accordingly. "So nobody knows what became of these people, though some say the most crossed over to Eng-land."[1] So in a second baptism of blood ends the Kingdom of God in Münster. ''Twas not the rage of his grace the bishop,' so the Evangelicals said, 'but the terrible vengeance of God, which thus punished the devilish doctrines of Sion.' When will mankind learn that human selfishness ever brings down its terrible curse, and that the future never forgets to enact grimmest judgment on the sins of its past? Rarely that judgment touches the individual defaulter; humanity at large must bear the burden of each man's peculiar sin.

What judgment his grace the bishop thinks fit to pass on the leaders of Sion at least deserves record. Rottmann has fallen by St. Martin's Church, fighting sword in hand, but Jan of Leyden and Knipperdollinch are brought prisoners before this shepherd of the folk. Scoffingly he asks Jan: "Art thou a king?" Simple, yet endlessly deep the reply: "Art thou a bishop?" Both alike false to their callings—

[1] *Warhaffliger bericht der wunderbarlichen handlung der Teuffer zu Münster in Westualen*, &c., . . . with woodcut of Jan of Leyden, 'King of the New Jerusalem and the whole world, *Etates* 26.'

as father of men and shepherd of souls. Yet the one cold, self-seeking sceptic, the other ignorant, passionate, fanatic idealist. " Why hast thou destroyed the town and *my* folk ? " " Priest, I have not destroyed one little maid of *thine*. Thou hast again thy town, and I can repay thee a hundredfold." The bishop demands with much curiosity how this miserable captive can possibly repay him. " I know we must die, and die terribly, yet before we die, shut us up in an iron cage, and send us round through the land, charge the curious folk a few pence to see us, and thou wilt soon gather together all thy heart's desire." The jest is grim, but the king of Sion has the advantage of his grace the bishop. Then follows torture, but there is little to extract, for the king still holds himself an instrument sent by God—though it were for the punishment of the world. Sentence is read on these men— placed in an iron cage they shall be shown round the bishop's diocese, a terrible warning to his subjects, and then brought back to Münster; there with glowing pincers their flesh shall be torn from the bones, till the death-stroke be given with red-hot dagger in throat and heart. For the rest let the mangled remains be placed in iron cages swung from the tower of St. Lambert's Church. On the 26th of January, 1536, Jan Bockelson and Knipperdollinch meet their fate. A high scaffolding is erected in the market-place, and before it a lofty throne for his grace the bishop, that he may glut his vengeance to the full. Let the rest pass in silence. The most reliable authorities tell us that the Anabaptists remained calm and firm to the last.[1] 'Art thou a king ?' 'Art thou a bishop ?' The iron cages still hang on the church tower at Münster; placed as a warning, they have become a show; perhaps some day they will be treasured as weird mentors of the truth which the world has yet to learn from the story of the Kingdom of God in Münster.[2]

[1] The Lutherans declared that Jan confessed to two of their number that he was an impostor ; the Catholics asserted that he went to the scaffold receiving the ministrations of a priest.

[2] Since the above was written, the cages have been removed.

NOTE ON BERNHARD ROTTMANN'S WRITINGS. — Hofmann and
Rottmann represented opposite poles of Anabaptist thought,—the directions respectively of spiritual and sensual fanaticism.   David Joris,
the author of ' *T'wonderboeck*, is the connecting link between the two
parties.   This is strikingly brought out by the Anabaptist Conventicle
held in Strassburg in 1538, when the followers of Hofmann refused to
accept the sensual elements of Joris's teaching (*F. O. zur Linden*, p. 393).
It was a friend of Joris, Hendrik Niclaes of Münster, who established
the *Family of Love*, and his disciple, Vitello, founded the first English
branch at Colchester in 1555.   Niclaes himself came to England about
1569, and it is to the Münster fugitives, as reorganized by Niclaes, that we
must look for the origins of our own Anabaptists.   The writings of Rottmann and *Twonderboeck* are thus of extreme interest for the beginnings
of English Anabaptism.   As it is improbable that an essay I had planned
on Rottmann will now be completed, I append a list of his writings:—

(1) Bekentnisse van beyden Sacramenten, Doepe vnde Nachtmaele, der
predicanten tho Munster.   (November 8, 1833.)   Extracts from this Confession are given by Bouterwek : *Zur Literatur und Geschichte der
Wiedertaüfer, Erster Beitrag*, Bonn, 1864, pp. 6–10.

(2) Bekantnus des globens vnd lebens der gemein Christe to Munster.
The date of this Confession—printed by Cornelius as the *Münsterische
Apologie* in his book *Berichte der Augenzeugen über das Münsterische
Wiedertaüferreich*, 1853, pp. 445–464—is not clearly determined, but it
preceded the *Restitution* (cf. *Bouterwek*, pp. 37–8).

(3) Eyne Restitution, edder Eine wedderstellinge rechter vnde gesunder
christliker leer, gelouens vnde leuens vth Gades genaden durch de
gemeynte Christi tho Munster an den Dach gegeuen.   (October, 1534).
I possess one of the few extant copies of the original ; it shows the
difficulties the Anabaptists had in printing.   The work was reprinted in
1574 in five hundred copies by the 'Second King of Sion,' Johann Wilhelm-
sen, but all the copies seem to have perished, and it has not been again
reprinted.   An analysis will be found in *Bouterwek*, pp. 18–33.

(4) Eyn gantz troestlick bericht van der Wrake vnde straffe des
Babilonischen gruwels, an alle ware Israeliten vnd Bundtgenoten Christi,
hir vnde dar vorstroyet, durch de gemeinte Christi tho Munster.
(December, 1534.)   No printed copy of this work appears to have survived.   Bouterwek reprints it in full (pp. 66–101) from a manuscript copy
made in 1663, and now in the Düsseldorf archives.

(5) Von verborgenheitt der Schrifft des Rickes Christi vnd von dem
dage des Henn durch die gemeinde Christi zu Munster.   (February, 1535.)
Printed copies of this tract exist in the library at the Hague and a few
other places.   It has been reprinted after a manuscript in the Cassel
archives by H. Hochhuth in *Bernhard Rottmanns Schriften*, I., Gotha,
1857—a publication which would have been very valuable, had it got
beyond the first *fasciculus*.

SOCIOLOGY.

Do I seem to say : 'Let us eat and drink, for to-morrow we die'? Far from it ; on the contrary, I say : 'Let us take hands and help, for this day we are alive together.'—*Clifford.*

XI.

THE MORAL BASIS OF SOCIALISM.[1]

Mächtig ist *Eins* nur auf Erden : die waltenden ewigen Mächte,
Welche die Völker bewegen ; und was in schnöder Verblendung
Diesen entgegen sich stellt und verwegen auf menschliche Macht trotzt,
Oder auf göttliche hofft, ein Koloss ist's auf thönernen Füssen !

It is scarcely ten years since our daily papers, noting the
rapid growth of the Socialistic party in Germany, congratulated
their readers on the impossibility of a like movement in this
country. To-day Socialism in England has immeasurably
outgrown its German progenitor. While in Germany
Socialism has remained the vague protest of the oppressed
worker, suffering under the introduction of the factory
system of industry, in England it has become already a
great social factor tending to leaven our legislation, and
likely, before long, to revolutionize our social habits. In
Germany it has remained an ill-regulated political protest
with an impracticable programme. In England, owing
partly to the vigorous emotionalism of Carlyle and Ruskin,
but principally to our more advanced economic development,
it has become a political tendency and a moral force long
before it has reached self-consciousness and formulated
itself as a recognized movement. As a recognized movement we shall find in the first place that various crude
manifestations will be singled out for fierce condemnation,
but that, after some contempt and misrepresentation, not a
little justified by the Utopian schemes of social reconstruction

[1] Originally written as a lecture, this paper, with some revision, was
published as a pamphlet in June. 1887.

propounded by the earlier Socialistic writers,[1] the doctrines
of Socialism will be at least listened to with respect, and
finally exert an acknowledged influence on all social and
legislative changes.

I have spoken of Socialism as a recognized movement, but
it is essentially necessary to mark the characteristics which
distinguish it from other political movements of this century.
The difference lies in the fact that the new polity is based
upon a conception of morality differing *in toto* from the
current Christian ideal, which it does not hesitate to call
anti-social and immoral. It is, however, the very fact that
Socialism is a morality in the first place, and a polity only in
the second, that has led to the introduction of the absurd
misnomer "Christian Socialist" for a section of the party
which vaguely recognizes the moral aspect of Socialism.
As the old religious faith breaks up, a new basis of morals
is required more consonant with the reasoning spirit of the
age. That view of life, which finds in this world only
sorrow and tribulation, a field of preparation for a future
existence, is more and more widely acknowledged to be
a superstition invented and accepted by the prevailing
pessimism of a decadent period of human development.
Harmful as the superstition has been, the common sense
of mankind has saved us from the logical consequences of
its full acceptance. At the very best, however, it has justified
poverty, misery, and asceticism of all kinds. The modern
Socialistic theory of morality is based upon the agnostic
treatment of the supersensuous. Man, in judging of conduct, is concerned only with the present life; he has to
make it as full and as joyous as he is able, and to do this

---

[1] It seems to me extremely unadvisable for Socialists to formulate,
at the present time, elaborate Socialistic organizations of the State.
The future social form is at present quite beyond our ken; it is sufficient
for the time to trace the probable effect of the Socialistic movement in
modifying existing institutions, and in influencing the legislation of the
near future. It is a waste of energy to build in the air co-operative
commonwealths, the destruction of which is no hard task for the hostile
critic; it is even harmful, since it associates the universal movement
with the easily controverted dreams of the individual Utopian.

consciously and scientifically with all the knowledge of the present, and all the experience of the past, pressed into his service. Not from fear of hell, not from hope of heaven, from no love of a tortured man-god, but solely for the sake of the society of which I am a member, and the welfare of which is my welfare—for the sake of my fellow-men— I act morally, that is, socially. Positivism has recognized in a vague impracticable fashion this, the only possible basis of a rational morality; it places the progress of mankind in the centre of its creed, and venerates a personified Humanity. Socialism, as a more practical faith, teaches us that the first duty of man is to no general concept of humanity, but to the group of humans to which he belongs, and that man's veneration is due to the State which personifies that social group. Yet even thus there is sufficient ground for the sympathy which is undoubtedly felt by Positivists for Socialism. Can a greater gulf be imagined than really exists between current Christianity and the Socialistic code? Socialism arises from the recognition (1) that the sole aim of mankind is happiness in this life, and (2) that the course of evolution, and the struggle of group against group, has produced a strong social instinct in mankind, so that, directly and indirectly, the pleasure of the individual lies in forward-ing the prosperity of the society of which he is a member. Corporate Society—the State, not the personified Humanity of Positivism—becomes the centre of the Socialist's faith. The polity of the Socialist is thus his morality, and his reasoned morality may, in the old sense of the word, be termed his religion. It is this identity which places Socialism on a different footing to the other political and social movements of to-day. Current Christianity is not a vivifying political force; current Christianity is the direct outcome of a pessimistic superstition, and can never be legitimately wedded to a Hellenic rationalism. Can we more strongly emphasize the distinction between the old and the new moral basis? To the thinkers of to-day crucified gods, deified men, heaven and hell have become intolerable nonsense, only of value for the light they have cast on past

stages of human development. These theories of the supersensuous, which our forefathers have handed down to us,
deserve all the respect due to relics of the Past. They are
invaluable landmarks of history, signposts to the paths of
man's mental growth. They were the banners under which
mankind has struggled, the symbols of his march across the
arid deserts of the Past, where the sources of knowledge
were few, and none ran copiously. Now that those deserts
are behind us, and we live in a fertile land, with wide fields
of truth only awaiting cultivation, with innumerable springs
of knowledge freely open to the thirsty, we can afford to lay
those symbols aside. Let us reverently hang these old
colours up in the great temple of human progress. Mankind, following them, has fought and won many an arduous
battle; but the best energies of our time can no longer rally
round them. They belong to history, and not to the glorious
actuality of that century in which we live. We are, it is
true, only just at the preface of the great volume of reasoned
truth, wherein is endless work for many generations of men,
yet we have, at least, found the only legitimate basis of
knowledge, the only fruitful guide to conduct. Rejoicing in
that discovery, we can lay aside the weird images of the
childhood of mankind, for History has taught us their
origin, and Science their value. The images are beautiful,
but they are lifeless; they are but idols carved by the ignorance of the Past. Still, like the Greeks of old, we may
glory in the beauty of our idols, long after the Intellect has
ceased to bend her knee in worship, or to sacrifice herself
upon the altar erected by the vague aspirations of a dead
humanity to a splendid shadow of itself. Yes! sympathy
with the Past we must have, but war, ceaseless war, with
that Past which seeks with its idols to crush the growth
of the Present! The right to re-shape itself is the one
birthright of humanity, and the 'vested interests' of priest
or of class, the sanctity of tradition and of law, will be of less
avail in checking human progress than the gossamer in the
path of the king of the forest.

It is because the old bases of religion and morality have

become impossible to the Present, that Socialism,—which gives us a rational motive for conduct, which demands of each individual service to Society and reverence towards Society incorporated in the State,—is destined to play such a large part in the re-shaping of human institutions. Socialism, despite Häckel, despite Herbert Spencer, *is* consonant with the whole teaching of modern Science, and with all the doctrines of modern Rationalism. It lays down no transcendental code of morality, it accepts no divine revelation as a basis of conduct; it asserts the human origin, the plastic and developable character, of morals; it teaches us that, as human knowledge increases, human society will tend to greater stability, because History and Science will show more and more clearly what makes for human welfare. The new morality, while recognizing the value of customary modes of action and of inherited social instinct, still looks upon knowledge and experience as the guides of human conduct. It trusts in the main to human reason, not to human emotion, to dictate the moral code. To give all a like possibility of usefulness, to measure reward by the efficiency and magnitude of socially valuable work, is surely to favour the growth of the fittest within the group, and the survival of the fittest group in the world-contest of societies. Socialism no less earnestly than Professor Huxley demands an open path from the Board School to the highest council of the nation. It is as anxious to catch talent, and to profit by its activity, as the most ardent disciple of Darwin.

It may seem to many of my readers that veneration for personified Society, or the State, and the identification of moral conduct with social action, are very old truths, which the world has long recognized. I venture to doubt this, or at least to think that, if recognized, they have never been given their true value, or been pushed to their logical outcome. I doubt whether all Socialists even yet grasp the large consequences which flow from their full admission. I propose to examine somewhat more closely these two fundamental principles.

At the present time it can hardly be said that there is any

veneration whatever for personified Society, the State. The State is brought to our notice, not as the totality of the society in which we live, but as government, and government we are accustomed to look upon as a necessary evil; we have no faith in its capacity for right ruling. To sacrifice our lives for government appears utterly ridiculous ; but to do so for the welfare of the State ought to be the truest heroism. It is the loss of veneration for the State which has made our government in all its forms something nigh despicable. We have been content to allow the State to be served by self-seekers, by men whose all-absorbing object has been to fill the pockets of themselves or of their family, whose highest patriotism has been to conserve the anti-social monopolies of their class. We have chosen our senators neither for their experience nor their wisdom, but for the glibness of their tongues and the length of their purses. So it has come about that the very name of politician is a term of reproach. Our legislation, our government, has been a scarcely disguised warfare of classes, the crude struggle of individual interests, not the cautious direction of social progress by the selected few. Veneration for the State has been stifled by a not unjustifiable contempt for existing government ; it has survived only on the one hand in an irrational feeling of loyalty towards a puppet, degenerating into snobbism, and on the other hand in a chauvinism, a claim to national pre-eminence, chiefly advanced by those who are contributing little to the fame of their country in art, literature, or science, still less in hard fighting. To bring again to the fore a feeling of genuine respect for personified Society, the State, to purify executive government, is obviously a hard but primary necessity of socialistic action. We must aristocratize government at the same time as we democratize it ; the ultimate appeal to the many is hopeless, unless the many have foresight enough to place power in the hands of the fittest.

Government has become what it is, because our respect for the State has grown so small, and not conversely. We have had fit men, and we could have put them in places of

trust; we could have demanded better action from our
rulers, had we had real veneration for the State. In early
Rome and at Athens such a feeling existed; it was, indeed,
a direct outcome of the old group kinship, the gentile organization of both those states. It is something more than
this respect for a widened family which we require to-day.
With modern habits of life, with the emancipation of women,
the strength of the family tie, one of the last binding links
of the old social structure, is disappearing. We must learn
to replace it in time by respect for personified Society, by
reverence for the State. The spirit of antagonism between
the Individual and the State must be destroyed. How low
our social spirit has fallen may be well measured by remarking how few recognize the immorality of cheating the State
in any of its industrial departments, say the Post Office;
how nearly all regard the tax-gatherer with a feeling akin
to that which mediæval burghers bore to the city hangman.
The man who goes whistling along, and with a heavy stick
knocks off the ornamental ironwork in the Embankment
Gardens, would think it highly immoral to whittle the arm-
chair of his friend; the woman who encloses a letter inside
a book-post packet would be indignant if you suggested that
she was capable of picking her neighbour's pocket. Yet in
both cases the offence against the State ought to be looked
upon as a far graver matter than the offence against
the individual. The clergyman who some years ago was
detected cutting out engravings from the books of a great
public library ought to have been publicly whipped and
ejected from society; yet the matter was hushed up,
apparently because it was only an offence against the State.
Had he stolen his churchwarden's spoons, a much less
heinous matter, he would undoubtedly have found himself
in the police court. So long as there is a large group of
persons who find pleasure in ripping up the cushions of
public carriages, in defacing public statues, in tearing down
the hawthorn bushes in the parks, and in generally
destroying what is intended for the convenience, or pleasure,
of the whole community—above all, so long as the majority of

the community treat such offences lightly, so long it is hopeless to think of vastly extending the property of the State.
Socialists have to inculcate that spirit which would give
offenders against the State short shrift and the nearest
lamp-post.   Every citizen must learn to say with Louis XIV.,
L'état c'est moi!   The misfortune is that wealth [1] has become
so individualized since the Reformation that the spirit of
communal ownership is almost dead.   This spirit, the joint
responsibility for the safeguard of common wealth, is one of
the most valuable factors of social stability, and the sooner
we re-learn it the better for our social welfare.   To preach
afresh this old conception of the State, so fruitful in the
cities of ancient Greece and the towns of mediæval Germany,
ought to be the primary educative mission of modern
Socialism.   If the welfare of society be the touchstone of
moral action, then respect for the State—the State as *res
publica*, as commonweal—ought to be the most sacred
principle of the new movement.

Let us turn to the other fundamental of socialistic morality
—the definition of moral conduct as socialized action—and
inquire whether, commonplace as the definition may seem,
it, any more than respect for the State, is a currently accepted
guide to conduct.   I fear we can only answer in the negative.
Whether we turn to practice or to theory, we shall find that
the notion of morality current has reference to some absolute
and, I venture to think, unintelligible code.   It is rarely, if
ever, based upon social wants as ascertained by past experience, or upon an accurate study of the tendencies of present
social growth.   We are very far indeed from recognizing the
momentous consequences, which logically flow from the
abandonment of the Christian morality and the Christian
conception of life.   Darwin has destroyed the old Ptolemaic
system of the spiritual universe.   We can no longer regard
all creation as revolving about man as its central sun.   We

[1] It has become so entirely 'property.'   When 'wealth' and 'goods'
were first used to describe that state of material prosperity, which is
well and *good* for men, individual ownership property had not yet been
evolved.

can no longer believe that the conduct of man is influencing the birth or destruction of worlds, or that his ' salvation' has any relation to the great physical laws which regulate cosmical evolution. Man's morality has no bearing on the ' infinite' and the 'eternal,' but solely on his own temporal welfare. Surely this Copernican view of human morality is one of the most obvious, the most unassailable, and yet the most revolutionary truths of our age. Yet how far we are from accepting it fully and loyally! The whole paraphernalia of Christian worship, with its complete perversion of the fundamental principles of human conduct, and its deadening effect upon human morals, is still spread far and wide over the land. Nay, what is even still more suggestive of our bondage to the Past is the fact that, a thinker, whose writings have perhaps done as much to enlighten—as they certainly have to obscure—the ideas of our century, finds the purport of the universe in the absolute necessity that man should be provided with a field for moral action! Thus it is that Kant and the neo-Hegelian reconcilers have given a new lease of life to a fallacious moral system by a process which is superficially rational. The influence of this neo-scholasticism, not only on the church, but on many of our popular teachers, is a factor which it is hardly wise to disregard. That it should have taken considerable root in a rational age proves how far the socialistic basis of morality is from universal acceptance.

At first sight the identification of morality and sociality may seem a principle that even our most conservative friends can accept. "If this is all Socialism means, we also are Socialists," they say. "We too are desirous of improving the condition of the poor." Follow the doctrine into its consequences, however, and they will soon discover the cloven hoof. They have not yet grasped that this view of life replaces that select body they term ' Society' (does not that abuse of terms alone fully condemn them ?) by the whole mass of the folk. It does not leave the welfare of large sections of the community to the caprice of the few ; it takes as of right what they would tithe for charity; it will inevitably

touch not only their emotions, but their more sacred pocket ;
it sweeps away an anti-social class monopoly, and with it
class-power. "You must either be working for the community, or leave it," is the ultimatum of the socialistic moral
code to each and to all. No amount of conscience-money
spent on the most ' philanthropic object' can atone for
individual idleness. The progress and welfare of society
demand for common use not only the stored labour of the
past, but the labour-power of each existing individual.
Without sharing in the social work of the present there shall
be no part for you in the goods of the present, or in the
wealth garnered by our forefathers. The socialistic toe
tingles with scarce restrainable impulse to eject in precipi-
tate fashion from the human hive the many endowed idlers
who with ineffable effrontery term themselves ' Society.'
The membership of Society, the moral right to enjoy the
fruits of social labour, can be based solely on the claim of
contributing to the welfare of Society in the present—to be
still working, or to have worked while the strength was there,
physically or intellectually, for the maintenance, progress,
or pleasure of our fellow-citizens. It is this fundamental
conception of modern Socialism, with its ennobling of all
forms of labour, which will revolutionize modern life, and,
once accepted as morality, will cause all political measures
to be examined from a new standpoint. From morality
Socialism will become a polity. It is a common accusation
against Socialists that they are only capable of destructive
criticism, but it is surely of primary importance to cut away
the old superstitions, the old mistaken notions of human
conduct, to create a wide-felt want for a new basis of action,
before a wooden and inflexible system of social reconstruction is propounded. The time for constitution-mongers has
not come, if, indeed, they are not always a bar to progress.
We want at present to inculcate general principles, to teach
new views of life. Society will reconstruct itself *pari passu*
with the spread of these new ideas ; the rate at which they
will become current, while depending to some extent on the
energy and enthusiasm of their propagators, will be far more

influenced by the failure of the old economic system, owing to the gigantic industrial and commercial changes which are in progress, and by the failure of the old Christian morality, owing to the rapid growth of rational methods of thought.

"Educate your workpeople," cry some of our leading scientists, "if you wish to maintain a position among competing nations in the world-markets." A falser reason for education it is hard to conceive, unless our scientists are prepared to prove that social welfare at home is impossible without successful huckstering abroad. It is worthy rather of the Lancashire cotton printer, who measures national prosperity by the import of china-clay, than of the genuine scientist. Let us educate our workpeople to face the difficulties which our society at home has to encounter ; let us train them to value intelligent labour as a means, not an end, to grasp that the general progress of society here, the raising of the common standard of comfort and intelligence, is of the first importance. After all, restriction, or removal, of population may be a more efficient aid to social progress than an endless rivalry with other nations in the monotonous labour of breeching the less civilized races of earth.

If I interpret socialistic principles at all correctly, they insist primarily on the moral need that each individual, according to his powers, should work for the community. The man or woman who does not labour, but, owing to a traditional monopoly, is able to live on the labour of others, or the stored labour of the community—which indeed requires, as a rule, present labour to utilize it—will be treated as a moral leper. The moment the majority have adopted this code of morality—and the economic development, taken in conjunction with the fact that the majority even at present do labour, will render its adoption rapid—then the legislation or measures of police, to be taken against the immoral and anti-social minority, will form the political realization of Socialism. This political realization of Socialism has already, although blindly and unconsciously, to some extent begun. Socialistic measures,—the limitation of the privileges of those who live on the labour-power of others, or on the stored labour of the past,—have become by no means an incon-spicuous feature of current legislation, and a feature which will yearly gain greater prominence.

There may be differences of opinion as to how the elimination of idlers from the community may best take place, but the majority of Socialists are convinced that, to destroy the private ownership of the physical resources of the country and of the stored labour of the past—to socialize the land and to socialize the means of production—are the only efficient and permanent means of restraining idleness, and the resulting misdirection of the labour-power of the community. We believe that, by destroying the pecuniary privileges of birth, and the class exclusiveness of education, we shall in reality be removing a great bar to the survival, or at least to the pre-eminence, of the fittest. It is for the welfare of society that it should obtain from all ranks the best heads and the best hands as its directors and organizers. This can only be secured by giving equal educational chances to all, by allowing no pecuniary handicapping of the feeble in mind or body. Here Socialism is at one with modern Radicalism, and is certainly not opposed to the teachings of Evolution.

At the same time Socialists are fully aware of the diffi-culties which lie in the realization of their ideal, and the more reasonable are fully prepared to face, and duly weigh, the arguments which may be brought against them. I propose to devote the remainder of this paper to a brief consideration of some of the more important of these arguments, which I may state as follows :—

(1) Socialism would destroy the rewards of successful com-petition, and so weaken the incentive to that individual energy, which is of such primary social value.

(2) No government can be trusted to fitly conduct the vast task of organization which Socialism would thrust upon it.

(3) The proposed socialization of land and of stored labour would destroy confidence, and check enterprise, to an extent which might have disastrous effects on the com-

munity long before the socialized State could be got into working order.

(4) The increase of population would very soon render nugatory any benefit to be derived from the socialization of surplus-labour.

(5) There is no means of measuring the value of an individual's contribution to the labour-stock of the community.

Let us take in order these objections, all of which deserve very careful consideration.

(1) *Socialism would destroy the rewards of successful competition, and so weaken the incentive to that individual energy, which is of such primary social value.*

If the result of socialistic reconstruction were to be the deadening of individual energy, it would undoubtedly not tend to the welfare of Society. But I believe that the importance of real incentive is fully recognized by all thinking Socialists, and that they would be the last to deny the social value of especially rewarding transcendent talent, or remarkable social energy. It is because the rewards at present given to such talent and energy are far more than sufficient to achieve their end, are utterly unsuitable in character, and most frequently go to anti-social cunning rather than to real worth, that I am compelled to look upon these rewards of the present competitive system as little short of disastrous to the community. I hold that social distinction, public gratitude, and State recognition, are the only suitable recompense, and at the same time are quite sufficient incentive to individual energy. There is no necessity for endowing for an indefinite period the posterity of a valuable member of society with a possibility of complete idleness. Such rewards as large grants of public money or land, perpetual pensions, or the accumulation by successful industrial organizers of stored labour or any other monopoly of the means of utilizing existing labour-power, are neither necessary, nor are they conducive to the general welfare of society. These incentives did not produce an Albrecht Dürer, a Newton, a Shakespeare, or a Watt, nor

induce them to do work of first-class social value. The
opportunity of a free education, given by a sizarship at
Trinity College, had more to do with the making of a
Newton than all the rewards of the competitive system. It
is the opportunity for self-development, the provision of a
field for its activity, and some amount of social recognition,
which are really needed to produce, and utilize, all forms of
talent in the community. The German trader will display as
much energy, fertility of resource, and downright hard work
in making £500 a year as an English manufacturer in
clearing £50,000. I do not think any real danger to the
incentive to energy is involved in the socialization of industry, while literature, science, and art have invariably
been found to thrive best with a minimum of pecuniary
honour, and a maximum of social recognition. The schools
of Athens, and the Churches of the Middle Ages, offer evidence enough on this point, while Galilei, at the height of
his reputation, had to *pay* for the printing of the *De Systemate
Mundi*.

Socialists assert that under a State-control of industry
the recognition of a new inventor by the State would be
as great an inducement to enterprise as the idea of twenty
per cent. profit is held to be at present ; more especially will
such honour have weight in the educated community of the
future. No practical Socialist advocates in the present stage
of human development an equal distribution of the profits
of labour as advantageous to society. He even recognizes
the importance, if necessary, of distinguishing by physical
rewards such energy and talent as are of great value to
the community. He is willing to admit that any one who
labours longer and better than another should reap a greater
return, but that this return shall be in its nature con-
sumable, not reproductive. It must not take the form of
a permanent tax (rent, interest, &c.) on the labour-power
and labour-store of the community. The socialization of
all means of production would render this impossible. It is
to the advantage of Society as a whole, when it has given
equal educational chances to its members, that the better

work should be encouraged by the better pay. The acceptance of Socialism, in short, does not involve approval of the
communistic principle of equalized distribution. It still
leaves room for the socially healthy rivalry of individual
workers, when that rivalry does not result, as in the present
competitive form of industry, in the standard of life permanently remaining for the great mass of toilers very close
to the point of bare subsistence.

(2) *No government can be trusted to fitly conduct the vast
task of organization which Socialism would thrust upon it.*

This objection has very real weight, as there cannot be a
doubt about the current distrust of all government under-
takings. I have already referred to the disrepute into which
the State executive has fallen, and endeavoured to point out
how serious a difficulty in the way of Socialism as polity is
this want of confidence in the State. Owing to the meagre
education in our present democratic Electorate, to the
intellectually and morally inferior class of men, who serve
as politicians, and to the resulting bad measures and widespread corruption—owing to the monopoly of wealth, which,
placing time and opportunity for political action in the
hands of a class, fosters class-legislation—owing to these
and other concomitant causes the State at present is dis-
credited. It is the mission of Socialists to reintroduce the
true conception of the State, to revivify respect for personified Society; to teach that the misappropriation of public
property is the first of crimes, and that the mismanagement
of public affairs is a disgrace, which, like the sin against the
Holy Ghost, can never be condoned. We must bring home
to each citizen the feeling of the Athenian vine-dresser,
or the craftsman of the mediæval town. Such an educational change can only be gradual; but, on the other hand,
Socialists neither strive for, nor expect, any but a gradual
assumption by the State of the means of production and
the stored labour of the Past. I may point to the
efficiency of the German post-office and to the scientific
perfection of the military organization of the same country,
especially the readiness of both to discover and adopt real

advances, as evidence that the State can successfully undertake and direct great enterprises. Even in our own country,
where faith in the State is much lower, it is difficult to
believe that a large railway company would be less efficiently
conducted if its managers were State officials, liable to
instant dismissal if failing in their duties, than if they were
private capitalists struggling to fill their own pockets. How
often is a false economy, or an anti-social line of action, adopted
with a view to immediate profit ? [1] Education is another of
the vast enterprises which the State has often undertaken
with the result of increased efficiency. It may be quite true
that in England there is a tendency in the State-code to
crystallize education, but even in this country, I firmly believe, our Board Schools are on the average more efficient
than the private schools of the voluntary system.[2] What
is wanted in matters educational, as in other State affairs in
our country, is their complete divorce from party politics.
We must educate the Electorate to such a degree that it
will not return stump-orators. This goal, I believe, will be
more and more nearly reached as the children who have been
educated in the State schools form a larger and larger part of
the Electorate. There is not, I contend, any inherent impossibility in the management by the State of large under-
takings ; the examples I have cited suffice to prove its
possibility. The only partial success of many others can,
I think, be accounted for by evils peculiar to our existing
form of government, and its singular anomalies. Socialists,
I cannot too often repeat, are not called upon to draw up
any constitution for an ideal socialized State. They are

[1] It is worth while noting that it is through the enterprise of private
companies that the lives of Londoners are endangered by a network of
over-head telegraphs ; in London the State already carries its wires
underground.

[2] The Girls' Public School Company has recently testified to the value
of our State system by the announcement that the majority of their
scholarships are annually gained by girls, whose primary education is
the work of Board Schools. This Company has to some extent opened
a path for the girl from State school to the University. How long will
t be before boys have a like advantage ?

quite justified, as any other party, in proposing a programme of immediately possible legislative changes. They believe that the realization of their ideal will be very gradual, and that, to be really efficient, it must be to a large extent tentative; the possibility of central organization, of organization by counties, towns, or communes, are certainly matters for discussion, but the comparative efficiency of each can only be tested by experience. As yet we have not even the results of a comprehensive system of local government to guide us, and any attempt to picture a fully-developed socialized commonweal is, I hold, unnecessary and ill-advised. To demand it of Socialists is about as reasonable as it would have been to have asked Jesus, the Christ, when propounding his new morality, to have waited before he did so, and drawn up a constitution for that World-Church, which was to include the Gentiles. There is little doubt that he would not have hit upon the historical development his teaching took in the Holy Catholic Church. He rightly left the matter to after ages, when councils and constitutions first became necessary. Socialism may well do likewise, it can content itself by showing that the State is not inherently incapable of organizing industry, and, strong in its conviction of the moral truth of the new movement, it can well leave the exact form of the socialized State to be worked out in the future.

(3) *The proposed socialization of land and of stored labour will destroy confidence, and check enterprise, to an extent which may have disastrous effects on the community long before the socialized State can be got into working order.*

It is suggested that these disastrous effects will result from the existence of a strong political Socialist party, and the adoption of socialistic legislation. There might very possibly, at first, be a partial feeling of insecurity, followed by some evil effects. At the same time any over-hasty phase of socialistic legislation would produce sufficient industrial disturbance to react quickly upon the labour Electorate, and so upon the over-hasty legislator. It would tend to counteract itself. Socialists recognize the fact that socialization, for the sake of the worker himself, can only be comparatively slow, and will have as far as possible to use and absorb all existing industrial enterprises. Revolutionary measures, which would paralyse the industry of the country, are simply impossible, because six millions of people would never submit to the starvation which a few weeks of idleness would inevitably produce ; indeed the stored labour of the community would hardly last *weeks*. We look forward, then, to a gradual change, which will be accompanied by an education, not only of the artizan, but of the capitalistic class. The Socialist has to teach that social approbation and public honour are worth more than pecuniary reward. The alteration of the standard of enjoyment from purely physical luxury to more intellectual forms of pleasure will do much to form a new goal for ambition, and so very materially lessen the evil effects which, it is asserted, must result from limiting the profits of private enterprise and discouraging all monopoly of surplus-labour.

(4) *The increase of population will very soon render nugatory any benefit to be derived from the socialization of surplus-labour.*

Hitherto I have assumed that the increased welfare of society, which Socialists hold would result from the socialization of the means of production and of stored labour, would be a *permanent* increase. Let us examine this question of permanency a little more closely. At each epoch in any given community there is a certain amount of labour-power and a certain amount of stored labour. Socialists assert that it is for the general good of the community that this labour-power and this stored labour, after providing the necessaries of existence for the entire community, should then be utilized in raising the standard of comfort of the whole body, and not that of individual members. This application of what I term 'surplus-labour' is prevented by the traditional or legal monopoly of individuals, which enables them to enforce upon the labourer a different application, namely, that after a low standard of comfort is provided for the masses, the surplus-labour shall be applied to indefinitely raising the standard of life of the monopolists themselves. The surplus energies of society are expended on the luxuries of the few. This condition of affairs would be to a large extent destroyed by the State ownership of capital and the State direction of labour-power. The present monopolists would be driven to provide themselves, by labour of social value, with such pleasures as they could obtain as its equivalent.

But, although I hold that the surplus-labour, thus socialized, would go at the present time a long way towards increasing the general comfort and pleasure of Society, I do not think this gain would be permanent, if the change were accompanied by an ever-increasing population. Up to a certain limit each increase of labour-power may raise, if socialistically organized, the general standard of comfort of a definite group of persons; by which I understand a group living on a definite area, having definite internal resources, definite means of communication with the outside world, and a definite series of products to exchange with neighbouring groups. When this limit, which is essentially local and temporal, is once reached, each accession of fresh labour-power tends to lower the general standard of comfort, and ultimately to force it down to that bare level of subsistence, at which the starvation check abruptly brings it up. It is this " limit to efficient population " which it is the duty of the statesman to discover, and to maintain, as far as possible, at each period of social growth. Removal of population, prohibition of immigration, and, if necessary, limitation of the number of births, are the means whereby the limit to efficient population may be approximately conserved. Does the existing organization of Society regard this limit? If not, would it be possible for a socialized Society to do so? These are the questions which form the population problem, and demand our consideration. The Socialist of the marketplace, who ignores them, places himself outside the field of useful discussion. We *must* recognize the problem; and, when carefully investigated, it will be found to offer one of the strongest arguments in favour of Socialism with which I am acquainted. We may even say that Socialism is the logical outcome of the law of Malthus.

Let us consider how the present economic structure of society bears on the problem of population. To begin with, we find that there exists a small body of thinkers, who believe that much of the social misery of the present would be relieved, were we, instead of attempting to transform the present economic relation of capital and labour, to devote our energies to inducing the working classes to limit their numbers. Such limitation, they hold, would, by increasing wages, raise the standard of comfort, and so, to a great extent, effect what Socialists desire. The standard of comfort once raised would be permanently maintained. To this I reply that, without an extremely large and scarcely probable reduction in population, the standard thus raised would be far below what would be reached by the socialization of surplus-labour, and that it would still leave untouched other anomalies of class-monopoly. Further, that there is absolutely no security that even such standard, if reached, could be maintained. Indeed it would be directly prejudicial to the capitalistic classes that it should be ; the export price of a commodity, depending largely on the cost of labour, would have to be lowered to the price fixed by that manufacturing country where the standard of life is lowest. The English trader would not only be unable to compete with his foreign rival, but, without protection, the home-markets would be flooded by the cheaper foreign ware. It cannot be to the interest of the monopolist class that labour should be dear, and there is not the slightest possibility that, under our present system of production for profit, not for use, any attempt on the part of the workers for limitation of population will be effectual in raising the standard of life. The moment the standard of living here is sensibly higher than abroad, we have an invasion of foreign labour accustomed to a lower standard of life, or a reduction in the home demand for labour due to the impossibility of exporting at the higher prices. Further, it is only natural that our capitalistic rulers should show no signs of hindering any foreign labour invasion, nay, they are often directly concerned in importing labour. We are periodically sickened with false sentiment as to a free country, as to free trade in labour, and the like— sentiment which, in the mouths of the speakers, is not the outcome of a well-thought-out social theory, but consciously or unconsciously takes its origin directly in the feelings of their pocket. Under a capitalistic form of Society the practical plutocracy which results will never hinder the importation of foreign labour with a lower standard of life ; it cannot for the sake of its own existence take any real steps to preserve the limit of efficient population.

It is one thing to limit population in order to *maintain,* another, to limit population in order to *raise,* an existing standard. The former is difficult enough, the latter almost impossible, yet this latter is practically what the non-socialistic Malthusians propose. The standard of life of a great proportion of the working classes is so near the bare level of subsistence, beneath which even the workhouse system does not allow it to fall, that there remains little to be maintained by restraint ; the attempt to raise the standard requires, if it is to be effectual, united action on the part of so many, and is, under our present social regime, so extremely unlikely to be successful, that restraint is not calculated to evoke much sympathy.

There is, indeed, little to induce the great mass of unskilled labourers to limit their numbers, more especially if that limitation imply an abstinence from one of the few pleasures which lie within their reach; a pleasure, too, which does not, like drinking, appear *immediately and directly* to reduce the weekly pittance. But the line between skilled and unskilled labour is not so rigid that the amount of the latter does not sensibly affect the wage-standard of the former; if skilled labour is for a time highly paid, a new machine will too often make it feel at once the whole weight of proletariat competition. The restraint of the skilled working class avails little, if there is no limitation of the proletariat, and if the capitalist is always seeking to lower wages, and so the standard of life, by the introduction of machinery. I think it is sufficiently

22

clear that the limitation of population in the capitalistic
organization of Society will hardly be attempted, and, if
attempted, would not be successful.

Let us now investigate the possibility of maintaining the
limit of efficient population in the socialistic organization of
the State.   In the first place, by socializing surplus-labour
the standard of comfort would be raised without having
recourse to restraint as a means.   Other than the merest
physical pleasures would thus be placed within the reach of
the worker; this, in itself, would give him a standard worth
maintaining, and tend to limit population.   Moral restraint
by men with rational pleasures is far more likely to be effectual than even a positive check in the present state of affairs.
But while I believe that the moral check will never in our
present social organization become usual, except in those
classes whose standard of comfort is far above the level of
bare subsistence, I am inclined to doubt whether, under any
form of Society, it will be adopted by the great mass of mankind.   We are dealing with one of the most imperious of the
animal instincts of man, and it may well be questioned, not
only whether such restraint is possible, but whether, having
due regard to the sanitary and social value of the instinct, it
is advisable to endeavour to restrain it.   With the approaching emancipation of women, and the decay of our foreign
trade, the problems of sex and of population will come more and
more into the foreground.   It is becoming of really urgent importance to discuss earnestly, scientifically, and from every
possible standpoint, the difficulties which present themselves;
to calmly weigh all the theories which may be honestly propounded, and not to dismiss every discussion as both unpleasant and unfitting.   The truly unpleasant and unfitting
conduct is to be brought daily face to face with these great
race-problems, and yet daily to ignore their existence, and
to condemn all, however earnest, consideration of them as
obscene and unprofitable.   Yet this has been essentially the
spirit of our modern social and political leaders.   .These problems which are uppermost in fact and thought have been
denied to have any existence, and those who would meet the

THE MORAL BASIS OF SOCIALISM.

difficulties of the labouring classes have been professionally reproved, socially ostracized, or legally silenced. There was a time when any discussion of the population problem was repressed; time was when even mention of the moral restraint of the disciples of Malthus was taboo'd; the time is still when Neo-Malthusianism is treated as outside the field of legitimate discussion. Far be it from me to assert that Neo-Malthusianism will solve the problem; but of this one thing I feel certain that the problem will grow more and more urgent, and that society will have to face and to solve it in one way or another. No amount of hypocrisy will suffice to hide its existence, and, if we are wise, we shall consider, while there is time, any solution which may be propounded in all its bearings, physiological and social. We cannot afford to reject any possible solution till we are scientifically convinced that it must be anti-social in its results. The apparent horror with which any discussion of this matter has been met is, I fear, to no little extent due to our present economical conditions. The same ultimate feeling of pocket, which, to some extent perhaps unconsciously, demands free trade in labour, demands also the repression of all free discussion of this great race difficulty. For the same reason that it is not to the interest of our modern plutocracy that the wages of labour should be high, for such reason we cannot hope, under the existing state of affairs, for any solution of the complex problem of population. It is because, with a socialization of surplus-labour, there would cease to be a class interested in the lowness of wages, that we trust to Socialism for a thorough and earnest investigation of the problems of sex. We are Socialists, because we believe that Socialism alone will have the courage to find a satisfactory solution. It alone can raise the standard of comfort to such a height that the worker will be able to procure other than the basest physical pleasures; so long as he is tied down to the bare means of subsistence it is idle, unreasonable, and even impertinent, to suggest that he should renounce his one unpaid-for excitement. Under Socialism alone shall we be able to confine the importation of foreign labour to those few

skilled artizans who have really something to teach our own
workers.   Under Socialism alone will it be possible to reap
the advantages of any limit of population, because one class
will not be interested in the over-production of another.
Then only will it be possible to consider dispassionately, and
without the suspicion of class bias, all the difficulties of the
problem.   With the socialization of surplus-labour it will be
to the interest of the whole community to maintain its labour-
power at that amount which gives the greatest surplus value,
to discover and maintain the limit of efficient population.
Indeed, the socialistic seems the only form of community
which can morally demand, and, if necessary, legally enforce,
restraint of some kind upon its members.

Thus the possibility of meeting and solving the population
problem is seen to be closely connected with the socialization
of surplus-labour.   But the possibility of the continued existence of Socialism depends, as was long ago remarked by
John Stuart Mill, on the solution of this very population
problem.[1]

(5) *There is no means of measuring an individual's contribution
to the labour stock of the community.*

We have seen that it is a fundamental principle of the new
moral code that each individual shall undertake labour of
social value, that is, not merely labour, but labour which is
really useful to the community. The reward of any individual
is to depend on the quality and quantity of the labour which
he has contributed to the common stock.   It is needful,
therefore, that there should be some general equality, some
practical coincidence, between this reward and the service
rendered to the community.   Putting aside the labour of
educating and amusing, which requires special valuation,
the reward of productive labour has in some manner to be
made proportionate to the amount of production. By the
consumption of certain quantities of stored labour and of
labour-power a commodity is produced, and placed at the
disposal of the community. The utility of this commodity
to the community is to be in some manner equated to the

[1] *Political Economy* (People's Edition), p. 226.

sacrifice of the individual, to the labour-power which he has usefully expended. The measurement of value by useful labour is the idea which naturally suggests itself. Protest as the orthodox economists may, it is useful labour, which, I firmly believe, can be the only moral, that is, socially advantageous, basis of exchange. Without attempting, in the brief space I have still at my disposal, any analysis of Karl Marx's theory of value, still less entering upon its defence, it yet may be profitable to inquire briefly whether even the admissions of its critics do not lead us to the same conclusions as the great economist draws from his theory; whether these admissions, indeed, are not sufficient to justify us in assuming that useful labour can be made a reasonable basis of exchange. A criticism of Marx which has met with the approval of some of our orthodox economists, and which is certainly lucid, if it be not unanswerable, is that published by Mr. P. H. Wicksteed in *To-Day* (October, 1884). I propose to refer to it in the following remarks. The really important features of Marx's theory are :

(1) That the cost of labour-power (say for one day) to the capitalist, when measured in labour-power, is less than the amount of labour put into the commodities produced by that labour-power in the same time (one day).

(2) That the exchange-value of a commodity is determined by the average labour required for its production.

(3) That the difference between the cost of labour-power in labour-power, and the exchange-value of the commodity produced, the surplus-value in Marx's theory (or, what it is perhaps better to term, the output of surplus-labour) goes into the pocket of the capitalist.

The first point will probably be admitted, as well as the third, if for a moment we use the word surplus-labour, and do not complicate matters by identifying it at present with surplus-value. These conclusions are, indeed, forced upon us if we take the total result of the labour of the industrial classes. This labour is not only sufficient to procure or prepare the bare necessaries of life for those classes, and such measure of comfort as they enjoy (*i.e.*, the cost of

labour-power in terms of labour-power), but at the same
time it provides the monopolist class with every imaginable
luxury and convenience which their fancy demands, or their
control of labour-power will extend to (*i.e.*, the surplus-labour
is monopolized).   It is obvious that there is a vast amount of
such surplus-labour, the results of which are either stored for
future use, or at once consumed as luxuries by the monopolists themselves. The monopoly, as opposed to the socialization, of this surplus-labour is the great economic fact of our
present social organization. It does not stand or fall with
Marx's theory that the essence of exchange-value is labour,
but Marx's discussion of that theory has first placed the fact
clearly before us in all its full hideousness. Now I contend
that the all-important outcome of Marx's theory is really
accepted, if on other grounds, by his critic. Mr. Wicksteed
admits " the fact that a man can purchase as much labour-
force [1] as he likes at the price of bare subsistence " (*To-Day*,
p. 409), and further tells us that there is " a *coincidence* in
the case of ordinary manufactured articles between 'exchange-
value' and 'amount of labour contained'" (p. 399). Thus
we see that, if the labourer can produce more than his bare
subsistence in a day of labour—a fact scarcely disputable—
Mr. Wicksteed himself really allows that the results of this
surplus-labour go, owing to the above *coincidence*, to the
capitalist. But this is precisely Marx's "inherent law of
capitalistic production."

Now our critic, by means of the laws first laid down by
Stanley Jevons (those "of indifference" and "of the variation of utility") logically [2] deduces that the coincidence
between exchange-value and amount of labour contained,
by which is meant socially useful labour, does really exist

---

[1] Rather labour-*power;* we cannot purchase *force,* but only the *capacity*
for changing various motions, *i.e.*, power. Force is not an entity at all,
but a mode of changing motion. The confusion has arisen from the
double sense of the German word ' Kraft.

[2] We are certainly not called upon to question this logic, if it leads
our opponents to a truth we were already on other grounds convinced of.

for all ordinary articles of manufacture. Now these are the very articles with which the socialized State would in the first place have to deal, and this fortunate "coincidence," whether it be deduced from a jelly theory of labour, or a jelly theory of utility, is just the practical fact which we require in order to measure, with some degree of approximation, the services of each member of the community, the magnitude of his contribution to the common labour-stock. Since in all ordinary manufactured articles the value *coincides* with the amount of labour contained, we are at liberty to take for such articles labour as the standard of value. This standard will be in those cases as convenient, and as legitimate, a medium of exchange as gold. If we now turn to other articles, the supply and quality of which is uninfluenced by labour—the "natural and artificial monopolies" of which Mr. Wicksteed speaks—it is perfectly true that the labour theory of value is inapplicable. But we do not think they would introduce confusion into the exchange system of the socialized State. When we analyze these natural and artificial monopolies we find :

(1) That the exchange-value of many is fictitious, being due to the survival of a barbaric taste, which would almost certainly disappear with the spread of education (*e.g.*, precious stones, gold and silver utensils and ornaments).

(2) That others, which, owing to special artistic merit, stand above competition from modern production, ought on any sound socialistic theory to be removed from the field of barter, and placed in local and national museums, or, at any rate, used to adorn public buildings.

(3) That some few natural monopolies, as, for example, a limited local supply of water, or output of salt, would require to have their distribution regulated by the State ; this is a not infrequent occurrence even under our present organization.

(4) That there is nothing to hinder, under a socialistic system, disproportionate amounts of labour being given by those who are inclined to do so for the majority of the remaining artificial monopolies. An enthusiastic china-

maniac may, in a socialistic community, devote the whole of a year's labour to purchase an artistically valueless, but absolutely unique pot—if he is so uneducated as to take pleasure in that form of self-sacrifice. His doing so would doubtless be a source of gratification to the supporters of the utility theory of exchange; it is not obvious how it would shake the foundations of a socialistic community, except as evidence of that want of common sense which is a primary condition for the stability of any form of society.

It seems to me unnecessary for the Socialist to assert that the *common something* in all commodities is the useful labour consumed in their production. It is sufficient if such labour can, in all ordinary cases, and with the approximation really sufficient in practical life, be taken as a measure of their value. Socialism insists that in the relation of the individual to the community the amount and quality of his contribution to the labour-stock can fairly be taken as a measure of his reward, since this contribution has practically a definite exchange-value in terms of all ordinary manufactured articles. It is this *coincidence* between the labour, or social value, of an individual and the exchange-value of wares, which is destined to introduce the moral element into the industrial system of the future. It suggests how Society can be as safely, and as reasonably, based upon labour, upon the social energy of its members, as upon the individual ownership of wealth, the monopoly by a few of the surplus-labour of the whole community.

I have endeavoured to give in this paper a brief sketch of the arguments with which, as it seems to me, a rational Socialist may meet some of the principal objections raised to the gradual reconstruction of society on socialistic lines. But such arguments will undoubtedly have far less weight in the minds of our opponents than the stubborn logic of fact, than those inexorable economic changes which the most obstinately conservative temperament must at last recógnize to be steadily taking place, ever in the direction of socialization. No appeal to human or divine power, no custom or tradition, will check the forces which are remoulding the wants and ideas of human societies. They stand outside us ; we can investigate, understand and follow, but we cannot control. There are some who interpret these changes as a national decadence, and accordingly paint the future in the blackest colours. They find the old religious notions toppling down like the old mediæval churches ; they do not see that both alike are worn out, and they would restore where they ought to rebuild. Finding the old conceptions of morality, social and sexual, in which they have been reared, unworkable in the present, they cry that there is no light, when, if they were couched for the cataract of prejudice, they could scarce face the gleams of the sun. On the other hand, the Socialist finds in the moral and economic changes in progress the development of mankind to a fuller enjoyment of life, the substitution for superstition of a faith in knowledge, the replacement of a worship of the unknowable by a reverence for concrete Society as embodied in the State. The Socialist teaches that the aim of industry is not supremacy in the world-markets, but the general welfare of the community, as evidenced by the raising of the general standard of physical comfort and intellectual development. Viewed from this standpoint the changes, which we see in progress, bring a feeling of unmixed satisfaction, and throw open a field of healthy social work and fruitful thought to all who would partake of that activity which is the joy of life. So far from our age being an age of stagnation, or of decadence, it is an age of greater movements than have been witnessed since the sixteenth century, and it is in our own country that two at least of these movements will more immediately bear fruit, and more powerfully influence the development of the rest of mankind. To work out the emancipation of women will be one of the gravest tasks, replete with the most far-reaching consequences, that England has ever taken upon herself. Socialism received from France and Germany as the ideal of Utopian dreamers, we shall return to them as a political possibility, not as a blind protest of suffering toilers, but as a workable social polity.

XII.

SOCIALISM :
IN THEORY AND PRACTICE.[1]

In the course of last year there was a great deal of discussion in the newspapers — and out of them—concerning the dwellings of the so-called poor. Numerous philanthropical people wrote letters and articles describing the extreme misery and unhealthy condition of many of our London courts and alleys. The Prince of Wales got up in the House of Lords and remarked that he had visited several of the most wretched slums in the Holborn district, and found them " very deplorable indeed " (!) The whole subject seemed an

---

[1] This lecture was originally delivered in February, 1884, to a Deptford working-men's club. It has since been twice printed as a pamphlet. The following dedicatory note to the first edition may serve to explain its object and its limitations :—

To E. C.

This lecture has been printed just as it was delivered. You would have wished it carefully revised. Other labour has hindered my touching it, and it now seems better to let its simple language stand. It was addressed to simple folk ; had it been intended for a middle-class audience it would have adopted a more logical, but undoubtedly harsher tone. The selfishness of the 'upper' classes arises to a great extent from ignorance, but these are times in which such ignorance itself is criminal. The object of this pamphlet will be fulfilled should it bring home even to one or two that truth, which I have learned from you, namely—that the higher Socialism of our time does not strive for a mere political reorganization, it is labouring for a moral renascence.

K. P.

Inner Temple, Christmas Eve, 1884.

excellent one out of which to make political capital. The
leader of the Conservatives wrote an article in a Tory
magazine on the dwellings of the poor. He told us that
things are much better in the country than they are in the
towns, that the great landlords look after the housing of the
agricultural labourers. It is the employers of labour, the
capitalists, who are at fault. THEY ought to provide proper
dwellings for their workpeople. This was the opinion of
Lord Salisbury, a great owner of land. But the Conservatives
having come forward as the friends of the working-man, it
seemed impossible, with a view to future elections, to let the
matter rest there. Accordingly, Mr. Joseph Chamberlain, a
Radical leader and capitalist, wrote another article in a
Liberal magazine, to show that it is no business whatever of
the employers of labour to look after the housing of their
workpeople. It is the duty of the owner of the land to see
that decent houses are built upon it. In other words, the
only men, who under our present social regime could make
vast improvements, threw the responsibility off their own
shoulders. "Very deplorable indeed," said Lord Salisbury,
"but of course not the landlord's fault ; why does not that
greedy fellow, the capitalist, look after his workpeople ? "
"Nothing could be more wretched ; I am sure it will lead to
a revolution," ejaculated Mr. Chamberlain, "but, of course,
it has nothing to do with the capitalist ; why does not that
idle person, that absolutely useless landlord, build more decent
houses ? " Then the landlord and capitalist smiled in their
sleeves, and agreed that it would be well to appoint a Royal
Commission, which meant, that after a certain amount of
philanthropic twaddle and a vast ocean of political froth, the
whole matter would end in nothing, or an absolutely fruitless
Act of Parliament.[1] Any change would have to be made at
the cost of either the landlord or the capitalist, or of both, and
whether we like it or not, it is these two who now practically
govern this country. They are not likely to empty their
pockets for our benefit. It is generally known how strong

---

[1] Four years afterwards we see it has ended in nothing of the least
practical value.

the interest of the landlords is in both Houses of Parliament,
but this is comparatively small when we measure the interests
of the capitalists.   You will be surprised, if you investigate
the matter, to find the large proportion of the House of
Commons which represents the interests of capital.   The
number of members of that House who are themselves
employers of labour, who are connected with great commercial interests, who are chairmen or directors of large
capitalistic companies, or who in some other way are
representatives of capital (as well as of their constituents) is
quite astounding.   It is said that óne large railway company
alone could muster forty votes on a division ; while the railway
interests, if combined, might form a coalition which, in
conceivable cases, would be of extreme danger to the State.
I have merely touched upon this matter to remind you how
thoroughly we are governed in this country by a *class*.   The
government of this country is not in the hands of the people.
It is mere self-deception for us to suppose that all classes
have a voice in the management of our affairs.   The
educative class (the class which labours with its head) and the
productive class (the class which labours with its hands) have
little or no real influence in the House of Commons.   The
governing class is the class of wealth, in both its branches
—owners of land and owners of capital.   This class naturally
governs in its own interests, and the interests of wealth are
what we must seek for would we understand the motive for
any particular form of foreign or domestic policy on the part
of either great State party.

   It may strike you that I have wandered very far from the
topic with which I started, namely, the dwellings of the
poor, but I wanted to point out to you, by a practical example,
why it is very unlikely that a reform, urgently needed by one
class of the community, will be carried out efficiently by
another governing class, when that reform must be paid for
out of the latter's pockets.   Confirmation of this view may
be drawn from the fact that the governing class pretend to
have only discovered in 1884 that the poor are badly housed.
There is something almost laughable in all the pother lately

raised about the housing of the poor. So far as my own experience goes—and I would ask if that is not a fact—the poor are not worse housed in 1884 than they were in 1874. The evil is one of very old standing. It was crying out for reform ten years ago, twenty years ago, forty years ago. More than forty years ago—in 1842—there was a report issued by a " Commission on the sanitary condition of the labouring population of Great Britain." The descriptions there given are of a precisely similar character to what was recently put before the public in the little tract entitled *The Bitter Cry of Outcast London*. In that report we hear of 40,000 people in Liverpool alone living in cellars underground. We are told that the annual number of deaths from fever, generated by uncleanliness and overcrowding in the dwellings of the poor, was then in England and Wales double the number of persons killed in the battle of Waterloo. We hear of streets without drainage, of workshops without ventilation, and of ten to twenty people sleeping in the same room, often five in a bed and rarely with any regard to sex. The whole essence of that report went to show that, owing to the great capitalistic industries, the working classes, if they had not become poorer, had become more demoralized. They had been forced to crowd together, and occupy unhealthy and often ruinous dwellings. The governing class and the public authorities scarcely troubled themselves about the matter, but treated the working classes as machines rather than as men. We see then that precisely the same evil was crying as loudly for remedy in 1842 as it cries now in 1884. We ask: Why has there been no remedy applied during all these years? There can only be two answers to that question : either no remedy is possible, or else those in whose power the remedy lies refuse to apply it.[1]

Is no remedy possible? A thoughtful Conservative recently stated that although he recognized the misery of the poorer members of the working classes, he still held no remedy was possible. The misery might become so intense

---

[1] 'Applying a remedy' connotes more than passing a Public Health Act. It means forcing vestries and local boards to carry out its spirit.

that an outbreak would intervene; still, when the outbreak
was over, matters would sink back into their old course.
There *must* be poor, and the poor would be miserable.[1] No
violent revolution, no peaceful reform, could permanently
benefit the poorer class of toilers. It was, so to speak, a
law of nature (if not of God) that society should have a basis
of misery. *History proved this to be always the case.*

It is to this latter phrase I want to call your attention—
History proved this to be always the case. Our Conservative
friend was distinctly right in his *method* when he appealed to
history. That is peculiarly the method which ought to be
made use of in the solution of all social and political problems. It is of the utmost importance to induce the working
classes to study social and political problems from the historical standpoint. Let us listen to no emotional appeals, nor
to the mere talk of rival political agitators. Let us endeavour,
if possible, to see how like problems have been treated
by other peoples in other ages, and with what measure of
success. The study of history is, I am aware, extremely
difficult, because the popular history books tell us only of
wars and of kings, and very little of the real life of the
people—how they worked, how they were fed, and how they
were housed. But the real mission of history is to tell us
how the great mass of the people toiled and lived; to tell us
of their pleasure, and of their misery. That is the only
history that can help us in social problems. Does, then,
history tell us that there always has been, and therefore
always must be, a large amount of misery at the basis of
society? The question is one really of statistics, and extremely difficult to answer; but, after some investigation, I
must state that I have come to a conclusion totally different
from that of our Conservative friend. I admit, in the words
of the man who worked for the poor in Galilee, that at all
times and places " the poor ye have always with you "; but the
amount of poverty, as well as the degree of misery attending
it, has varied immensely. I have made special investigation

[1] This seems to be the doctrine recently expounded to " Church
Paraders," March, 1887.

of the condition of the artizan class in Germany some three to four hundred years ago, and do not hesitate to assert that anything like the condition of the courts and dwellings of poorer London was then totally unknown. If this be true, the argument from history is false.   The artizan class has occupied a firmer and more substantial position in times gone by than it at present occupies.   If it has sunk in the scale of comfort, it can certainly rise.   In other words, a remedy for the present state of things does seem to me possible. Should any of you want to know why the working classes were better off four hundred years ago than they are at present, I must state it as my own opinion, that it was due to a better social system.   The social system of those old towns, so far as the workman was concerned, depended on his guild, while the political system was based as a rule upon the combined guilds. Thus the union which organized the craftsmen and their work, which also brought them together for social purposes, was practically the same as that which directed the municipal government of their city.   If you would exactly understand what that means, you must suppose the trades unions of to-day to have a large share in the government of London.   If they had, how long do you think the dwellings of the poor would remain what they are ? Do you believe the evil would remain another forty years ? or that in 1924 it would be necessary to shuffle out of immediate action by another Royal Commission ?

As I have said, the guilds of working men had originally a large share in municipal government.   The city guilds, as you know, are still very wealthy bodies, and have great authority in the city.   This is all that remains in London of the old system of working-men's guilds taking a part in the management of the city's affairs.

In old days, then, the labouring classes were united in guilds, and these guilds had a considerable share in local govern- ment.   The social and political system was thus, to some extent, based upon *labour*.   Such an organization of society we call *socialistic*.   The workmen of four hundred years ago were better off than are the workmen of to-day, because the old institutions were more *socialistic*—in other words, society was organized rather on the basis of labour than the basis of wealth. A society based upon wealth, since it grants power and place to the owners of something which is now in the hands of a few individuals, may be termed *individualistic.* To-day we live in an *individualistic* state. I believe the workman of four hundred years ago was better off than his fellow now, because he formed part of a *socialistic* rather than an *individualistic* system. I believe a remedy possible for the present state of affairs, because history seems to teach us that the artizan has a firmer and happier position under a socialism than under an individualism. It also teaches us that some forms of socialism have existed in the past, and may therefore be possible in the present or future. I hold, and I would ask you to believe with me, that a *remedy is possible.* If it is, we are thrown back on the alternative that the governing class has refused or neglected to apply it. We have seen that the evil did not arise, or did not accumulate to such an extent, where society was partly based upon labour ; we are, therefore, forced to the probable conclusion, that the evil has arisen, and continues to subsist, because our social and political system is based upon wealth rather than upon labour —because we live under an individualism rather than under a socialism. It is the fault of our present social system, and not a law of history, that the toilers should be condemned to extreme misery and poverty.

We have now to consider the following questions :—What do we mean by *labour* and a social *system based upon labour ?* By what means can we attempt to convert a system based upon wealth to one based upon labour ; in other words, how shall we proceed to convert our present individualism into a socialism ? In the latter question it will be necessary to include the consideration of the attitude which the artizan class should itself take with regard to organizations for socialistic change, and how it should endeavour to take political action, especially with regard to the two great capitalistic parties.

Let me first endeavour to explain what I understand by

labour.   You may imagine at first, perhaps, that I refer only to labour of the hand—such labour as is required to make a pair of boots or turn a lathe.   But I conceive labour to be something of far wider extent than this.   I hold the term to include all work, whether work of the head or of the hand, which is needful or profitable to the community at large. The man who puts cargo into a ship is no more or less a labourer than the captain who directs her course across the ocean ; nor is either more of a labourer than the mathematician or astronomer whose calculations and observations enable the captain to know which direction he shall take when he is many hundred miles from land.   The shoemaker or the postman are no more labourers than the clerk who sits in a merchant's office or the judge who sits on the bench.   The schoolmaster, the writer, and the actor are all true labourers. In some cases they may be overpaid ; in many they are underpaid.   Men of wealth have been known to pay the governess who teaches their children less than they pay their cook, and to treat her with infinitely less respect. I have laid stress on the importance of labour of the head, because I have met with certain working-men, who believed nothing but labour of the hand could have any value ; that all but labourers with the hand were idlers.   You have doubtless heard of the victory gained last year by English troops in Egypt.   Now, how do you suppose that victory was gained ?   Were the English soldiers a bit braver than the Arabs ?   Were they stronger ?   Not in the least.   They won the victory because they were better disciplined, because they had better weapons, —shortly, because what we may term their *organization* was better.   That organization was due to labour of the head. Now, what happened in Egypt is going on in the world at large every day.   It is not always the stronger, but the better organized, the better educated man who goes ahead. What is true of individual men is true of nations.   The better organized, the better educated nation is victorious in the battle of life.   We English have been so successful because we were well organized, because we were better educated than Hindoos, Zulus, and the other races we have

23

conquered.   You must never forget how much of that
organization, that education, is due to labourers with the
head.   Some of you may be indifferent to the great empire of
England, to this superiority of Englishmen, but let me assure
you that, small as in some cases is the comfort of the English
working classes, it is on the average large compared with
that of an inferior race—compared, say, with the abject
condition of the Egyptian peasant.   I want, if possible, to point
out to you the need for sympathy between labour of all kinds
—that labourers with the hand and labourers with the head
are mutually dependent.   They are both true labourers as
opposed to the idlers—the drones, who, by some chance
having a monopoly of wealth, live on the labour of others.
I would say to every man—"Friend, what is your calling,
what are you doing for society at large?   Are you making its
shoes, are you teaching its children, are you helping to
maintain order and forward its business?   If you are following none of these occupations, are you relieving its work hours
by administering to its play?   Do you bring pleasure to the
people as an actor, a writer, or a painter?   If you are doing
none of these, if you are simply a possessor of wealth,
struggling to amuse yourself and pass through life for your
own pleasure, then—why, *then*, you are not wanted here, and
the sooner you clear out, bag and baggage, the better for us—
and perhaps for yourself."   Do you grasp now the significance
of a society based upon labour?   The possessor of wealth,
simply because he has wealth, would have no place in such
a society.   The workers would remove him even as the
worker bees eject the drone from their hive.

Society ought to be one vast guild of labourers—workers
with the head and workers with the hand; and so organized
there would be no place in it for those who merely live on the
work of others.   In a political or social system based upon
labour nobody on the mere ground of wealth could lay claim
to power.   How far we are at present from such a Socialism
may be best grasped by noting that wealth has now almost
all political and social power; labour may have the name
but has little or none of the reality.

We have now reached what I conceive to be the fundamental axiom of Socialism. *Society must be organized on the
basis of labour*, and therefore political power, the power of
organizing, must be in the hands of labour. That labour, as
I have endeavoured to impress upon you, is of two kinds.
There is labour of the hand, which provides necessaries for
all society; there is labour of the head, which produces
all that we term *progress*, and enables any individual society
to maintain its place in the battle of life—the labour which
educates and organizes. I have come across a tendency in
some workers with the hand to suppose all folk beside themselves to be idlers, social drones, supported by their work.
I admit that the great mass of idlers are in what are termed
the ' upper and middle classes of society.' But this arises
from the fact that, society being graduated solely according
to wealth, the people with the most money, and who are
most idle, of course take their place in these viciously named
' upper classes.' In a *labour scale* they would naturally appear
at the very bottom, and form 'the dregs of population.' It
is true the labourer with the head is, as a rule, better clothed,
housed, and fed than the labourer with the hand, but this
often arises from the fact that he is also a capitalist. Still, if
the labourer with the head, whose labour is his sole source of
livelihood, is better clothed, housed, and fed than the artizan,
it does not show that in all cases he is earning more than his
due; on the contrary, it may denote that the artizan is earning far less than his due. The difference, in fact, often represents the work which goes to support the drones of our
present social system.

At this point I reach what I conceive to be the second
great axiom of true Socialism. *All forms of labour are equally
honourable.* No form of labour which is necessary for society
can disgrace the man who undertakes it, or place him in a lower
social grade than any other kind of work. Let us look at
this point somewhat more closely, as it is of the first importance. So long as the worker looks upon his work as merely
work for *himself*—considers it only as a means to *his own*
subsistence, and values it only as it satisfies *his own* wants,

so long one form of work will be more degrading than another. To shovel mud into a cart will be a lower form of work than to make a pair of shoes, and to make shoes will not be such high-class labour as to direct a factory. But there is another way of regarding work, in which all forms of real labour appear of equal value, viz., when the labourer looks at his work, not with regard to himself, but with regard to society at large. Let him consider his work as something necessary for society, as a condition of its existence, and then all gradations vanish. It is just as necessary for society that its mud should be cleared from the streets, as that it should have shoes, or again, as that its factories should be directed. Once let the workman recognize that his labour is needful for society, and, whatever its character, it becomes honourable at once. In other words, from the social standpoint *all labour is equally honourable.* We might even go so far as to assert that the more irksome forms of labour are the more honourable, because they involve the greater personal sacrifice for the need of society. Once let this second axiom of true Socialism be recognized—the equality of every form of labour—and all the vicious distinctions of caste, the false lines which society has drawn between one class of workers and another, must disappear. The degradation of labour must cease. Once admit that labour, though differing in kind, as the shoemaker's from the blacksmith's, is equal in degree, and all class barriers are broken down. Thus, in a socialistic state, or in a society based upon labour, there can clearly be no difference of class. All labourers, whether of the hand or the head, must meet on equal terms; they are alike needful to society; their value will depend only on the fashion and the energy with which they perform their particular duties.

Before leaving this subject of labour there is one point, however, which must be noticed. I have said that all forms of labour are equally honourable, because we may regard them as equally necessary for society. But still the effect on the individual of various kinds of labour will be different. The man who spends his whole day in shovelling up mud will hardly be as intelligent as the shoemaker or the engineer. His labour does not call for the same exercise of intelligence, nor draw out his ingenuity to the same extent. Thus, although his labour is equally honourable, it has not such a good influence on the man himself. Hence the hours of labour in such occupations ought to be as short as possible; sufficient leisure ought to be given to those engaged in the more mechanical and disagreeable forms of toil to elevate and improve themselves apart from their work. When we admit that all labour is equally honourable, and therefore deserving of equal wage, then to educate the labourer will not lead him to despise his work. It will only lead him to appreciate and enjoy more fully his leisure. This question of leisure is a matter of the utmost importance. We hear much of the demand for shorter hours of labour; but how is the increased spare time to be employed? Many a toiler looks with envy upon the extravagant luxury of the wealthy, and not unnaturally cries: "What right have you to enjoy all this, while I can hardly procure the necessaries of life?" But there is a matter in which I could wish the working classes would envy the wealthy even more than they might reasonably do their physical luxury—namely, their power to procure education. There is to me something unanswerable in the cry which the workman might raise against the wealthy: "What right have you to be educated, while I am ignorant?" Far more unanswerable than the cry— "What right have you to be rich while I am poor?" I could wish a cry for education might arise from the toilers as the cry for bread went up in the forties. It is the one thing which would render an increase of leisure really valuable to the workers; which would enable them to guide themselves, and assist society, through the dangerous storms which seem surely gathering in the near future. Leisure employed in education, in self-improvement, seems to me the only means by which the difference in character between various forms of labour can be equalized. This is a matter in which the labourers with the head can practically assist those with the hand. Let the two again unite for that mutual assistance which is so necessary, it between them they are to reorganize society into one vast guild of labour.

If we pass for a moment from the possibilities of the present to those of a distant future, we might conceive the labourers with the hand to attain such a degree of education that workers of both kinds might be fused together. The same man might labour with his pen in the morning and with his shovel after mid-day. That, I think, would be the *ideal* existence in which society, as an entire body, would progress at the greatest possible rate. I have endeavoured, then, to lay before you what I understand by labour; how all true labour is equally honourable and deserving of an equal wage. If many of the anomalies and much of the misery of our present state of society would disappear, were it organized on a Socialistic or labour basis, it becomes necessary to consider in what manner the labour basis differs from, and is opposed to, the present basis of wealth.

In order to illustrate what the present basis of wealth means, let me put to you a hypothetical case. Let us suppose three men on an island separated from the rest of the world. We will also suppose there to be a sufficient supply of seed, ploughs, and generally of agricultural necessaries. If, now, one of the three men were to assert that the island, the seed, and the ploughs belonged to him, and his two comrades for some reason—or want of reason—accepted his assertion, let us trace what would follow. Obviously, he would have an entire monopoly of all the means of sustaining life on the island. He could part with them at whatever rate he pleased, and could insist upon the produce of all the labour-power, which it would be possible to extract from these two men, in return for supplying them with the barest necessities of existence. *He* would naturally do nothing; they would till the ground with *his* implements, and sow *his* seed and store it in *his* barn. After this he might employ them in work tending to increase his luxuries, in providing him with as fine a house and as gorgeous furniture as they were capable of producing. He would probably allow them to build themselves shanties as protection from the weather, and grant them sufficient food to sustain life. All their time, after providing these necessaries for themselves, would be devoted to his service. He would be landlord and capitalist, having a complete monopoly of wealth. He could practically treat the other two men as slaves. Let us somewhat extend our example, and suppose this relation to hold between the one man and a considerable number of men on the island. Then it might be really advantageous for all the inhabitants, if the one man directed their labour. We may suppose him to be a practical farmer, who thoroughly understood his business ; so that, by his directing the others, the greatest amount possible would be produced from the land. As such a director of farming operations, he would be a labourer with the head, and worthy as any man under him to receive his hire. He would have as great a claim as any one he directed to the necessaries of life produced by the labourers with the hand. In a Socialistic scheme he would still remain director ; he would still receive his share of the produce, and the result of the labour of the community would be divided according to the labour of its members. On the other hand, if our farm-director were owner of all things on the island, he might demand not only the share due to him for his labour of the head, but also that all the spare labour of the other inhabitants should be directed to improving his condition rather than their own. After providing for themselves the bare necessities of life the other islanders might be called upon to spend all the rest of their time in ministering to his luxury. He could demand this because he would have a monopoly of all the land and all the wealth of the island ; such a state of affairs on the island would be an individualism, or a society based upon wealth. I think this example will show clearly the difference between a society based upon labour and one based upon wealth. Commonplace as the illustration may seem, it is one which can be extended, and yet rarely is extended, to the state of affairs we find in our own country. We have but to replace our single landowner by a number of landowners and capitalists, who as a group will have a monopoly of land and of wealth. They can virtually force the labouring classes, who have neither land nor capital, to administer to their luxury in return for the more needful supports of life. The degree of comfort to which they can limit the labouring classes will depend on the following considerations, which, of course, vary from time to time :—First, their own self-interest in keeping at least a sufficient supply of labour in such decent health and strength that it can satisfy their wants ; secondly, their fear that too great pinching may lead to a forcible revolution ; and, thirdly, a sort of feeling—arising partly perhaps from religion, partly perhaps from inherited race-sympathy—of dislike at the sight of suffering.

The greater demand there is for luxury on the part of the wealthy, the smaller is the time that the labouring classes can devote to the improvement of their own condition and the increase of their own comfort. Let us take a possible case, which may not be the absolute truth, but which will exemplify the law we have stated. Suppose that the labouring classes work eight hours a day. Now, these eight hours are not only spent in producing the absolute necessities of existence, and the degree of comfort in which our toilers live, but in producing also all the luxuries enjoyed by the rich. Let us suppose, for example, that five hours suffice to sow and to till, and to weave, and to fetch and carry—shortly, to produce the food-supply of the country, and the average comfort which the labourer enjoys as to house and raiment. What, then, becomes of the other three hours' work ? It is consumed in making luxuries of all kinds for the monopolists, fine houses, rich furniture, dainty food, and so forth. These three hours are spent, not in improving the condition of the labourer's own class, not in building themselves better dwellings or weaving themselves better clothes, nor, on the other hand, are they spent in public works for the benefit of the whole community, but solely in supplying luxuries for wealthy individuals. The wealthy can demand these luxuries because they possess a monopoly of land and of capital—shortly, of the means of subsistence. This monopoly of the means of subsistence makes them in fact, if not in name, slave-owners.

Such is the result of the individualistic as opposed to the socialistic system. We see now why the houses of the poor are deplorable—namely, because that surplus-labour which should be devoted to improving them is consumed in supplying the luxuries of the rich. We may state it, indeed, as a general law of a society based upon wealth : *that the misery of the labouring classes is directly proportional to the luxury of the wealthy*. This law is a very old one indeed; the only strange thing is that it is every day forgotten.

Having noted, then, wherein the evil of the social system based upon wealth lies, we have lastly to consider how far, and by what means, it is possible to remedy it.

The only true method of investigating a question of this kind is, I feel sure, the historical one. Let us ask ourselves how in past ages one state of society has been replaced by another, and then, if possible, apply the general law to the present time.

Now, there are a considerable number of Socialistic teachers—I will not call them false Socialists—who are never weary of crying out that our present state in society is extremely unjust, and that it must be destroyed. They are perpetually telling the labouring classes that the rich unjustly tyrannize over them, and that this tyranny must be thrown off. According to these teachers, it would seem as if the rich had absolutely entered into a conspiracy to defraud the poor. Now, although I call myself a Socialist, I must tell you plainly that I consider such teaching not only very foolish, but extremely harmful. It can arise only from men who are ignorant, or from men who seek to win popularity from the working classes by appealing to their baser passions. So far from aiding true Socialism, it stirs up class-hatred, and instead of bringing classes together, it raises a barrier of bitterness and hostility between them. It is idle to talk of a conspiracy of the rich against the poor, of one class against another. A man is born into his class, and into the traditions of his class. He is not responsible for his birth, whether it be to wealth or to labour. He is born to certain luxuries, and he is never taught to consider them as other than his natural due; he does as his class does, and as his fathers have done before him. His fault is not one of malice, but of ignorance. He does not know how his luxuries directly increase the misery of the poor, because no one has ever brought it home to him. Although a slave-owner he is an unconscious slave-owner. Shortly, he wants educating; not educating quite in the same sense as the labouring classes want educating: he probably has book-learning enough. He wants teaching that there is a higher social morality than the morality of a society based upon wealth. Namely, he must be taught that mere ownership has no social value at all—that the sole thing of social value is labour, labour of head or labour of hand; and that individual ownership of wealth has arisen in the past out of a very crude and insufficient method of representing such labour. The education of the so-called upper or wealth-owning classes is thus an imperative necessity. They must be taught a *new morality*. Here, again, is a point on which we see the need of a union between the educative and hand-working classes. The labourers with the head must come to the assistance of the labourers with the hand by educating the wealthy. Do not think this is a visionary project; at least two characteristic Englishmen, John Ruskin and William Morris, are labouring at this task; they are endeavouring to teach the capitalistic classes that the morality of a society based upon wealth is a mere immorality.

But you will tell me that education is a very long process, and that meantime the poor are suffering, and must continue to suffer. Are not the labouring classes unjustly treated, and have they not a right to something better? Shortly, ought they not to enforce that right? Pardon me, if I tell you plainly that I do not understand what such abstract 'justice' or 'right' means. I understand that the comfort of the labouring classes is far below what it would be if society were constituted on the basis of labour. I believe that on such a basis there would be less misery in the world, and therefore it is a result to be aimed at. But because this is a

result which all men should strive for, it does not follow that
we gain anything by calling it a ' right.' A ' right ' suggests
something which a man may take by force, if he cannot
obtain it otherwise. It suggests that the labouring classes
should revolt against the capitalistic classes, and seize what
is their ' right.'

Let us consider for a moment what is the meaning of such
a revolt. I shall again take history as our teacher. History
shows us that whenever the misery of the labouring classes
reaches a certain limit they always do break into open
rebellion. It is the origin, more or less, of all revolutions
throughout the course of time. But history teaches us
just as surely that such revolutions are accompanied by
intense misery both for the labouring and idling classes.
If this infliction of misery had ever resulted in the reconstruction of society we might even hope for good from a
revolution, but we invariably find that something like the old
system springs again out of the chaos, and the same old
distinction of classes, the same old degradation of labour, is
sure to reappear. That is precisely the teaching of the
Paris Commune or again of the Anabaptist Kingdom of God
in Münster. Apart from this, the labourers with the hand
will never be permanently successful in a revolution, unless
they have the labourers with the head with them ; they will
want organization, they will want discipline, and this must
fail unless education stands by them. Now, the labourers
with the head have usually deserted the labourers with the
hand, when the latter rise in revolt, because they are students
of history, and they know too well from history that revolution has rarely permanently benefited the revolting classes.
You may accept it as a primary law of history, *that no great
change ever occurs with a leap ;* no great social reconstruction,
which will permanently benefit any class of the community,
is ever brought about by a revolution. It is the result of a
gradual growth, a progressive change, what we term an
evolution. This is as much a law of history as of nature.
Try as you will, you cannot make a man out of a child in a
day : you must wait, and let him grow, and gradually educate

him and replace his childish ideas by the thoughts of a man.
Precisely so you must treat society; you must gradually
change it by education if you want a permanent improvement
in its structure. Feeling, as I do, the extreme misery which is
brought about by the present state of society based upon
wealth, I should say to the working classes : Revolt, if
history did not teach us only too surely that revolution
would fail in its object. All progress towards a better state
of things must be gradual. Progress proceeds by evolution,
not by revolution. For this reason I would warn you against
Socialistic teachers who talk loudly of ' right ' and ' justice '—
who seek to stir up class against class. Such teaching
merely tends towards revolution ; and revolution is not
justifiable, because it is never successful. It never achieves.
its end. Such teachers are not true Socialists, because they
have not studied history ; because their teaching really impedes our progress towards Socialism. We might even take
an example from our island with its landlord - capitalist
tyrannizing over the other inhabitants. We have supposed
him to be a practical farmer capable of directing the labours
of the others. Now, suppose the inhabitants were to rise in
revolt, and throw him into the sea, what would happen ?
Why, the very next year they would not know what to sow,
or how to sow it ; their agricultural operations would fail,
and there would very soon be a famine on the island, which
would be far worse than the old tyranny. Something very
similar would occur in this country if the labouring classes
were to throw all our capitalists into the sea. There would
be no one capable of directing the factories or the complex
operations of trade and commerce ; these would all collapse,
and there would very soon be a famine in this island also.
You must bring your capitalist to see that he is only a
labourer, a labourer with the head, and deserves wage accordingly. You can only do this by two methods. The first is.
to educate him to a higher sociality, the second is to restrict
him by the law of the land. Now, the law of the land is.
nothing more or less than the morality of the ruling class,
and so long as political power is in the hands of the

capitalists, and these are 'uneducated,' they are unlikely to restrict their own profits.

If, then, my view, that we can only approach Socialism by a gradual change, is correct, we have before us two obvious lines of conduct which we may pursue at the same time. The first, and I am inclined to think the more important, is the education of the wealthy classes ; they must be taught from childhood up that the only moral form of society is a society based upon labour; they must be taught always to bear in mind the great law—that the misery of the poor is ever directly proportional to the luxury of the rich. This first object ought to be essentially the duty of the labourers with the head. Let the labourer with the hand ever regard himself as working in concert with the labourer with the head ; the two are in truth but members of one large guild, the guild of labour, upon which basis we have to reconstruct society. The second line of conduct, which is practically open to all true Socialists, is the attainment of political power; wealth must cease to be the governing power in this country, it must be replaced by labour. The educative classes and the handworkers must rule the country; only so will it be possible to replace the wealth basis by the labour basis. The first step in this direction must necessarily be the granting of the franchise to all hand-workers. This is a very practical and definite aim to work for. Now, I have already hinted that I consider both great political parties really to represent wealth. Hence I do not believe that any true Socialist is either Liberal or Conservative, but at present it would be idle to think of returning Socialistic members to Parliament.[1] Socialists will best forward their aims by supporting at present that party which is likely to increase the franchise. So that to be a true Socialist at present means, I think, to support the Liberal Government. This support is not given because we are Liberals, but because, by it, we can best aid the

[1] This was written in 1883. The extension of the franchise, incomplete as it is, has since considerably increased the possibility of returning Socialistic members for at least one or two towns.

cause of Socialism. But with regard to the franchise, there is a point which I cannot too strongly insist upon. If the complete enfranchisement of the hand-worker is to forward the Socialistic cause, he must be educated so as to use it for that purpose. Now, we have laid it down as a canon of Socialism that all labour is equally honourable; in a society based upon labour there can be no distinction of class. Thus, the true Socialist must be superior to class-interests. He must look beyond his own class to the wants and habits of society at large. Hence, if the franchise is to be really profitable, the hand-worker must be educated to see beyond the narrow bounds of his own class. He must be taught to look upon society as a *whole*, and respect the labour of all its varied branches. He must endeavour to grasp the wants and habits of other forms of labour than his own, whether it be labour of the head or of the hand. He must recognize to the full that all labour is equally honourable, and has equal claims on society at large. The shoemaker does not despise the labour of the blacksmith, but he must be quite sure that the labour of the schoolmaster, of the astronomer, and of the man who works with his brains, is equally valuable to the community. Here, again, we see how the labourer with the head can come to the assistance of the labourer with the hand. In order that the franchise may be practically of value to the artizan, he must grasp how to use it for broader purposes than mere class aims. To do this he requires to educate himself. I repeat that I should like to hear a cry go up from the hand-workers for education and leisure for education, even as it went up forty years ago for bread; for the mind is of equal importance with the stomach, and needs its bread also. Apart from the franchise, there is another direction in which, I think, practical steps might be taken, namely, to obtain for trades-unions, or rather, as I should prefer to call them, labour-guilds—an influence or share in municipal government. Let there be a labour-guild influence in every parish, and on every vestry. As I have said before, I cannot conceive that the housing of the poor would be what it is if the trades-unions had been represented in the government of London. Such a representation would be the first approach to a communal organization based upon labour, and ultimately to a society on the same foundation. You can hardly support your trades-unions too energetically, and you have in this respect taught the labourers with the head a lesson. These labourers with the head are just beginning to form their labour-guilds too—guilds of teachers and guilds of writers—and it is to these labour-guilds, and to your trades-unions, that we must look for much useful work in the future.

These surely are practical aims enough for the present, but I may perhaps be allowed to point out to you what direction I think legislative action should take, supposing the franchise granted to all hand-workers. As I have endeavoured to show, any sudden change would be extremely dangerous ; it would upset our old social arrangements, and would not give us any stable new institutions. It would embitter class against class, and not destroy class altogether. We must endeavour to pass gradually from the old to the new state ; from the state in which wealth is the social basis to one in which labour is the sole element by which we judge men. Now, in order that wealth should cease to be mistress, the individual monopoly of the means of subsistence must be destroyed. In other words, land and capital must cease to be in the hands of individuals. We must have nationalization of the land and nationalization of capital. Every Socialist is a land-nationalizer and a capital-nationalizer.

It will be sufficient now to consider the first problem, the nationalization of the land. Mr. George says : Take the land and give no compensation. That is what I term a revolutionary measure ; it attempts to destroy and reconstruct in a moment. If history teaches us anything, it tells us that all such revolutionary measures fail ; they bring more misery than they accomplish good. Hence, although I am a land-nationalizer—as every Socialist must be—I do not believe in Mr. George's cry of ' No compensation.' Then we have another set of land-nationalizers, who would buy the landlords out. Let us see what this means. The landlords

SOCIOLOGY.

would be given, in return for their lands, a large sum of
money, which would have to be borrowed by the nation, and
the interest on which would increase for ever the taxes of
the country. In other words, we should be perpetuating the
wealth of the landlords and their claims to be permanently
supported by the classes that labour. That is not a *socialistic*
remedy. It would seem, at first sight, as if there were no
alternative—either compensation or no compensation. Yet
I think there is a third course, if we would only try to legislate for the future as well as for the present. Suppose a Bill
were passed to convert all freehold in land into a leasehold,
say, of 81 to 100 years, from the nation. Here there would
be no question of compensation, and little real injury to the
present landowner, because the difference between freehold
and a hundred years' leasehold (especially in towns) is comparatively small. At the end of a hundred years the nation
would be in possession of all land without having paid a penny
for it, and without violently breaking up the present social
arrangements. In less than a hundred years with the land
slipping from their fingers the children of our present landowners would have learnt that, if they want to live, they must
labour. That would be a great step towards true Socialism.
Precisely as I propose to treat the land, so I would treat most
forms of capital. With the land, of course, mines and
factories would necessarily pass into the hands of the nation.
Railways would have to be dealt with in the same fashion.
The present companies would have a hundred years' lease
instead of a perpetuity of their property.

These are merely suggestions of how it might be possible
to pass to a stable form of society based upon labour—to a
true Socialism. The change would be stable because it
would be gradual ; the state would be Socialistic because it
would be based upon labour ; while wealth, in its two important forms—land and capital—would belong to the entire
community.

Some of you may cry out in astonishment : "But what is
the use of working for such a Socialism? We shall never live
to see it, we shall never enjoy its advantages." Quite true, I

reply, but there is a nobler calling than working for ourselves, there is a higher happiness than self-enjoyment—namely, the feeling that our labour will have rendered posterity, will have rendered our children, free from the misery through which we ourselves have had to struggle ; the feeling that our work in life has left the world a more joyous dwelling-place for mankind than we found it. The little streak of social good which each man may leave behind him—the only immortality of which mankind can be sure—is a far nobler result of labour, whether of hand or of head, than threescore years of unlimited personal happiness.

XIII.

THE WOMAN'S QUESTION.[1]

The legislator ought to be whole and perfect, and not half a man only ; he ought not to let the female sex live softly and waste money and have no order of life, while he takes the utmost care of the male sex, and leaves half of life only blest with happiness, when he might have made the whole state happy. . . . There appears to be need of some bold man who specially honours plainness of speech, and will say what is best for the city and citizens, ordaining what is good and convenient for the whole state, amid the corruptions of human souls, opposing the mightiest lusts, and having no man his helper but himself, standing alone and following reason only.—*Plato.*

THE rapidity with which women in this country are obtaining an independent social and political position—the near approach of their complete emancipation—is one of the most marked features of our age. Yet, like so many other social changes, we allow it to take place in a tentative and piecemeal fashion, without first intelligently investigating whither the movement is leading us, and how far it is not really undermining the whole basis of existing society. The remoulding of existing society may itself be desirable, but it is also advantageous that we should see the whole bearing of what is taking place in this revolution of the relations of sex, and endeavour, so far as is humanly possible, to guide the movement into such channels that it may gradually change the foundations of society without at the same time depriving it of all stability. It is the conviction that the emancipation of women will ultimately involve a revolution in all our social institutions, which has led me to attempt a statement of some of the numerous social and sexualogical problems

[1] Printed for private circulation in 1885.

with which the woman's question abounds. These problems remain to a great extent unsolved, partly on account of their difficult nature, partly because the danger of being classed with charlatans and quacks has restrained investigators of genuine historical and scientific capacity. Not until the historical researches of Bachofen, Girard Teulon, and McLennan, with the anthropological studies of Tylor and Ploss, have been supplemented by careful investigation of the sanitary and social effects of past stages of sex-development, not until we have ample statistics of the medico-social results of the various regular and morbid forms of sex-relationship, will it be possible to lay the foundations of a real science of sexualogy. Without such a science we cannot safely determine whither the emancipation of women is leading us, or what is the true answer which must be given to the woman's question. It is the complete disregard of sexualogical difficulties which renders so superficial and unconvincing much of the talk which proceeds from the 'Woman's Rights' platform. We have first to settle what is the physical capacity of woman, what would be the effect of her emancipation on her function of race-reproduction, before we can talk about her 'rights,' which are, after all, only a vague description of what may be the fittest position for her, the sphere of her maximum usefulness in the developed society of the future. The higher education of women may connote a general intellectual progress for the community, or, on the other hand, a physical degradation of the race, owing to prolonged study having ill effects on woman's child-bearing efficiency. This is only one example of the many problems which are thrust upon us; and those who are the most earnest supporters of woman's independence ought to be the first to recognize that her duty to society is paramount. They must face sex-problems with sexualogical and historical knowledge, and solve them, before they appeal to the market-place with all the rhetorical flourish of 'justice' and of 'right.' They must show that the emancipation will tend not only to increase the stability of society and the general happiness of mankind, but will favour the physique and health of both sexes. It is this want of preliminary sexualogical investigation which renders nugatory much of what John Stuart Mill has written on the subject, and in a somewhat less degree the more powerful work of Mary Wollstonecraft. With the view of strongly emphasizing this need of preliminary investigation I have put together the following remarks; I do not profess to give opinions, but to suggest problems. It has been difficult to avoid individual bias, and I cannot flatter myself that I have been really successful. I shall be satisfied, however, if my paper should convince even a small number of the earnest men and women, who are labouring for woman's freedom, that there are certain problems which demand more than emotional treatment; they require careful collection of facts, and the interpretation of such facts by scientific and impartial minds.

In order to group the problems I am about to suggest, I shall first draw attention to what I think will generally be admitted as the fundamental distinction between man and woman. It lies in the capacity for child-bearing, not necessarily in the activity, but as well in the potentiality of the function. This capacity is the essence of the physiological difference between men and women; and the first problems which arise before us spring from the effects of the child-bearing potentiality on the physical and mental development of woman. Are these effects of such a kind as to make a fundamental distinction in social and political position between man and woman? Do they connote a physical and mental inferiority on her side? The question is not so easily answered as some old-fashioned folk and some new-fashioned platform agitators seem to imagine; it must be treated from the scientific and historical basis only, and even then any definite answer will not be easily obtained. Yet the problem is radical, and without some solution it is difficult to see how we can profitably advance in our discussion. Some have argued that history shows the position of women always to have been secondary; others have pointed out that the tendency towards complete emancipation has been constantly increasing of late years, and have cited the generations it took to convince mankind at large of the justice of slave-emancipation. Here we may note, however, the argument that the negro-emancipation has wrought its best effects in an improved moral tone among the white population. The negro, although free, remains intellectually and morally the white man's inferior. We may ask whether the emancipation of women may not have a like excellent effect on the moral tone of men, but in nowise raise women to an intellectual equality. Closely associated with this problem is that of the like or unlike inheritance by male and female children of their parents' intellectual capacity. Is the girl at a disadvantage in this respect as compared with the boy? Does she start life handicapped? If we admit the inferiority of women at the present time—and the tone of the great mass of men, especially the characteristics they peculiarly desire in a wife, is strong evidence of it—we have still to determine whether it is a necessity for *all* women. Is child-bearing a check on intellectual development, and so the subjection of child-bearing women a part of an inevitable natural law? How, again, are we to treat non-child-bearing women? Does a like inferiority exist here? Or must we, with a recent writer in the *Westminster Review*, draw a broad distinction between the two classes? This question is extremely important with regard to the increasing number—now roughly, 20 per cent.—of single women in the community. Are these women hampered in their physical or intellectual development by merely potential functions? The writer of a recent pamphlet[1] has spoken of the stifled cry of the unmarried woman, the Rachel-like appeal, "Give me children, or else I die." It is an open question how far there is a physiological basis to this cry. It has, however, led certain disciples of James Hinton to replace his chief argument for polygamy, namely, the evil of unsatisfied sexual desire, by an appeal to the insatiable and passionate wish of women to give society what they alone can give. Our present social arrangements are such that there is no demand for children; the acquisition

[1] *The Future of Marriage.* An Eirenikon for a Question of To-day.

of a great tract of land is viewed by our governing classes not as a field for fresh population, but as opening up a new market for traders' profits. Hence, under our present social system, woman's prerogative function—child-bearing—is of small account, and would probably be exercised to a much less extent than it is, were it not associated with the gratification of sexual desire. If race-evolution has implanted in women a physical craving for children, it is obvious that it remains unsatisfied in more than 20 per cent. of womankind. We may ask whether this affects the physical health of women, whether as such it may not act as a check on intellectual activity? Thus either child-bearing or its absence may possibly act as a hindrance to woman's development. Such are the sort of arguments which may be produced against woman's being able to occupy an equal position with man ; they are not arguments against her being admitted to equality, but against her power of maintaining it. In most historical forms of society the honour in which women have been held depended to a, considerable extent on the value which society then placed on children. Hence we see the extreme importance of social and political questions to woman, notably those relating to great social changes and to population ; but these are matters whereon she has hitherto had little or no opinion, and wherein she has hitherto been allowed no voice. The creator of a new machine, which throws a quantity of labour upon the market, and so decreases the demand for population, is at present deemed a public benefactor ; the woman who can bring forth a new human being is at a discount. It is possibly due to this fact, that the position of woman in America and our colonies is found to be superior to that of woman in England.

I have, perhaps, said enough to point out the important problems which centre round this prerogative function of woman. For our present purposes I shall divide women into two classes, child-bearing and non-child-bearing women [1]; the distinction is an evil one in some respects, but will perhaps

[1] Corresponding to the *parous* and *nulliparous* women of gynaikological writers.

suffice to mark two different kinds of problems. Let us consider first those which relate to the single woman.

If 20 per cent. of womankind remain single, we must consider whether it be not absurd on the face of it to talk of woman's proper place being the home, and her sphere the family; to hold that the first duty of society is to educate women to be mothers (We may well question, however, if this duty be frequently, or fitly, performed). Granted that there is a large and increasing number of single women, we shall have to consider whether they are hopelessly handicapped by the present competitive constitution of society. Are they merely surplus machines which cannot be turned to their proper purpose, or do they form a contingent whose labour will ultimately be of the utmost importance to the community? The problem as to the inferiority of the single woman can only be solved by an investigation of her intellectual and physical condition. Putting aside the question of any child-bearing desire affecting her welfare, it seems probable that she may be *less*, certainly not more, influenced by sexual impulse than the single man. On the other hand, her physical activity is probably more—though, perhaps, to a lesser extent than is generally supposed—affected by her sexualogical life than man's by his. Whether a single woman is physically—I use physically in its broadest sense, not only of strength, but also of power of endurance—equal to the single man, is a question which wants very fully investigating. That the average woman—including both child and non-child-bearing classes—is at present held physically inferior to man, is best evidenced by the smaller wages she receives for manual labour. Whether the non-child-bearer would not fetch as high a price in the labour market as man, if the competition of child-bearing women, who are necessarily at a disadvantage, and of prostitutes, who have other means of subsistence, were removed, is an important problem. The astounding powers of endurance exhibited by domestic servants and by the peasant girls of Southern Germany and Italy, seem to point to no physical inferiority, when once the physique has been developed.

When we turn to the intellectual position of women we find a condition of affairs which ought to occupy much attention. Woman's past and present subjection probably depends to as great an extent on her presumed intellectual as on her presumed physical inferiority. We must face the problem of her being naturally man's intellectual inferior; her prerogative function of child-bearing may possibly involve this. If it be so, we can only accept the inferiority, and allow woman to find compensation for it in other directions. Possibly, however, the present average intellectual inferiority may be due to centuries of suppression, which have produced an inherited inferiority. Mental difference is closely related to physical; and there seems as much reason for woman's inheriting a less fully developed mental organ than man, as for man's inheriting rudimentary organs which are fully developed in the woman. But we shall have further to consider—and here I fancy we approach nearer the core of the matter—whether *present* suppression be not a more potent cause than past; whether the fact that, bad as men's education undoubtedly is, the great mass of women as yet receive nothing worthy of being called intellectual training, is not the root of all this presumed mental inferiority? What women can do when they compete with men intellectually has been well brought out by their recent university and college successes. At the same time I must note that these institutions at present draw picked women, but hardly picked men. Either of the two reasons I have given : inheritance of a less fully developed brain, or want of intellectual training, deserves careful investigation, because it seems probable that remedies may be found for both. The intellectual and physical training of single women ought to receive the special attention of the state, because to them will fall in all probability much of the work of the community in the future, because the great restrictions which are at present placed on their development are such an obvious evil. The general tone of the family, of society, of the state, with regard to single women, is at present at a very low ebb. The first puts restrictions on individual study and activity by absurd

domestic and social demands ; the second checks to a great
extent freedom of action and intercourse by still more absurd
social prejudices ; while the third, the state, giving women no
voice in public affairs, leaves their interests practically un-
represented in legislature and executive. Nowadays neither
intellectual nor physical inferiority excludes from the franchise
—possibly they ought to do so. There must be some reason
apart from these which gives the dullest yokel a vote and
excludes a Mary Ann Evans ; the only obvious difference is
the child-bearing potentiality. Why it should exclude is by
no means clear. Yet there may be some deep race experience,
some more valid cause to be produced for this apparent self-
assertion of men than the historical origin of our institutions
in an age when might was right, and most women, being
child-bearers, were, by reason of it, rendered dependent on and
subservient to men. Granted that woman's emancipation is
desirable, still I am not sure whether all its ardent advocates
have fully recognized the fact that her enfranchisement and universal suffrage would at one stroke *theoretically* place the entire
power of government in her hands, for she possesses a majority
of upwards of half a million in this country. If there were a
proposal—which does not seem improbable in the future—to
construct a woman's political party, this would be indeed a
momentous, I will not say an undesirable, revolution.

Whether the throwing open of all public institutions and
professions to women be or be not advisable is a problem
for much consideration. In our *present* state of society (I
emphasize *present*) it may not be so easily answered as some
at first may think. Is it or is it not possible for the sexes
to mix freely in all relations of life ? The hitherto almost
complete separation of the sexes in the business of life has
led to what appears to me a very artificial relation between
them. It is a fact which we have to face and to consider
that, whereas friendship between a man and a married woman
is possible, close friendship between single men and women
is almost impossible. It may be due to something inherent
in human nature, the existence of a sexual attraction produced by the struggle of group against group in the battle of

life, or it may be due to an artificial relation, the outcome of a false social system. It may be needful that existing society should put its veto on such friendships, but we may still question whether it be not a real hindrance to human development. So far is this restriction carried in some ranks of life at present that, if a single man and woman are once seen walking alone together, society points its finger; if they are seen twice, society pronounces them engaged; if this be denied, on the third occasion it damns, not the man's be it noted, but the woman's reputation. The nigh complete separation of the sexes from youth upwards in the upper and middle classes of our present society is a point which demands our careful investigation. Is it expedient? may it not hinder general progress? is it even healthy? The boy at the public school and the university is kept, to a great extent, from woman's society. He is then thrown into it in an extremely artificial manner at a time when his sexual impulses are most rapidly developing. George Eliot, I think, felt this keenly when, in the last years of her life, she said that far too much of family influence is "ruthlessly sacrificed in the case of Englishmen by their public school and university education." The same process occurs to a great extent with the girl. Neither boy nor girl fully and clearly understand what influences them; and thus the making or marring of the whole future of life too often depends entirely on the blind direction of a sudden sexual impulse. How many men, how many women, wonder in after life what attached them to their present partners? They try to believe that characters have changed, because they are unwilling to admit that they had neither the inclination, nor the knowledge, nor the opportunity to study character before marriage.

Whether the co-education of boys and girls would not be advantageous is a problem demanding thoughtful consideration. Possibly the continual association of women of equal position and intelligence with men from boyhood upwards might have a good influence on the general moral tone; might lead some men to understand that sex-friendship had other pleasant and more worthy elements than mere sexual passion. It might thus go some way in hindering prostitution, or, at any rate, in enforcing some degree of refinement on the prostitute. To this it may be replied that in our *present* social organization it would often lead to long engagements, against which there appears to be considerable objection from the medical side.

If comparative separation of the sexes in youth be advisable, we have still to note the possible desirability of fuller sexualogical knowledge, which might be imparted by home or school education. Men and women are not only surprisingly ignorant of each other's modes of thought and phases of feeling, but, extremely often, of each other's constitution; nay, not only of each other's, but occasionally of their own. The question is an extremely difficult, but immensely important one, especially for teachers and parents, having regard to what is said to be a growing evil in boys' public and girls' private schools. Some parents believe that ignorance is the best safeguard, but ignorance may hinder a child from knowing the very danger into which it has fallen. Want of sexualogical knowledge, or even a false sense of shame may prevent parents speaking out freely in these matters. It is a question whether society has not through its schoolmaster a right to interfere between parent and child.

We must not forget that the emancipation of woman, while placing her in a position of social responsibility, will make it her duty to investigate many matters of which she is at present frequently assumed to be ignorant. It may be doubted whether the identification of purity and ignorance has had wholly good effects in the past[1]; indeed it has frequently been the false cry with which men have sought to hide their own anti-social conduct. It is certain, however, that it cannot last in the future, and man will have to face the fact that woman's views and social action with regard to many sex-problems may widely differ from his own. It

[1] If we may trust Alexander Dumas fils, 80 per cent. of marriages in France are made in ignorance, and regretted within a month.

is of the utmost importance, then, that woman, not only on account of the part she already plays in the education of the young, but also because of the social responsibilities her emancipation must bring, should have a full knowledge of the laws of sex. Every attempt hitherto to grapple with prostitution has been a failure—what will women do when they thoroughly grasp the problem, and have a voice in the attitude the state shall assume with regard to it ? At présent hundreds do not know of its existence ; thousands only know of it to despise those who earn their livelihood by it ; one in ten thousand has examined the causes which lead to it, has felt that degradation, if there be any, lies not in the prostitute, but in the society where it exists; not in the women of the streets, but in the thousands of women in society who are ignorant of the problem, ignore it, or fear to face it. What will be the result of woman's action in this matter? Can it possibly be effectual, or will it merely tend to embitter the relations of men and women ? Possibly an expression of woman's opinion on this point in society, and the press would do much, but then it must be an educated opinion ; one which recognizes facts, and knows the innumerable difficulties of the problem. An appeal to chivalry, to a Christian dogma, or a Biblical text, will hardly avail. The descriptions we have of Calvin's Geneva show that puritanic suppression is wholly idle. What form will be taken by the opinion and reasoned action of women, cognizant of historical and sexualogical fact ?

Perhaps it may be that women when they fully grasp the problem may despair, as many men do, of its solution. They may remark that prostitution has existed in nearly all historic times, and among nearly all races of men. It has existed as an institution so long as monogamic marriage has existed, —it may be itself the outcome of that marriage ; I do not know whether any trace of a like promiscuity has been found in the animals nearest allied to man—I believe not. The periodic instinct has probably preserved them from it. How mankind came to lose the periodic instinct, and how that loss may possibly be related to the solely human institution of marriage, are problems not without interest. On the one hand, it has been asserted that prostitution is a logical outcome of our *present* social relations, while, on the other hand, it is held to be historically a survival of matriarchal licence, and not a *sine quâ non* of all forms of human society. There is very considerable evidence to show that a large percentage of women are driven to prostitution by absolute want, or by the extremities to which a seduced woman is forced by the society which casts her out. This point is important. It may, perhaps, be that our social system, quite as much as man's supposed needs, keeps prostitution alive. The frequency with which prostitutes for the sake of their own living seduce comparative boys, may be as much a cause of the evil as male passion itself. The socialists hold the sale of woman's person to be directly associated with the monopoly of surplus-labour. Is the emancipated woman likely to adopt this view ? and if so, shall we not have a wide-reaching social reconstruction forced upon us? That emancipated woman would strive for a vast economic reorganization as the only means of preserving the self-respect and independence of her sex is a possibility with the gravest and most wide-reaching consequences. We cannot emancipate woman without placing her in a position of political and social influence equal to man's. It may well be that she will regard economic and sexual problems from a very different standpoint, and the result will infallibly lead to the formation of a woman's party and to a more or less conscious struggle between the sexes. Would this end in an increased social stability or another subjection of sex ?

Woman may, however, conclude that the alternative is true—that prostitution is not the outcome of our present economic organization, but a feature of all forms of human society. She must, then, treat it as a necessary evil, or as a necessary good. In the former case she will at least insist on an equal social stigma attaching to both sexes, if she does not demand, as in the instance of any other form of anti-social conduct, so far as practicable its legal repression. In the latter case, that is, if its existence really tends in some way to the welfare or stability of society, women will have to admit that prostitution is an honourable profession; they cannot shirk that conclusion, bitter as it might appear to some. The 'social outcast' would then have to be recognized as fulfilling a social function, and the problem would reduce to the amelioration of her life, and to her elevation in the social scale. Either there is a means of abolishing prostitution, or all participators must be treated alike as anti-social, or the prostitute is an honourable woman—no other possibility suggests itself. Society has hitherto failed to find a remedy, perhaps because only man has sought for one; woman, when she for the first time fully grasps the problem, must be prepared with one, or must recognize the alternatives. There cannot be a doubt, however, that in a matter so closely concerning her personal dignity, she will take action, and that, if only in this one matter, her freedom will raise questions, which many would prefer to ignore, and which, when raised, will undoubtedly touch principles apparently fundamental to our existing social organization.

Hitherto I have roughly endeavoured to suggest problems which arise only from a consideration of the position of the non-child-bearing woman—I have, of course, only touched the veriest fringe of a vast subject, but it is needful that I should pass on to others more directly related to the second or child-bearing class of women.

The recognized state of the child-bearing woman is, under our present social conditions, marriage. Even if we admit generally the advantages of this institution, we may ask whether emancipated and economically independent woman-hood will permit social stigma to be put upon those of their number bearing children and upon the children born out of marriage. They may demand that society and the legislature shall reconsider the position of such women and children. The demand, if granted, might involve very revolutionary changes in our present views on the devolution of property, and in the general laws of inheritance. It might ultimately result in something like a return to the ancient matriarchal principle of tracing descent through the female.

Turning to marriage itself, we may remark that the permanency of the existing type has been questioned by more than one recent writer. It has been argued that this institution is plastic, and that its present form is not necessarily the fittest, but possibly only a phase in its evolution. Indeed a well-known modern advocate of polygamy has asserted the unfitness by postulating prostitution as the necessary reciprocal of monogamic marriage. Without in any way being able to assent to the characteristically illogical arguments of this advocate, I must yet confess that there seems to me no prospect that the educated woman of the future will regard marriage and its duties from the same standpoint that man has done; it is difficult to conceive that she will sanction the Church-Service view of the institution, that she will be prepared to limit her sphere of activity to marriage, or her function in life to child-bearing. The disgust generated by the ecclesiastical conception of marriage will go far towards destroying all faith in the religious character of the institution. Questions of its duration and of its form will not seem beyond discussion, and a characteristic prop of existing society may rightly or wrongly be shaken by the complete emancipation of women. The religious sanction having collapsed, and social welfare, rationally investigated, being the only possible sanction left, a number of problems lying at the very root of the institution will demand investigation. Arguments of the following kind will have to be faced, confirmed, or refuted. It will be asked whether the binding of man and woman together for life be either expedient or necessary—whether it may not be a real hindrance to progress, and this in more respects than one? Whether marriage, after all, be not the last, and therefore the greatest, the least recognized superstition which past barbarism has handed down to the present? We shall have to search for the real social grounds upon which the institution may be defended. Can we argue that because monogamic lifelong union exists among certain Christian peoples, whom we are accustomed to look upon as in the van of civilization, therefore it must be a needful condition of progress? Might not the same argument have been used at one time for slavery, at another for the Holy Catholic Church, and even now be used for prostitution? Is not this last as much a social institution of our Christian civilization as marriage? It will not do to translate the law of "survival of the fittest" into "whatever is surviving *is* fittest." Fittest for the age in which it exists, but may not that age be passing away? Will or will not the independence of woman shake this institution? I merely suggest the problem; this is not the time to attempt, were it possible, any solution. I would only add that, personally, I see no reason why two persons, who may be in no way responsible to a third, should be bound together for life, whether they will or no. The birth of a child undoubtedly makes them responsible to a third being, and may be a strong social reason for making marriage permanent, at least till the child has reached its majority. If we except this case, where young children might suffer, may not the question be raised whether marriage should not be a socially recognized but far more easily dissoluble union? Can marriage, lasting when the sympathy which led to it has died out, do ought but make two lives miserable? The life-long tie may be needful so long as society casts a slur on a woman who is separated from her husband, so long as a woman is not in as good an economic position as a man— that is, so long as separation would cast her helpless on the world, or so long as she is a mere plaything with no individual activity. But let us put the case of equal education, of equal power to earn a livelihood, of equal social weight, what woman, under these circumstances, would desire to continue a union which had become distasteful to either party? The union enforced in such cases by our present system is surely a nightmare which even Goethe's *Wahlver-wandtschaften* fails to paint. On the other hand, so long as marriage is entered upon without any study of character, upon the bidding of some slight sexual inclination or fancied sympathy—as so frequently happens at the present day— any relaxation of the marriage tie would certainly lead to an anti-social spread of sexual irregularity. How will the self-dependent woman of the future regard this problem ? What line have such women taken in the past ? With the past to guide us it seems not improbable that, when woman is truly educated and equally developed with man, she will hold that the highest relation of man and woman is akin to that of Lewis and George Eliot, of Mary Wollstonecraft and Godwin ; that the highest ideal of marriage is perfectly free, and yet, generally lifelong, union. May it not be that such a union is the only one in which a woman can preserve her independence, can be a wife and yet retain her individual liberty ? I suggest no solution to these problems, but I believe that without facing them we cannot fully grasp whither the emancipation of woman is likely to lead us.

Taking marriage as it is, we may ask how far it necessarily cramps a woman's growth? This is not a question we can lightly answer. There are many women who affirm it distinctly does. Admitted this is true in the present state of subjection, will it be possible to remedy the evil in any state so long as the wife is a child-bearer ? Can such a woman ever hope to equal intellectually the single woman ? If not, how will it be possible for her to meet the average man with a like mental force, and so preserve her individuality ? The possibility of woman's individual development after marriage is important ; all the more so, as certain ardent advocates of woman's higher education have put forward as a plea for it, the happiness which would arise if woman were only educated so as to understand her husband's ideas and enter into his pursuits. A baser argument for woman's education it is hard to conceive. It denies her an individuality, even as the Mohammedan denies her a soul.

But there is another problem of marriage, which is all-important, and which the advocates for emancipation are called upon to face. How will it ever be possible for the child-bearing woman to retain individual freedom? She cannot during child-bearing and rearing preserve, except in special cases, her economic independence, she must become dependent on the man for support, and this must connote a limitation of her freedom, a subjection to his will. How is this to be met, or does the very fact of child-bearing inevitably produce the subjection of women? The happiness of any human being is commensurate with the sphere of its individual activity, its freedom to will; how infinitely narrowed this is for woman in the average marriage is obvious enough. How far this can be changed by a truer education of both sexes is a very complex problem. By such means a more social tone might be introduced into men and women's conceptions of their mutual relations and duties, into their respect for the individual's sphere of freedom. Perfect legal and political equality might strengthen this respect in the family, but I fail to see how, without perfect *economic* equality, the freedom of woman can ever be absolutely maintained. Yet without a complete reorganization of society how can there be economic independence for the child-bearer? Here again the emancipation of woman seems to call into question the economic basis of existing society.

It is not only the *form* of marriage, but the feelings and objects with which it is entered upon, that are likely to be questioned and remoulded by the woman's movement. Protestantism cannot be said to have formed an elevated conception of the conjugal relation,[1] and there can be little doubt that the cultivated woman of the future will find herself compelled to reject its doctrines on this point. It has repeatedly taught that early marriage is a remedy for vice, and disregarded the social misery which arises not only from improvidence, but also from that ill-considered choice of life-partners, which is customary to passionate youth. Only render early marriage possible, and prostitution will disappear, is a current opinion, especially among evangelical parsons. Let boys and girls marry the moment they feel the sexual impulse, insisted Luther, and we shall have no vice. The problem of early marriage and the difficulties which stand in the way of it, at least for many in our present social state, is undoubtedly important; but the above reason for early marriage seems to me the most degrading ever discovered by the Christian Church, which

[1] See the *Sketch of the Sex Relations in Primitive and Mediæval Germany* for some account of the nature of Luther's teaching.

has never taken a very ideal view of wedlock. The passion, which cannot be bridled out of marriage, will hardly be bridled in marriage. On this account early marriage, for the reason advocated by Luther, seems unlikely to be the basis of a happy lifelong union, which requires some sympathy of aim and much similarity of habit. It will hardly aid the stability of society or the permanence of the institution; from Protestantism, indeed, has arisen divorce.

So long as monogamy subsists, restraint for the man is as much a duty in as out of marriage, and Luther's cure for prostitution is by no means a social one. To what extent this restraint is not exercised, or again to what extent prostitution is a supplement to monogamic marriage, are points on which it is difficult to obtain information, but which are not without direct issue on the future equality of woman. Evidence of the resort of married men to prostitutes, as an almost recognized custom among the rural population, was brought to my notice some years ago; further evidence of its frequency among the working classes in London has been supplied to me by hospital friends; while its prevalence, to some extent in a different form, among the upper classes can hardly be denied. The early-marriage theory as a remedy for sexual irregularity has been pushed so far that various methods have been suggested for rendering it economically possible under the present pressure of population. The whole question of Neo-Malthusianism is fraught with immense social and sexualogical difficulties. As a mode, indeed, of preserving the wife from the cares of a large family, and of enabling her to retain her economic independence, it may possibly commend itself to the woman of the future. It raises, however, a very grave problem of race-permanence : Will the material prosperity and the individually greater efficiency of a limited population, counterbalance the advantages of unlimited production ? It may require another Franco-German war to answer this problem to the satisfaction of the evolutionist.

If we now turn to the intellectual sympathy and similarity of habit which alone appear likely to contribute to the stability of marriage, we shall find that historically they have been much overshadowed by the more sensual side of which we have been treating. Sexual impulse (taken, however, in the broadest sense) has almost always been the cause of marriage. The man or woman, who quietly sat down to argue with themselves whether such a one would or would not suit them as a partner for life, would be the scorn of poet and of "moralist." If we take our modern poets, from Goethe downwards, not one has represented a woman with whom an intellectual man, in his saner moments, would think of passing his life. Gretchen is a type of the whole round of their ideals, and she, the perfection of womanhood, is the perfection of dolldom. It may be questioned whether this following of mere instinct, this want of intellectual influence, has not reduced marriage to a mere lottery, and so brought it into deserved contempt with many thinking men and women. It is indeed hard to conceive how marriage can be otherwise, unless greater freedom in friendship between single men and women becomes habitual.

If the ideas I have described are at all likely to replace the old Protestant conception of marriage, then it is obvious that the education and emancipation of woman will go far to revolutionize both men and women's sexual ideals. Yet we may rightly demand that the new ideals shall be shown to be consistent with race - permanence, before we possibly sacrifice future efficiency to increasing the present freedom and happiness of women.

Hitherto I have been suggesting problems which bear essentially on the position of women, or which raise questions of the relation of man to woman in a somewhat ideal future. They are questions which only those will discuss who have to some extent raised the veil of life; who allow that no human institution is so holy that it can out-top the sacred right of human reason to probe its foundations; that the whole truth is only to be reached by the rational process which starts with universal questioning; that the conviction of knowledge—the one true creed—can only be attained by those who have completely grasped the catholicity of doubt. There are, besides, certain general problems of philosophical.

and scientific interest to which I may briefly refer. Thus there are some writers who assert that man's sexual instincts have been so abnormally developed that they have become a disease. I do not say that this opinion is true ; I think possibly anthropological investigation would show it to be false. Perhaps the very fact that the opinion is held proves that these instincts are more restrained than of old ; that we now term disease what formerly was held natural may possibly be a sign of their decreased vigour. We may question whether the public tone has not changed since the days when the highest honour a German town could show its princely guests was to throw the public brothels open to them free of charge. It may be that our princes are still as sensual as in those days of old, but our towns offer up turtle rather than women in honour of royalty. On the other hand, there is something to be said from the evolutionary standpoint for the increase in sexual instinct. Those nations which have been most reproductive have, on the whole, been the ruling nations in the world's history ; it is they who have survived in the battle for life. The expansion of England has depended not so much on the dull brain of the average English man or woman as upon their capacity for reproducing themselves. If race-predominance depends, then, to any extent upon race-instinct for reproduction, that race which survives will have this instinct strongly developed. Strongly developed sexual instinct may accordingly be a condition for race-permanence, and may thus tend to increase among the surviving races. This is only a suggestion, which we may do well to bear in mind ; there are, of course, many other factors which help to turn the balance—race-physique, energy, and foresight. It must also be sexual instinct not abused, but manifesting itself in increased birth-rate. There remains, however, a possibility, and it is one which I think is worthy of our attention, that sexual instinct may never tend to decrease, but even to increase in the predominant races of mankind. If child-bearing women must be intellectually handicapped, then the penalty to be paid for race-predominance is the subjection of women. In this respect we may remark

how in Greece the wives, or child-bearing women, were in
complete subjection, they were held in social honour merely
as legitimate child-bearers ; on the other hand, the prostitutes and mistresses, as a rule non-child-bearing, were often
the intellectual equals, the genuine comrades of the men.
The fact is noteworthy not only for the complete change
which has taken place in this latter relation in modern times,
but also for the light it throws on possible limitations to the
emancipation and education as well of child-bearing as of
non-child-bearing women.   It almost suggests that child-
bearing will ultimately differentiate the female sex.

Another general problem is that of the law of inherited
characteristics.   If it be true, that the more highly educated
members of a community have less or more restrained
sexual instinct, and so fewer children than their more animal
fellows, then there will always be a restriction on inherited
intellectual development.   The race will not tend to develop
greater brain power nor a more refined nature.   May not this
possibly be the reason why the progress of the great mass of
the people is so dishearteningly slow? Our middle classes are
now filled with men whose intellectual powers would have
astounded a mediæval philosopher ; but place a modern
working man beside a mediæval craftsman, and morally or
intellectually should we be able to mark an absolute progress? I doubt it. Both Darwin and Galton have emphasized the loss to the Middle Ages produced by the ascetic
life of its best men and women—thousands of the noblest-
minded of those days left only a personal, not a transmitted
influence to posterity.   Much the same tendency is visible
to-day ; educated men and women often marry late or not at
all. The writer in the *Westminster Review* already referred to
holds that in the future the best women will be too highly
developed to submit to child-bearing; in other words, the
continuation of the species will be left to the coarser and
less intellectual of its members.   This seems to me a very
serious difficulty, demanding the most thorough investigation.
Educated men and women may even in this respect owe a
duty to society, which society, as it is at present constituted,

hinders them from fulfilling. The right to bear children is a sacred right, and in a better organized society than the present, would it not be fitting that either the state should have a voice in the matter, or else a strong public opinion should often intervene? Shall those who are diseased, shall those who are nighest to the brute, have the right to reproduce their like? Shall the reckless, the idle, be they poor or wealthy, those who follow mere instinct without reason, be the parents of future generations? Shall the consumptive father not be socially branded when he hands down misery to his offspring, and inefficient citizens to the state? It is difficult to conceive any greater race crime. Out of the law of inherited characteristics spring problems which strike deeply into the very roots of our present social habits. It is not one, but a whole crop of questions which will be raised when the old ideal of sex-relationship is once shaken. It involves a change in the whole nature of woman's occupations and enjoyments, and a corresponding outcry on the part of those who have ministered to them or profited by them. Picture the change which even the growth of a public opinion among women will involve; the old literature and special press will become extinct, because social and political questions will be of equal importance to man and woman. *Damen-Lectüre*, that peculiar curse of the German woman, would vanish into nothingness. That any general literature should be written especially for woman's reading would be too absurd to require criticism. Women and their views would be influential factors in the public press, because publishers and editors would soon recognize that for commercial success they must respect the opinions of a moiety of their possible customers. Not only journalistic literature, but even the very appearance of the streets would mark the change which must follow on woman's emancipation. Her assumption of definite social and political responsibilities would revolutionize the sight which meets our eyes between three and four in the afternoon in any fashionable London thoroughfare. Hundreds of women—mere dolls—gazing intently into shop windows at various bits of coloured ribbon.

The higher education of women, so far as it has gone at present, has hardly touched the fringe of this great mass. Perhaps nothing is more disheartening than this sight, except the mob of women in these very same streets between twelve and one at night. Both phenomena are calculated to make one despair utterly of modern civilization. Scorn and sympathy are inexplicably mingled ; on the whole our scorn is greater for the woman of the day, and our sympathy for the woman of the night. The latter suggests a great race-problem, and is an unconscious protest against the subjection of woman and a decadent social organization. Can as much be said of the former, the shopping doll, the anti-social puppet, whose wires (well hidden under the garb of custom and fashion) are really pulled by self-indulgence ?

How often do men take to heart the too obvious fact that they are to a great extent responsible for the way in which the life of the subject-sex has been moulded ? How to reach, to influence the average man and woman is one of the most difficult problems with which those who are working for woman's emancipation can possibly concern themselves. Those only who have endeavoured, without appeal to prejudice, to move a commonplace man or woman can fully grasp what I mean. Put aside all dogmatic faith, all dogmatic morality, regard the sexual relation as in itself neither good nor evil, only so in the misery it brings to the individual or the race, and then try to influence the average human ! If you have sufficient Hellenism in you to regard all exercise of passion as good in moderation, provided it be productive of no mediate or immediate misery ; if you see no virtue in asceticism, but only something as unworthy of humanity as excess, then how infinitely difficult you will find it to influence the average mind !

I am very conscious that in mentioning the above problems I have only skirted the great field of social difficulties. To many with a wider experience, a more scientific training, and a truer power of insight into human nature, there will appear no problem where all is to me obscure. Especially to the woman many of these difficulties will appear in a totally different light, while to her, others, which have remained unmentioned, may seem of far greater importance. I quite recognize that man alone cannot understand or formulate the difficulties which form the woman's question ; that " there will be very little hope of real reforms unless men and women know one another's aims and views in detail, and then accept to some degree the same standard, the same ideal for the community." Nevertheless, we must not forget that the woman's question is essentially also a man's question. It opens up great racial problems, and 'goes to the very basis of our existing social structure. I have endeavoured to show that the complete emancipation of woman connotes a revolutionary change in social habits and sexual ideals certainly not paralleled since that subversion of mediæval modes of thought and action which took place between the years 1460 and 1530. Let us take warning from the results of that revolution, and endeavour to see what we are doing and whither we are going.

In concluding this necessarily insufficient outline of a difficult and complex subject, I would ask the reader to note that every historical change in the relative position of man and woman has been accompanied by great economic and social changes. The sex-relationship has itself been the basis of most of the rights of property. Social economy and sex-relationship have changed together, ever in intimate association. Hence it seems to me to follow that the present movement for the emancipation of women cannot leave our social organization unaffected. Every change in sex-relation has brought momentous changes to the family, and to the public weal as well. The mother-age and the father-age connote totally diverse family and tribal organizations. It is difficult to imagine that the perfect social and legal equality of men and women,—the goal to which we seem tending,—will not be accompanied by the entire reconstruction of the family, if not of the state. It may become still more important than at present for the state to hold the balance between man and woman, to interfere between parent and child, to restrain mere physique from dominion in the field of labour. There have been periods in the world's

history when there was an approach to equality between
the sexes, but those periods have been marked by an equality
in freedom, rather than by an equality in restraint.   By
restraint I do not mean asceticism, but such regulation
of the sex-relations as permits a folk to reproduce itself in
sufficient numbers for permanence, and the older generation
to transmit its tribal knowledge and traditions to the younger.
These matters are necessary for the stability of the state,
they are incompatible with complete sexual freedom.   The
right and wrong of the sex-relations (morality in its narrow
sense) is synonymous with the stability and instability of
society.   If the growing sex-equality connote sex-freedom—
a return to general promiscuity—then it connotes a decay of
the state, and it will require a second Pauline Christianity
and a second subjection of one sex to restore stability.   But
sex-equality must either be marked by the cessation of
prostitution among men, or, if it remains, the like freedom
to women.   I see no other alternative.   We shall have the
choice between equal promiscuity and equal restraint.   The
misfortune for society is that the former is a much easier
course to take than the latter, and one which history shows
us has generally been adopted.

Yet there is one ray of hope, which may after all foretell
the dawn of a new social era.   If it be so, the equality of the
sexes will not again connote the return of a swamp-age
such as befell the tottering Roman Empire.   That the past
subjection of woman has tended largely to expand man's
selfish instincts I cannot deny ; but may it not be that this
very subjection has in itself so chastened woman, so trained
her to think rather of others than of herself, that after all
it may have acted more as a blessing than a curse to the
world ?   May it not bring her to the problems of the future
with a purer aim and a keener insight than is possible for
man ?   She may see more clearly than he the real points at
issue, and as she has learnt self-control in the past by sub-
jecting her will to his, so in the future she may be able to
submit her liberty to the restraints demanded by social welfare, and to the conditions imposed by race-permanence.

XIV

A SKETCH OF THE SEX-RELATIONS IN PRIMITIVE AND MEDIÆVAL GERMANY.[1]

Die Mütter! Mütter!—'s klingt so wunderlich !

IN tracing the historical growth of a folk, there are two questions which it is needful to keep prominently before us,

[1] I have had considerable hesitation in printing this paper unaccompanied by the analysis of German folklore, mythology, and hero-legend, upon which the statements of the earlier pages are really based ; they appear merely deductive, but are nevertheless the outcome of a lengthy, if ill-directed, historical inquiry. The paper was written some time ago, and although, as the mass of material increases, I see reason to modify in one or two points the statements I then made, still, the *general* drift of social growth as it is here described has in my opinion been amply confirmed. The chief point which requires modification is the want of sufficient stress laid upon *group-marriage* (see p. 406). This phase of social growth I now recognize has played an enormous part in the development of pre-historic Germany, and the proofs I can adduce of its existence and influence would, I think, have satisfied the sceptical McLennan. I have determined to publish the paper in its present form because it throws light on the preceding essay, and may help to explain the origin of the ideas which are formulated in the succeeding one. It represents, to some extent, the passage of the writer's mind from agnostic questioning through historical inquiry to a definite social theory. My collection of facts bearing on the social condition of early Germany I hope ultimately to classify and publish. But this will hardly be for some years. Meanwhile I would ask the reader to take nothing on faith, to treat this paper as one of fanciful suggestions, till the sparse leisure moments of an otherwise occupied life may have sufficiently accumulated for me to convince him by reasoned treatment of facts, that the suggestions have a real historical basis.

namely, (1) What were the successive stages in that growth; (2) What were the physical causes which produced their succession?

The answer to the first question is embodied in what I may term *formal* history. The formal historian has to construct from language, from tradition (folklore and saga), from 'archæological finds,' and ultimately from monument and document, the *form* of growth peculiar to a given folk. Only when this very necessary formal history is in its broad outlines established, can the *rational* historian enter the field and point out the physical causes which have produced each particular phase of development. This distinction between formal and rational runs through all branches of human knowledge. Formal history has made, of recent years, great advances; it may be said to have had its Kepler and Koperni-cus, but the Newton or Darwin, who shall rationalize it,—who shall formulate axioms of historic growth in complete harmony with the known laws of physical and biological science,—has yet to arise. He awaits the completion of formal history.[1]

Of one point we may be quite sure. Since the entire development of our species is dependent on the sex-relations, the rational historian of the future will appeal, to an extent scarcely imagined in the present, to the science of sexualogy and to the formal history of sex. The formal history of sex is becoming a recognized branch of research; it is a neces-sary preliminary to a science of sexualogy, and to the ultimate acceptance of the laws of that science as factors in the *rationale* of historic growth. What is this but to assert that the higher statescraft of the future—historically and scienti-fically trained—will recognize the sex-relations as funda-mental in the organization of the state?

In the present paper I shall place before you a slight sketch of what I hold to be the formal history of sex among the Germans. In the course of this sketch I shall suggest various causes which have probably produced the

[1] Herder attempted it,—and failed,—because pre-Darwinian, he was really pre-scientific.

development described. I shall, in fact, make various excursions—possibly of a rather idle character—into the field of rational history. I cannot ask you at present to examine with me at any length the material upon which I have based my formal history.

If many of the statements of my paper appear to you to sound wonderful, exaggerated, or even impossible, I would ask you to suspend judgment till you have analyzed the evidence I hope one day to place before you.

The Germans belong to a folk-group which, at some distant date, common features of language, custom and folk-lore, show to have sprung from a common stock. This folk-group is usually termed Aryan, and the first home of the Aryans was formerly placed in Asia. This view has, of recent years, been contested, and Northern Europe has replaced Asia in the opinion of some first-class historians. Be this true or not, the fact that we have to bear clearly in mind is, that the Germans did not pass through the preliminary stages of their civilization within their present geographical limits.

In the stone age, in the ages of cave and pile dwellings, a race of men occupied geographical Germany which was not Aryan—so much we know, if but little else, concerning them. The Germans developed from brutedom towards manhood, passed through the long centuries of primitive culture outside geographical Germany. When we learn to know the Germans historically they have reached a fair stage of civilization—a stage, however, which is not greatly in advance of what they had received from the common Aryan stock. Let me recall to your minds briefly what that Aryan civilization amounted to. It bred cattle, milked the cow and the goat, kept flocks of sheep, swine, geese, and poultry, had tamed the dog, and discovered butter and cheese. It sowed corn, prepared mead out of honey, roughly spun, wove and sewed clothes out of wool and flax ; it used roads and discovered fords ; it made ships, wagons, and houses of wood, and also had learnt the potter's art. It had weapons, spear and shield, bow and arrow, possibly only of stone and wood. It had villages, folk-meetings, folk-customs, petty chiefs,

and tribal organization. Further, it could count to near a thousand, reckoned time by months and years, had the elements
of medicine, a complex mythology, and believed in the immortality of the soul. Above all, the family life was fairly developed, our usual grades of relationship being recognized.[1]

The Aryan migration must be looked upon, then, as that of
a semi-agricultural folk. An agricultural folk does not, like a
purely hunting folk, lightly leave its dwellings and pastures.
Possibly some social oppression, some subjection of the
'plebs,' drove the Aryans from their first homes. Be this
as it may, we have to note that the Germans remained
much behind the Aryans who migrated further southwards.
This may, very probably, be accounted for by the nature of
the country into which stress of circumstances drove them ;
the huge forests of Northern Europe checked their development, the hunting instincts of the people were encouraged
or resuscitated ; the growth of the patriarchate was thus
delayed, the complete annihilation of the matriarchate post-
poned. Our first historic notices of the Germans bring
before us clear evidences of the existence of the mother-age ;
the power of woman, although no longer at its zenith, is far
from the nadir ; the contest between man and woman for
supremacy is not concluded. The existence of that contest
is one of the causes of the rapid reception of Christianity by
the Germans; it was the religious weapon needed by the man ;
the old faith, if remodelled by the man, had yet been invented
by the woman and did not admit of being readily used as a
weapon against her. It is this retardation of the subjection
of women which renders German primitive history of such
value in the general history of culture. The Aryan civilization, if we except tribal organization and possibly herding of
cattle and use of weapons, is the civilization of the woman—
of the mother-age ; and, as I have remarked, the German of
Tacitus has not got immeasurably beyond it. The development of sex-relations in mediæval Germany is only intelligible
when we bear in mind that the conflict between man and

[1] Much of this paragraph requires modification in the light of recent
work.

woman only terminated with the complete subjection of the latter in the sixteenth century. What the Greeks had accomplished in the age of Pericles—the 'domestication' of the woman—the Germans achieved in the age of Luther.

Let us endeavour to form some rough scheme of the phases of sex-relationship in early Germanic culture. Anthropology shows us that while many savage races have passed through, or are passing through, similar phases, they do not give us a universal law of evolution. Possibly they do not hold for every member of the Aryan stock; that they hold for the Greeks, has, to my mind, been sufficiently proved by Bachofen,[1] for the Slavs by Zmigrodrki,[2] while all that I have been able to glean with regard to Indian sex-relations is, I venture to think, confirmatory.

The following are the stages to which I wish to draw attention :—

(1) *The Period of Promiscuity.*

In this period mankind is not far from the brute stage. There is no conception of relationship, and sexual intercourse is absolutely promiscuous. The food of man is raw, whether vegetable or animal, and he is a creature of the woods. Sex-relations have the chance character of perfectly wild nature. The plant drops its seed, and it fructifies or not as surrounding circumstances admit. The man pursues animals for his food, or woman when he would gratify his passions. Traces of this stage abound in Aryan myth. The promiscuous period, or raw-food age, has for essential characteristics the wood and the swamp. God-conceptions, if such they can be called, are of the darkest, most inhuman type. They are the natural forces of the wood, particularly at night; the creatures of the swamp, which is the symbol of unregulated fertility. These natural forces are the foes of mankind, particularly of comparatively helpless children and women; they take the form of beast, or half-beast, half-man. As they prey upon the helpless, so arises later the conception of propitiating them by the sacrifice

[1] Bachofen: *Das Mutterrecht,* 1861.
[2] Zmigrodrki: *Die Mutter bei den Volkern des arischen Stammes,* 1886.

of children and captives. These human sacrifices, occasionally followed by cannibalism, are typical of a whole group of myths, German, Greek, and Slavonic, which are only reminiscences of the late promiscuous period. We find also survivals from this age in the folklore of childbirth and marriage from every part of Germany.

Let us turn to the position of the woman who has been rendered pregnant by the man, and then left by him to her own devices for self-preservation. Granted that, at any rate in an advanced state of pregnancy, she is no longer an object of pursuit on the part of the male, still she has a difficult task before her in self-preservation during the period of childbirth. I put self-preservation in the first place, although undoubtedly the mother-instinct to preserve the young would be evolved by natural selection early in the course of human development ; the impulse, however, of self-preservation would probably be foremost in an age when the mother was not unaccustomed to the destruction of children. Further, we must note that among primitive races the period of suckling is extremely prolonged, amounting often to two or three years—even more. During the whole of this time the woman must, by a well-known physiological law, abstain from intercourse with the man. As she is of less value to him, so she is largely left to provide for herself. We have, then, in these facts, the prime motor towards human culture. The birth of civilization must be sought in the *attempts of the woman at self-preservation during the times of pregnancy and child-rearing.* What the man achieved in the promiscuous age was due to the contest for food with his fellows and with the beasts. He invented and improved weapons; but the woman, handicapped as she might appear to be by child-bearing, became on this very account the main factor in human civilization. The man's contributions in this early period are a mere nothing as compared to the woman's. Take the earliest German or Scandinavian mythology, remove all the goddesses ; what is left ? An utterly impossible state. No agriculture, no wisdom, no medicine, no tradition, no family, no conception of immortality. Now take away all the gods ;

we have left quite a possible phase of civilization, without, however, war or sea-traffic ; hunting remains, although much less emphasized ; some, indeed, might even suggest war—or at least occasional contest between man and woman.[1]   This social organization is that of the *mother-age*, and is the work of women.   Women evolved it in their struggles for self-preservation during pregnancy and child-nurture.   The part woman has played, and, I venture to think, will play, in civilization differs from man's part exactly in this element of child-rearing.   Take away this element, and the like character of the struggle for existence will lead the non-child-bearing woman along the same lines of development as man.   What woman has individually achieved for civilization is, I think, due to her child-bearing function.   It raised her to intellectual and inventive supremacy, it made her the teacher and ruler of man in the mother-age.

Let us attempt to sketch the rational side of this formal change from promiscuity to the mother-age.

The pregnant woman owing to the instinct of self-preservation seeks the cave, the den, or some retreat in the darkest part of the forest; there she collects leaves, sticks, or whatever will protect her.   She must shelter herself from man and the beasts.   She must also hoard food for the days or weeks when she can neither hunt nor seek roots and berries.   This is the more important if the birth takes place towards winter.   Here are wants enough urging her towards invention, developing her cunning and her positive knowledge.   The den or cave becomes the basis of the home, for the child depends for a long period on the mother ; she communicates to the child her knowledge of roots, and her methods of preserving food.   She becomes the centre of traditional culture; she hands down to the child her primitive beliefs; she shapes religion and custom.   Round the den arise the first attempts at agriculture ; roots and berries are thrown forth, and collect alongside human excrement and other refuse.   The fertility produced by a chance neighbourhood is ulti-

[1] For a like result based upon Slavonic tradition, see Zmigrodzki, p. 222.

mately made use of as a basis for food supply.   The woman
becomes the first agriculturist ; nor does·the folklore of
childbirth forget to commemorate this fact.   Probably long
before the first child can maintain itself, the mother is again
pregnant, not improbably by a different father; the woman
has now a double burden upon her, a double call for invention and ingenuity.   The child-mortality is probably very
great, exposure of children and their sacrifice frequent ; still
natural selection points to the survival of that type of woman
who provided for several children ; we see the woman
increasing the capacities of the den, increasing her knowledge of roots and of agriculture.   I have already referred
to the long period of suckling among primitive races ; during
this time must have arisen a contest in the woman between
duty towards the child and sexual inclination.   Probably in
many cases it ended in the desertion of the child, or in its
formal sacrifice by man or woman.   But from this contest
arises the most marvellous stage in the mother civilization.
Mankind at some period of its growth has tamed the animals
and used their milk and flesh for its food supply.   To man
or woman do we owe this boon ?   To those who have
examined the folklore of childbirth, there cannot be any
hesitation as to the answer.   In great part, if not entirely,
to woman.   The cow, the swine, butter and milk, the cock
.and hen, are all associated with the German and Slavonic
childbirth traditions in a fashion which admits of one interpretation only.   The needs of the child-bearing woman, her
struggles for the preservation of self and children, her desire
to shorten the period of suckling, led to the domestication of
animals.   The woman surrounded by a group of children
becomes in the long lapse of centuries the centre of civilizing
force.   From this group springs the family based alone on
the mother ; the man learns of the woman the elements of
agriculture, the tending and breeding of at least the smaller
domestic animals, the properties of roots and herbs.   She forms
religion and tradition, and she naturally reverences women,
not men, goddesses, not gods.   The oldest, the wisest, the most
mysteriously powerful of the Teutonic deities are female.

The Altvater Wuodan must sacrifice his eye to learn their mysterious knowledge. I even find traces in 'Fru Gude,' an earth-goddess, of a primitive female form of Wuodan himself. The natural powers deified by the woman are of two kinds. She has fled from the sight of man, she and he are at feud during pregnancy and child-nurture. She is guarded from man at this time by beings of the den and cave, goddesses of the dark and the night, at war with man. To approach the pregnant woman is dangerous to the man, she is surrounded by spirits hostile to him; but there are other beings around her too, hostile to *her*, the old nature forces, half-animal, half-man, of the promiscuous period, ready to take her life and that of her children. These are, as it were, the personified difficulties with which she has to struggle for self-preservation. Round the woman at childbirth collect a group of infernal beings unfriendly to man and woman alike. Later folklore represents them by a crowd of witches and devils eager to destroy child and mother. How shall she escape them? Place against the door an axe, a broom, and a dung-fork; let her eat certain roots; bring in sacred milk and cheese, or slaughter a cock. Then they cannot touch her. These are symbols of the means taken by the woman for self-preservation in the earliest ages—symbols of her work of civilization. They are more akin to the brighter spirits, who are there to protect her, the prototypes of the goddesses we find in later German mythology. Thus it comes about that the woman in childbed is to the German peasantry of to-day something at the same time pure and impure. The witch is there ready to harm both husband and wife, but the angel, the good deity, is there likewise, and the woman who dies in childbirth avoids purgatory and goes straight to heaven.

Jacob Grimm said of the German goddesses, years before modern investigations had brought the *mother-age* to light:

" In the case of the gods the previous investigation could reach its goal by separating individuals; it seems advisable, however, to consider the goddesses collectively as well as individually, because a common idea lies at the basis of them all, and will thus be the more clearly marked. They are conceived of peculiarly as *divine mothers* (*göttermütter*), travelling about and visiting mortals; from them mankind has learnt the business and the arts of *housekeeping as well as agriculture, spinning, weaving, watching the hearth, sowing and reaping.* These labours bring peace and rest to the land, and the memory of them remains firmer in pleasing traditions than war and fighting, which, like women, the majority of the goddesses shun."[1]

A truer, although unconscious, tribute to the civilizing work of women can hardly be imagined. If we add to the arts mentioned by Grimm, the art of healing, the elements of religious faith as a tradition, and, as far as the Germans are concerned, apparently the runic art of writing, we have a slight picture of what women accomplished in the centuries which intervened between the promiscuous period and the complete establishment of the father-age.

(2) *The Mother-Age* (*Matriarchate*).

In this age raw food has been supplemented or replaced by milk and butter; hence the period has been called the milk-and-butter period. The den has developed into the home or house of which the mother is the head. She is the source of all traditional knowledge and of all relationship. Her children are by different, and very probably unknown, fathers; such property as there is, descends through her. In the earlier phases of the mother-age, when the food supply and the shelter of the den were limited, the boy would, as he grew older, go off hunting for himself, and become like other men. As the supply and comfort of the den increased to that of the hut, there would undoubtedly be two types of men, the huntsman who went forth, and the agriculturist who stayed at home, remaining under the influence of his mother. As a rule the daughter would also remain at home, and, when she reached puberty, consort temporarily with some man. The earliest Aryan names of relationship denote merely sex-functions. Daughter and son are not correlated to father and mother; the one is simply the 'milk-giver,' the other the begetter.' The word 'mother' is connected with a root signi-

[1] *Deutsche Mythologie*, i. p. 207.

fying the 'quickening' one. The conception of father could hardly be very prominent during the promiscuous period and the earlier portion of the mother-age. Its signification is double—the ' protector' and the ' ruler '; this points at least to the later mother-age, if not to the patriarchate, or father-age.[1] Till the mother had established the comparative comfort of the den, there was no inducement for the father to stay by her and protect or rule the offspring. The father-instinct has been evolved in some animals, notably birds, in the struggle for existence. I do not know whether it has been found in any carniverous, and therefore hunting mammal ; especially I doubt whether it existed in man before the mother-age.

The above remarks will suggest the prominence of the women in the primitive family. The man remains at first outside it—he is a hunter. His whole knowledge is the ' mother-wit' he has received in the den. The woman stands on a higher level ; she has become *located*, and has an interest in the soil. No longer the swamp, but the field becomes the symbol of sex-union. In both cases it is Mother Earth which is productive, but it is no longer the unregulated fruition of the swamp period :

> Her plenteous womb
> Expresseth its full tilth and husbandry.

The conception of sexual union in folklore becomes tilth, the goddess of childbirth is the goddess of agriculture.

The superior position of woman leads, however, to a division of mankind into two classes : the agriculturist stays in the family, the huntsman leaves it, and remains in a lower grade of culture. Probably the same promiscuous sexual relations between the women, of what we may now venture to call the family, and the men outside continue, but the agriculturists, the men of the family, have now to be provided for. This provision seems to have been made in a variety of ways which we find clearly marked in early mythology and folklore. I note the following :—

(1) They have promiscuous sexual relations, like the hun-

[1] A. Kuhn : Zur ältesten Geschichte der indogermanischen Völker, Bd. I., 1850. Deecke : Die deutsche Verwandtschaftsnamen, 1870.

ter, with women of other families, still retaining their place
in their own. Their offspring are quite independent of them,
and belong to a family in which they have no position.

(2) They have sexual relations with the women of their
own family, their sisters. Brother-sister marriage and group-
marriage are the very usual relations pointed to by German
as well as Greek mythology, folklore and philology.

(3) They unite themselves to women of other families, and
transfer themselves to those families; in this case their
position seems to have been unstable, if not dangerous, even
when they brought, as in later days, dowry with them.

(4) They capture women from other families, and introduces them into their own. This was probably also a dangerous method, if the women were not paid for.

With regard to the modes in which the agriculturists satisfied their sexual instincts, (3) and (4) apparently belong to a
later state of development than (1) or (2). They pass over
into the father-age, and the fourth develops into the ordinary
forms of marriage by capture and by purchase. But there
is an important point to be recognized here : three out of
these four forms tend towards permanency in the sexual
relation, and limitation in its field, or ultimately to a lasting
monogamy. It is quite true that brother-sister and group-
marriages led in many cases to polygamy or polyandry, but
even here there was permanence and limitation. The Teutonic
mythology dates from an age when brother-sister marriage was
becoming monogamic. The agriculturist in the mother-age
developed a regulated sex-relation on the side of the man,
and in our earliest traces of German culture we find monogamy
general, if not absolute.

But although the property in the wife can be shown by
her capture, and the husband-right thus established, it is a
different matter with the child. That the child follows the
womb and that ownership is shown by the labours of childbirth, was a principle which our forefathers held for centuries,
and found extremely difficult to circumvent, as with the decay
of the mother-age the sexual father rose into importance. The
same method of claiming father-rights has been discovered

among the natives of Africa, South America, and the Celts of Strabo's time. It was that the husband also should simulate the labours of childbirth, and take to bed at the same time as his wife, if he wished to be held as the father and proprietor of the child. We find several traces of this naïve device in German folklore. It belongs to a later period of development than that which we are at present considering, but it is intimately connected with the marriages by purchase and capture, which marked the end of the mother-age. Thus Strabo tells us of the primitive people of Spain—that they suffered a most ' foolish governaunce by women '; that the women possessed the property, and it passed from mother to daughter; that the latter gave away their brothers in marriage, and that the men took a dowry with them into the houses of their wives; that the women performed all agricultural work, and became so hardened by it that childbirth was nothing to them. ' Indeed,' Strabo remarks, ' *they on these occasions put their husbands to bed and wait upon them.*' Strabo's account of the Cantabri has been ridiculed by an unbelieving age. Modern research, however, and the discovery of the matriarchate, are doing much to re-establish the good faith, not only of Strabo, but even of that supposed arch-liar Herodotus.

Let us return for a moment to the hunting, as distinguished from the agricultural portion of the population. It presents, as it were, the man's side of primitive civilization. It has improved its arms, become skilled in the artifices of the chase, and, according to Lippert, domesticated herds of cattle, probably beginning, like the Egyptians, with the antelope or some kindred form of easily tamed deer.[1] From the huntsman develops the nomad, and here arises the culture of the man in opposition to the culture of the woman. Where no men, or few, have become agriculturists, we have a distinction of food between men and women ; they live apart and feed apart —a state of affairs which evidently existed in some primitive German tribes, and is still to be found in parts of Central Africa. On the other hand, where the agricultural element

[1] *Die Geschichte der Familie*, p. 41.

is strong, there becomes a division and a conflict between the nomadic and agricultural sections of primitive man. Their interests are opposed, especially in matters of sex. The primitive agriculturist reared among women has not the fighting skill of the nomad. The nomad has not the easy access to women. With him woman must be captured, but owing to the long period of suckling—without assuming any great disparity in the number of men and women—we must suppose sexually fit women to have been comparatively scarce. Hence arises contest with the agriculturist, poly-andry, and often a comparatively inferior position of woman, as a captive or chattel, among nomads.

The permanency of the sex-relation among the agricul-turists, the necessity for organization in matters of defence, which must be entrusted to the men—these are the beginnings of the father-age. But, as Lippert [1] has pointed out, the man appears as tribal organizer, ruler, or tribe-father, before his position as sexual father is recognized. The first conception of father is 'ruler,' 'protector,' not progenitor. The first stage towards the father-age is the need of a physical protector. The mother still rules the house, but the 'Altvater' rules the fight, often indeed guided by the women. For the woman is still essentially the wise, she is the source of traditional reli-gion, and the care of the gods is essentially hers. About the hearth arise the first conceptions of 'altar' and 'sanctuary.' She writes with her staff in the ashes the will of the gods, and her pots and kettles reappear in every witch-trial of the Middle Ages. Her spirit lingers round the hearth even after death, and to-day the solitary student sitting over his fire, or the peasant when his family are out, will tell you they have been *mutterseelen allein*, meaning absolutely alone. Unrecog-nized relic of the mother-age,—they are alone at the hearth with their mother's soul!

If I might venture on a fanciful suggestion, which, how-ever, seems to me to receive much confirmation from German folklore, I should say, that it was a conflict between nomadic and semi-agricultural populations, which drove the Germans,

[1] Ibid. pp. 6, 7, 218, *et seq.*

if not all the Aryan stock, from their earlier dwelling-places. Be this as it may, our first historical traces of the Germans are of a semi-agricultural people, among whom the mother-age has not yet passed away; the women are priestesses and rulers of the house, the deities are in great part goddesses; learning—runic lore—is in the hands of the woman, and folk-custom recognizes in much her superiority to man; the man may be *Altvater*, or tribal ruler, but as sexual father, he is not yet fully recognized. But it is the period of struggle, the man is asserting himself, a regulated sexual relation has appeared, the possibility of a sexual father is there, and the power of woman is on the decline. But the victory of man is not easy; it takes long centuries to fully confirm it, and traces of the mother-age remain throughout mediæval times. The transition from the mother- to the father-age is, indeed, marked by the appearance of women of gigantic stature and nigh infernal nature. There is as yet no sanctity in the relation of wife and husband; the wife is the result of purchase or capture, and she does not lightly submit to the loss of the mother-power. The old legends of contest between men and women are not such idle fancies as some would have us believe, and very dark shadows indeed do such figures as those of Ildico, Fredegunde, and Brunhilde cast across the pages of history. Such women, indeed, are only paralleled by the Clytemnestra and Medea of a like phase in Greek development. Nor does the poet fail even among the Germans to represent the contest between man and woman for the mastery; it is the victory of the new day- or light-gods over the old night- or earth-goddesses. Wuodan replaces Hellja and Mother Earth, Siegfried conquers Brunhilde, Beovulf defeats the offspring of the swamp goddess Grindel, and Thor fights with Gialp and Greip, the daughters of Geirrod.[1]

It is this struggle between the mother- and father-stages which is all-important in considering the phases of development in the sex-relations. As external marriage took the place of group-marriage, the capture of the bride must have met with active opposition on the part of the mother; equally hostile

[1] *Corpus Boreale*, Mythic Fragments, i. p. 127.

must she have been to the necessary changes in the customs
relating to the devolution of property. The mother-in-law,
or the chief-woman of the wife's family, becomes a peculiar
object of hatred to the husband; she is his special foe, and,
in some primitive tribes, they never afterward exchange a
word or meet under the same roof.[1] Evidence of the like
feeling is very apparent in German folklore. To such
bitterness did the marriage by capture lead, to such blood
feuds, that we find in early German tradition great merit
ascribed to those rulers who ordered that the wife should
be obtained by *purchase*, not by *capture*. Driven from the
commanding position of house-mother, and deprived of her
mother-rights in the matter of property, the last fortress of
the Teutonic woman was her sacerdotal privileges. She
remained holy as priestess, she had charge of the tribal
sacrifice and the tribal religion. From this last refuge she
was driven by the introduction of Christianity among the
Germans. In the Roman world that view of the sex-relations symbolized by the swamp had long given place to a
regulated sex-system, which had culminated in the strongest
father-rights possibly ever attained by any folk. The reaction against these father-rights had led, in the course of
centuries, to what appears, at least in Rome itself, as a
revival of the swamp-age. A regulated sex-relationship
had become impossible to the body social, for it had adopted
equal license, not equal restraint, as the keynote to sex-
equality. Upon this field appeared Christianity with the
difficult task of reconstruction and the terrible narrowness
of the Pauline doctrine. It succeeded, with the aid of
Chrysostom and Jerome, in damming out the swamp, but at
the entire cost of woman. Woman is to be, so long as she
is considered a creature of sex, entirely subject to the man.
She is mentally and physically his inferior, and must obey
him. Considered as an asexual being, she can attain to a
position in the ecclesiastical world, but on this condition only.
Thus it is not the character of mother, but the peculiarity of
chastity which marks a woman as holy, grants her religious

---

[1] Lippert, quoting from *Nachtigals Reisen*, pp. 44–45.

importance as a saint. This may have been necessary to stem the Roman swamp, but it was not a version of Christianity likely to be popular with a folk still in the mother-age, and it led to not a few eccentric heresies. Taking, however, the Germans as we find them in the midst of the transition from mother- to father-age, the Christianity of Paul and Jerome was to the men by no means an unpleasant faith. There was much in it which favoured the spread of the father-power, and when Christ was reduced to a warrior-chief, and the disciples to his head-men—much as we find them in that earliest German version of Christianity, the old Saxon Heliand—then, indeed, it might be accepted as a suitable faith for the father- or hero-age. On the other hand, the women, the priestess-mothers of the old faith, were unlikely to receive warmly this version of subjection and chastity. They and their deities became the object of hatred to the Christian missionaries, and later of alternate scorn and fear to pious ascetics and monks. The priestess-mother became something impure, associated with the devil, her lore an infernal incantation, her very cooking a brewing of poison; nay, her very existence a perpetual source of sin to man. Thus woman as mother and priestess became woman as witch. The witch-trials of the Middle Ages, wherein thousands of women were condemned to the stake, were the very real traces of the contest between man and woman. For one man burned there were at least fifty women, and when one reads the confessions under tortures of these poor wretches, a strange light is thrown over the meaning of all this suffering. It is the last struggle of woman against complete subjection. There appears in these confessions all the traditional lore of the mother-age; the old gods and goddesses are there, and the old modes of thought; nay, the very forms of sex-relationship due to the promiscuous age and the mother-age reappear. Nor was it only tradition, there can be little doubt of a sexual cult, and childbirth rites lasting on into the father-age and the Christian Middle Ages. I hope on another occasion to throw some light upon this secret sexual cult as evidenced by German witch-trials.

(3) *The Father-Age (Patriarchate).*

This age cannot be said to have been fully established among all Germanic folks till the reception of Christianity. Its essential features, of course, the rule of the *Altvater*, the capture or purchase of wives, the reckoning of descent by the father's side, and the inheritance of property by sons only, are all manifest in the heroic age—the age of the Germanic folk-wanderings and of the Vikings. The hero-legends of the *Heldenbuch* and of the *Edda* testify to this state of affairs only too clearly. But we find at the same time, even in these very legends, as well as in early custom and law, an anomalous position of the woman. The hero-age is a period of transition. Christianity is necessary to make the father-age universal, and complete the subjection of the woman.

But Christianity left a loophole to the woman, which is of singular importance ; it allowed her to play a really important part in the state on condition of her leading the ascetic life. It threw open its schools to men and women alike ; and, provided the woman retained her virginity, she might rise to any degree of intellectual eminence. As abbess of an important nunnery she had a social and intellectual influence, which is not always sufficiently recognized. The history of culture in Germany shows a series of women like Hroswitha of Gandersheim and Herrad of Landsberg, who were scarcely equalled, certainly not surpassed, by any men of their time. The popular theology of the age expressed the new position of woman in the phrase, ' Eva (a mother and a wife) had deprived man of paradise ; Ave (*Ave=Maria* (sic)—a virgin) had restored salvation to him.'

We have thus again a great division drawn across womankind ; the non-child-bearing woman is holy, and has a career before her ; the child-bearing woman is of an inferior caste, and is a necessity of the weak and sinful nature of man. It must not be supposed that this was merely the view of the Church Fathers, or of scholastics and monks. It passed into folk literature and the proverbial philosophy of the people, and remained there long after it had ceased to be the opinion of the educated. A comparison of monkish and folk writings would, did space permit, bring this clearly before the reader. If every peasant and burgher did not hold the same view of wedlock as an 'endless penaunce,' which is expressed by a mediæval English poet who has been saved from the 'hell' of marriage when he to wed 'saught fyrst occasioun,'[1] still every peasant and burgher looked upon the woman as an inferior being, ever ready to contest his authority and lead him into evil. Nor do I think, considering that the subjection of women, and the establishment of the father-age, were not of remote date, that this feeling was by any means unreasonable. Be this as it may, there is small doubt that the folk accepted the theologian's view and divided women into a higher and lower order of beings, the virgin and the wife. For centuries woman as wife almost disappears from the sphere of political and social influence.

The contrast, however, between the beauty of virginity and the comparative degradation of motherhood could not be maintained in human life, full as it is of sexual tendencies. The way in which the contradiction was solved presents us with one of the most remarkable instances of the close relation which always seems to exist between intense religious enthusiasm and sexual excitement.

The Germans were in far too primitive and natural a state to shake off entirely their old polytheistic faiths, and while, on the one hand, witchcraft maintained its place, on the other the influence of the old reverence towards women, due to the mother-age, made itself felt in the new religion. Owing to the Jews having chosen Jahveh, not Astoreth, as their tribal god Christianity presents the strange spectacle of a religion without a goddess. As such we recognize that it is not the construction of an agricultural people, but of one among whom women held a very secondary place. Jews and *late* Greeks together were not likely to give to the world a religion of the woman. Hence, when this religion of the man came among a people full still of the beliefs and feelings

[1] But of his grace God hath me preserved
Be the wise councell of aungelis three ;
From hell gates they have my silf conserved
In tyme of vere, when lovers lusty be.

of the mother-age, although it came as an instrument towards the subjection of woman—yet the spirit of the folk was too strong for it; they demanded and obtained a goddess.[1] If the ideal woman be no longer the mother, at least a virgin goddess shall be added to the Christian pantheon; the tritheistic faith shall become tetra-theistic, and ultimately polytheistic. Some Protestants are apt to look upon this change in Christianity as the mark of the Devil; to me it seems the great triumph of mediæval Christianity. With it, it threw off Hebraism and later Hellenism, and became Germanic. It became a matter of feeling and imagination; it was possible for a great art, a great literature, and a great theology to grow up under it. It became a means by which the Germanic element could influence civilization as the Greek and the Indian had done. The condition of the reception of Christianity by the Germans was the fuller reception of the mother-element by Christianity—the woman—even in the shape of a virgin.

The new goddess, once incorporated in the Christian mythology rapidly replaced in affection and reverence the older gods. Every virtue, every form of praise, in the most exaggerated language, was heaped upon her. The ascetic monk, deprived of the natural outflow for his sexual feelings, gave expression to it by songs to the Virgin, which, as the years rolled by, gained a stronger and stronger sensual colouring; the most remarkable, not to say dangerous, similes were used; all the ardour of the sexual passion is poured out in these Latin Virgin-songs. Nor did the matter end here: the strolling scholars adopted these Virgin-songs, modified and extended them—so that we find occasionally the same lines in a sacred hymn and in a rollicking, drinking lovesong. The Virgin became merely a peg on which every expression of the wildest passion could be hung. The hymn to the Virgin became the basis of a new phase in the sex-relationship.

[1] Although the Germans did not invent mariolatry, which had its origin not improbably in the direct transformation of the priestesses of Ceres into priestesses of the Christ-Mother, yet mariolatry was from the earliest time an essential and much emphasized feature of German Christianity.

In the cloister-manuscripts, among these extravagant hymns to the Virgin, we find the first love-songs. Little more than translations of the Latin Virgin-hymns, their scope is yet obvious ; whether used by the monks, or, what is very probable, written by them for the knights, they are purely songs of sexual love, songs in adoration of an earthly, and not heavenly, mistress. They are the germs of the *Minne-sang*. We have reached the age of the German *Minnesinger*, the beginning of what we in England term *chivalry*, but what the Germans denote by *Minne*, a word which in the oldest German signifies spiritual love, as for the gods, but in Middle High German has almost a purely sensual meaning. Woman —at least in the upper classes of society—is to regain a place of influence. She has, indeed, revenged herself upon the theology which placed chastity above motherhood. But her power over men is to be based not upon the rights of a mother, but upon the charms of a mistress. Man is her slave so long as she retains her beauty, or his fancy be not sated. It is the Periclean period of German development ; Hetairism triumphant, only with a difference—the woman is paid for her sexual service in a more spiritual form. She remains before the law and the church subject to man, but she rules him through the senses. That is the strange out-come of the father-age in Germany ! We are too apt to look upon the chivalry of the Middle Ages from the standpoint of nineteenth century romance-writers — to consider it as the single-minded service of a generous manhood towards a noble but weaker womanhood. Such a service may be, I venture to think occasionally is, a feature of nineteenth century life, certainly it was not a prominent factor of *Minne-dienst*. It was, indeed, a service on the part of the man, often arduous and prolonged ; but there was always one end in view, and that, the gratification of sensual passion. Those who have studied the great Arthurian epics in their original forms, and have some acquaintance with the vast mass of lyric poetry due to the *Minnesinger*, will undoubtedly agree with this conclusion. It was, indeed, a time of unre-stricted sexual indulgence on the part of both men and women. The maiden, the *âmie,* and the married woman were all alike the object of homage on the part of the knight but the favour which fair ladies gave to the victor in the tournay was of the most material kind. Chastity was prudery, and long-continued reserve on the part of either man or woman ill-breeding; the only disgrace, discovery and mutilation by an enraged husband; the only crime, forcible seduction. The *âmie* was received in all knightly society, and free-love—only restrained in one or two cases by a formal etiquette—the morality of the day. Nay, even to the field, the *âmie* and the recognized prostitute followed the knight. The crusaders were accompanied by a second army of women, and such were the sexual extravagances in the Holy Land, that the failure of the second crusade is attributed by the old writers to the license alone.

This marked characteristic of courtly society was imitated by the burgher, and to a less extent by the peasant, so that the period is distinguished by a scarcely paralleled freedom in matters of sex. The love of boys, probably arising in the cloister, infected Germany, although it never appeared so markedly as in England and France. Women, especially married women, were perpetually found in intrigue with monk and priest, who for their own sake preserved a secrecy, which the knight at the drinking bout might forget. Not a few mediæval songs discuss the comparative merits of the sacerdotal and knightly lovers, generally to the advantage of the former. But I have said enough to indicate the character of the period. At first sight it appears like a return to the swamp-age—a period of social collapse like the last years of the Roman Empire.

But it is really something very different; this age of chivalry has given Germanic civilization one of its grandest factors, one which in our modern world has played a great part in the sex-relationship. Let us recall the fact that we are still in the father-age, that marriage by purchase has only recently taken the place of marriage by capture; that the father has yet power to give or sell his daughter to whom he pleases; that even yet he occasionally offers her

THE SEX-RELATIONS IN GERMANY.

to the victor in a tournay; that every woman is legally in some man's hand, or, as the Germans termed it, in *mund*. Note all this, and then recognize the advance—when the woman is allowed to freely dispose of her person, when it is once admitted that she has a choice in sexual matters. It is a great step indeed towards the modification of the harsh sex-relationship peculiar to the father-age. But this is not all; the century of the Hohenstaufen is the age of great plastic development; things Germanic were then moulded to the form under which they have often lasted to the present day. It was a freethinking age, as well as a freeloving age. It was an age which built cathedrals, and fought the pope. In architecture and decorative sculpture Germany achieved what few nations have ever equalled. We talk much of the Parthenon and its friezes, but how shall we compare them with the western façade of a Gothic minster? In epic and lyric poetry how little have after-ages that can rival *Tristan und Isolt* or the love-songs of Meister Walther! It was the boyhood of German vigour, and not the senility of a dying empire, which produced this age of sense. The relation of man to woman was primarily sensual, but it was a sensuality idealized by the highest phases of art. It was an age of music and of song, of noble buildings, of flowing drapery and graceful forms of dress. It is the peculiarity of this period of German civilization that, while as in Imperial Rome the sex-relationship became a free choice for both sexes, yet also as in the Periclean age of Athens sensuality was idealized by art. It was human sense superseding brute sense. Put these two things together—sexual instinct guided by co-option and idealized by artistic appeal to the emotions—and we have the basis of that which, with a good many centuries of spiritualizing, has developed into what we term *love*. There is an element in the love of Romeo and Juliet—still more in that of Faust and Gretchen, sensual as both alike are—which I have never come across in the classical authors with whom I am acquainted; there is a certain inexplicable tenderness which it is quite impossible for me to analyze, but which I believe is due to mediæval chivalry.

We have, then, towards the close of the thirteenth century a new stage in sex-relations which is tolerably wide-spread. The woman was legally in complete subjection to the man, but socially co-option was established, and there was a tendency to idealize sexual attraction. This result had not been obtained without a considerable weakening of the customary sexual restraints. I now pass to the last period I shall lay before you, and which, from one of its leading features, I shall characterize as :—

(4) *The Age of Prostitution.*

The prostitute, whom Tacitus informs us had no existence among the primitive German tribes, became a recognized personage in the age of chivalry. It is not very easy to trace what the exact causes were which led to the reimposition of sexual restraint on the married woman ; they are partly, of course, due to the re-establishment in the thirteenth century of the influence of the Church, and to the purer character of that influence; partly to the decay of the old knight-culture. The knights owing to their increasing poverty could no longer indulge in the courtly gathering, in music and in song; the archer, and later the arquebusier, made the knight useless in the field, and the man of learning—the theologian or the jurist—was of more value at the council board. With the disappearance of chivalry and the rise of burgher-culture came a new phase of the sex-relation ; the woman had free option in the choice of a husband, but once married she was legally, and to a large extent socially, in complete subjection. On the other hand, the free sexual relations of the age of chivalry continued to exist in the form of prostitution. Prostitution began to play a great part in the social life of the mediæval cities ; it must also be noted that at the same time the line between capitalist and worker became more prominent, and a town proletariat made itself visible. The prostitute in the mediæval city played a singular part ; she was alternately honoured and abused. She was made use of to grace the banquet of the town-council or the reception of emperors ; but she was often compelled to wear a distinctive dress, or was deprived of all legal rights. Nothing is more characteristic of the absolute subjection of woman than the treatment of prostitutes and the police regulations concerning them in such towns as Nürnberg, Frankfurt, and Augsburg. They present us with one of the most instructive examples of the result of allowing men alone to legislate on matters of sex. The prostitute was treated in the first place not as a woman, but as a necessary, although troublesome, part of the town-property, which had to be disposed of as might seem for the time most convenient. Only occasionally had she to thank the Church for a little human consideration. Long before the spread of venereal disease at the end of the fifteenth century, the maintainance by the town-councils of brothels, generally placed in charge of the hangman or the town-beadle, had become universal. A typical instance of the moral feeling of the time is the vote of public money by the town-councils for the decoration and free opening of the public brothels when there was a visit from distinguished strangers. Some phases of this old life undoubtedly throw light on one or two kindred problems of to-day.

It remains for me to note the influence of the Reformation upon this last period, marked as it is by monogamic marriage and organized prostitution. Let me first state the exact results of chivalry following upon the father-age :—

(1) Free option for the woman in marriage, accompanied by what is usually termed love. After marriage complete 'domestication' of the wife; she plays no part in the state or outside the home.

(2) Prostitution organized by men, with only the slightest social or legal rights allowed to the prostitute.

(3) The ascetic life for both men and women, offering the only means by which the middle-class woman could obtain knowledge and power. The convents in the fifteenth century show, in some cases, a remarkable revival of earnestness; in others, they have sunk to the level of brothels.

We are apt to look upon the Reformation as a purely religious movement, neglecting the far more important social revolution which produced and accompanied it. The beginning of the sixteenth century is the birth of Individualism—

a phase of development which, while producing infinitely
rich results for human knowledge, has often been little less
than disastrous for the physical well-being of society. The
discovery of the New World and the concurrent decay of the
old faith led to an entire reconstruction in the relation of
master and handicraftsman. The whole organization of
trade and of labour was destroyed and remodelled. The age
of the capitalist, of the trading company and of the specu-
lator began. Hochstetter and Welser of Augsburg formed
'rings' in the wine and corn markets, Koberger of Nürnberg
ruled the publishing trade of Europe; capital started on its
long years of labour-exploitation, and the handicraftsman
soon felt the pinch of the new methods of production. The
Catholic Church with its strong socialistic doctrine, the
Canon Law with its exaltation of manual labour, and the semi-
religious guilds—the bulwark of the handicraftsman—were
driven out of the best part of Germany as snares of the Antichrist. The evil first made itself felt in the decreased capacity of large classes of the community to marry, and a
resulting increase in prostitution. As I have already pointed
out, the existing convents were of two kinds—the one class,
owing to the spirit of moralists like Geiler, Wimpfeling, and
Thomas à Kempis, was filled with really earnest men and
women; the other contained monks and nuns ready for, or
actually practising, every form of sexual indulgence. The
Reformers made no distinction, they raged against all forms
of ascetic life as 'the service of the woman in scarlet'; they
demanded the closing of all the convents. The effect may
be easily imagined. Monks and nuns of the inferior kind
rushed from their cloisters, and too often did penance for
their past sin of asceticism by the extreme of sexual excess.
It is no exaggeration to say that throughout Germany more
monks were converted to Lutheranism by the strength of
their sexual passions than by their enthusiasm for the Wittenberg 'evangely.' The sexual relations of the mass of early
Protestant divines, and even of some of the chief reformers,
form a remarkable, although little regarded, side of Reforma-
tion-history. At the same time with the licentious the

earnest class of monks and nuns were expelled from their homes. A woman like Charitas Pirkheimer, driven with her nuns out of the St. Clara nunnery at Nürnberg, is the last type of the educated nun. In correspondence with the leading Humanists, enthusiastic for the new knowledge and the old literature, she was driven at the instigation of the brutal and uneducated Ossiander from her convent. Her diary is one of the most suggestive books to which the modern reader can turn for light on the dark problems of that time. It is the last glimpse we get of the great value which the ascetic life even in the sixteenth century had been to an enslaved womanhood. Henceforward domestication or prostitution were the only careers open to the German woman.

As I have remarked, the first result of closing the convents was an increase in licentiousness. The economic changes at the same time in progress tended in the like direction. It was impossible for the Reformers to disregard this increase; they admitted it, attributing it, as they did many other things, to the peculiar activity which their piety aroused in the Devil. Like many good people of to-day, they held up their hands in horror at the extent of what they termed vice, they preached against it, and they got stringent laws passed against it, but they never took the trouble of investigating the social causes which produced it. Once term sexual extravagance sin, and attribute it to the Devil, then it is illogical to seek for any further cause of its existence. The Devil was a convenient whipping-post, and as the obvious manifestation of his presence was the prostitute, the Protestant town-councils were not long before they closed the town-brothels. The prostitutes, like the nuns, were turned out upon the streets and bade to go their way, occasionally driven with exemplary harshness out of the towns; which action, as it did not touch the real economic cause of the difficulty, tended rather to increase than decrease the rate at which licentiousness was spreading. Luther, more clearly than any one, seems to have marked the social problem at the bottom of the sex-difficulty, and he proposed a remedy—one of the most heroic kind. We have seen that the Reformation destroyed the ascetic life,

and more forcibly even than Catholicism branded the prostitute as a social outcast. We have, in the last place, to
consider its teaching as to marriage.

Under the influence of chivalry marriage had become a
matter of co-option, and mere sexual instinct had been
ennobled by art, and to a great extent spiritualized. A good
deal of the love which ends in marriage has doubtless a
sensual basis, but the pure gratification of sexual appetite is
usually kept in the background, or remains quite in abeyance.
It was this factor in marriage which Luther did not hesitate
in the plainest of language to again bring to the fore.
"Marriage," said the early Christian Fathers, "is a lower
state than chastity. *If* man or woman cannot remain
chaste, let them marry for their bodies' sake." While this
degraded marriage, it at least left an *if* to save humanity.
Luther left no *if*. "When God made man and woman He
blessed them and said to them, 'Increase and multiply.'
From this verse we are certain that man and woman shall
and must come together in order to multiply. . . . Since so
little as it stands in my power that I should not have the
form of a man, so little is it in my power to remain without
a woman. Further, so little as it stands in your power that
you should not have the form of a woman, so little is it possible for you to remain without a man. Since this is not a
matter of free-will or advice, but a necessary natural thing;
what is man must have a woman, what is woman a man. This
word of God's: 'Increase and multiply,' is not a command,
but more than a command, namely, a divine work that it is
not possible for us to hinder or to neglect, but is even as
necessary as that I have the form of a man, and more
necessary than eating and drinking, bodily offices, sleeping
and waking." [1]

"If one promises to fly like a bird, and does so, then there is
a miracle from God. Now it is just as much when a man
or woman vows chastity. Since they are not created for
chastity, but as God said: 'Increase and multiply.' Who
must refrain from bodily easement, when he yet cannot;

[1] *Vom Eelichen Leben*, 1520.

what would happen to him? (*Wer seinen Mist oder Harn halten müsste, so er's doch nicht kann; was soll aus dem werden?*)[1] Luther asserts chastity is possible for the impotent alone, and he who does not marry is perforce an adulterer, or commits worse vices.

It may have been necessary then to stigmatize the ascetic life in this fashion—I will not enter upon that now—but the doctrine of the impossibility of restraint was certainly calculated to increase the sexual licence of the age. Sexual intercourse, Luther tells us, is never without sin, but it is a needful sin, and marriage renders it legitimate.[2] It is here where the worst feature of the Reformation doctrine of marriage comes in,—all sexual relations outside marriage are criminal. Luther goes so far as to assert that the adulterer ought to be stoned—('Dead, dead with him to avoid the bad example'![3]). Marriage is established for the legitimate gratification of the sexual instinct—that is the basis of the institution. The licentiousness of his age Luther proposes to stem by early and general marriage: the primary object of marriage is the satisfaction of the sexual appetite. It is obvious that this doctrine raised the sexual appetite into an irresistible natural force, and must lead in practice to most disastrous results. Thus, when Philip of Hesse finds one wife not sufficient, Luther allows him a second, because appetite cannot be restrained; when Marquard Schuldorp marries his niece, Luther writes a book in his defence,[4] because appetite cannot be restrained; when Henry VIII. of England writes to Melanchthon on the matter of his divorce, Melanchthon recommends him instead to take a second wife, if his appetite cannot be restrained. Nay, this teaching touches the inmost privacy of married life. The wife is to be a mere breeder of children. "One sees how weak and sickly are unfruitful women. But the fruitful are

[1] *Schreiben von August,* 1523, *De Wette,* 2, 372.
[2] *Von dem ehelichen Stande,* p. 44.
[3] Ibid. p. 28.
[4] *Grundt vnd orsake worup Marquardus Schuldorp hefft syner suster dochter thor Ehe genamen,* 1526.

sounder, fresher, and stronger.   If a woman becomes weary
and at last dead from bearing, that matters not ; let her only
die from bearing, she is there to do it.   It is better to live a
short and sound life, than a long and sickly one." [1]   If the
wife refuses to submit to such a life, what then ?   " Then it
is time for the man to say : ' Will you not, so will I another ;
will not the wife, so let the maid come ' "—a doctrine which
is supported by the biblical example of Vashti and Esther.[2]
I have remarked on the sexual licence of the time, and on
the economic depression ; the Reformers, advocating marriage as the cure for licence, were still obliged to recognize
the depression.   How is early marriage possible when the
handicraftsman has nothing to support a family with ?   " We
have to meet a great and strong objection," preaches Luther.
" Yes, they say; it were good to marry, but how shall I
support myself? . . . This is, indeed, the greatest hindrance
to wedlock, its ruination, as well as the cause of all whoredom.   But what shall I reply thereto ?   It is unbelief and
doubt in God's goodness and truth.   Hence, no wonder, where
it exists, that vain whoredom follows and every misfortune.
Here lies the rub : they wish first to be sure of property,
whence they can obtain food, drink, and clothes.   They
want to draw their head from the noose,—' In the sweat of
thy brow, thou shalt earn thy bread.' . . . Hence, to conclude, who does not find himself suited to chastity, let him
early find work and take to wedlock in God's name.   A boy
at the latest when he's twenty, a girl at the latest when she's
fifteen or eighteen.   Then they are still sound and fitted thereto, and let God take care how they and their children are
to be supported.   God creates children, and will certainly
support them." [3]   These doctrines on marriage, which I have
exemplified from Luther, repeat themselves in the writings
of many reformers.   It will be seen how at variance they
are with the conceptions of the Catholic Church.   St. Jerome
declared that virginity fills heaven ; the Reformers described
this as blasphemy.[4]   " The smallest sin is theft, after that

---

[1] *Von dem ehelichen Stande,* p. 41.   [2] Ibid. p. 29.   [3] Ibid. p. 43.
[4] *De servo arbitrio, Opera, Wittenberg,* 1554, ii. 472.

comes adultery, then murder, and last the ascetic life." The Catholic Church held marriage a sacrament—that is, it gave to the physical facts a spiritual meaning. "Marriage is an outward bodily thing," said the Reformers, "as any other worldly bargaining." This new conception of the sexual relation was not only opposed to the Catholic standpoint, but is, in my opinion, distinctly inferior to the faith of chivalry. It reduced marriage to a purely sensual relationship—to a physical union the idea of which would be repugnant to every modern man and woman of culture. It tended to check the idealizing of the sex-relation, and, at the same time, to degrade woman to a mere breeder of children. The Reformation completed the subjection of woman by destroying the cloister-life; its view of woman may, in fact, be summed up in the following words of its chief hero :—

"The woman's will, as God says, shall be subject to the man, and he shall be master (Gen. iii. 16); that is, the woman shall not live according to her free-will, as it would have been had Eve not sinned, for then she had ruled equally with Adam, the man, as his colleague. Now, however, that she has sinned and seduced the man, she has lost the governaunce; and must neither begin nor complete anything without the man; where he is, there must she be, and bend before him as before her master, whom she shall fear, and to whom she shall be subject and obedient."

This is the unqualified doctrine of the father-age, unblushingly based on the Hebrew myth, which in the early days of the father-age had come to man's aid.

For three centuries after the Reformation the history of woman in Germany was a blank. Domestication or prostitution, subjection or social expulsion, were almost the only possibilities for her. Perhaps no modern nation has been so backward as Germany to start the work of emancipation, or has been so lukewarm in the support it has given to the higher education of women. It has organized a special class of books for their feebler intellects, and many an 'educated' German will say to his women of the masterpieces of literature, like the savage of Polynesia, *Ai tabu*—

this food is forbidden you. That is a cry which contrasts strangely with the *mother-wit* of primitive man, with the literature of chivalry written in the service of the lady-love, or even with the select circle of learned and earnest women to be found round several of the early Fathers. I do not attribute the modern subjection of women to the teaching of the Reformers, it is really an outcome of the father-age ; but the repulsive side of German courtship, and the complete domestication of the German woman are, I believe, in no small degree due to the manner in which the ascetic life was in the sixteenth century first abused and then abolished.

XV.

SOCIALISM AND SEX.[1]

At last they came to where Reflection sits, that strange old woman, who has always one elbow on her knee, and her chin in her hands, and who steals light out of the past to shed it on the future.

And Life and Love cried out : " Oh ! wise one, tell us, when first we met, a lovely radiant thing belonged to us—gladness without a tear, sunshine without a shade. Oh ! how did we sin that we lost it ? Where shall we go that we may find it ?"—Ralph Iron.

THERE is a principle lying at the basis of all growth, which was first made manifest by the naturalist, but will one day receive its most striking corroboration from the scientific historian. This principle is somewhat misleadingly termed 'the survival of the fittest.' A slight change for the better would be made were we to term it the 'survival of the fitter.' In all forms of existence—in brute and human life, in brute and human habits, in human institutions, religions and philosophies—the fittest is never reached, has never come into existence, and cannot therefore survive. When it does, evolution will cease,—a final epoch that may for the present be classed with a certain catastrophe termed the 'day of judgment,' which formerly played a conspicuous part in mediæval cosmogony ; we may leave them both to that storehouse of unintelligible lumber whence paradoxers and supernaturalists draw their material. I, the more matter-of-fact sensationalist,[2] content myself with recognizing

[1] This paper, originally read to a small discussion club, was printed in *To-Day* (February, 1887), and afterwards issued as a pamphlet.

[2] I use this word to exclude on the one side the absurdities of materialism of the Büchner type, and on the other the muddle-headed mysticism of some of our neo-Hegelian friends. A sensationalist is one who does not attempt to get beyond his sensations and their laws.

that every form of life, every human institution and mode of thought, is ever undergoing change ; not change by hap incalculable, but to a great and ever wider extent foreseeable and capable of measurement both as to magnitude and direction. There is no absolute code of morality, no absolute philosophy nor absolute religion ; each phase of society has had its special morality, its peculiar religion, and its own form of sex-relationship. Its morality and its religion have been stamped as immorality and superstition by later generations. Promiscuity, brother-sister marriage, infanticide, the subjection of women, and the serfdom of labour have all in turn been moral and again immoral. No property, group-property, tribe-property, chief-property, and individual property in both land and movables have all had their day, and foolish indeed is the man who would term one absolutely good and another absolutely bad. One thing only is fixed, the direction and rate of change of human society at a particular epoch. It may be difficult to measure, but it is none the less real and definite. The moral or good action is that which tends in the direction of growth of a particular society in a particular land at a particular time. In this sense, to avoid all preconceptions of the absolute, I shall use the word *social* for moral, and *anti-social* for immoral. An action which is social (or moral) may have arisen from custom, from feeling, or from faith, but to understand *why* it is social (or moral) requires knowledge. It requires knowledge of the historical growth and the consequent present tendency of a particular phase of society. Hence we see why it is that many actions arising from feeling, custom, or faith are anti-social ; if custom could dictate a moral code, I fear Socialism would at present have little basis of support ; it must throw itself back on rational judgment based on historical study. For this reason I cannot look upon Socialism as a mere scheme of political change : it is essentially a new morality, the subjection of individual action to the welfare of society ; this welfare can only be ascertained by studying the direction of social growth. Socialists must claim to be, and act as, preachers of a new morality, if they would create that en-

thusiasm which only human love, not human hatred, can
arouse. Therein lies the only excuse for the absurd title of
'Christian Socialist.'[1] Socialism as a polity can only become possible when Socialism as a morality has become
general; as a polity it will then only be a matter of police,
a law restraining a small anti-social minority.

In all social problems there are two questions which need
investigation: (1) What is the ideal we place before ourselves? (2) How shall we act so as best to forward the
realization of our ideal?

Before I attempt to consider these questions in their relation to the problem of sex, it is needful to explain what I
understand by the term 'ideal.' By 'ideal' I do not denote
some glorious poet-dreamed Utopia, the outcome of individual
wishes, inspiration or prejudice, but solely the direction
wherein it seems to us from the history of the past that the
history of the immediate future must surely progress. Our
ideal is the outcome of our reading of the past, the due
weighing, so far as lies in our power, of the tendencies and
forces at present developing humanity in a definite direction.
It is the one absolute we have got upon which to form a
judgment, and so the test of moral or social action. We are
students of history, not because we are Socialists, but
Socialists because we have studied history.[2]

We have now to ask the following questions with regard
to the sex-relationship. What is its ideal form? How can
we best work towards its attainment?—that is—What is the
true type of social (moral) action in matters of sex? It is
because I hold that the present sexual relationship is far

---

[1] It reminds me of a well-known lady doctor who terms herself *Christian physiologist*, as if socialism and physiology were not groups of facts
associated by laws independent of any form of faith!

[2] A leader of the 'Anarchist Group' recently read a paper in my hear-
ing which deduced anarchy as a necessity of the coming ages by a
metaphysical process quite unintelligible to me since the idealist days of
German student life. I ventured to ask him if he thought the same
conclusion would be reached by the historical method. He had not
applied it, he said, but he was quite certain that that method could not
contradict his process.

removed from the ideal (the relationship of the future), and that the present marriage law tends to hinder our approach to the ideal, that I have written this essay.

Briefly let me state here, for it is impossible at present to enter on any lengthy historical investigation, that I believe the forces and tendencies of the present as evidenced in the history of the past are working strongly against our present relationship of sex, and are not unlikely in the near future to sweep it as completely, and as roughly, out of existence as rational knowledge is sweeping away metaphysic, freethought Christian theology, and socialistic doctrines orthodox political economy. I will try to enumerate shortly the tendencies I have found at work, and point out how they must come into conflict, and ultimately modify entirely our present legal and customary views on the relations of sex.

I have spoken of one principle of the law of evolution, the survival of the fitter. According to the Darwinian theory, this survival is chiefly brought about by sexual selection and the struggle for food. All-mastering as these factors are easily seen to be in the development of the brute-world, they appear at first sight insufficient to explain the growth of man and the changes in human institutions. The scientific student of history, however, will find them just as forcibly at work in directing the course of man's progress from barbarism to civilization. The future Darwin of the history of civilization will probably recognize that his subject falls into two great divisions—the history of sex and the history of possession, into the changes in sex-relationship and the changes in the ownership of wealth. The explanation for the most part of these two main groups of changes lies in sexual-selection and in the struggle for food.[1] One by one various forms of sex-relationship have succeeded each other, there has been no permanent type, and the historical growth of the relationship

[1] Herder attempted a philosophy of history on the basis of metaphysic and naturally failed. The philosophy of history is only possible since Darwin, and the rationalization of history by the 'future Darwin' will consist in the explanation of human growth by the action of physical and sexualogical laws in varying human institutions.

has at each stage agreed closely with the state of development
of the other social and legal institutions of the age.   Legalized
life-long monogamy is in human history a thing but of yesterday, and no unprejudiced person (however much it may
suit his own tastes) can suppose it a final form.   Thus it is
that a certain type of sex-relationship and a certain mode of
ownership are essential features of the present stage of human
growth.   In the past others have marked the successive
stages reached by man in his long course of evolution.   To
each fresh type of sex-relationship has corresponded a new
mode of ownership—a peculiar phase of human society.
When the sex-relationship was pure promiscuity, then possession was based on finding and keeping so long as the
finder had strength to retain ; with brother-sister marriage
and with group-marriage, property was held by the group,—
communism in the group ; with the matriarchate, at least
in its zenith, property could be held by individuals, but
descended only through women ; with the patriarchate property was held only by the men, and descended through
them,—woman was a chattel without any right of ownership.
With the centuries as the last traces of the patriarchate
vanish, as woman obtains rights as an individual, when a
· new form of possession is coming into existence, is it rational
to suppose that history will break its hitherto invariable law,
and that a new sex-relationship will not replace the old ?

The two most important movements of our era are without
doubt the socialistic movement and the movement for the
complete emancipation of women.   Both of them go to the
very root of the old conception of property, and to the careful
observer connote a corresponding change in the old relationship of sex.   To the onlooker the Socialist and the advocate
of ' woman's rights ' are essentially fighting the same battle,
however much they may disguise the fact to themselves.
Change in the mode of possessing wealth connotes to the
scientific historian a change in the sex-relationship.   It is
because I hold Socialism will ultimately survive as the only
tenable moral code, that I am convinced that our present
marriage customs and our present marriage law are alike

destined to suffer great changes. It is not a question of sensuality, or of sexual experiment, but of indomitable law. Variations are taking place in our views and actions with regard to sex, which are but forerunners of the new type ; a type which possibly for many centuries will hold the field. Sexual experiments are no experiments in the real sense of the word, they are the variations in the present, some of which are destined to survive as the rule of the future.

So far as may be possible in a paper of this kind, let me examine the leading principle of modern Socialism as a moral code, and its bearing on the current relationship of sex. I may state this principle as follows :—

A human being, man or woman, unless physically or mentally disabled, has no moral right to be a member of the community unless he or she is labouring in some form or other for the community—that is, contributing to the common labour-stock.

By no 'moral right' I simply mean that it is *anti-social*, and therefore deserving of the strongest social censure, or even punishment, if any person lives in, and therefore on the labour of, the community without contributing to the labour-stock.

It follows as a necessary result of this our first principle that it is anti-social : (a) to live on inherited property, (b) to receive interest on accumulated property. For, in doing either, the human is in reality taxing the labour of others for his or her support, and is not repaying that taxation by an equal labour-contribution to the common labour-stock. I am quite aware that these dictates under our present social regime are very hard to accept, and harder to act up to, but I am convinced that they will have to be accepted as the basis of the moral code of the future. A human may labour and acquire, but he has no social right to endow himself or his posterity with that idleness which merely connotes a living on the labour of others. There is a point here which deserves special notice, because it bears on a remark I shall presently make of the wife and her home-life. The endowed idler, to a great extent owing to his monopoly of possession, misdirects the labour of others and gives it an anti-social direction ; he employs labour in creating luxuries for himself, labour which ought to be employed socially in improving the dwellings of the people, on the ordering and beautifying of the public streets, on the building of public institutions, and for the like social purposes.

The society of the future will apply the above principle as a test of right conduct to all its members, be they men or women. But that men and women shall be able to live socially there must be a field of genuine labour freely open to them. This is only possible under two conditions : (1) economic independence of the individual, and (2) a limitation of population. Both these conditions go, I think, to the very root of our present sex-relationship. They denote an entire change in the position of husband and wife, and a very possible interference of society (the state) in the heart of the family,—at least in the family of the anti-social propagators of unnecessary human beings.

By 'economic independence of the individual,' a term likely to be misunderstood, I denote the maintenance due to the individual for genuine contributions to the labour-stock of the community. The moral dignity of the individual is preserved only so far as his or her labour is a *genuine* contribution, and not the fulfilment of somebody else's caprice or of an anti-social desire for pure luxury.

In order that a woman, to use a theological expression, may save her own soul, may preserve her moral dignity,—in order that she may fulfil the moral code of the future,—she must have economic independence. I think men in this respect are apt to underrate the feelings of women. A man might be quite willing to put half his income at the disposal of a friend, but how few are the men, who (unless such gift would enable them to perform a recognized public service) would not feel a loss of moral dignity in accepting it ! They so far obey the socialistic code, that they refuse to live without return on the labour of others—their friends ; unfortunately they have rarely any objection to live without return on the labour of others who are *not* their friends. But it

28

SOCIOLOGY.

seems to me that the majority of women under our present
social system are bound to live on men's labour. A man
may be willing enough to give, but the woman cannot
morally afford to receive. Women must have economic
independence, because they cannot act truly so long as they
depend for subsistence on father, brother, husband, or lover,
and not on their own labour. It may be suggested that a
woman often brings property to the husband, and contributes
as much as, or more than he to the joint establishment. This
might be rendered still more frequent were there likely in
the future to be a return, however partial, to the matriarchal
principle. Some signs of such a return are indeed to be found,
but I think it could only be of a very transitory kind, for it
seems opposed to the fundamental principle of Socialism,
namely, that the property of the individual shall not be inherited property, but the outcome of his own labour. Very
few, indeed, are the cases wherein the property a woman
brings to marriage is the outcome of her own labour; it may
render her economically independent of her husband, but it
makes her economically dependent on the community. The
community, not her husband, will thus be supporting her;
this is in many instances a still graver social offence. My
reader, I fear, may be impatient to suggest as a further
plea for woman's idleness, that her home-duties are really
her labour-contribution to the community. So far as such
duties have to do with the rearing of children, I at once
admit that they *may* indeed form an all-important contribution to the social stock. But the possibility of this depends
entirely on the social (moral) right of the particular man and
woman to propagate under the present pressure of population. By physique and mental power a particular man and
woman may be fitted to carry on the race, or they may
not. If they are fitted, it does not follow that they have a
social right to an unlimited family. Indeed the men and
women who are socially fitted to be parents of the future
race, and at the same time rearers and educators of that
race, are not nearly so frequent as current habits might
lead us to imagine. The birth of children is a responsibility,

the moral gravity of which is far from being properly weighed by the average husband and wife of to-day.

Let us put aside for the present the social value of such part of women's home-labour as is spent in rearing and educating children, a function which she may, indeed, often exercise better on a wider field than that of the home. Let us confine ourselves for the present to childless families, to those where the children are not educated at home or have left home, and to the home-life of single women. The home-duties of the woman are those towards husband, father, brother, or paramour. These are the labour-return the woman makes for her support by the community, they form the basis on which she can claim to be moral, the source from which her feeling of independence, and her sense of contributing to society something for what she receives from it, must arise. It is difficult for me to suppose any man would accept cheerfully a similar dependence on the dearest friend, and it is surprising that customary modes of thought allow so many women to submit to such chattel-slavery. I have no hesitation in asserting that the home-duties of the non-child-bearing woman do not in the great majority of cases satisfy the standard of the socialistic code. If the woman is called upon to labour, it is to labour beyond the household limits. The great changes introduced into domestic economy during the last fifty years by machinery, by the wholesale production of provisions, by the division of labour, by the flat-system, &c., have revolutionized home-life, and " what the housewife and her attendants sixty or eighty years ago had good reason for doing, has now become a pastime of no value, the machine mocks the individual woman's hand." [1] The reader will probably be able to call to mind, not only several cases where a single man or woman successfully manages his or her own home, but instances where the husband and the non-child-bearing wife follow their own professions, and yet their home is not a scene of hopeless disorder. I could myself produce much evidence on the same side from the life of the Swabian and Baden peasantry. Many a farmer's wife

[1] Marianne Hainisch : *Die Brodfrage der Frau, Wien*, 1875.

undertakes not only her home-duties, but the whole business
of a village inn ; or, again, while her husband is occupied in
the forest, she with the aid of knave and maid manages
entirely the little farm and its homestead.   I have seen
her ploughing, dunging, reaping and thrashing, milking and
making butter ; I have sat with her in the evening by the
kitchen fire, and the home did not seem neglected, nor her
spiritual life utterly void.   At such times I have learnt that
woman's labour has a social value which must carry her in
all classes beyond home-duties.   Much of the time spent by
women of the middle-classes in increasing the comforts and
ornaments of home, with the corresponding round of 'shopping' and the purchase of nicnacs and trifles, is simply anti-
social, a misdirection of the labour of others.

There may indeed be some who will say : " But you
are neglecting the value of home-comforts and woman's
function in producing social happiness ? "   To this I reply :
If it be the function of women not to labour in the same
manner as men, but to be centres of comfort, sympathy, and
happiness in social life, then to be consistent we must apply
this rule to *all* women.   We must stop every woman from
receiving wages for her labour.   We must prohibit entirely
her employment for wages in factories, mills, post-office,
shops, and domestic service ; to be consistent we must prohibit paid prostitution and paid literary work.   Are, then, the
great mass of women who now labour to be left to chance
dependence on men, or to be supported by the state ?   As
woman's function would be different from man's, and involve
immunity from social-labour, so there would be for her a
different code of morality.   Women would indeed have a
glorious time of ease were this millennium ever reached ; my
only regret is that men also could not share it !   It seems to
me, however, that all assumption of a distinction in social
function between men and women, which reaches beyond the
physical fact of child-bearing, is absolutely unwarranted,
and calculated to reduce women again to the position of toys,
of creatures having no souls, and incapable of acting according to the higher social code laid down for men.   The

labour of woman is a fund of infinite value to the community,[1] and her right to have educational and professional institutions thrown open to her is based upon her duty
to contribute to the common labour-stock of the community.
The moral force behind the ' Woman's Rights ' platform is
woman's duty to labour. Such labour, I am sure, is not in
the great majority of cases synonymous with ' home-duties.'

My argument, then, reduces itself to this : Economic independence is essential to all humans in order that they may
develop their full individuality, and freely obey the highest
code of morality. The current type of sex-relationship
which confines the wife to the home, and permits of little, if '
any, free action and free labour on her part, is inconsistent
with this economic independence, and therefore is a type
destined to extinction. The socialistic movement with its
new morality and the movement for sex-equality must surely
and rapidly undermine our current marriage customs and
marriage law.

Hitherto I have treated the question from the woman's
side, but to the thoughtful man surely the present legal
sex-relationship must appear equally unbearable, even
repulsive. The idea *will* suggest itself that the woman
possibly married him for a livelihood or for a position ;
possibly she remains with him for the same reasons, or
because she thinks she has a duty towards one who has so
long supported her, or again, it may be, because she feels
the customary social ostracism following on separation would
be unbearable. The charm of friendship is the spontaneity
of its nature ; two humans remain friends so long as they
find in each other sympathetic attraction ; it is the very
danger of rupture that produces mutual forbearance, and
renders friendship so frequently life-long. To be bound to
treat a person as a friend after sympathy had vanished would
be intolerable, yet this is too often the outcome of life-long

[1] Were labour socially organized, the introduction of female labour
would increase the number of workers, and so decrease the amount
required of the individual, without increasing the number of mouths to
be fed.

monogamy. Is it any wonder that men as well as women shrink from such a union? Deprive life-long legal monogamy of its ' customary respectability,' or men and women of their sex-instincts, which can only be ' respectably ' exercised in this mode, and we do not believe a single man and woman would again sign the register which replaced the freedom of friendship by a life-long Siamese twinship. *The economic independence of women will, for the first time, render it possible for the highest human relationship to become again a matter of pure affection, raised above every suspicion of constraint, and every taint of commercialism.*

Those who consider legalized monogamy necessary because women have not yet economic independence, and because man is by nature so knavish that he must needs take advantage of woman's dependence, have obviously clear ends to work for in the emancipation of women and the propagation of the socialistic morality. But one result of maintaining without exception legalized monogamy may well be noted ; namely, that more and more men and women, as we get nearer the epoch when possession and sex-relationship will change in character, are likely to remain unmarried ; the transition from one type to the other will thus be more abrupt, more revolutionary than evolutionary. It may well be doubted whether this mode of change will be more advantageous to society as a whole, than that whereby society would grow accustomed to the new type by its appearance as a more and more frequent variation.

I am now in a position to state what I hold the new type of sex-relationship will be, and how law or social opinion will act with regard to it. We will start from its fundamentals—the economic independence of women, and the duty as well as right of all to labour, involving as we have seen a limitation of population. As other Socialists I demand that all shall labour, and that a field of labour shall be provided for all. Differing, however, from the majority of Socialists,[1] I believe that the existence of such a field

---

[1] Marx by abusing Malthus has not solved the population difficulty. Leroux's theory—that the food-supply is a question of dung, and that the

essentially demands a limitation of population.[1]   Now it will
profit little that the social man and woman without constraint

excrement of each individual if properly applied suffices to produce his
quota of food,—and Dühring's doctrine—that each additional labourer
increases the labour-stock, and so the social-capacity for producing food
—are alike naïve, as they beg the question by presupposing a *field* for the
dung and the labour. Engels would apparently find such a field in the
valley of the Mississippi, or he suggests the remedy of emigration ; this
remedy Hyndman, on the other hand, declaims against as a capitalistic
expatriation. Bebel's treatment of the problem is as wanting in logic and
historical accuracy as the rest of his writings. Champion has recently
preached the pernicious doctrine that the country is " frightfully under-
populated ! " The minor Socialists will not face the problem, but practically shelve it. The real solution is simply that the limitation of population is possible in a socialistic community, but not in a capitalistic one.
Kautsky seems to stand alone among Socialists in accepting the
Malthusian law and its consequences.

[1] I have more fully on another occasion treated of the relation of
Socialism to the problem of population, and pointed out how the acceptance of the law discovered by Malthus is an essential of any
socialistic theory which pretends to be scientific. I would, however,
recommend to the reader the following passages from John Stuart Mill's
Political Economy (People's Edition, pp. 220, 226) :—" Every one has a
right to live. We will suppose this granted. But no one has a right to
bring creatures into life, to be supported by other people. Whoever
means to stand upon the first of these rights must renounce all pretensions
to the last. If a man cannot support even himself unless others help
him, those others are entitled to say that they do not also undertake the
support of any offspring which it is physically possible for him to bring
into the world. . . . It would be possible for the state to guarantee
employment at ample wages to all who are born. But if it does this, it
is bound in self-protection, and for the sake of every purpose for which
government exists, to provide that no person shall be born without its
consent. . . . One cannot wonder that silence on this great department
of human duty should produce unconsciousness of moral obligations,
when it produces oblivion of physical facts. That it is possible to delay
marriage, and to live in abstinence while unmarried, most people are
willing to allow ; but when persons are once married, the idea, in this
country, never seems to enter any one's mind that having or not having a
family, or the number of which it shall consist, is amenable to their own
control. One would imagine that children were rained down upon
married people direct from heaven, without their being' art or part in
the matter ; that it was really, as the common phrases have it, God's will
and not their own, which decided the numbers of their offspring."

limit the number of their offspring, if large anti-social sections of society continue to bring any number of unneeded
human beings into the world. Society and law will in some
fashion have to interfere and restrict the anti-social in the
matter of child-bearing. For this reason I think the sex-
relationship of the future will not be regarded as a union for
the birth of children, but as the closest form of friendship
between man and woman.

It will be accompanied by no child-bearing or rearing, or
by these in a much more limited measure than at present.
Hence one of the chief causes of woman's economic dependence will disappear. Her sex-relationship will not
habitually connote sex-dependence. I must here make a
distinction which appears to me fundamental, although
objections have been raised against it, namely, between
child-bearing and non-child-bearing women. A woman may
pass and repass from one class to the other, but the position
of society with regard to the two classes is essentially
different. With the sex-relationship, so long as it does not
result in children, we hold that the state of the future will in
no wise interfere; but when it does result in children, then
the state will have a right to interfere, and this on two
grounds : first, because the question of population bears on
the happiness of society as a whole ; and secondly, because
child-bearing enforces for a longer or shorter interval
economic dependence upon the woman.

The reader will note that we have assumed that the
non-child-bearing woman of the future will possess economic
independence, and that there will be no legal or state
distinction between the man and such woman. It may be
asked whether such economic independence, such sex-equality
is really possible ? I believe it will be so in the future, I
doubt whether it is so in the present. The Post Office
employs women-clerks, not because of their equality with
male-clerks, but because their decreased efficiency and
increased sick-leave are more than compensated by the
diminished wages. This fact lies at the basis of much of

the employment of female labour under our present system.[1] But the lesser physical strength and general intelligence of the average woman of to-day are no real arguments for those who would maintain her present enslaved condition. The student of the history of civilization will find that there was a time when the woman *physically* was practically on a par with the man, while *mentally* she was his superior.[2] There is no rigid natural law of feminine inferiority, and what we see now in certain classes of our current society is the outcome of the generations during which woman's physical and intellectual training has been neglected. Every teacher or examiner who has had to deal with women students will admit their capacity to grasp the same intellectual training as men. The wanderer in the mountainous lands of Southern Germany, Switzerland, and Northern Italy knows to what extent woman's physical strength can be developed by a healthy outdoor life. I have often rested in a Tyrolese Alp, miles away from the nearest hamlet, where for four or five months one or two maidens had charge in all weathers of forty to fifty cows. Morning and evening these cows had to be milked, cheese had to be made, and occasionally butter

---

[1] Examples of this are common enough ; I will only cite the following striking instance just brought to my notice. A London firm of lemonade manufacturers recently discharged twelve men to whom they had paid 4s. a day *per* head, and replaced them by sixteen women who could do the same work, but to whom they only paid 1s. 8d. a day. The firm thus saved, by employing in greater numbers less efficient workers at starvation wages, 11s. 4d. a day. This was of course only an act of self-preservation on the part of the manufacturers, the real sources of the evil lie much deeper, namely, in competitive production and unchecked population. Owing to these influences more and more men in London are being supported by women's labour. This fact taken in conjunction with the great disproportion of the sexes in the metropolis points indeed to a painful form of return to the matriarchate. Were the capitalistic phase of society enduring, we might expect to find ultimately the male of the working classes reduced to the sole function of drone, to the mere procreator of workers !

[2] The evidence I have collected on these points is far too complex and copious to be reproduced here. Suffice it to say that it seems to me highly probable that among the Aryans women first practised agriculture, created primitive religion, and discovered the elements of medicine.

carried down into the valleys. Still early in the morning
after milking, one or both women might be seen one or two
thousand feet above the Alp, almost on the snow-line, mowing
green fodder, and later carrying it down in masses that many
a man would fail to lift.   In bad weather, in mist and snow,
the cows had to be sought for and brought home; at other
times they had to be driven to pastures which could only be
reached by crossing considerable snow-fields. Yet, notwithstanding the physical severity of their task, these Tyrolese
Dirndl are among the healthiest, freshest, and happiest women
I have met.   I am not pointing to any abnormal cases of
mental and physical power in women, they are merely types
of what training easily produces.   I have faith, then, that
when one or two generations of women have received a sound
intellectual training, and when the physical education of girls
is as much regarded as that of boys, then a non-child-bearing
woman will be the economic equal of man, and so preserve
her independence; for she will be his physical and mental
equal in any sex-partnership they may agree to enter upon.
For such woman I hold that the sex-relationship, both as
to form and substance, ought to be a pure question of taste,
a simple matter of agreement between the man and her, in
which neither society nor the state would have any need or
right to interfere.   The economic independence of both man
and woman would render it a relation solely of mutual
sympathy and affection; its form and duration would vary
according to the feelings and wants of individuals.   This
free sexual union seems to me the first outcome of Socialism
as applied to sex.   I am, although a Socialist, no advocate
of state-interference for its own sake, only when it appears
of social value as capable of hindering the anti-social
oppression of one individual by a second more favourably
situated.   *Children apart*, it is unbearable that church or
society should in any official form interfere with lovers.
Were it not customary it would seem offensive; it has
become customary as a protection for a subject class.   When
marriage is no longer regarded as a profession for women,
and nigh the only way in which they can gain the comrade-

ship of men and a wider life,—when the relations of men
and women are perfectly free, and they can meet on an equal
footing,—then so far from this free sexual relationship leading
to sensuality and loose living, I hold it would be the best
safeguard against it. Men and women having many friends
of the opposite sex with whom they were on terms of close
friendship, would be in far less danger of mistaking fancy or
friendship for love, and the relation of lovers would be far
less readily entered upon than at present, when in some social
circles man and woman must be lovers or exhibit no sign of
affection. Every man and woman would probably ultimately
choose a lover from their friends, but the men and women
who, being absolutely free, would choose more than one, would
certainly be the exceptions — exceptions, I believe, infinitely more rare than under our present legalized monogamy,
accompanied as it is by socially unrecognized polygamy and
polyandry—by the mistress and the prostitute.[1]

If the above, to any extent, express the solution of the
sex-problem for the non-child-bearing woman, whose economic independence will preserve her individuality, how are
Socialists to regard her sister, the child-bearing woman?
Here again it seems to me needful that she should first be rendered economically independent of the husband and lover. In
the society of the future the birth of a child will have social
sanction or it will not. If the birth is sanctioned, then I
hold that the woman in bearing a child is fulfilling a high
social function, and on society at large, on the state, falls
the correlative duty of preserving her economic independence. The state, not the individual, should in one form or
another guard that its child-bearing women do not lose their
independence owing to their incapacity to undertake other
forms of social labour while bearing and rearing its future
citizens. Let not the reader picture to himself huge state
lying-in hospitals, free nurseries and the like ; I see no reason
why dismal barracks of this kind should replace our ordinary

[1] Some of the above remarks I owe to the letter of a friend, who
has expressed my own views in truer words than I could have found for
myself.

home-life, nor why the father's affection for his children, even as it exists to-day, should be based solely on the fact that he is bound to support their mother; there is surely a deeper root to it than *that!* Nay, I imagine that as friends dwell together now, so lovers will seek to do in the future; that as they will not have children without the mature consideration and desire of the woman, if not of both, so they will desire to have those children about them, to form round themselves a home-life. But in this home-life the wife, no longer a chattel, will possess an economic independence insured by the state.

Let me take a *purely hypothetical* example—on the details of which I lay no stress, and which is not given to raise idle discussion on its value—let me suppose that on an average three births to a woman has been found sufficient at any epoch to maintain the limit of efficient population. Some women would doubtless have more, others less or none; in such cases there might well be a communal balance, a sanctioned addition to the local average; but for each sanctioned birth it would be the duty of the commune or state to contribute a certain annual sum for the maintenance of the mother while child-bearing and rearing incapacitated her for other social labour, and this not with the view of decreasing the father's interest or responsibility in his child, but solely to render the mother a free individual. As the national wealth increased, a larger number of births or a greater annual allowance for maternity might be made. This seems to me the only satisfactory method of placing the child-bearing woman on a true footing of economic equality with the man, of destroying her chattel-slavery to the husband. Obviously a birth beyond the sanctioned number would receive no recognition from the state, and in times of over-population it might even be needful to punish positively, as well as negatively, both father and mother. That there is a possibility of limiting the number of births the example of France sufficiently testifies. With the general raising of the standard of comfort, which would result from a socialization of surplus-labour,—with the increased independence of women, due to their complete emancipation,—it is very probable that there would be small occasion for the state to interfere in the matter; the number of births would fall as it has done in France. It is sufficient here to note the possibility, the manner of checking the population lies outside the sphere of this discussion. It is a problem requiring the careful and scientific investigation of the state itself,—only by such investigation shall we be able to determine what is social or anti-social, what is healthy or unhealthy, in the proposals of both primitive and neo-Malthusians.[1]

Such, then, seems to me the socialistic solution of the sex-problem : complete freedom in the sex-relationship left to the judgment and taste of an economically equal, physically trained, and intellectually developed race of men and women ; state interference if necessary in the matter of child-bearing, in order to preserve intersexual independence on the one hand, and the limit of efficient population on the other. To those who see in these things an ideal of idle dreamers and not a possibility of the future, I can only reply : Measure well the forces which are at work in our age, mark the strength of the men and women who are dissatisfied with the present, weigh carefully the enthusiasm of the teachers of our new morality socialistic and sexual, then you will not class them as dreamers only. To those who would know their duty at the present, I can but say : The first steps towards our ideal are the spread of Socialism as a morality, and the complete emancipation of our sisters. To others who, like the aged poet, halt and are faint at heart, seeing in the greatness of our time only pettiness and lust, we must bid a sorrowful but resolute farewell—" Father, thou knowest not our needs, thy task is done, remain and rest, we must onward—farewell." We are full of new emotions, new passions, new thoughts ; our age is not one of pettiness and lust, but replete with clearer and nobler ideas than the past, ideas that its sons will generate and its daughters bring to birth. Dangers and difficulties

[1] The need for state action in the matter has been well pointed out by Jane Hume Clapperton in her suggestive book *Scientific Meliorism*, p. 427. 1885.

there are, misery, pain, and wrong-doing over and enough. But we of to-day see beyond them ; they do not cause us to despair, but summon us to action. You of the past valued Christianity—aye, and we value freethought; you of the past valued faith—aye, and we value knowledge ; you have sought wealth eagerly—we value more the duty and right to labour; you talked of the sanctity of marriage—we find therein love sold in the market, and we strive for a remedy in the freedom of sex. Your symbols are those of the past, symbols to which civilization owes much, great landmarks in past history pointing the direction of man's progress, even suggesting the future, *our* ideal. But as symbols for our action to-day they are idle, they denote in the present serfdom of thought, and serfdom of labour, and serfdom of sex. We have other ideals more true to the coming ages — freedom of thought, and freedom of labour, and freedom of sex—ideals based on a deeper knowledge of human nature and its history than you, our fathers, could possess. Term them impious, irrational, impure, if you will; 'tis because you have understood neither the time nor us. We must leave you sorrowfully behind, and go forward alone. The age is strong in knowledge, rich in ideas ; we hold the future not so distant when our symbols shall be the guides of conduct, and their beauty brought home to humanity by their realization in a renascent art.

His omnia, quae de Mentis Libertate ostendere volueram, absolvi.

UNWIN BROTHERS,
THE GRESHAM PRESS,
CHILWORTH AND LONDON.

www.ingramcontent.com/pod-product-compliance
Lightning Source LLC
Chambersburg PA
CBHW030937110726
47900CB00004B/1030